A SPELL OF EMPIRE

The Horns of Tartarus

A SPELL OF EMPIRE

The Horns of Tartarus

Michael Scott Rohan
and Allan Scott

ORBIT

An *Orbit* Book

First published in Great Britain in 1992
by Orbit Books

Copyright © Michael Scott Rohan and Allan Scott 1992

The right of Michael Scott Rohan and Allan Scott to be
identified as authors of this work has been asserted
by them in accordance with the Copyright,
Designs and Patents Act 1988.

A CIP catalogue record for this book is
available from the British Library

ISBN 0 7088 8360 5

Phototypeset by Intype, London
Printed in Great Britain by
Cox & Wyman Ltd, Reading, Berkshire

Orbit Books
A Division of
Little, Brown and Company (UK) Limited
165 Great Dover Street
London SE1 4YA

Dedication

To Rosemary and Deb, spice of our lives, for valiantly coping with melancholy Danes and mad Frenchmen

Acknowledgements

For help, encouragement and as much responsibility as the authors can offload, our thanks
to John Jarrold; Richard Evans; Maggie Noach,
agent extraordinary; Rob Holdstock, onlie
begetter; Andrew Wille; and not forgetting
Robert Maxwell, last seen circling some
sharks.

And to the shades of Jeffrey Farnol, Rafael
Sabatini, Frans Gunnar Bengtsson, Alexandre
Dumas . . .

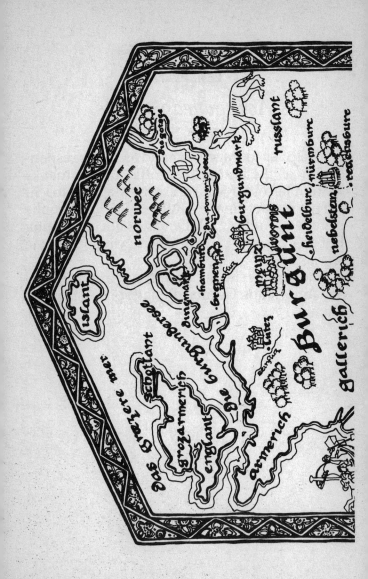

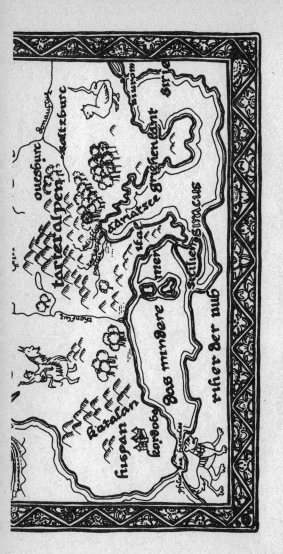

Map of the Burgundian Empire some 700 years after the death of Attila, from the Imperial Library in Worms. The map, painted on wood, was discovered after a mysterious fire in the students' quarter – it had been re-used as the headboard of a bed in one of the more exclusive bordellos.

History Lesson

The sublime Emperor Constans, born to the Purple, Lord of New Rome, or Constantinopolis, or Byzantium – depending upon whether you were flattering the Emperor, writing a history book, or just trying to ask the way – stamped furiously into his marbled audience chamber, his sparse hair disordered, his crown of gilded laurels bent at a rakish angle over one ear, striving vainly – and messily – to shake the richly assorted clods of horse dung off his stiff gilded robes. From below came the buzz of angry altercation as his personal guard of Saxon, Teuton and Scandinavian tribesmen forced the crowd back down the steps, removing the odd head here and there in their artless barbarian fashion, and barred the palace doors. He rounded angrily on the sleek old man who had glided in, apparently on oiled wheels, and was contemplating the Emperor with a far too expressionless face.

'Hokay! All-a right!' said the Emperor coldly. He made a point of not speaking Greek too well, as if to underline that he was technically at least still an Italian. 'So, what's a-da matter this-a time?'

Stephanos, his personal scribe, adviser, food-taster and stage manager, waved his hands in the twisted shrug that was the nearest to helpless frankness a Byzantine official could manage. He began checking off a list on his ring-laden fingers. 'The Leek-Greens are rioting because their chariot teams didn't win. The Blues are rioting because theirs did. The Red and White *demes*

1

are rioting because they want to keep up with the wealthier supporter's clubs. The Christians are rioting because they can't agree over the nature of Christ, and because you don't restore them to the official faith. The Jews are rioting in case you do. The devout pagans are rioting because they're being threatened by all these monotheists. The worshippers of the dark gods of Tartarus are rioting because what else would you expect them to do? And the everyday Greeks—'

'*Si?*'

'Because it breaks the *monotonos*, I suppose.'

The Emperor howled for a slave while he began a futile effort to wriggle out of his soiled finery. 'Jeesama Christ!'; Like most of his line since Constantine he had flirted with Christianity, but it had taken root only in his swearing. 'What a-da people I'm-a ruling! What a-da people! Jeesa-ma Christ!'

'Would that be in His divine nature, O excellency?' inquired the slave politely. 'Because, saving your Worship, despite the ridiculous Orthodox contention that He could somehow have two, divine and human, divisible, it surely must be more respectful to believe that—'

'*Out!*' roared the Emperor, wrapping the noisome cloak around the slave's head and shoving him staggering away. He slumped down in his throne of gilded porphyry, and raised his fists to heaven.

Unknown to him or to anyone else, a nexus of history trembled invisibly on the brink of resolution. It swelled and bobbed in an instant of electric silence, broken only by the distant sound of the slave falling downstairs. It was quite an old nexus, having been born in the turmoil after the death of the emperor Constantine, when it became clear that his attempt to make Christianity the official Imperial religion hadn't quite caught on. By now it was positively overripe and bursting with implications; and it was determined to be settled one way or the other.

The Emperor slammed down his fists on the arms of the Imperial throne, accidentally activating the mechanism of clockwork and counterweights arranged by what would now be called the Imperial special effects department to impress barbarian visitors. There was a clanking whirr, a strong smell of olive oil, and the emperor was hoisted sixteen feet up in the air, while bronze lions roared and brass peacocks flapped their wings.

'*Mamma mia*! That does it! *That-a does it!* I've had-a my bellyful of this city of lunatics and-a chariot hooligans and religious maniacs and-a crazy clockwork tinkerers and-a *retsina* louts out here on the edge of the world, *entendi*? My *bellyful*!' repeated the Emperor. The nexus of history tipped happily over and burst. 'I'm-a going back to where it's-a civilised, and-a people can murder each-a other inna peace anna quiet and not-a tear down half-a city every time!'

'But excellency!' stammered Stephanos from below, staggering against an unseen shower of implications. 'Roma – so ruined – and so far from the capital of your Empire – all the heart of the Imperial administration—'

'That's all-a right!' declared Constans with a grand, all-embracing gesture. He slumped back into the throne and crossed his legs. It was amazing how problems seemed to melt away once you came to a decision.

'They-a coming too! Where-a Emperor is, is-a Empire, *no*? So. It is-a settled. But we not-a going to Roma. We go to Sicily, to lovely rich-a Syracusa, where the sun shine and men-a know how to live! Make-a da arrangements, Stefano! *Sei pronto!*'

'But – majesty—' protested Stephanos faintly, feeling ancestral reins of influence and rivers of patronage slip out from between his shaking fingers. Sheepishly he began to work the lever that lowered his royal master safely, if rather jerkily, back to earth. 'It's so far to the

3

south – cut off by sea – so remote from the direct lines of Imperial communications northward! These barbarians in Germania and Gaul, these Angles and Saxons and Franks and these Burgundians, Nibelungs as they called themselves after they allied with that uncouth Attila person! They're powerful already, and there's more of them pouring in all the time! What if they band together? They could found a whole new Empire up there in the Transalpine lands!'

The sublime Emperor Constans stood up, plucked the ruined laurels from behind his ear, contemplated them a moment – then threw them down and stamped on them. 'Let-a them! They're-a welcome. Me, I'm-a go take a bath! Let them!'

And that's exactly what they did.

Prologue

Night lay heavy over the ancient city of Worms, high capital of the vast Nibelung Empire. Elsewhere, perhaps, in the palaces of its lords and the high houses of its richer merchants, blazing braziers and festoons of candles might lift the mantle a little, music and song drive back silence; even in the lowest dives of the Rhineside districts dockers would be carousing with their drabs around a fire of flotsam and litter. But here in the university quarter the shutters were made fast, and scarcely a chink of light escaped between them; even the moon could not lift the darkness in the narrow, winding streets they overhung, and a deep silence reigned. But it was the silence not of sleep, but of thought, the thought that delves deep into mysteries darker than the darkest night. Behind many of those shutters, by the light of a single candle or cheap tallow dip, strange substances were mixed, decayed old scripts were scanned and arcane rites performed which might, in the day of their fruition, move the world more profoundly than a whole generation of merchants, lords and dockers together. For this was the realm of knowledge, and the hour of magic.

In the large and draughty room where the doctor of alchemy Schweiker Strauben had allotted his apprentice Volker a place to sleep there was no light at all, save a silver thread of moonlight at one ill-fitting shutter. The darkness didn't worry Volker; his fingers knew every contour of the old cittern better than his eyes, and they slid deftly to their stops as the music poured out into the room. It was his great love and leisure, this music; there was no greater pleasure for an apprentice, at least one as poor as he was. But tonight his heart was hardly in it; he'd strum a few chords, then break off and glance anxiously up at the ceiling, to where even now his master was working. He didn't worry about disturbing him; in fact Strauben liked him to play, saying that it helped him concentrate. It was just what the old man was up to that concerned him, this evening and many like it in the past few weeks. He'd half a mind to go up and knock on the elaboratory door, though he knew it would get him nowhere.

Strauben had changed. He'd seemed like a worthy old fellow when Volker had first come to him, a year or two past, austere and withdrawn but kindly enough in an absent-minded way; and he'd never been less than a good master. But Volker had soon come to realise that as an alchemist Strauben was a failure, and knew it. He had made a great name twenty years ago with a pioneering thesis on the natural harmonies of matter, the 'music of spheres', but all his attempts to research it further had led nowhere. These six months past the last of them had gradually petered out, and he seemed to have no new ideas to replace it; at least, none he'd talk about. He'd become not just withdrawn but completely cut off. By day he'd potter through meaningless labours, with hardly a word for Volker; he seemed to be waiting impatiently for night, when after their scant supper he would retreat into the elaboratory again, shutting Volker out. And then there would be . . . things. Worrying things. Sounds, strange sounds filtering down through the boards from above; some he could identify—

He stopped playing abruptly. There was the first, the creak and bump of furniture shifting. Old fool! He'd do himself an injury mucking about like that! Then the squeak of chalk on the boards, or sometimes a brush rasping, painting something in minute, intricate-sounding strokes. Then the voice, sometimes simply muttering aloud, sometimes clearly chanting, now rising, now falling, a monotonous moan like the wind in the chimney. After that, other sounds, infinitely stranger, and odours – gods, those stinks! There was the chant beginning now; it could go on and on for hours, lulling him to sleep only to waken him, half the night later, with nightmarish visions dancing in his head. Dancing – was the old fellow doing that too, the way those feet thudded on the boards, hopping about and kicking up his scrawny shins? He shivered; it should have been funny, that idea, but instead it unnerved him. He didn't want to face what it suggested. Even the merest suspicion of such goings-on would bring every witch-hunting fanatic in Worms down the back of their necks, and right now the city was louse-ridden with them. He strummed an angry chord, then jumped as something answered him out of the darkness, a metallic ring like a soft cymbal. Volker looked up to the ceiling and saw the orrery of painted bronze that hung there still vibrating, its planets shaking on their gearwheel courses and turning new faces to the thin sliver of light. He swung off the bed and padded over, cursing the cold flagstones. Something had struck it . . .

The chant was rising now, a note of intensity and excitement in the old man's voice that he had not heard for many months. He held out a hand, and something warm dripped into his palm. Dripped? He lifted it to his face, then gagged and ran for the pitcher and basin to splash away the foulness; blood and dung and rotting offal were the least of it. More of it was dripping down as the boards flexed, and the stench was filling the room, catching acridly at his throat, while overhead the bouncing and crashing grew louder. And behind all that noise there were other sounds, ghastly ones. He grabbed his jacket, and kicked his feet into his boots. This had to stop, and now! Come morning he'd give the old loon a proper earful, but for now he was going out; he'd little money to spare for another bed, but sooner sleep in the gutter than beneath what was going on up there.

Then he stopped dead. Something had fallen with a crash, something big – and now something else. And as he looked up he saw the boards creak and bulge suddenly, as if some immense weight had settled upon them, and a single wisp, of steam or of smoke, puff down between them into the shaft of moonlight. Old Strauben was not chanting now, he was shouting. Or screaming. Volker darted across the room, hurtling out of the door and into the narrow stairwell. The stench seemed to pour down on him as he clattered up the springy boards, enveloping him in its invisible embrace. His lungs convulsed, refusing to take it in; it was growing worse by the minute, an overwhelming, suffocating wash of foulness. He had to force himself up against it, like climbing up a waterfall, and draw himself up on to the landing on all fours. He reached the door, scrambled up and beat on it. The screaming was louder now, louder but somehow thinner; and beneath it he seemed to hear another note, a deep gurgling sound with the rhythm of a chuckle, though there was nothing merry about it. It was the kind of gloating sound a cat might make when toying with a mouse, undisturbed by Volker's hammering and cries. He leaned against the door and pushed hard; and it seemed to him that the wood quivered under tension, as if something upon the far side pushed back with greater strength. He could not move it in the least, and suddenly he fell back with a cry, rubbing his shoulder; the wood was getting hot.

In desperation he stepped back across the landing, nerving himself. He was more afraid than he had dreamed he could be, he knew it was a foolish and futile thing he was about to try. But the old man had been good to him. He flung himself off the wall opposite, and cannoned with all his weight into the door. He was not heavily built, but even that strain seemed too much for the tortured timbers; they exploded outwards with a roar, and a great tongue of red flame licked out over his head.

Tongue indeed; for as he reeled back, shielding his face, he saw the door pillars sweat and bulge, and the lintel above them curve suddenly. Warping in the heat, was his first instinctive reaction – till they bulged out after him like vast obscene lips, slobbering fire. In sheer terror he hurled himself aside, and that saved him, for he fell head-over-heels down the stairs once more. Bruised and shaking, he staggered to his feet and back into his own chamber, knowing there was no more he could do. The foul drip lay slathered across the room: the books on the shelves whose worn bindings he had polished, the papers on the great table, the worn trenchers on the dark dressers, the clothes chest he left open at night to air it. He could not bear to touch anything it had contaminated, not even the worn spinet he had been learning to play. But his best cloak was safe, and his cittern and hautbois, and he caught them up, along with the two books that lay beside his bed, his present studies. On the dresser only a salt-cellar, one of Strauben's few pieces of silver, had escaped the drip, and he seized that also. Smoke was billowing in the hallway outside, but he had no intention of escaping that way; seizing the shutters, he hauled them back and flung wide the casement beyond. The fire above roared hungrily at the fresh inflow of air. He inhaled once with deep relief, then sprang nimbly on to the sill, crouched there an instant, and leaped out into the cool darkness.

He landed in mud. There was no drain in the alley that ran behind the old houses, but it felt infinitely cleaner than the foul air within. Looking up, he saw plumes of smoke escape between the roof tiles, with here and there red glows like malevolent eyes peeping through. Smoke billowed up through the open window, and tongues of flame played across the ceiling. He had one glimpse of the orrery, glowing scarlet and white, swinging crazily; then the beautiful instrument fell free and dropped blazing into the dark, like true stars falling.

Outside in the street voices were calling, feet clattering on the cobbles. Volker had been wise not to go that way; folk were gathering, folk who would want to put out the fire, to know just how and why it had started. He wouldn't be the one to tell them. Let it burn, and with it all trace of Strauben's folly. He picked himself up, and began to run, though he didn't know where. The rising column of flame lit his way, and showed him the vast wavering shadows of the crowd gathering. The witchfinders would not be far behind, circling like vultures over any unexplained calamity, eager – too eager – to find someone to blame. Only when he was some streets away did he stop and stare back at the glare that danced over the rooftops. It hadn't been put out, then, but neither was it spreading; and both those things were good. He found himself shedding a few tears for the old alchemist; in his way he had been a good and a kindly master, something of the father Volker had never known. Even if, in his extreme of fury and frustration at failing to master his own legitimate science, he'd been driven to dabble in demonology – and had demonstrably failed to master that as well.

Pitying the old man made it easier to avoid self-pity. He shivered. He'd some excuse: he had been cast out almost penniless and utterly alone, without a single friend to turn to, and with little or no skill to support himself. True, he had his degree – but the theses his tutors had admired and encouraged were no substitute for practical experience, and two years as Strauben's

10

assistant had given him less of that than he had imagined possible. His prospects looked dismal, right enough. Then he drew himself up to his full height, which was considerable, and pulled his cloak closer about his lean shoulders. He was young, wasn't he? And strong? There must be plenty of jobs he could do, if he didn't mind swallowing his pride. And he had freedom. No bonds of duty, family, or religion held him back; he was free to wander where he willed in the world. He'd seen little enough of it so far – his home city of Bremen, Worms, the roads between. Yet, huge as these cities were, the Empire was vaster yet. From the cold borders of the Norselands to the warm coasts of the Mittelzee in the south, from the barbarous steppes of the East to the wide seaboard of western Galle, over huldra-haunted forests and kobold mountains, over nymph-swum lakes and pirate-ridden rivers its vast mantle spread – although sometimes a little threadbare in patches. And beyond that mighty sweep lay another as rich, that few now living had ever visited – the Southern Empire, vast and decadent, last heir of vanished Rome, sprawling about the Middle Sea like the corpse of one of the Titans Jupiter struck down, gangrenous and crumbling, yet still seething with malign life.

And beyond that immense sway there must be other, stranger lands still. In so wide a world there must surely be a place for him somewhere, a new life to lead . . .

The problem would be staying alive to find it.

Chapter 1

Volker glared contemptuously at the specks of coloured light skipping about like fireflies in the smoky air, and struggled not to feel envious or despondent. One of them wiggled suddenly and made as if to shoot up his nose; despite himself he swore and slapped at it, though he knew it was the simplest of illusions, the cheapest and flashiest of magic. The skinny little man who had directed the lights with his waggling fingers smirked broadly and bowed, while the tavern regulars around the ratting pit hooted. Some threw bones and crusts at Volker, and even the occasional dead rat. They were getting used to him, which wasn't too surprising. He had been standing in that same hiring line every day for the last two weeks.

The Mutzelbacherkeller was a huge low-roofed cellar. The building above had once been the headquarters of a waggoners' company – but its owners had failed to compete with the new canal link to the Danube. Since those heady days the inn had come down in the world, a long way down. Even so, its hiring line was supposed to be the best in Nürnberg for entertainers, especially those boasting magical skill. That was why silk sleeves brushed the greasy tabletops, and fine leather boots scuffed circles in the sawdust on the floor. With both music and magic to offer, Volker had thought he might do well here. After all, Nürnberg was the oldest Free City of the Empire, commercial capital of the Burgundmark – all its lands east of the Rhine – and richer, if anything, than Worms itself. Also, it was a university centre, almost as illustrious as Heidelberg or nearby Regensburg, but much more liberal. It had seemed the best place to run. The capital, after all, was too hot to hold him, what with demonfire on one hand and witch-burners on the other. Finding another master would take time, but his skills should pick him up some cash while he looked.

He knew better now. He'd known better after the first two humiliating days. He was ten times the magician of any other in this line, with their hedge-wizard skills and half-baked marketplace patter; but he could not do that trick with the lights, nor conjure up crude carica-tures of leading citizens as the man before him had – nothing at all like that. And he wasn't enough of a musician to make up. He'd been careful to keep his music a hobby. Becoming anything like a professional player would have seemed like a bad joke, as if the blood he'd always despised and rejected was showing through. So he couldn't join the kept players of a noble-man, expected to read off anything from a sarabande to a symphony at a few minute's notice. And he couldn't reel off all the bawdy street songs from memory the way the feeblest busker could, even with only three chords and a broken d-string, nor play the lumbering *ländler* dances they favoured for weddings and jollifications round here. There was definitely more to being an entertainer than he'd thought.

He had stood in other hiring lines, of course; but scriveners and shophands had their special skills as well, and even a bootblack with a reference could beat a bootblack without one. He'd never have dreamed how many experienced bootblacks and undergrooms and footmen – even tall and personable footmen – seemed to be running loose around Nürnberg just now. There was no hiring line for experienced magician's appren-tices, and if there were he wouldn't have dared join it.

13

Strauben's death had caused gossip, and with the taint of demonology at his back nobody would have hired him, even if the witchfinders didn't start pulling out his toenails just in case. Moodily he watched the very fat man next to him conjure up a miniature nymph, on the porky side herself, and set it dancing on his palm. Volker found nothing remotely erotic in her meaty wigglings; in fact they only reminded him that he was hungry. The proceeds of pawning the salt-cellar had kept him alive, barely; but there was only tonight's dinner left of it, and a meagre dinner at that. For the last week he'd been dining only every other night. And the bluff, jolly fellow who was the last hirer tonight seemed the typical merry merchant type, richly dressed and leaning on a silver-headed ebony cane. He was no more likely to hire Volker than all the others had. It hardly seemed worth staying in the line.

But here was his turn, and he might as well summon up the best trick he could think of. From his pocket he produced one of his last coins, a cheap copper thing, and spun it a moment on his palm; then he breathed on it, and muttering words in an ancient tongue he flipped it high in the air:

A Mercurio! Denarius in argente enitesce!

It caught the torchlight with a sudden silvery gleam as it dropped into his outstretched palm, and with a flourish he held out what looked like a silver thaler. The burly man took it in red, meaty fingers, and examined it carefully. 'That's useful!' he said cheerfully. 'Doesn't look like an illusion, either. Risking the laws 'gainst coining, aren't you?'

'It's not meant to be an illusion,' explained Volker hastily. 'Just a simple transformation spell. Before I blew on it I turned the acid in my breath to a weak solution of spirits of nitre and quicksilver; it reacts with the

14

copper to become a thin film of amalgam. Looks silvery at first, but it goes on reacting – turns black in a minute or two, then rubs off, so!'

It seemed a feeble trick to him, and the tavern louts thought so, too. But to Volker's surprise the merchant rounded on them, and silenced their hooting with a single angry bark. 'That's real magic!' he said, in some surprise. 'Simple alchemy, but real. Called on Mercury, didn't you? God of alchemists . . .' He chuckled. 'And thieves. You know a thing or two, don't you, my lad? Any other skills?'

'Well, aside from reading and writing, only music, I'm afraid,' said Volker lamely, 'but I play several instruments—'

The merchant stepped back a little, and looked Volker up and down. He felt a cold chill as those eyes passed over him; suddenly they seemed dark and fathomless and not at all jolly. 'Yes,' said the merchant musingly. 'Yes, of course. You would, wouldn't you?'

Volker flushed angrily. Was it that obvious? And suppose it was, why should even a rich bastard go tearing out of a man the things he most wanted to bury? 'I'm no minstrel or player,' he said coldly. He was ruining his best, his only prospect, but he couldn't hold back his pride. 'It's just a hobby with me. Nothing more.'

The merchant nodded, apparently undisturbed. 'All the same, it's in your blood,' he said calmly, adding, 'whether you like it or not.' Volker flushed. 'But this once, at least, it may serve you; it has decided me. I hadn't hoped to find a lettered man here. My name's Ulrich, Ulrich Tragelicht of Worms, dealer in wines and spices and anything else that'll turn a profit. If you're game for a long journey, and maybe a hard one, you're exactly the servant I'm looking for. Will you join me?'

A long journey? Volker blinked in amazed relief. It could hardly have suited him better. He could go somewhere else and find a new apprenticeship, or at least stay away till matters here had blown over. As for hardship, well, he could soon have his bellyful of that just by staying where he was. Volker squared his shoulders and bowed as he had seen servants do. 'I'm Volker Seefried of Bremen. I'll be honoured to!' The merchant nodded, and called across the gaping heads of the loiterers for the two cups of wine that were the traditional bond of hire.

'But not here!' he told the landlord sternly, glaring at the noisy crowd about the ratpit. 'Show us to a clean table in a quiet corner! I'm surprised the city ordinances haven't banned this filthy sport.'

Volker smiled sourly. 'They do – officially. But it's tolerated – they say it encourages the poor to catch rats.'

Ulrich twitched his whiskers disdainfully, and followed the grovelling landlord to an alcove by the main fireplace. There they toasted one another. Volker took a long draught, and felt the new wine run cold and deep into his empty stomach; the merchant sipped austerely, and put his goblet down at once. Again he looked at Volker with that same piercing gaze, that turned his jolly face to . . . something else. 'Seefried, eh? I've heard that name in Bremen. A wealthy merchant family. Strange . . .'

Volker smiled ruefully. 'That's my family, sir – but my branch of it hasn't much hope of wealth.'

Ulrich shrugged. 'Perhaps. But truth to tell, I expected a name in another tongue altogether.'

Volker flushed: 'Seefried was my mother's name. My father's I choose not to bear.' He had meant to say no more, but when the merchant looked at him expectantly, tapping his cane lightly against his shoe, he found himself telling the whole story, unable to hold it back. 'She came from the merchant family you know of, yes. My father – he was as you have guessed. Of another kind altogether—' He stopped, waiting for the

16

merchant to fill in the hateful name himself; but he didn't.

'One of the *Huldravolk* ,' said Volker at last. 'One of the Old Peoples. A *Huldrawicht* of the Odenwald, the High Forests.' He spat out the words as if they poisoned him. 'One of the few who live near men, and have some trade with them. He . . . he went away when I was young. Just vanished. Perhaps something happened to him. I think he just got tired of humans – like any wild beast! He abandoned us without a thought. In poverty. My mother's kin might have helped us, but she broke with them to marry my father – she was too proud to go begging to them. My father had kin still in the woodlands; it was their duty to aid us. And they did – as little and as grudgingly as they could. After all, we were humans. My mother died young, worn out. Now I want nothing of theirs, not even the name. I would spill their blood from my veins if I could.'

'But you cannot,' said the merchant severely. 'Nor their shape from your body, their thought from your mind – as witness your love of music. This is folly, my young friend.'

'My mother loved music,' said Volker angrily. 'My father was a huntsman, a skin-trader – practically tone-deaf, by his people's standard! She gave me music, not him.'

'And your way with magic? In huldra the two go together – in humans, more rarely. Which brings me to my problem.' He sat back, took a deeper draught and patted his belly, and became the merry merchant once again. 'I use magic and music to sell my wares; a good show pulls in the customers. *And* sweetens 'em for an extra two or three thalers in the hundred on the prices. Trouble is, none of my present staff could manage this journey; it's a long one – and no, I'm not saying where to just yet. What I need is two or three new helpers, same as my partners in the venture are taking, men

17

young and strong enough to serve on the road, but with talents we can use at the far end. They're hard to find. Now I've found you – and your first job'll be to find me the others!'

Volker swallowed uneasily. 'I've no experience of hiring . . . Surely you . . . ?'

'Not I. This is meant to be a secret, this journey, for any number of reasons; never know who might be keeping eyes and ears open. Competitors, robbers – comes to much the same thing in this trade. I can hire one young fellow with no questions asked; but if I'm seen touting about for sturdy bravos with talents magical and musical . . . you follow? And sturdy they must be, two or better still three fellows who've knocked around a bit and can look after themselves. You're a strong lad, I don't doubt; but we'll need experienced fighters on this road.'

Volker shook his head helplessly. 'I don't want to let you down! I wouldn't know how to choose such people, even if I can find them!'

Ulrich's beard twisted in a lop-sided smile. 'Bring those you choose to the *Goldener Hirsch* inn, four days from now. I'll cast an eye over them, and unfold all to you – and them. But use your own judgement first; you've brains, they'll serve you. And you've a good heart, when you're not filling it with follies! Choose those you trust, those you're drawn to, and I'll wager you won't go far wrong.' He grinned suddenly, and tossed a purse on to the table. 'Tell them their pay will be excellent; and so will yours, little as you seem to care. Here's for your expenses! And your first should be some dinner. You'll look less elven-pale with some blue trout and a mug of ale inside you. At the *Goldener Hirsch*, then!'

His shoulder still stinging from the friendly thump of Ulrich's hand, Volker sat hefting the unopened purse in his hand. From its weight he could guess there was gold in there, a neat amount. Either this Ulrich was mad, or he could size men up with the accuracy of an insult. He'd decided Volker was honest; and the worst of it was, he was right. Volker smouldered with resentment. He'd half a mind to run off with the lot, just to prove him wrong; only he was too damn proud. And Ulrich might have guessed that, too. What gave that fat old fraud the right to read a man like a book? Volker sighed, and hefted the money. The right to buy the book, of course. Being a servant wasn't going to be easy. But he had been given his orders, and he'd better get on with them – starting with dinner. Ulrich had even guessed his weakness for trout. Sheer perversity made Volker order a steak.

It might just as well have been the fish. Ravenous as he was, he hardly noticed what he was eating. His new responsibility took all the savour out of it. How in all the length and breadth of the Empire was anybody supposed to set about finding a pack of reformed musical brigands? And discreetly, at that!

Two evenings later, lurking behind the door of the snug with the row from the rat-pit grating on his ears, he still had no answers. The cudgel of untrimmed oak poised above his head was about as near as he'd got. Unemployed musician-magicians seemed to be as common as bootblacks, and a pretty feeble lot they were. By now he had scared several dozen out of half a year's growth. None who came in answer to his carefully phrased placards had shown the slightest ability to 'look after himself' . . . No, not quite true. A fair number showed startling agility when the cudgel whistled past their ears, and some had demonstrated a fine turn of speed. One had leapt clear through the window. That had cost Volker extra to placate the landlord; the window had been closed at the time.

Useful as these skills might be, they weren't quite

what Ulrich had meant. Being a peaceful and sensitive soul himself, Volker felt some sympathy with his victims; but the fact remained, all of them were even softer than he was. Not one had shown the kind of spirit he'd want in a companion on a different journey to the gods knew where. Neither, he told himself, would this next one. The tread approaching the door was heavy and slow; probably another bulge-bellied lutenist, or another Italian eunuch singer; the last had screamed in a voice so high Volker was almost had up for rape. He hefted the cudgel, fighting down the urge not to miss for a change, so disgusted he felt; but he muttered the simple spell that would deflect it, just as before. As the door swung back on the newcomer he brought it whistling down.

For one mad moment he thought he'd hit himself, so solid was the impact that jarred along his arm. Then he heard a nasal, accented voice say, very reproachfully, 'A man should not do that. Someone might get hurt.' Something, a gale maybe, plucked the cudgel out of his hand. Then the gale blew a tree down on his head. '*Saa*. You see?'

Those damned coloured lights were back, Volker decided, wittering around his head again. But what was he doing flat on his back, and why was the cudgel waving about in front of his nose? 'One light tap I give you. You have a face too honest for any such *nithing*'s work. But I think it best that in two, maybe three breaths you tell a tale I believe, or you shall eat this twig without salt and pepper.'

Volker sat up with an effort, though the room insisted on swaying. Above him loomed what appeared to be a mass of sandy-brown hair, with somewhere in the midst of it a straight, rather prominent nose; above high cheekbones, tanned to the same shade as the hair, a pair of ice-blue eyes fixed him with a highly alarming stare. 'I think,' mumbled Volker, rubbing his head, 'that concludes the first part of the interview . . .'

The newcomer's name was Thorgrim, called, he said, Thorgrim Thryhyrning, for reasons he didn't go into. But even before he heard it, Volker knew where he was from. The accent was unmistakable, and so was the look, up to a point. He had seen and heard Norse barbarians often enough in Bremen, where their traders came now and again to buy the civilised luxuries that fierce and hardy folk had developed a remarkable taste for. Unlike most Empire citizens Volker knew that they weren't all giant raving loons in breechclouts and horned helmets. Aside from the occasional berserker, that was; and this one looked almost offensively calm.

He was no giant; Volker, yanked back on his feet with one effortless heave, topped him by a good handspan, though the Norseman was much more heavily built. And he didn't look uncivilised, too much the other way, if anything. His hair and beard, though dense, were elaborately barbered and curled and perfumed; his metal-studded leather jerkin, though it looked rather worn, was lined and trimmed with rich grey fur, and his full hose were in the latest eye-aching fashion, gaudy black and yellow stripes. The high boots they were tucked into, though very battered, were imported Cordoban work, crucially expensive city footwear. But he bore none of the ornaments that were every Norseman's portable savings, save a heavy gold-hilted knife at his hip, and empty sockets yawned among the gold where gems had been pried loose. He might have looked funny, like an overdressed mountebank; but that knife, and the weapon like a huge-bladed spear or pike that he scooped up off the floor – there was a well-used practicality about them that gave Volker, clutching at the wall for support, no urge to laugh at all. He put the Norseman at about ten years older than him, and maybe twice the strength. A pretty active ten years, at that. The blue eyes measured up Volker with deceptive mildness. '*Naa*. An interview? You hear, perhaps, that Norsemen make drums of skulls, and you will tune mine? I heard you sought *skalds* or spellsingers—'

'You?' demanded Volker, detaching himself gingerly from the wall. 'You're a musician?'

Thorgrim's blue eyes fixed him with that stare once again. 'That seems unlikely to you. But our princes will not have slaves to sing their praises. Alfvinn Reykjadale's-Chieftain, he was my father. His third son, me, he causes to be raised as a *skald*, so that someone may sing of his great deeds. Then he is slain by Eystein Fart before he does much worth singing about. And so there is feuding—' he fingered the shaft of his halberd suggestively '—and I must fare south awhile with Oskel the Skin-Trader, down the Rhine to Strasbourg. There I serve the Archpriest three years as *hærethman*—'

'As what?'

'Bodyguard. In his house-troop. Also I play in his band. Second sackbut. Then the Archpriest tightens his purse-strings. Band disbanded. Sackbuts sacked.' He stamped the round steel butt of his weapon irritably on the floor. 'So I wander this great Empire with my father's old halberd Hlavisbana to look for honest labour in lousy fleabitten taverns, and instead we are set on from behind doors . . .'

'Please sit down!' said Volker hastily, waving him towards the better of the two chairs and the wine bottle on the table. 'Help yourself,' he added, staggering to the other chair and managing, somehow, to slump into it. 'All right, so you're a musician. But my – er, I also require some magical ability . . .'

'That I have also,' grunted the Norseman from behind his wine cup, 'a little. It comes to me when I am deputed to guard a *fjolkingis*, a witchfinder you would say, in the Archpriest's service. A bad man, that, little better than the Tartarists he hunted. But in his service I found a skill, and that – uncommon.' He fell silent, as if unsure how much to give away, fingering the hammer-shaped amulet that hung at his throat. Volker couldn't help noticing the ruby that glittered at the base of its shaft – one jewel, at least, the Norseman had kept.

'You came for a job,' Volker reminded him. 'I'll need a demonstration, maybe—' He gulped at his wine, and the drumming in his head eased. 'Wait a minute . . . I've just had one, haven't I? With the cudgel! You were *expecting* it!'

The Norseman shrugged, rather sheepishly. 'Half-told is ill told. *Ja*, I knew. It came to me while we searched for places where ill magic was being worked, that I knew them at once. I was not believed at first, but later it saved many innocents from being put to the question, or worse. For that he did not love me, the witch-hunter; he would have tried me, but the Arch-priest pronounced me clean. It is this way with me, that I have no magic – but when a man uses magic near me, I know it. In my guts I feel it. If it is strong enough, I know where. Sometimes, very strong, very close, I can even tell who. You and your little stick-spell, it was a small matter; for as the saying goes, *no door speaks of what lies behind it*, and it is my way always to check. That is all.'

Volker whistled, impressed. 'That's not quite what I expected, but it's a powerful talent! It could come in useful—'

The beard split in a crafty grin. '*Naa ja*? Useful for what? '

'I don't know myself. Not yet. We'll all be told before we're hired.'

'But it is a matter of hazard, that is plain. Hence the twig. It seems you are looking for the kind of *skald* who does not step lightly through strange doors?'

'Something like that,' admitted Volker. 'There can't

23

be many, and I couldn't think of a better way to find them.'

'Not so bad, at that,' conceded Thorgrim reluctantly. 'Though perhaps it is not so simple to find another with my placid nature. Most, I think, will first break your neck, and ask why later . . .'

'I thought of that; but magic and music, those kinds of skills make a man more likely to think before he acts. Anyway . . .' he smiled shamefacedly, and rubbed his head. 'I thought I'd be able to stand them off – long enough to explain, anyway. Some hope! I hardly even saw you. I think you're just the type my master's looking for. I'm just not sure that *I* am.'

Thorgrim chuckled good-naturedly. 'There is more to you than your seeming, I think. So when shall we see this master of yours?'

'In a day or so. But I've got to find others first – at least a couple more like you.'

'Luck, my friend,' said Thorgrim drily. 'Tell me the meeting-place, and you shall find me there.'

'I was hoping you might help me . . .' Noting a certain lack of enthusiasm, he added, 'I'd make it worth your while, of course. But this time *you* hold the club.'

Thorgrim thought it over a moment, then chuckled again, and raised his wine cup.

The next two days passed all too swiftly, and so, it seemed, did the few remaining musician-magicians in town. If the firstcomers had moved fast when Volker swung at them, the rest surpassed themselves when they saw Thorgrim. One with more magical ability than most tried to levitate up the chimney, wedged himself tight, and had to be hauled down kicking and screaming amid clouds of soot and old bird's nests. Volker's hopes sank.

'Tomorrow,' he muttered, staring moodily down at the dinner he had hardly touched. A day or two earlier he had been starving; now he had lost his appetite. Besides, everything tasted of soot. 'My first task, and I fouled it up.'

Thorgrim shrugged and stole a length of blood-sausage from his plate. 'You have found me. I think it not so strange that there should be few in these soft lands to match me. There is no making a stone bleed – except, maybe, in the forest heartlands or the high mountains, where the older powers still endure. I am wondering if our journey will lie through them.'

Volker shuddered. 'Surely not. There can't be many customers in the wilds—' He broke off as the bell above their heads tinkled, the tapster signalling that another customer was on the way.

'Yes, well, try going a bit easier on this one!' warned Volker as Thorgrim took up station, the end of the sausage still dangling from his mouth. 'Spell or not, swing wider!'

'Well for you to say!' grumbled the barbarian past mouthfuls of sausage. 'Making miserable lute-pluckers spoil their breeches, that is poor work for a man—'

They were taken completely by surprise. The door burst open as if it had been kicked. A large figure careered through it, rebounded off the doorpost with a wild shout, and reeled straight into the path of Thorgrim's cudgel. The spell had no time to deflect it again. There was a hollow clonk, a roar like a ruptured centaur, and the black-clad man collapsed on to his knees, clutching his head.

'*Merde de Minotaure!*' he bellowed, his pale face suffused with fury. His pointed beard bristled, and one of the upturned moustaches above it wilted to give him a lop-sided sneer. '*Qui a osé?*' He spotted Thorgrim and screamed with such fury that even the Norseman blinked. The newcomer shot out a hand, surrounded by a heavy lace cuff, and shouted in a different tongue:

25

*Vinifer vineaticus Dionyso! Torrenter in mascarpionem effer-
vesce!*

From between his stabbing fingers a jet of scarlet liquid
blasted out, caught the startled barbarian in the chest
and shot him bodily off the ground to slam hard against
the opposite wall.

For an instant the torrent held him there like an insect
pinned to a card, a time in which it ought to have
flooded the tiny room. Instead it vanished utterly, leaving only a heavy, fragrant odour on the air. Thorgrim
slid to the floor. Volker, horrified, moved to help him,
but seeing the wheezing Norseman already picking
himself up he turned to the newcomer. He had started
to rise, but as Volker took his arm he shook him off
absently and sniffed at the air. Then he gazed in astonishment at his fingers and touched them to his lips.
'*Un bon soixante-six – ou cinquante-neuf, voyons . . .* ' he
muttered raptly to himself. '*Première cuvée, coté sud du
colline . . .*'

Without warning he whirled around unsteadily and
caught the startled Volker in a bone-crushing bear-hug.
'My friends!' he shouted, in perfectly clear Burgundian.
'This is a great night! At last I have succeeded in calling
up the true, the blushful queen of wines, the one and
only *Sein d'Aphrodite*! You shall drink it with me!' He
sent Volker spinning across the room, seized a cup from
the table and thrust his fingers into it. Liquid boiled
over the rim, he flung it to his lips and gulped. A wild,
haunted look came into his eyes, and he sat down
heavily on the bench. 'I am betrayed!' he whispered.
'Again – nothing but water!'

'Try again!' suggested Thorgrim, fascinated. So was
Volker; this was potent magic, and no illusion-juggling.
With a look of deep resolution the hefty man flung the
water hissing into the fire, plunged his fingers into the
cup, and this time sniffed nervously at what appeared.

26

Then he sank his head into his arms and quietly began to weep. Curiously Thorgrim picked the cup up, twitched his wide nostrils over it and suddenly drained it with a smack of the lips. 'A man should not weep with no cause,' he observed, wiping from his moustache. 'The ale is passable.'

'*Ale!*' wailed the man, pounding the table. '*But where are the wines of yesteryear?*'

Abruptly, as if he had just remembered, the scowling face of before popped up. 'What bestial trick is this? I come to offer you the incomparable benefit of my services and you set upon me in this coward fashion? *Canaille*, I will teach you—' He was on his feet with a surge that almost overset the table, his hand already in the basket hilt of a long straight sabre, halfway from its sheath. Thorgrim snatched at his halberd, but Volker held up his hands between them.

'*Freiherrn!* Gentlemen! Peace, please, while we explain! And,' he added, eyeing the sabre, 'drink a glass of wine as some amends . . .'

The newcomer looked them both up and down out of glittering brown eyes, somewhat bloodshot. Absently he lifted a finger and curled his moustaches back into shape. Roundheaded and bull-necked, he bulked formidably in the dim light of the dingy little parlour, taller than Thorgrim and broader than either of them. His doublet of figured black velvet hung unlaced across his barrel chest to reveal an elaborately ruffled and laced shirt of white silk, his glossy black hair flowing back in unkempt waves across its wide ornate collar. They were costly clothes, obviously made closely to his measure; but the elbows of the doublet shone with wear, and the lace was speckled with spatters of dull brown that might have been wine, or blood, or both. If Thorgrim looked like a barbarian dressed as a gentleman, this one, thought Volker, looked like a gentleman dressed as a barbarian.

Suddenly he gave a snort of disgust, and the sabre swept from its sheath. Volker seized the cudgel, Thorgrim hefted his halberd, but the newcomer swung around and with his sword's point flipped up a wide-brimmed black hat from the floor where it had fallen. He blew the dust from it, straightened its cockade of white plumes, and slid the sabre back into its sheath.

'Well? I await your feeble excuses with interest, and I will drink your wine if it is palatable.'

Volker rang for wine, then introduced himself and Thorgrim, and began trying to explain what the cudgel had been for. 'It wouldn't have hit you, if you had not, er . . . stumbled.'

An angry cloud swept over the burly man's face. 'Is it that you are implying I was drunk?' he growled.

'Yes,' said Thorgrim matter of factly. The other man's face crumpled with fury; he seemed about to burst, but instead he gave a rumble of laughter and sat back.

'You are not mistaken, *foi de Guillac*! Do you think it easy for I, I, Guy de Guillac, Seigneur de Josselin et de Pontivy, Draconnier Hereditaire of all the lands north of Morbihan, Knight Commander of the Tributary Dukedom of Armorica, to come and seek common employment – *employment!* – as a mere entertainer? No! It could not be! Five hundred ancestors weep within their vaults tonight! So I must needs console myself. A trace over the brim, it may be. And, my faith, I have never been sobered more quickly, nor my head ached more speedily! Not to mention a mouth not unlike the floor of the ancestral vaults – ah, you are kind!' There was a brief interval of fast swallowing, then he held out his cup for a refill; so did Thorgrim. They regarded each other with a certain professional respect, and drained their wine noisily. '*Aaahh!*' sighed the lord of Josselin and Pontivy, settling back on the bench. 'Hardly the *Sein d'Aphrodite*, but it will serve. Now, tell me, what

28

manner of mountebank do you seek that you must test their nerves with a cudgel?'

Before Volker had finished the Armorican noble sprang to his feet and paced around the room. 'I see it all! Yes! This is better than I could have guessed! I will certainly join you!'

'Generous of you,' grunted Thorgrim.

'Is it not? But I am inimitable!'

'But are you – I mean, is such a noble gentleman as yourself fitted to the task?'

The big man stopped dead, mouth dropping open. 'I? But who is better? In my very cradle I am trained as a warrior. I am a belted knight, I fight in three campaigns under my lord duke of Armorica, in one under the Emperor himself. Ever since I am exiled from my humble demesnes through the intrigues of the Archpriest of Condate and his closet-Tartarist cabal on the flimsy pretext of having hunted his scrofulous tithe-gatherers with boarhounds, I have lived as a freelanced knight, a *Landsknecht* as you say in the Empire.'

'A mercenary? I see,' said Thorgrim. 'They are ten a thaler round the Empire just now, even the best. You would have done better turning professional jouster, or hiring out as a champion for trials by battle.'

'The Draconnier is no paid assassin!' rumbled de Guillac sulkily. 'Nor a skulker at sports grounds, ready to strip any man of his armour. I have my pride! I am not one of the perfumed brainless fops of the Gallic aristocracy, nor one of your boneheaded Burgundian *Junkers*! The Lords of Guillac have always been educated men. I am master of all the skills you demand!' He snatched up Volker's cittern and struck an impressive flourish of chords upon it, then a lilting little tune. 'I play also hautbois and ophicleide, and I sing, *bas-profond*. The rudiments of music are taught us in our cradles, and of magic also. As you have witnessed.'

'I think you are kept busy in those cradles,' said

Thorgrim, straight-faced. Volker looked a question at him, and found it returned. So the decision was once again up to him. *Choose whom you trust*, Ulrich had said. He had begun to trust the genial Norseman, but this outrageous Gallian – or more accurately Armorican – was a harder proposition altogether. His magical skill was obvious, but his appearance was against him. The pointed beard and moustaches around his jutting chin and blunt nose had an arrogant, devilish tilt, heightened by the ironic tilt of his brows; an intelligent-looking devil, though, with that high forehead. And with a sense of humour, for all his bluster. He'd laughed off that whack on the head.

That decided Volker. 'Very well, then. I'll take you to my master tomorrow. It's he who must make the final choice.' After all, it was unlikely he would find anyone better. It would have been good to have a third, but now, at least, he could feel that he had not failed Ulrich.

The Gallian rose and bowed with an elaborate flourish to each of them in turn. 'Then, masters, I suggest we quit this soot-stinking parlour and drink a small glass or two upon our agreement. And what diversion does this ill-conditioned hovel offer, I wonder?'

Volker did not want to drink any more, but he did want to get out of the little snug; the cloudy wine fumes still hanging in the air were giving him a headache. As for entertainment, he hoped the man didn't mean the rat-pit; he'd already spent too long beside it, and he loathed rats. But de Guillac sniffed ostentatiously and gave the crowd a wide berth. 'Stinking beasts!' he said, taking in rats, dogs and audience, and Thorgrim grunted his assent.

'No sport for a man,' he said stolidly. 'Drink up, my friends, and away to the *Tröllenkopf*, where they have sword-jugglers and fire-eaters . . .' De Guillac shrugged unenthusiastically, and the Norseman added craftily

'Or the *Blue Harpy*. They have exotic dancers, Libyan style . . .'

'Ahhahh!' said the Armorican happily, twirling an extra curl in his moustaches. 'Have you ever seen Libyan dancers of the stomach, Master Volker? No? And you aspire to be an educated man! Let me tell you—'

His lecture was rudely interrupted by a loud crash. The door at the head of the stairs was flung back. A blinding beam of evening sun slanted down into the smoky gloom. Many of the regulars cringed back from it like night creatures under a stone, fearing a raid by the City Watch or the Imperial Excise. But the silhouette was too slender to be either. It was the slim figure of a girl that came cantering two at a time down the rickety stairs, long hair flying out behind her, a long staff bouncing at her shoulder. With a shriek of rage she plunged through the gap her appearance had cleared.

'Oi!' yelled the outraged landlord. 'Where d'you think you're—' But she was already at the rat-pit, and to Volker's horror she leaped right over the rim and down into the little arena. A flurry of squeaks and snarls arose from the startled terriers and their prey, but she plunged through and across to the door on the far side, and flung it open. 'Stop the bitch, somebody!' bellowed the landlord. But before any of the thugs could move she reappeared with a shriek of triumph, clutching a wooden cage.

'Landlord!' she yelled furiously, jumping up on to the barrier of the pit. 'Mutzelbackher, you boar's fewmet! Not paying enough, was it, the pit? Punters getting bored, so you've got to go breeding more rats – oh yes, those special late-night shows! I've heard! But not just plain ordinary rats, you stupid bastard, no – *they've got to be black rats*!'

With the force of her anger she heaved the cage high and hurled it across the heads of the startled crowd. It

31

crashed down into the main fireplace and exploded into pieces among the blazing logs. The drinkers dived for cover as shrilling things little smaller than cats came boiling out of the ruin, biting and tumbling among the flames; a few burst blazing out of the fire and went scattering across the floor, snapping in their last agony at themselves and anyone or anything else they passed.

'Don't you know what you were *doing*?' screamed the girl. 'Those things are deadly! Every bloody distemper out of Tartarus they carry! And not just breeding them – you've been letting them escape! Three I caught in the sewers round here tonight alone! Want to set the Black Plague on the whole bloody city? The Watch'll have your hide for this, and not before time either! They'll shut you down—'

The fat landlord loomed out of the shadows, sweating heavily about his jowls. 'Shut me, will they?' he wheezed. 'You little whore, I'll see you flayed first! Here, boys!'

An angry growl answered him; many of the rat-pit gamblers sprang to their feet. The girl tossed her head defiantly, but Volker read the sudden nervousness in her very stance. She twitched the staff he'd taken for a ratcatcher's pole down from her shoulder; it was a longbow. But as she bent and strung it, a huge lout snatched at one end and began to yank on it, amid coarse howls of encouragement.

Volker clenched his fists. 'Shouldn't we help?' he demanded uncertainly.

Thorgrim shrugged. 'Why?'

The Armorican nodded. 'It is her lookout. My faith, lad, she is a ratcatcher, they are rarely tender souls. A little harmless roughing about may remind her not to rush in so stupidly next time.'

Suddenly the girl, in danger of being pulled down, looked up to the door and whistled loudly. Volker expected a ratcatcher's savage little dog. Instead he ducked like all the others, as something wide and white whistled through the air. Between girl and thug it swept, seeming to touch neither – but the thug squealed and spun around. The gamblers growled, and Volker caught his breath. Bloody furrows were scored down the man's face from eye to chin.

Down from the vaultings the white shadow swooped, to settle on the girl's shoulder, and with a high shrieking cry it spread its wings behind her head like a protective crest. It was an owl, a huge owl of no breed Volker knew, its back grey-mottled but its breast pure blazing white behind her rich brown hair. Its eyes flashed as bright as hers, eerie, numinous, forbidding. Thorgrim nodded quietly, as if he had noticed something.

Ignored by the others, the lout lurched roaring away. The girl snapped home the bowstring, and with liquid speed plucked out an arrow, notched it and drew to her ear. But the landlord's obscene goadings overcame the startled superstition of the crowd, and with a menacing rumble they closed in. Their mood had changed, bullies balked of their fun turning suddenly resentful. The girl swung her bow back and forth, but at every swing the thugs ducked closer. The owl's head twisted around suddenly, its jarring cry rang out. She whirled, there was a thrum and a hiss, and the man who had crept up through the open rat-pit door yelled and cartwheeled over with a long shaft quivering in his upper arm. In the same instant she notched and drew another arrow, and swung back to cover the growling mob. Fast as she was, Volker realized, she could manage no more than one or two shots; and there were at least twenty. He tensed suddenly; metal glinted among them. The knives were out, if no worse.

He sprang up, but Thorgrim's heavy hand landed on his shoulder. 'So, it goes too far, yes. But best leave this to us. You wait a chance to get out the girl.'

'*Mille sabords*, yes!' muttered the Armorican. 'A pretty

hide she has, rat-scented or no. A shame if such a rabble were to cut it up!' He thrust his plumed hat at Volker. '*Allons!*'

With a speed Volker would never have expected from such hefty men they launched themselves across the room. Those few more reputable customers who hadn't already fled hastily scuttled out. Thorgrim's halberd butt ploughed a path through the startled bullies; with a challenging bellow that made the girl jump he scythed the long blade at their legs, and they leaped back in stumbling disorder. De Guillac, without even drawing his sword, seized the nearest and sank his heavy boot into the man's ample stomach, then, as he folded, felled the man behind with a blow to the throat and sprang through the gap to the tabletop behind. A sword slashed down at Thorgrim's head; he parried deftly, and the sword skidded down his halberd blade and caught in a deep notch at the base. The ironbound shaft twisted sharply in the Norseman's heavy hands. With a crystalline ring the sword was snapped off at the hilt. The flat of the halberd smacked down on the ex-swordsman's head; he slid down under the others' feet and failed to reappear.

Weapons cut at de Guillac. With a shout of laughter he dodged them, sprang down on the far side of the table and ducked out of sight. Jeering at his cowardice, the attackers sprang up after him, only to be sent flying as he surged up again, bringing the table with him. Knives were flung, even an axe, but he heaved the overturned table up before him and they thudded harmlessly into the thick wood. Then, with an angry roar and an audible crack of his shoulders, he swung the long table chest-high and hurled it bodily at his shrinking assailants. Three went down beneath it, as many more went sprawling. De Guillac jumped on to it like a springboard, crushing the wind out of those beneath, and fell upon the rest. That left only three or four to harry the girl. One swordsman she dropped with an arrow in the thigh, struck aside a knife blow with her bowstave and notched another arrow before they could strike again.

Volker waited as he'd been told to, clenching his fists and shivering with the unfamiliar excitement of the fight. Two knifemen jumped Thorgrim, front and back. A quick fore and aft swing hammered the blade down flat on the head of the front man, then, one-two, brought its steel-ball butt up smartly between the legs of the man behind. Both lost interest in the immediate proceedings. Volker winced. His blood was in turmoil. Thorgrim and de Guillac were still grossly outnumbered. They were obviously being careful not to kill; would their opponents let any little thing like that bother them? And the girl – while here he was left hat-holding like a milliner's dummy!

An axe-wielder slashed at de Guillac, then dropped his weapon with a yell as an arrow skewered his arm. The girl snatched at a new arrow, fumbled – and the remaining thugs closed in. Volker threw down the hat. To Tartarus with that, he'd make his damned moment! He snatched the cudgel from his belt and charged.

The first man, a huge fat bully, half turned with dagger upraised, but Volker's long reach took him by surprise. The cudgel struck a pleasantly musical note on his shaven pate and knocked him in a heap. The second, a skinny little shred, ducked, wove, and thrust with a darting needle of a dagger, so insignificant that Volker simply plunged in and whacked him on the head with the cudgel. He dropped, but with a strange tearing sound. Volker swallowed as he saw the little dagger rip free from his jerkin below the armpit. It had come within a hair's breadth of his heart. The third man, as tall as himself, loomed up, Volker struck out – and the world exploded in stinging light. Abruptly, confusingly, he was flat on his back on the filthy floor again, the cudgel a splintered stump in his numbed fingers and above him the dull sheen of a sword. It seemed to fill the world as it fell.

Dimly, from vast distance, he heard a shrill command. *'Roll, idiot!'*

The blow sent filth leaping from the trodden floor where he'd been. Then the high voice spoke again, words he only half understood.

Diana lucina! In frumenta zizania – spargete!

All his senses quivered. Something like a vast invisible soapbubble seemed to burst overhead and shower its essence on the men around him – just as the sword-wielder snarled and struck again. His blow went wild, he lost his balance, stumbled roaring right over Volker and barged the landlord. The landlord took it personally, thumped the swordsman on the nose, tripped painfully over Volker's gangling shins, was caught by another man – and thumped him too. The swordsman aimed a terrible blow at the landlord, but his upswing sank his sword deep in one of the beams. Volker kicked him on the kneecap and scrambled up, only to be felled by the man the landlord had punched. Somebody else cold-cocked the staggering swordsman and turned to the landlord with an ingratiating grin – for which he received a bullet head in the stomach, sending him flying into a heap of empty casks. The landlord straightened up with a satisfied air, then jerked as a chair flew to matchwood flinders against his shaven skull. He toppled rigidly over the edge into the rat-pit, where he was immediately set on by yapping terriers.

The girl tossed aside the chair's remains and reached down to Volker. 'Up you come, elf-legs!' Volker bridled, but she jerked him easily to his feet. He was still too winded to speak and more than a little dazed by the nimbus of that soundless detonation. He'd recognized it from the words, an appeal to some goddess or other to sow tares among the wheat – a confusion spell. Simple magic, but tricky enough to handle in a tight spot; a neat piece of work, and it had saved his neck. He'd plenty to thank . . .

Wait a minute. Thank who? That hadn't been Guy de Guillac's rumbling drawl. It sounded more like . . . Oh, no. Here was Thorgrim, grinning like an urbane wolf, and behind him the Armorican, panting hard, his sword still in its scabbard.

'Timely aid for our young friend!' growled Thorgrim. 'Now I think it good that we clear a way out of this place!'

'Suits me!' snapped the girl, slinging her bow over her back and standing shoulder to shoulder with the men. The Armorican nodded breathlessly, and twisted his head round to the bewildered Volker.

'Keep close behind us! And don't forget my hat!' Hastily Volker snatched it up, and grabbed his cloak and cittern from beside the bar. *'Now!'* shouted de Guillac, and for the first time drew his sabre. Hunched close together the three charged for the stairs, halberd and sabre swinging a path. None of the remaining gawkers seemed inclined to challenge this human wall. They shrank back, and Volker, hobbling along behind, passed unhindered, with the great owl wheeling above their heads.

But as they clattered up the creaky wooden steps the girl looked back and stopped so suddenly she almost knocked Volker over. Behind them the landlord scrambled groggily over the edge of the rat-pit, beating feebly at the two terriers attached to the seat of his pants. The girl leant over the creaking rail and yelled something that, if it was true, made either his ancestry or his anatomy pretty remarkable. Then she whirled and fumbled with her belt; either she meant to launch an arrow at him, or drop her hose. Thorgrim cursed and more or less dragged her up to the door by the scruff of her neck.

He slammed it hard behind him. Together he and the Armorican upended one of the large tables outside and leaned it against the door. 'Hey, it opens inward!' exclaimed the girl, holding an arm out to the owl. 'That won't stop them . . .'

Thorgrim grinned. 'You think not? Wait and see – but not here. *Only fools gabble at a foeman's gate.*' Despite his words, he set off at a very leisurely stroll. Volker was more inclined to run, but Guy, too, showed no sense of urgency; he just kept looking over his shoulder. They had reached the far edge of the little court when a fearful racket of crashes and shouting reached them, and a faint tremor underfoot. It was exactly the kind of noise you would expect several men crashing arse over apex downstairs to make, especially if they were inextricably entangled with a large table.

Thorgrim nodded calmly. 'Best we fill our bellies at some other board for a while, perhaps.'

The girl nodded. 'Don't worry. Once I sic the Watch on old Mutzelbacher they'll close him for a year at least.'

'In that case,' grunted Guy, 'may I suggest you take a little trip awhile, out of town altogether. For reasons of good health.'

The girl looked him up and down. 'Listen,' she began, 'don't think I'm not grateful for you all rushing in to help and everything when you don't know me from Embla. But most times I can look after myself—'

'Look after yourself?' exploded Volker, nursing his head. 'Just charging in like that, running off at the mouth? Of all the fool tricks—'

'Hmm,' observed the girl, as if belatedly noticing him. Her eyes were large, as brown and lustrous as her hair, but she narrowed them as if she was looking at some small and unpleasant insect. 'Now of course *you'd* never go galumphing in just anyhow, would you? So nobody would have to waste a good spell just saving your stupid butt – right?'

Volker scowled. 'Next time I'll save myself the trouble . . .'

She wasn't listening. 'So I blew up a little, that's all. Lousy enough being a ratcatcher without morons making it worse! Plague rats, *ugh*!'

'Then why stick to it?' inquired Thorgrim mildly. 'One more reason to get away. He is right, this Gallian; he and I leave town anyway, but I shall sleep the sounder for it. As the saying goes, *Sleep lowers the strongest guard, and no man's throat is safe upon a mattress*. You show some skill as a fighter, and some also in magic. You could find a hundred less lowly ways to earn your bread!'

De Guillac twirled his moustache. 'You could, for example, do us the honour of joining our company!'

'That was in my mind,' agreed Thorgrim.

'Here, wait a minute!' protested Volker. 'That's for me to say! I choose who's right and who isn't! And she doesn't fit!'

De Guillac threw his hands wide in florid disagreement. 'You sought a third? Here she is, tumbled into your lap – your pardon, *mam'selle*, merely a figure of speech! But what possible objection can there be to one with so shapely an . . . an . . . .'

'Yes?' smouldered the girl. 'You were going to say?'

De Guillac gestured apologetically, eyes twinkling. 'So shapely an owl – is it not? The word had quite escaped me.'

Thorgrim's grin split his beard. 'It seems to me she would not be wholly unwelcome.'

'Hey, don't I get any say?' demanded the girl. 'I'm not just sailing off into the blue with a bunch of guys I don't know – not even their names! Think I need to go buying trouble?'

'See? See? She just doesn't . . . measure up.'

'Measure up? Name of a damned blue demon!' Guy threw his hands up to the skies for patience.

Volker, flushing, wished he'd chosen a better way of putting it. Nothing measurable about her could possibly be described as wrong. She was tall, lissom, hardly shorter than himself, with chestnut hair all but long enough to sit on. No wonder the others were interested. In fact she was looking more attractive by the minute, standing there with hands on her hips and an indignant flush on her high cheekbones, her lips pursed angrily and her dark eyes flashing. Volker told himself it was her character he couldn't stand; he hated brash women, and her manner grated on his nerves. As a shy teenager in a squalid quarter of Bremen he'd shrivelled when fishwives and street-girls called coarse invitations after him. It had never occurred to him, then or since, that they actually liked the look of him. The girls he dreamed of were pastel princesses, silently passionate, or – in more realistic moments – free spirits with brains and education, good company. This one's barging and bawling had put him off, and that elvish taunt of hers had just finished the job. Damned if he'd suffer that sort of thing on a trip that might last months! It didn't occur to him to wonder why he'd still been so eager to help her. 'She's . . . not the type my master meant, that's all. She's no skill in music, for one thing.'

The girl snorted. 'Well, *Master* Fokler—'

'*Volker!*'

'All right, all right, keep your codpiece on! And while you're about it my name's not *she* – it's Dani! Danitzia! Don't worry, wild horses wouldn't drag me anywhere you went – but as it happens I can play an instrument!' And from one of the pouches at her belt she produced a row of wooden tubes bound into a wide slab.

Volker snorted. 'Panpipes! We mean *real* music!'

The girl snarled 'These *are* real music! You think I'm just an ignorant peasant, don't you? I've studied it,

40

studied hard! I can read all five kinds of tabulature –
can you? I know harmony, counterpoint – *and* I can
write in all the modes—'

Volker bridled, though he fought not to show it. He
was fine on the commoner tabulatures, but he'd never
applied himself enough to learn the technicalities of
composition. She might be bluffing, but he didn't dare
call it. 'No!' he said firmly, forcing down the feeling he
was making an idiot of himself again. 'It's my choice, I
say she's not fit for it, and that's all.'

'Not fit for what?' she blazed. 'For anything you are?
Listen here, you long superior streak of misery –
anyhow, what makes you think I'd come anywhere
with you this side of Tartarus? Answer me that!'

'The man finds, the master chooses,' put in Thorgrim.
'Why not let this Master Ulrich make up his own mind?'

'No!' said Volker as firmly as he could. 'I don't know
much more than you about him, but one thing I'm sure
of – he'll never approve of her!'

'An excellent choice,' said Ulrich, putting down his
winecup and wiping his lips on a napkin of fine linen.
The *Goldener Hirsch*, a tall half-timbered stone building
standing right on the main square between the immense
guildhalls, was a far superior breed of inn. 'I approve
of them all!'

Volker swallowed. 'All?' he croaked. 'Even the girl?'

'Why, yes!' frowned Ulrich. 'A lapsed votaress,
almost certainly a priestess – don't find *them* every day!
Nor the others, for that matter. They're all of high cal-
ibre, better men than I'd hoped to find at such short
notice. I congratulate you.'

'A lapsed priestess,' said Volker, leaning heavily on
the carved back of the merchant's chair. 'I'd never have
guessed.'

'You didn't know? Lapsed, or a penitent, maybe,
labouring under the displeasure of her goddess. Surely

41

the owl made you wonder? A familiar, the gift of a goddess such as only practitioners of her mysteries may have. But which goddess, eh?' Ulrich crossed his hands over his belly, and looked crafty. 'Minerva Brynhilda, maybe, for an owl's her emblem, but a smaller one, not that ferocious snowy breed from Bretain. It's of a piece with all else about her – the bow, the magic. Hunting! It all smacks of that! Even her ratcatching, the lowliest task that would still let her remain a huntress. So, it's likely enough Diana Skadia she served, and sorely offended. I wonder how?' He mused for a moment. 'No. Best not ask till we know her better. There are depths to that young woman, as there are to you, young man! Now go call your fellows up to our chambers here; they must be introduced to the company. And then, at last, I may speak freely of our venture!'

Volker bowed, his mind still whirling, and went down the stairs into the main body of the inn. Thorgrim and the others sat at the table where he had left them; but since Ulrich had summoned him they had collected an impressive array of jugs and bottles. The men were definitely merry. Thorgrim was telling some complicated story with very strange gestures that were making Dani splutter with laughter as she drank. They rose as he approached, obviously expecting the summons, and he saw the clear flask of fruit juice by Dani's plate, another telling detail, now he knew what to look for. These nature cults didn't exactly ban alcohol, but they tended to make a virtue of avoiding it.

Even so this rowdy she-urchin, batting back Thorgrim's coarse jokes and Guy de Guillac's elaborate compliments, hardly seemed the type to serve a goddess, even a pretty robust one like Diana. Still, the magic of the mystery cults was strong and ancient, and perhaps she'd acted differently when Ulrich had interviewed them one by one that afternoon. The merchant had that kind of effect on people. Even Guy and Thorgrim looked subdued as they tramped into the spacious dining hall and bowed before him.

He sat solid as a carving in the place of honour, above the salt. The four other men who shared the tables' head were dressed as richly as himself. Behind them, and at the ends of the long table, sat some fifteen more, all in livery of some kind. They all eyed the newcomers suspiciously as Ulrich named them. A few of the liveried men were clearly domestic servants, bland of face and manner, but the majority were different, lean men with faces seamed and scarred and hardbitten, and unreadable eyes. Thorgrim nodded to them casually as Ulrich introduced him, but de Guillac stared back with immense disdain, twirling his moustaches into a sneer. 'Cornes d'Actaeon!' he muttered to the others. 'A fine boiling of a crew! One or two barber's powder-puffs – the rest cutpurses or cut-throats! Wharfsweepings – not worth a tin thaler the gross!'

'Not all!' murmured Thorgrim. 'There are soldiers or sailors among them, that straight-backed old fellow for one.' He pointed to a grizzled veteran who seemed to hold himself at a distance from the rest. Volker had noticed the curious stains on the man's hands – stains more fitting for an alchemist than a soldier – and noted the respectful tone in the merchant's voice as he spoke the name of Joachim Landau.

Ulrich frowned at them, and they fell silent. 'My followers, I make known to you my partners in this little venture. On my left hand here, Master Rudiger Goldfüss of this city, well-known merchant-general.' Goldfüss was a big blond scowling man with eyes so habitually narrowed their colour was hard to see. His curt nod tipped his forelock into his eyes. 'On my right, first, Master Ekkehard Haagen, Augsburg's largest dealer in wines and luxury goods, and by him Master Balthazar Beck of Mainz, jeweller and goldsmith—' These two were opposites, to each other and to the images of their trades. Beck was plump and merry-looking, his nose red-veined and bulbous, while Haagen was tall and thin and bald, as mean and sour-looking as his worst vintage. 'And of course,' continued Ulrich, 'the oldest member of our party, Master Diderik Gundelfingen, like myself of Worms, who deals in fine furs and choice leathers.' Master Diderik looked even more like his own stock, brown as a berry and so bent and shrunken and wrinkled that he might very well have been seasoned in his own tannery; but his eyes sparkled very black and bright in his walnut face, and he alone condescended to greet Volker and the others.

'Welcome, welcome, my children,' he cackled cheerfully, waggling his fingers at them. He seemed to fizz with a vitality that belied his age. 'My, my, this is going to be a merry little adventure, isn't it, eh? Eh? Heh-heh, and a fine pretty lass as well – my, you young folk are fine and enterprising these days!'

Goldfüss smiled, his eyes narrowing to invisibility. 'Well, old fellow, we'll see how enterprising when they hear whither we're bound! Tell 'em, Master Ulrich!'

Ulrich inclined his head slightly. 'Thank you; I was about to. Seat yourselves, all you serving-men, and listen.' He perched himself on the leading edge of the table, and paused a moment while benches were pulled around. Master Diderik beckoned Dani over to sit beside him, patting his cushions excitedly. 'So, then. You'll all, I think, have heard of the southern land, home of the old Empire, known as Italia? And of its northern region, called Alpina for the mountains above it?'

If he'd spiked every seat in the room he couldn't have made them jump more effectively. The hiss of breath was simultaneous, and Volker noticed many pairs of eyes – even in the toughest faces – turning to seek the door.

'Alpina?' growled a man in brown livery. 'It's called

bloody Alpina Tartara – and not for nothing! That's haunted land, Hades' own doorstep!'

Ulrich shook his head. 'Not so! The name comes from the river Tartaro that runs through it. But creatures of the Old World live on in the mountains, yes; and many of them owe allegiance to Tartarus. Barbarians come in from north and east, too, across Thrace and Macedon; and Tartarus is strong among them also. But there also the spirit of Old Rome lives on. Many little realms and petty princedoms of men linger. Turbulent and short-lived though they are, they often fight very valiantly against the threatening forces from the Outer Lands. Without their buffering the east flank of our northern Empire would never be at peace, and southern Italia might be overwhelmed completely. Still, I agree. Alpina remains a place of dangers, well-nigh impassable, especially to we merchants, who can't travel light enough to run! The princelings can be as rapacious as any Old Worlders. But in the last few years one prince has won a succession of victories, first against his fellows, then against the barbarians. And a month or two since, word came to us that he's won a great victory against the worst Old Worlders infesting his lands, and driven them back into the mountains. How long that triumph'll last, who can say? But for a short time, a year or so, the lands should remain relatively clear; and he is more interested in encouraging trade than plundering it, for the moment. The five of us saw a rare opportunity, so rare we cannot ignore it. There are travelled men among you; have any ever reached the Southern Empire, and seen its great capital at Syracusa? Or do you know any who have?'

Volker looked up, startled. So did many others, and the rest simply blank. What did the southern capital have to do with all this? To his surprise it was Thorgrim who spoke. 'Men of my kindred have told me much. Some have taken longships there, to trade or to raid.

45

The raiders dangle from palm trees, or pull an oar in the galleys, which they may do well enough without their eyes. It is a very great city.'

'It is. And the traders?'

'Out of ten ships, perhaps one will return – but that one laden with riches from windvane to dragonhead. The rest fall foul of pirates, Italian or Libyan outlaws in the Middle Sea. Or Moorish corsairs near the narrow straits they name Gebr'al'Tarik, and you the Pillars of Hercules. Or the accursed Easterners – they swarm in through the sea you call Black and lair among the little islands like flies over dung.'

Master Goldfüss snorted and thumped the table. 'They do indeed. And if only one in ten Norse longships can get through, how will civilised merchants fare? The southern Empire grows stale; the pirates control the seas at its fringes, and ofttimes coasts and islands also. Corsica's a nest of them. They bleed tolls from a strong fleet, so there's no profit there; weaker ones they crush and squeeze like fruit ripe for the picking. Either way, it's poor business! For twenty years or more the Syracusa run's been dead, or good as, yet the South is howling for our furs and skins and spirits and subtle manufactures at almost any price. And their silk and spices and gems'd fetch an Elector's ransom at any market in the Empire.' He smacked his full lips. 'If only we could get past the pirates, and we can!'

Balthazar Beck nodded and beamed expansively. 'All thanks to our esteemed Master Ulrich here! For we mean to go not by sea, but by river!'

A rumble of surprise filled the room, but Guy shook his head fiercely. 'If you mean the old route down the Rhone to its delta, then messires, I fear you'll have little better fortune! Neither Empire has been able to police that of recent years. There are pirate encampments all along the Gallic coast there now!'

Beck's green eyes twinkled. 'No, my good sir, I know

of the Rhone as well as you. That is why Alpina comes into it. Down the Danube we go to the Alpine Mountains, crossing them—' Ulrich coughed. 'Quite so – at a place and by a means master Ulrich knows of, and our rivals do not. And thence through the rivers of Alpina to the Mare Adriatica, and a straight run towards Sicilia and fair Syracusa with her golden paving! We'll come back the same way – and we'll come back rich!'

Haagen nodded slowly. His sardonic voice had more humour than his sour face showed. 'Filthy . . . stinking . . . rich!'

'And that means you also,' observed Ulrich, raking the servitors with his suddenly piercing glance. 'You'll share the profits, as well as the perils. These will be great – but not as deadly as they might otherwise have been. We are all going, even Master Diderik; we wouldn't, if we thought there was no chance of coming back. And remember those profits! If they are as high as we expect, the least share will set any of you up for life. Well, does anyone no longer wish to come?' He swung his silver-headed cane, as if to single out anyone who wanted to speak.

Panic snatched up Volker and all but galloped off with him. A long journey! To the far ends of the Empire, he had thought, beyond them even – to Bretain or barbarian Kiev, the Norselands even – the stars knew that would be dangerous enough! But all the way to *Sicily*! Swallow his pride, speak up, that'd be the sensible thing to do. Right now, before it was too late. Why not? But every time that cane gleamed in his direction he was tongue-tied. If somebody else would just speak . . . But they didn't, just stood around looking sheepish, like himself. And there was something else, too. The journey was everything Ulrich had promised, and more, in terms of danger. But just a – a *peddling* trip? He liked the idea of being rich as well as the next

47

man. But he felt vaguely disappointed. Somehow he felt there should be more.

While he was still struggling with himself Ulrich laid down his cane and beamed merrily. 'That's settled, then. Every man jack of you tags along! I thank you. A hard decision, no doubt, but I think it's the right one. You see now why we needed secrecy! Determined rivals could steal a march, or hinder us in some way. But now, I think, it'll be too late; we sail at dawn, and you'll all remain within the inn here until we take you to the wharves. Eat and drink and make merry at our expense; but keep silent and keep sober! No speaking of this even to those who know, in case you're overheard; remember, it's your profits at risk. Till dawn, then, fare you well!'

Volker swallowed. At dawn! Now he knew how fishes felt when they snapped up the bait, only to find it sticking in their throats. Well and truly hooked . . .

Ulrich dismissed the company with a wave, but motioned to Volker and the others; Dani had some trouble detaching herself from old Diderik. 'I want you three to get friendly with your fellows,' Ulrich told them. 'With eyes and ears aflap, eh? Rivals we've definitely got, and there may be a spy in our camp, one reason I hired you so secretly. No, Volker, not you! I have other work for you. Helping me pack my bags, for one. Come!'

The merchant had packed so much himself that Volker was surprised he wanted help. His big chests were almost full, and the only other baggage lay on the bed, one small satchel and a much longer case of black leather, the kind that usually held musical instruments. Ulrich scooped up the satchel and began to bustle around delving in drawers and transferring things from the trunks, while Volker gathered the last few garments lying around. Something about that black case aroused his curiosity; he couldn't see Ulrich as the musical type.

Remembering a near-disaster with his own cittern, he told himself he should make sure that its contents were securely fastened down. But his fingers had barely slid back the catches when Ulrich all but flung himself across the wide room, seized the lid and slammed it down. Volker heard a strange soft crackle and caught a whiff of a pungent, thundery odour. He knew it only too well, from some of Strauben's more spectacular transmutation experiments; it came from the release of great energies.

He stared open-mouthed at Ulrich. The merchant met his gaze levelly for a moment, then said 'Ah, well. No doubt small harm's done. I always meant to show you, in due course, when we were far from the ways of men. But you may as well look now. Take up my cane, there; touch the silver head to the locks – so! Now – say *Quiesce!*'

Volker, astonished, repeated the command to lie quiet, as he might to a savage watchdog. Ulrich said nothing, only nodded, and after a second's hesitation Volker slid back the catches again. He caught his breath.

Inside the case, on a bed of fine velvet, lay a horn, of a kind he had never seen before. It was almost five feet in length, with a wide bell mouth, its nubbled surface pierced at intervals – wide intervals – with holes of different sizes. Many of these were blocked by plugs of silver padded with felt, mounted on an intricate silver cage which surrounded the whole horn; a system of keys opened some holes and stopped others in what was clearly a sophisticated tuning system. Volker lifted it, and marvelled.

'Well?' asked Ulrich quietly. 'Think you could play it? One day you may have to.'

'I . . . I might; but it looks difficult.' He lifted the silver mouthpiece to his lips, but Ulrich reached out and took it from him.

'No, don't practise just now! There'll be better times.'

Volker grinned. 'Yes, of course, master. I might rouse the whole inn.'

'You might indeed!' agreed Ulrich with surprising grimness. Swiftly he put the horn back. 'Now, in any event, the case will open for you as easily as for me; and for no others. That case has been made safe – *very* safe. Interesting, that you noticed it; few ordinary men would, even if you popped it under their noses! Hide it, though, and hardly a mage among men could find it. Strong magic lies within it, so strong magic must surround it. That horn is more important than you could ever dream. Men died to recover it, and I don't doubt that more will die before its journey ends. It's intimately bound up with the true purpose of this little jaunt of ours.'

Volker stared. 'T-*true* purpose?'

Ulrich smiled; and though it sat easily on his broad beaming and bushy beard, it was not the smile of any common merchant. 'As I said. A purpose for which I put together this entire venture. Oh, it's genuine enough, had to be, to make a convincing cover. A timely quest for profit, nothing wrong with that. But it cloaks a deeper purpose, boy, that only I know of. So far; for soon enough you'll have to know, too. To be the helper I need, you must know the plan as well as I do myself.' He tapped the satchel. 'This is as safe as the horn-case. There's some account of our route in here, maps and all, and some other notes. You can pass the first few days of the journey studying those. But the core of it all I dare not write down, and neither must you. I'll give you the gist of it straight, and that you must tell nobody, not even your three fellows – not yet, at least, not till I have probed them more deeply. They're plainer humans, and you are not – no, don't fly off your handle! The Old World blood in you makes you trustworthy. Ever wonder why your late master fell, and you not? Plain humans are more easily snared by the false promises of black sorcery, and the rewards of Tartarus. And those adventurous or greedy enough to undertake this journey might be easier still to corrupt. It is something worse I fear among us than a rival commercant.'

He shut the satchel with a snap and tossed it down on the bed beside Volker, who sat there speechless, trying to absorb the implications of what he'd heard. Could Ulrich be off his tiltcart? Certainly. He just didn't look it, that was the trouble; in fact, for all his jovial manner Volker had never met anyone who could radiate that much stern authority. Or could that itself be a sign of madness?

'Come then,' said Ulrich, as if he guessed Volker's confusion. 'Is the chest packed? And your own bags? Then call the porters, and have them taken down to the wharves. You and I, we'll go for a stroll that way. We have much to talk about.' He took up his silver-headed cane and shouldered the horn-case by its leather sling, brushing off Volker's attempt to take it. 'Carry the satchel. You'll find it heavier than you expect.' And so it was.

Beyond the inn door the cobbles gleamed slick with drizzle, and the old uneven streets were deserted. 'So much the better,' was all Ulrich remarked. Volker sighed and followed, thanking his stars he'd at least got his cloak out of hock. Thunder grumbled in the distance, and far-off flickers heralded a real storm. Ulrich glanced this way and that about him as they walked through the ways, evidently on the lookout for anyone following or even straying too close. Around a crooked corner a wide square opened, a shopkeeper's quarter dominated by a tall clocktower that was crowned by one of the city's famous mechanical clocks. Several of the shops had left their canvas awnings out, and beneath the shelter of one of these Ulrich at last stopped. Volker joined him, and silently they watched the clock strike.

The figure that slid out in a whirr of clockwork represented an armoured knight of the Ordo Teutonicus, victoriously bestriding some cringing Old World monster with wings; that made it a pretty old clock. Everyone knew that these days any Teutonic Knight was less likely to fight such a thing than – never mind. A hundred years ago the Empire had decided it no longer needed such uncomfortable hatchet-men, much given to sleeping in their armour and abstaining from almost everything – everything normal, anyhow, including washing. They had all been despatched to convert the barbarian Baltic lands from Tartarist heresies. If anything, though, the conversion had gone the other way. The Knights had found Tartarism just their cup of slimy alkaline water, and now their great gloomy fortress communities were riddled with it. The grotesque model whacked at the bell with his uplifted sword. 'The eleventh hour!' said Ulrich sourly, glancing around to be sure they were completely alone. 'Fair warning from the forces of darkness! But who'll heed it?' Then he turned to Volker with a strangely apologetic smile.

'It's not so easy, this. Secrecy gets to be a habit; grows on you, like. Expect you've guessed I'm no merchant – or is that true? I've been one for ten long years now, and a damn good one too; times are I've forgotten, literally forgotten I was ever . . . anything else. If you've ever to play a part, lad, choose the right one and live it up to the hilt. I got rich, because I needed to, both as cover and to fund my plans. Ten years; and I'm older than I look. But there was a time when I was something more, a name to be reckoned with. In the Learned Order of Jupiter Donarus, would you believe? High in its councils and influential in its politics, and in those of the Empire itself. A Deputy Prior of the Imperial Abbey itself, in Worms; Master Magus of the Eleventh, or Hidden, Degree; and appointed one of the

Imperial Inquisitors to the Praetorian Council, charged with investigating and assessing the activities of Tartarist heretics. How's that, eh?'

Volker fought the urge to plaster down his hair; it was trying to stand on end. This jovial moon-faced character beside him, if he was to be believed, could once have filled the Imperial torture chambers at the merest nod of his head, or the gibbets around the execution ground, especially with apprentices whose masters had just vanished down a demon's maw. If, that is, he didn't just turn them into earthworms and set them loose in a chicken run. Rumour had it that Inquisitors were fanatically dedicated, instinctively ruthless, utterly merciless and (unlike most Imperial officials) totally incorruptible, because, suggested other rumours, they found their work too enjoyable to let any little thing like wealth or influence get in the way. And an Inquisitor who was one of the twenty or so greatest mages in the Empire . . .

Some kind of response seemed called for, but the best Volker could manage was 'Quite a job.'

Ulrich smiled. 'It had its good side. You found out things; and sometimes those things began to fit together, and make a pattern. A rumour or two, for example, let slip under – call it questioning. A minor cult, ancient, obscure, almost moribund, grown suddenly arrogant. Some long-lost magical secret now found. Petty whispers, ten a thaler; but the deeper I looked, the firmer they grew. The cult did exist; tiny, elusive, so impossibly secret even for Tartarists that it could hardly recruit any new members, yet suddenly bidding high for power in their dark hierarchy. I loosed my best hounds on its trail; the agents I sent to infiltrate it never returned. The raids I sprang on its meeting places, far apart, well concealed, found nothing but the lingering demoniac stink, long cold.' Volker remembered the dripping foulness, but said nothing. 'An obsession, my superiors told me. Neglecting other more immediate concerns, they told me, without getting any closer. Or was I getting too close? So close, that someone in high places sought to stop me?'

There was a cold edge to Ulrich's voice. 'My resignation was written for me; my penance set out, promotion to a tiny priory in barbarian Baltic territory, barely within the Empire's borders. Dutifully I set out there; but I never arrived. Agents still loyal to me helped me vanish, and start a new life, in a new guise. Not the one you now see; one that would give me an introduction to known Tartarist circles. I had not given up the scent.' Distant lightning flickered among the clouds, and in that bleak grey gleam Volker suddenly saw the inquisitor in Ulrich's eyes.

'Of course, without Imperial resources it took a little longer; fifteen years to be precise. Even that might not have been enough, if the cult's own ruthless secrecy had not turned against it. They found themselves in urgent need of new magical talent, and were forced to relax their strictures a little. I was there waiting. At the cost of ordeals and deeds I hardly dare remember I was admitted to their circle. At last I learned their secret, and what they were preparing to do with it. As soon as could be their conclave was stormed with all the power I could muster. It was barely enough. I never saw the face of their master, but he was almost my match – and he had help to call on.' Thunder growled, like the echo of a memory, and the rain hissed stronger, bouncing and spattering among the cobbles. 'The men who helped me died, badly. I fled alone, because there was no more I could do – but in the confusion I had seized the horn. Again, alone now, I put on a new self, becoming this Ulrich you know; and I settled down to study what I had won. Ten years of study, and of preparing.'

Volker looked at the black case, and shivered. 'But . . . couldn't you just destroy it?'

'Perhaps. Perhaps not. Not easily, in any event. You, young alchemist, you should know how deadly dangerous it can be to meddle with something before you understand it fully; I might destroy only myself and leave the horn for the cultists to recover. And I'd learned enough to know how dangerous that might be – and why they had not yet used it, save as a threat to overawe their rivals. They had only found half their weapon, Volker. The thing that horn was torn from had two.'

Volker remembered the strange feel of that nubbled black surface beneath his fingers, and swallowed. 'There's another?'

'There is. But not in their hands. Long ago, when the world was young, the two were ripped apart and hidden, hidden well. There is great power in this one, even on its own; but strangely enough, not for evil. Undirected, rather, unfocused, neutral, following the will of its wielder. Probably the other would be the same, on its own. But together, I guess, it might be a very different tale. The cultists thought so; and that was why they had such need of magic. They were setting this horn to search out its fellow.'

'Search?' demanded Volker, tottering on the brink of a vast and unsettling understanding. 'How could one horn search for another?'

'All too easily, to a man of skill – or should I say, a player? For its power lies in its music, Volker. Hence all that silver valve work they put upon it, to refine their control; though little good it did them! The kind of man who becomes a Tartarist has hardly a note of music in him; they could not tap a tenth of its power. But I – whatever that says about me, I have even less. I have been tone-deaf since my childhood, Volker. A cruel irony of fate, that one of the greatest master mages in the Empire should be denied that one simple skill.'

Volker slid over the brink, slithering and scrabbling down towards one dark inevitable conclusion. But before he could speak, Ulrich nodded. 'Yes, you have it; that's why I chose you – and the others. You see, lad, before I could stop them, the cultists had found the other horn.'

'*Found* it?'

'Aye – but not laid hands on it, or the world would've echoed with it ere now. With those horns in their hands they could unleash such a force out of black Tartarus as it hasn't seen for millennia.'

The rain was slackening, now, the thunder growing more distant; the storm seemed to be passing. Ulrich chuckled. 'But much good their discovery did them! Properly wild, they were. They'd narrowed it down to Italia Transalpina. In the dark forests that skirt the southern peaks of Alpina Tartara it lies hidden, hidden and not unguarded. To find it exactly and break its defences they must go much closer; and that they couldn't do! It's the weakness of Tartarus that one hand'd as soon chop off another as help it. That pest-hole country was as barred to them as to us – until now. They'll be on the lookout for signs of either horn. They'll be making their move any day now. And that's why I set up this little jaunt, prepared these last ten years. We can forestall 'em. We've got the horn, and players for it. We'll beat them to the mountains, we'll find the second horn, and we'll take the two of 'em together where they can do no more harm.'

He clapped his hands like a man beating away the dust of a job well done, and stepped confidently out on to the glistening cobbles. 'So now you know. That's going to be your real job, and it's one you alone—'

A tremendous thunderclap cut off his words, and a sudden torrential deluge of rain. The calm had only been the eye of the storm passing; it was back in force. Volker hesitated a moment, torn between ducking back to shelter, or running for the wider doorways across the square; and it was a moment too long. Another crashing peal burst on the heels of the first. Ears ringing, they looked up and saw, as if in a dream, twin lightnings branch and meet behind the mechanical clock, silhouetting the knight's figure in a blast of baleful glare. And in that instant the demoniac beast beneath it gaped its ornately carven jaws, spread its wings of weatherscored lead and launched itself and its rider down off the clock, straight through the downpour towards them.

Volker had no time, no chance to move, not even to cry out; it was that swift. Down upon him it swooped, stone teeth gleaming, stone talons outstretched for the kill – then suddenly he was thrown back and Ulrich was before him, cane uplifted, crying words that crackled like brittle steel, louder even than the storm:

Apollone! Calor abite! In frigorem – fugite!

There was a sudden blast of steam, a rush of blue light and furnace-hot air; then a resounding crash, a shrill cry and a noise like shattering masonry, and nothing after but the hissing rain.

Volker sprang up, still dazed, peering this way and that in the downpour; but there was nobody in the square. Then he looked down, and saw Ulrich sprawled at his feet. All around him lay fragments of stone, barely recognisable as the statue, each in a little halo of ice upon the pavement. The merchant was truly the master of magic he had named himself; to save Volker he had contrived to blast every trace of heat from the carving, shattering it like a century of frosts. But himself he had not saved; one stone talon lay in a pool of scarlet, and it had slashed his throat across.

Horrified, Volker knelt down and tried, with shaking hands, to staunch the flow of blood; but he could see at a glance it was too late. White bone gleamed in the wound, and the eyes were open and staring as the raindrops splashed upon them. Ulrich must have died even as he fell. And with him, unfulfilled, had died his great purpose and plan.

The full horror of it began to dawn on Volker. The attack had been aimed directly at him alone; Ulrich could surely have escaped it. This man of awesome power had thrown away his life, and with it all that he had laboured for, all he had planned throughout a quarter century and more – just to save one life. His.

What Volker felt most was anger. *'Why?'* he shouted – screamed, almost, above the storm. He clutched the dead man's collar and shook him. *'Why? Why lay that weight on me, damn you? Why?'*

Because . . . you are needed.

He had not expected an answer.

A vast void of fear seemed to open beneath him as he stared across the corpse, to where blood and rain pooled together – so much blood, more than it seemed one single body could ever hold. From there the voice had come, a strange voice, low, gurgling and hissing, such as might very well sound from a severed windpipe. But it didn't. It was a voice made of the very splashing of the rain itself, mingling with the blood, and somehow forming that dull sound into speech.

Within my blood . . . if shed . . . a spell to bear my message . . . the journey must go on . . . you must lead it . . . yooouuuu . . .

Volker howled in disbelief but the voice paid him no heed. The wind whipped up the rain into savage gusts, and the words wavered. Volker listened, but as he caught word after word he clutched his head in growing horror.

They knew . . . who is dangerrr to themm . . . struck first

*at youu . . . in satchel, gold . . . maps . . . all yoouu
need . . . horn will guide you . . . use your powers . . . your
natures . . . huldra and humannn bothh . . . find both . . .
destroy . . . Templa Volcana at Syracusa, if nowhere
elssse . . . fare yoooou well . . . remember musicc . . .
remember . . . me . . .*

The rain lashed down with sudden intensity,
rebounding in flashing droplets from the paving. The
roar of it drowned all other sounds. Across the stained
flagstones it sluiced with driving force, and the dark
pool dissolved before it, drew off in wavering threads
and washed away along every cranny and crevice in
the stone, until at last it drained into the shadows
beneath, and faded utterly away. On the clock above
wheels whirred. The next figure came lurching out,
hunched and sullen under hood and cloak, and with
the scythe in its skeletal hands it struck twelve slow
strokes on the bell. The day of departure had begun.

Chapter 2

'The bargain is broken, and there's an end of it.' Haagen's thin face, almost skeletal in the harsh shadows cast by the single hanging lantern, showed no trace of sympathy or understanding. The chill morning air, unwarmed by the new-lit stove at the end of the curtained cabin, made mist of his breath.

Volker met him with stubborn politeness. 'Not by Master Ulrich. And I hope not by you, either – sir.' His voice was firm, but in the face of the merchants' sceptical frowns he could feel his confidence trickling away. Even Diderik's laughter-crinkled old eyes were narrowing into suspicion.

'Come now, my boy, come now. Surely you know more than you've said?'

'There's nothing else I can tell you,' repeated Volker, stubbornly. 'My master is detained by unexpected business here in Nürnberg. You heard his instructions at the inn – to set out down the Regnitz at first light.' He looked round at his companions, hoping for support, and found none. Thorgrim sat with both hands clasped under his chin, a study in impassivity. De Guillac sucked on a long clay pipe, twirling his mustachios in a way that suggested profound cynicism. Dani gave him a look that would have melted glass. He wondered uncomfortably if a priestess of Diana could detect a lie.

Beck shook his head helplessly, wringing his chubby hands together. 'Without your master this venture's impossible! Haagen's right.'

'You rely on him, so you let him down?' inquired Volker. 'I don't know how I'm going to explain that to him!' *Let's hope I don't get the chance too soon.*

'He's your master,' sniffed Haagen, 'not ours. We're as much sharers in this company as he is; he leads it because he's the obvious man, but it's by our consent. He has our trust. You do not. You bring us orders you say are his, but no proof or token of his authority. Why should we obey?'

'Well, why not?' protested Volker. 'He told me to get the expedition started without waiting for him, and that's the simple bloody truth!' *A bloody truth it had been, too.* 'I've no reason to lie – any more than I have to betray his confidence. How could I gain?'

Beck frowned deeply, an expression that hardly suited his cherubic features. 'But this – this business of your master's. Surely it couldn't have prevented him from at least coming here, to tell us something so momentous himself? There's something you're not saying, boy, something we need to know.' Sweat beaded in the furrows of his forehead, even in this cold air. With a sudden qualm Volker realised that Beck was frightened. Why? Did he know something? About the sending against Ulrich, for instance? If so, then he knew that the *Walross* itself, and everyone on board, might be attacked at any moment. Maybe Beck was the spy Ulrich had feared; or perhaps he was something worse . . .

But Volker himself had been the target, and he was still alive. Better yet, Ulrich had destroyed the sending, which meant their unknown opponents had been caught on the raw. For all they knew, Ulrich was even now tracking them down, readying a counter-attack with his own considerable powers. So far Volker had avoided outright lies. He hated them, and besides they had an amazing habit of coming home to roost. But if he was economical, no, absolutely cheeseparing with the truth now, he could win the merchants' confidence, and at the same time throw Ulrich's enemies on to a false scent.

'Very well, then, Master Beck. This much I *can* tell you, since nothing less will still your doubts. Master Ulrich was waylaid and attacked in the street, and not by common robbers. He thought it a deliberate bid to hold us here in Nürnberg; perhaps the first of many . . .'

The merchants shot alarmed glances at each other. 'You mean – we're all at risk?' demanded Goldfüss.

'If we don't leave *now*,' said Volker firmly, 'as Ulrich bids us!'

The merchants looked at one another doubtfully. Haagen was shaking his head again, and so was Diderik. 'Boy, boy, you don't understand. The whole damned venture *is* Ulrich. Every detail, every scrap of knowledge, has come from him. It was he who chose these boats; aye, and armed 'em with that devilish bombard gun. Barges that'll take to the sea at a pinch, and they're hard in the handling. I'd never trust *Walross* or *Walfisch* in any other hands.'

Goldfüss nodded agreement. 'And the country, the route – Ulrich has all the secrets of that. We've none of us travelled half so far in the south. We'll not go straying round those parts without our guide!'

'Ah!' said Volker, doing his best to look relieved. 'No, of course he wouldn't expect you to do *that*! You'll have his guidance there, be sure of that!' *If I can make head or tail of his damned notes, that is.* He havered for an instant; should he tell the merchants about them? No use; either they wouldn't be convinced, or they'd want to take them, which would never do. But he had to say something! Get them out, get them started, that was what mattered – somehow, anyhow, before their luck ran out. In desperation he blurted out the slender slice of truth that might just tip the balance. 'You see – though this must be a secret – we can expect to find him at Regensburg. Or find word from him there.'

His natural honesty shrivelled. Anyone could *expect*, after all. And as to where Ulrich was now—

It was an unwise thought. It shattered his defences, brought back the image he'd struggled to forget. The staring eyes lit suddenly from within, a light that washed the last colour from beneath the ash-pale skin, leaving the ivory of naked bone. The tiny needles of light flickering at the dead mage's temples, sparkling across his body in a spatter of silver fire. The tunic swelling, like a sudden gasp of lifeless lungs, then sagging inward. The mask that was Ulrich's face writhing and crumbling like a figure on a witchfinder's balefire . . .

Volker caught himself, hoping his face had not betrayed him. Where Ulrich was now, that was a question for the philosophers. As well in Regensburg as anywhere, and none but a necromancer could say otherwise.

Thorgrim grinned. *'Naa?'* It was the sort of noise that might greet unlikely boasts in a Norse drink hall. 'Ahead of us? He grows wings, our Master Ulrich?'

Volker gathered what was left of his confidence. 'He left early, and by road. You have a problem with that?'

For an endless moment the Norseman's ice-blue eyes locked with his; then he lifted an eyebrow and shook his head. 'No problems. And for the boats, they will be safe enough under my hand.'

Volker let out his breath, slowly. Thorgrim's lopsided smile was transparently honest. One man, at least, had no idea Ulrich was lost beyond the summoning of the most powerful necromancer. Against the chance of his own death the master mage had prepared one final desperate sending, ensorcelling his own blood to form an elemental messenger. But he had failed to allow for the chance it might be raining. To deliver that last desperate message, halting as it was, Ulrich's own flesh had been consumed. Among the scorched and blood-soaked pile of velvet, silk, furs and leather, Volker had found only a few handfuls of coloured powder and crystals, as though the substance of a living man had somehow been reduced to the salts, essences and catalysts of an alchemist's elaboratory. Those, the furs and all else he had consigned to the river, as reverentially as he could. Ulrich had been too disturbing a character to awaken much affection during their short acquaintance. His whole personality had been a bluff, genial mask concealing sombre, unfathomable depths; but awe, respect, reverence – that Volker could give him. And, of course, gratitude.

And someone here had caused his death, someone Volker knew, perhaps one of the ones he himself had recruited. The extraordinary de Guillac, who had appeared so conveniently; his erratic sorcery might be no more than a convenient cover. This mysterious Dani, who had argued so furiously against coming with them; and then joined the company without a murmur as soon as she'd met Ulrich. Beck, who seemed so anxious to discredit him. Any one of them might have seen him leave with Ulrich – and known they would he heading for the boats . . .

'*Open, in the Emperor's name!*'

A thunderous bang on the cabin door brought everyone round the oaken chart-table to their feet, and Thorgrim's head to a low deck-beam with an equally thunderous crack. Volker winced in sympathy. The Norseman appeared to hesitate slightly, blinked at the beam with an air of mild surprise, then unperturbedly reached for his halberd.

De Guillac stayed his hand. '*Hé la! Du calme, mon coco!* We are – are we not? – innocent travellers with nothing to fear.'

'*Open in there! Instantly, or we'll have this door d-owb!*'

The first cold daylight fell gracelessly on an Imperial officer and a knot of yawning, shivering guardsmen. The officer's sash identified him as an agent of the *Burgunderischerreichliches Rheinflussgebuchtlandwachts*, the combined Imperial river police and excise service. His uniform was frilled and flounced in the excruciating height of dandyish fashion; the unfashionable scarlet spots were being added by a spectacular nosebleed.

The Armorican held up his own lace-bordered hands in benign horror. 'Well, Monsieur did say upon the instant, did he not? Behold, I fling it wide in haste to obey, and—' He shrugged. 'I am desolated. I am crushed.'

The officer said something fairly forcible, but it got lost in the lace handkerchief he was trying to stuff up his nostrils. De Guillac doffed his hat and bowed low. 'Ah, you are most gracious indeed to offer such an apology, my dear . . . lieutenant? You find us, alas, not yet at breakfast. How may we assist his excellent majesty?'

The lieutenant said something even more forcible, glared at his far too straight-faced followers, then ducked into the cabin. Storked might have been a better expression, thought Volker, though that was a little unkind to the bird. The lieutenant's arms and legs had apparently been borrowed from a longer body, and his head from a smaller one. It was mostly the improbable hat that gave it the stork effect. The scuffed six-inch points on his shoes wilted suggestively, and his hose sagged in a mare's nest of cross-gartering, while the bulging costrel below his belt and the bulging belly above marked him as a serious drinker. His escort, however, were fair specimens of the species bullet-headed thug, each armed with a poleaxe and a heavy, basket-hilted sword. Breastplates clanked and plumes brushed the deck beams as five of them followed him in; over their shoulders Volker saw others lining up on the quay and boarding the *Walfisch*. His heart sank. They meant business, evidently; and they looked more than a match for his unarmed companions and the *Walross* crew together.

'You are the odour of this bessel?' honked the lieutenant.

Guy looked devastated. 'The . . . ? *Ah, mais jamais de la vie, monseigneur*. These well-known, widely respected and it goes without saying quite immensely *influential* gentleman have that hon—'

The lieutenant glared at the four merchants as they straggled out of the cabin. 'By my inforbation, gentleben, you have contrabad on board.'

Volker's heart sank. Every sailbarge on the river carried contraband; it was the only way they could turn a decent profit. By the same token every *Landswachtsmann* was normally bribable, at customary rates; but in this case it looked very much as if someone else had bribed them first. *Someone with enough money to hand-pick his men. Assuming anyone'd want to use hands on this lot.*

'Search freely, my friend,' Diderik piped up from somewhere behind Volker's left elbow. 'We have nothing to hide.'

The lieutenant nodded curtly and pushed past de Guillac, signalling one of his men to follow him. The others tramped back out on to the foredeck and lounged there, a beefy barrier effectively penning in the crew. Goldfüss's glare nailed Diderik, still blinking benignly, to the wall. '*You* may have nothing to hide, you daft old gnome! I for one have a living to make!'

Volker sighed. It made no difference. If the lieutenant had been paid to find contraband, he would find it, and there was an end of their venture – which made de Guillac's smug smile all the more inexplicable. And why was he waggling his fingers like that? Some spell? Dani and Thorgrim were eyeing the Armorican with an odd intensity; and suddenly Volker saw Dani's fingers flash an unmistakable answering signal. With a shiver of excitement, he understood; battle-speech was passing, of a subtle and silent kind. But what could they hope to do?

The guardsman's head vanished below the hatch. The lieutenant looked down to find his footing on the steep companionway, and with nicely measured force de Guillac brought the hatch-cover down on his head. The lieutenant slid from sight; there was a muffled crash as he landed on the patrolman beneath, but the closing hatch stifled it. De Guillac shot its bolt, and the end of the heavy chart table, propelled by Thorgrim and Dani, slid smoothly across it. Even as it landed de Guillac threw open one of the wide cabin ports on the starboard side, away from the land, and Thorgrim plunged through it, reached up and drew himself out. Dani rolled across the table and slid after him.

It had taken perhaps five seconds, and made no sound loud enough to alert the patrolmen outside, their eyes on the uneasy crew. De Guillac winked at the startled merchants, and motioned them to the door. He produced the key from his lace cuff with an ironic flourish. Smirking, he slipped it into the keyhole behind him and noiselessly locked the door.

For a long moment nothing else seemed to happen. The merchants put on a very good show of standing around arguing with one other. The guardsmen on the dock stamped their feet on the cobbles, blowing their hands to keep them warm. A few loafers drifted towards the barges, anxious to see the show and equally anxious not to get involved. A warehouse door creaked open, and two fascinated labourers put down the crates they were carrying to stare. Then, slowly, the whole scene began to move.

The *Walross* was adrift.

The guard had seen it too. The nearest turned menacingly on the merchants, but a curt *'Herop!'* from Thorgrim drew his eyes up. He had a wonderful view of descending boot soles, however brief. The Norseman landed at a stumbling run, scattering merchants and guardsmen alike, and turned just in time to catch the tips of two poleaxes with the barge pole he had used to push them clear of the quay. De Guillac picked up the third man bodily by his chest armour and dropped him neatly overboard like a chef making lobster thermidor.

The men on the dock stormed up the gangplank to join the fight – and clattered into the river like an accident in a scullery as the barge drifted away from the quay. Goldfüss and Haagen cheerfully bundled Thorgrim's first victim over the side while the Norseman himself backed away from the other two at a run, far faster than they could follow, lashing out with the pole. Then, suddenly, he let it drop and as they stumbled over it he set one hand on the rail, the other on the coach roof and swung himself at them feet-forward. The guards, caught amidships in both senses, doubled up and folded, winded and easy meat for the merchants – but Thorgrim's success, like his battle-cry, was cut short as his backside hit the deck with bruising force. De Guillac sucked in his breath with elaborate sympathy. *'Ouf!* But it is the fortunes of war, my friend! *Gare aux fesses!'*

The *Walross* was secure but a chaotic mêlée swirled across the long, open foredeck of the smaller barge. De Guillac grabbed a rope, noticed Thorgrim hobbling to his feet, and quietly let it go again. After a moment's thought he uncorked a familiar-looking costrel, sniffed at its contents and tilted a fair amount down his throat. His face twisted into a horrible grimace. *'Quel aventure funeste!'* he growled sorrowfully. 'The lieutenant's wine takes after him – a lout masquerading as a gentleman!'

'Well?' growled Thorgrim. 'Is this a time for wine-tasting?'

'This sour thin essence of malodorous goat's armpit, my friend, does not deserve the name of wine – but as you may have observed, a certain inspiration is occasionally required to refine my powers to their incomparable maximum. *Esperons que ça suffira.* Now let me see . . .'

He hesitated, then muttered a few rapid words under his breath, rippling his free hand in a series of intricate passes, ending in an immensely impressive gesture like a striking snake. It certainly seemed to achieve something. Within seconds the chaotic brawling on the *Walfisch*'s foredeck had become a wholesale rout, with the guardsmen on the receiving end. Amid a rising clamour of weapons two of them hurled themselves into the river in blind panic. De Guillac smiled smugly, but his face fell sharply as two of the barge's crew followed, and the *Walfisch* was left totally out of control. Attackers and defenders alike were taking to the river or shinning up the rigging, while the smaller barge drifted slowly into the main current in a series of lazy circles. As de Guillac's language graduated from the unlikely to the unspeakable, Volker suddenly understood what was happening. In a rising metallic crescendo like the prelude to Armageddon, two dozen assorted weapons were madly battling one another without the slightest assistance from their owners. Up in the rigging, three guardsmen and the remaining members of the *Walfisch*'s crew clambered over and around each other like rats on a rope in their desperate efforts to escape.

'Fortunes of war?' suggested Thorgrim.

The veins stood out at de Guillac's temples. *'Vous savez ce que je vous en dis, moi, de vos fortunes emmerdées?'*

'Never mind,' said Volker hastily, instead of what the Armorican was about to add. 'We'd best fish our lot out of the river. How long's that spell going to last, *Monseigneur* de Guillac?'

By way of answer de Guillac bellowed a counterspell.

Its force alone should have brought every weapon on the barge clattering to the deck. Instead, the clangour gradually died down to the level of two or three ordinary smithies, as though some monstrous clockwork device were slowly running down. Guardsmen were scrambling back on board, but they seemed strangely reluctant to pick up their weapons; an inconclusive fist fight was developing, with one or two still active weapons joining in.

'We help?' inquired Thorgrim.

'Why not?' said Goldfüss. 'You, Joachim, get the tiller and steer us towards them. Manfred, Gottfried, help our men out of the river. The rest of you, stand by to board the *Walfisch*.'

As the larger *Walross* manoeuvred alongside, Thorgrim leapt on to the gunwale and launched himself across the narrowing gap between the two barges. Landing a little more gracefully than before, he brushed two pirouetting longswords aside with his trusty bargepole and rapped a guardsman's helmet down over his eyes with the butt, causing him to jack-knife over the starboard rail. De Guillac, not to be outdone, jumped on board the *Walfisch* just as two miserable-looking guards were scrambling back on to the safety of the deck. He banged their helmets together with a most melodious clang, and they slid sadly back into the water.

Goldfüss, meanwhile, was happily tidying the port rail of the *Walross* in much the same way, while Diderik seemed totally absorbed in something at the stern. Haagen and Beck disappeared into the cabin with a huge, bell-mouthed arquebus and as the guards on *Walfisch* were beaten down and cast into the river they reappeared, prodding along the lieutenant and his assistant, relieving them of various small items they had picked up in their search. Neither man looked anxious to put up a fight. Diderik, however, seemed to be caught up in some deadly struggle; Volker was about to help him when he saw that the other half of it was Dani, her long hair a tousled mess of rats' tails, and her shirt soaked well beyond the tiresome demands of decency.

'Thank you, Master Diderik – no, truly, I can manage perfectly – *oh!* – well – there's really no need to— *yeep!*'

Volker turned aside too late to hide his fit of giggles. She extricated herself with difficulty, and let her fixed smile drop as she rounded on Volker. 'Well, thank *you* too, Master Fokler. What *would* we have done without you!'

That stung, all the more because she was right; he'd done nothing. He'd just left all the thinking, all the fighting, all the magic to these hired hands. Why in all the world had Ulrich put *him* in charge . . . ?

For just one reason. Not to punch heads with the Imperial guard, not to bicker with this temperamental little biddy, not to worry about his wounded pride. His job was to take the horn to Syracusa and destroy it. And now, if he only used his head, he could take advantage of a perfect opportunity. 'If you'd listened to me,' he said coolly, 'we'd have left at dawn. But no. You had to stay here and argue yourselves into a fight.'

Dani flushed, opened her mouth to say something, and closed it again. Beck laughed. 'Boy's right, Haagen. All that talk came near costing us our cargo.'

Haagen nodded, and poked the lieutenant with his arquebus. 'Time for some answers. You, you pin-headed lankin – *who sent you*?'

The man flapped his hands feebly. 'Beg you, sir – unhand the doublet – month's wages – really no idea what you mean – just doing my job, sir . . .'

'An understrapper,' snarled Haagen. 'A snivelling understrapper. Norseman, this fish is too small. Would you help me throw it back in the river?'

'No!' screamed the man. 'My pourpoint! My silk hose! *My new—!*'

71

A mouthful of river-water cut short his protests. The hat, a multi-coloured jellyfish, sank slowly into the depths as it drifted downstream. Guy uncorked the wineflask he had acquired, and, with the air of a high priest at a christening, ceremonially anointed the spluttering lieutenant with its contents.

'*Pax tecum, filius*,' he rumbled. 'So fair a costrel demands a worthier filling!'

'Don't just stand there!' bubbled the lieutenant to all and sundry. '*Give me a hand!*'

As Thorgrim's crisp commands brought the two boats under control once again, they glided out into midstream and away. From along their decks and the surrounding quayside arose the sound of all and sundry, onlookers and participants alike, politely clapping.

At first, as it cut across the open country around Nürnberg, the river was a busy highway between fields flecked green with growing shoots, or dotted with cattle and horses. Ragged children danced along the bank, shouting cheerful abuse that sometimes reached the level of a minor art. Each new vessel gave another opportunity to display their talents – and brought Volker to the gunwale, scanning the river for a patrol boat or some other, less obvious, enemy. Sailbarges like their own drifted downstream with enviable ease, bringing produce from the farms, or skins and furs from forest villages further south. Fishing boats, low in the water from the day's catch, drew hoots of derision from the children as they carried their stinking cargoes to the quayside market at Nürnberg. But one vessel stood out from all the rest: a sailing ship with its prow and stern carved into the fearful shape of a wyvern poised to spring, and its black banners writhing with obscene emblems. Taking in the coiled and barbed tail that formed its stern castle, the arrow-ports in the outspread wings supporting its forecastle, and the bombard half-concealed between the gaping jaws of its figurehead, Volker had no doubts.

'Thorgrim. I think we have company.'

The Norseman glanced round, shrugged expressively, and continued to whittle an obscene-looking figure from a piece of driftwood.

Volker carefully suppressed his irritation. 'It's not so much their taste in decoration,' he said, 'though the gods alone know where they get it from. It's just that I don't like bombards trained down my throat.'

De Guillac turned from a leisured study of Dani's back, lifted his spyglass, and smiled. 'That, my excitable young friend, is the *Winged Serpent*. I should be greatly surprised if her master could train a pet monkey.'

'Isn't she a warship?'

'More of a whoreship,' said Thorgrim. 'For fat merchants – and playacting aristos.'

The Armorican grinned. 'The pig of an owner sells bad food, new wine and old tarts. The bombard is to frighten other pirates who would steal their gold more honestly.'

Volker scanned the unlikely carvings under the wyvern's wing. 'They have strange pleasures.'

'They like a breath of Tartarus,' said de Guillac. 'It is as close as they come to excitement.'

As the ship drew nearer Volker could hear muffled sounds of music and drunken merriment. For a moment he thought the *Winged Serpent* a crewless vessel, held on course by some artifice of magic. Then, with a screech of tackle and a crack of canvas, the black mainsail opened like a dark flower, and he saw the warped and sinister creatures that hung in the rigging and crawled along the yardarms. He knew them only from street carvings, but they were certainly satyrs – they had the misshapen, goat-horned heads, the hairy, malformed legs bent into a permanent crouch, and the general air of misery he would have expected from creatures of the First Creation. Even so, there was something odd about them . . .

An expressive curse rang out from the top of the mainmast, followed by a splash and a string of dockyard obscenities delivered with all the fluency of a riverman born and bred. For a moment Volker seemed to be looking at an unlikely hybrid with the body of a satyr and the face of a bewhiskered, lantern-nosed sailor, purple with fury and embarrassment. Then he saw the tired-looking mask floating lazily downstream and realised why one small child with a catapult was finding the whole business so funny. The *Winged Serpent* passed downstream through a barrage of laughter, leaving a mingled smell of greasy cooking, cheap perfume, and exotic incense as a last reminder of her passage.

As day wore on, the tilled flatlands around the city gave way to marshes and reedbeds. Flocks of birds circled overhead, ready prey to the archers in flatboats seeking meat for some Nürnberg merchant's breakfast, or down and feathers for his bedchamber. Soon the *Walross* and the *Walfisch* were alone in a wilderness of sedges, bordered at its southern edge by a line of trees and undergrowth like the ramparts of a vast city. As evening approached, the forest marched to meet them, until both banks became walls of unbroken shadow. This was the Wald, the immense primeval forest that still carpeted so much of the northern Empire and made the rivers its major thoroughfares. Roads had been driven through it in many places, with settlements along their course like islands in a still, dark sea; but the rivers could carry more traffic, and in greater safety. It was a proverb that mysteries were woven among those branches – not all evil, but alien to man, survivals of the Old World that predated even the first Empire, relics of the time when man's dominion was limited to the circle of light around his campfire. Volker leaned on the rail, staring into the deepening shadows on the bank. Even the bravest traveller would not willingly choose a mooring-place on such stretches of the river, where the trees arched out over the water and thrust out entangling roots.

No rest for the crew tonight. But why should I be afraid . . . ?

'I think,' said Thorgrim, 'that the forest will not grow more welcoming for your watching it. But we, my friend, we have nothing to fear. There are spells bound about these boats of ours, strong spells.'

Volker looked a question mark. Was Thorgrim trying to tell him something?

'Such spells are not achieved without great wealth – or great power.' The Norseman fingered his hammer-amulet, as if he sought some protection of his own. 'And our fat moneybags is also a mage of some ability. You had guessed this, perhaps?'

Volker did his best to sound surprised, but he was more deeply disturbed. Thorgrim had seen through Ulrich's disguise sooner than expected, but it had only been a matter of time. Surely the mage had planned for this as carefully as for all else . . . ?

'Yes,' Thorgrim assured him solemnly. 'An unusual talent for a merchant, though not, I think, unprofitable. I sensed spells he had woven about himself in the inn; they had the same feeling as these.'

Volker half-smiled. 'Which is why you backed me up this morning? Because you knew of the spells?'

The Norseman's answering smile was mild and cherubic. 'In part. Master Ulrich has gone to much trouble. He must be very tender of our lives – or his cargo.'

Volker shivered. Only he knew that Ulrich's spells had proven too weak to protect their wielder. Or had he chosen it that way? There was a price to pay for magical protection. Often they enclosed the user in a thaumaturgic cage of such complexity that he could scarcely work any magic of his own. Perhaps Ulrich had wished to leave his powers unfettered. It would have been just like him.

But if he, the careful planner, could not stand against their unknown enemies, then what chance did any of them have against the numberless perils ahead? Of all their party, de Guillac alone deserved the name of mage – and his talent seemed as erratic as his temper. At the moment, though, the Armorican was more concerned with the fall of his elaborately carved ebony dice. He seemed to be losing with surprisingly good grace, and winked at Thorgrim as yet another throw was added to his run of bad luck. Only Dani, breathing softly into her panpipes, looked outward towards the dark and silent aisles of trees on either bank.

'Others than Ulrich have power over things of the forest,' remarked Thorgrim. 'That one, too – her pipes make more than music.'

Unwillingly, Volker began to realise that the girl had not exaggerated her skill. And yet it disturbed him. He felt an irrational impulse to snatch the pipes from her lips and break them over his thigh. Her eyes seemed unfocused, as if they looked beyond the shadows of the forest to some place, some being, that was the master of all forests. The great white owl sat at her shoulder, eyes hooded, head swaying slowly in time to her music, snared, perhaps, by the same magic . . .

Volker cursed silently. A hoyden with a gutter tongue and a vixen's temper, that was all she really was. Yet, for a moment he had seen something else, something the pipes had conjured out of darkness, something that spoke to a part of him he had thought buried beyond recall . . .

Volker awoke from a spectacular nightmare into an equally spectacular electrical storm. Jagged tridents of lightning split the sky, and the forest echoed with answering thunder. His head throbbed, his back ached from the hard boards, and one of Mutzelbacher's rats had been nesting in his mouth. The others around him were sleeping soundly and more (or less) noisily. He vaguely remembered a great deal of ale, a seemingly endless dice game, a long, drunken argument about magic, gambling, and the laws of chance, and a brief, rather noisy brawl during which he had finally passed out. Now, relieving internal pressures via the forward rail, he tried to ignore the miniature smithy that had set up shop in his skull, wincing at the clank of metal.

No. That was real. And it was coming from the bows, from the draped canvas outline that concealed that mystery of military sorcery, Ulrich's carefully chosen ultimate weapon – the bombard, or gun.

They had been around for a century or more, but so dark was their reputation that priestly councils in both Empires were still debating motions to have them declared devices of Tartarus and excommunicate their users. Not surprisingly, this kept them relatively rare and mysterious. They had been invented by the alchemist-priest Rogier, so Volker understood something of their basic principles; but for most people they smacked of demonolatry and were too fearful to touch. Which did not seem to bother whoever was rolling off the canvas cover.

'What – what're you doing there?'

'My mystery, young sir.'

'Your . . . ?' A thick provincial accent made the word doubly baffling, but the voice sounded placid, undisturbed, an unlikely saboteur.

'Joachim Landau, master bombardier, at yer service.'

Volker recognised him now, by his dim outline; this was the soldierly old fellow Thorgrim had commented on. 'I'm sorry. I thought—'

'Aye, aye. Vigilance is all, as my old sergeant used ter say.'

Volker studied the revealed bombard curiously. It

was a weird device, cast in the form of a seven-headed hydra; each long neck formed a separate gun barrel facing back over the creature's tail. This left its scaly backside pointing at the enemy, neatly adding insult to threat – beneath its curled tail was the mouth of a wider barrel fully eighteen inches in diameter. Each barrel had its own powder chamber linked to a master chamber in the form of a human skull clasped between the hydra's forepaws, and the whole assembly was protected by a heavy wooden mantlet.

'Well, I'm no expert, but it looks fiendish enough to me. Complex, though. Is it a good weapon, master Bombardier?'

The man rubbed his grizzled chin and gave a slow, grudging nod. 'She's a mite new-fangled for my liking, but your master'd have no other. Eight chambers, and every one cast metal – "None of yer iron stave-barrels", says Master Ulrich, "I'll have cast metal or none at all." '

'He w-is a knowledgeable man.'

'Aye. Spoke as I told him, save for the eight chambers. They'll make for a devilish kick and poor aiming. I'd trust 'er at forty paces, no more; else she'll shy 'er shot clear around the clock, any which way.'

'I still wouldn't hang around. Maybe he expects crowds of enemies, where we're bound. You're from . . . ?'

'From Regensburg, young sir. Twenty year in the militia, and nought ter show for it but a few scars and a niggardly pension. Set my heart on a journey to far parts – and by Vulcanus Voland, here I am nine days' sailing from Regensburg.'

'Well, with any luck we'll be going a bit further than that!' Volker stifled a yawn. 'But what leads you to unveil your mystery at this hour of the morning?'

'Just a feeling, sir. You'll forgive an old campaigner his foolishness.'

'No foolishness,' said a thick voice that Volker barely recognised as Thorgrim's. The Norseman looked about a thousand years old: he was shaking de Guillac, who looked little better, roughly by the shoulder.

'Hnh? *Mais pas encore, Marianne . . .*'

'Quiet, my friend. There is need of your skill.'

'What is it?' breathed Volker. 'What do you see?'

Another flurry of lightning gave the answer, revealing the tumbled stonework of a shattered tower, half-overgrown with climbing plants.

'*Couilles d'auroch!*' rumbled the Armorican. 'A ruin. A nothing. Go back to your nightmares, *espèce d'anacoluthon*, and leave me to my dreams.'

Thorgrim ignored him. He held the hammer-amulet reversed, as if the ruby glistening faintly between his fingers could somehow focus his curious talent. 'There is . . . something here. Close by. Else I should not have woken you.'

'Magic being used?'

'Not magic. Things magic clings to – with a smell of Tartarus. Twisted things. And one that searches.'

'It knows we are here?'

'I cannot be sure. Something protects us – Ulrich's spell, perhaps.'

'*Oi!* For Frigg's sake!' One of the merchant's hired men, a bullet-headed young thug, sat up, scratching his bristling scalp with a noise like a rasp. 'What's a man gotta do t'get a Frigg'n nights' sleep round here with you Frigg'n old women making a Frigg'n row all the—'

There was a splintering crash, and a long, black tongue sprang out of his midriff. Volker threw himself sideways as the man folded up, writhing, revealing the iron harpoon shaft that pinned him to the gunwale at his back. Behind them *Walfisch*'s alarm bell was drowned in yelling; they too were under attack. Volker had barely found his feet when a second harpoon crashed through the aft cabin of the *Walross*. Goldfüss and Haagen burst through the door just in time to trip over a third harpoon as it hammered down through the deck and into the cargo hold. Beck scuttled close behind; there was no sign of Diderik. Shock held Volker dazed for a few precious moments. Only as they snapped taut did he see the heavy cables each harpoon carried, cables that were drawing them inexorably towards the dark bulwarks of the forested bank. Thorgrim hacked at the nearest cable with his halberd, but the blade glanced off the thickly-twined hemp as though it were mirror-polished steel, and tipped the startled Norseman on to the deck.

'*Svinelem!* Volker! It's protected! You must counter the spell!'

Almost automatically Volker glanced at de Guillac, but the Armorican was urgently mumbling and gesticulating to himself. *The difference between magicians and idiots*, thought Volker, *is mostly results . . .* Gritting his teeth, he touched the nearest cable. A thrill of power jolted up his arm, throwing his hand back with a dark weal across the palm.

A strong arm drew him behind the bombard mantlet. 'Your Norse friend has the right of it,' said the bombardier, unclipping one of the brown leather bags from his belt and shaking it with methodical efficiency. 'Powerful magic on that cable.'

'Really?' grated Volker, shaking his burned hand. 'I'd never have guessed.'

The harpoons had done their work. Now the hidden catapult was firing heavy iron quarrels and volleys of slingshot stones. Volker and the bombardier were shielded by the mantlet, but the crew had only the gunwales. One or two were returning fire as best they could, but the bank was still out of bowshot and there was no clear target. Unless they cut loose they would be easy meat for the wreckers. Again Volker reached out for the cable, probing its protection, and again a flare of power flung back his hands. Haagen's bald pate mirrored the flash as the merchant crawled on his belly across the deck, arquebus in hand, with Beck following close behind.

'You! You there! Bombardier! Load me this weapon!'

'Just a moment, sir, just a moment. Now let me see – still some fifty strides, aye, aye, that'll be another drachm less a scruple for the main chamber. Or maybe half a scruple. Aye, that's it.'

'Damn your impertinence!'

'Best leave him to it,' said Volker, ducking another whistling volley of stones. 'He may be our only chance.'

'But you're a magician, damn it. Can't you—?'

'No I can't. Especially if you keep talking.'

Haagen opened his mouth, thought better of it, and closed it again. He and Beck glared at the bombardier's methodical preparations, practically dancing up and down, while Goldfüss and Thorgrim chivvied crossbowmen to the rail. Then de Guillac barged them aside, leaped up on to the coach roof and stretched out an arm towards the bank in a massive, grandiose gesture. With an echoing thunderclap a whirling ball of purple flame sped from the Armorican's fingertips and arced high across the river, lighting the water below with the same eerie colour as it dropped towards the wreckers. For a moment it revealed running figures, piles of stone and earth, and a tall, cowled shape with its hand upraised. Then de Guillac's missile struck.

It was very impressive, Volker had to admit. The flash sent streaks of blue and purple fire rocketing skywards in a shower of glittering sparks, efficiently ruining everyone's night vision. The gnarled and twisted body of an ancient oak flared briefly into a network of traceried light, as though every vein of every leaf were pulsing with molten silver. Then, smoking, it sagged and wilted like an overblown flower. This was definitely high-class magic, and all in all the only thing more that Volker, blinking away a dozen dancing after-images, could have wished was that it had been anything like on target, instead of twenty yards or more straight up the slope. The Armorican's pride in his powers was evidently justified; now if they could only do something about his sighting . . .

From the direction of their attackers a loud and juicy rasping noise echoed across the water.

Only the bombardier took not the slightest notice of the fireball, de Guillac's string of abominable oaths, or the barrage of jeering and insults from the bank that followed. He was measuring out the charges for the smaller chambers with imperturbable thoroughness, and when an arrow embedded itself in the planking by his right leg he brushed it aside like some annoying little insect.

'Titans of Tartarus!' roared Haagen, 'Fire, man, fire!'

'All in good time, Master Haagen, all in good time. Why, here am I with the wadding scarcely loaded, let along the balls. Yer don't want to hurry these things, not these days yer don't when good linen's such a price and yer can't hardly get yer first rate lead for love or money no more—'

Suddenly a soft whisper cut across the night, and the next moment a snapping, splintering thump. 'Get down, oaf!' he heard de Guillac hiss. 'They saw you then!' Volker barely heard him, but he tried to shrink smaller all the same, no easy task for him. They must have come within range of some marksman's magical night vision, and he'd ventured a shot – in hope of catching their helmsman, probably.

Dani was launching a string of arrows that glowed briefly as they fell. 'Minor magic,' thought Volker derisively. 'Priestess's spells . . .' And what good did it do to pierce the darkness of the woods momentarily? It only showed the hopelessness of their position. The winches and the catapult were well dug in behind piles of earth and stone, and the wreckers' bowmen were hidden by a tangled web of trees and undergrowth, all but impenetrable in these momentary flickers of light. Soon the barges would be reeled in like salmon, and it would be hand to hand against unknown numbers, probably too many. And well-armed. Volker cast about for some weapon he could wield, and settled for a heavy rigging pin. He felt more than ever like a fool. If he could only make a showing here, it might win him some authority – but how? The bare wooden deck of a riverboat held little scope for alchemical magic, and with weapons he was like a child among these hardened men, who took such abilities for granted. Thorgrim and de Guillac and even Dani, they had faced battle before; but for him this would be a baptism of fire . . .

Fire. He tried to stifle the memory of an old river barge burning by the Bremen quayside. It had made excellent tinder.

Volker hefted the belaying pin and crept forward. Then he became aware that something was gritting under his hands. He touched fingertips to mouth; salt, as he had thought. A stone must have cracked a salt barrel, and set the expensive stuff leaking over the deck. He hefted a handful, and a cold thrill of excitement trickled into his mind. Perhaps it needn't be wasted.

'Thorgrim!' He moved again, and it crunched loudly.

'Shut *up*!' growled Thorgrim in exasperation. Another arrow came swishing at the sound.

'Suppose we could *really* see them?'

'Wait!'

Dani at the stern lifted a hand just barely into the light, and signalled. For answer the Norseman wove a rapid pattern with his fingers. Without replying, Dani stood up, drew, aimed and released, all in one ripple of movement. For a moment there was silence – and then a yell out of the darkness. 'That for their marksman!' grunted Thorgrim. 'Owls need no magic upon their night-eyes.'

Volker got the idea. Thorgrim and Dani had lulled their pursuers into thinking the *Walross* an easy target, and the masthead light had let them see each other's signals. The enemy, with no reason to believe the barge so well protected, had made an incautious move; now their best man was down, and they were learning their mistake. But the battle was still unequal. The moment had come to turn tide.

'Thorgrim!' he breathed. 'I may be able to mark your targets for you!'

'Then do it!' growled the Norseman. 'Arrows stay not for words!'

Volker gritted his teeth. Then, scooping up the broken barrel of coarse salt, he whispered the words of a purification spell, simple but seldom used. And as it happened, the only other thing he'd need was water . . .

He ripped open the barrel and with all the strength of his long arms he flung it over the side. It bounced off one of the harpoon cables, spraying a long white trail of moonlight-glittering salt, and toppled into the water. It bobbed for a moment, then sank. For a moment more nothing happened.

Then the river erupted. Beneath the water a flower of orange fire opened, and a great bubble belched up to break the surface. A reek like demon's breath tainted the breeze, which scooped it landward; the jeering turned into an explosion of coughing and spluttering. The baleful light flared and spread upward in a coruscating whirlpool, drifting downsteam towards the bank. Every figure on the bank stood transfixed in a ghastly orange glare, the archers frozen in the act of taking cover, the catapult crew behind their rampart in the act of reloading. Their weapon was armed and ready, but they stood transfixed with terror, staring at that impossible fire as if some monstrous river demon had joined the battle.

'Shoot!' yelled Thorgrim, even as Dani's bowstring thrummed. The boatmen's crossbows snapped, and a hissing rain of bolts descended on to the bank. Several found marks, and the dark figures raced about like ants in disorder, yelling apparently to the catapult crew.

'Ah,' said Joachim approvingly. 'Were you gentlemen still wanting me to—'

Haagen's jaw dropped. 'You mean – you're actually *ready*?'

'Have been these last few minutes, sir,' said Landau, a little hurt. 'If yer'll just help me to swing this 'ere barrel around, like—'

Merchants and men flung themselves on the bombard and swung it about, trampling on each other unheeding. Stones and arrows rattled and rang off the mantlet, and they ducked away wildly as Landau, totally unmoved, made his final fine sighting adjustments. He clicked his tongue, shook his head and drew a smouldering fuse from the clip on his belt. 'It's a shocking sloppy job, it is! But if yer gentlemen are in such an all-fired hurry, then when yer all stood clear—'

'In the name of all the gods, man!' yelled Beck. '*Shoot!*'

A puff and fizz burst out from where he thrust the taper, and a thunderclap burst on the prow of the *Walross*, rocking the barge so wildly that she all but keeled over. Smoke enveloped them. Muddy river-water slopped across the deck as Volker grabbed desperately at the rail, dodging three or four cannon-balls that had been thrown clear of their racking. The after-images of de Guillac's flare were mild by comparison with the shapes that seemed to be dancing in front of his eyes, and inside his head someone was beating a bass drum with a pounding, insistent rhythm. But it was nothing to the scene from Tartarus some forty yards in front of him.

The charge from the assorted dragon orifices had ploughed up the bank like a stampede of demons, shredding the sheltering undergrowth and whatever it concealed, felling many of the wreckers and sending the rest stampeding in every direction, smashing a great trench through the earthwork, sweeping up winches, catapult, crew and all in its path and blasting the horrible mess right up the bank with the general effect of a giant scythe. Bushes blazed, severed branches swung, cracked and fell. Wreckers ran or hobbled in all directions; some, their clothes ablaze, dived for the water. The trunk de Guillac had blasted swayed on its last few splinters, smoking and crackling, then gave up and toppled headlong, picking off a few crawling wreckers.

The bombardier clicked his tongue. 'Ar. Sloppy. Just like I said. A devilish kick, and useless to man nor beast past forty paces.'

Dani's bow gave a sudden thudding snap, startling Volker; what on earth was the point now? Then he saw the figure in a shredded, flapping cowl, scrabbling up the bank towards the shelter of the trees. A flicker seemed to chase him; the figure jerked, threw up its long sleeves and cartwheeled untidily down into the lurid water. The cables the sorcerer had protected hung limp and useless from the shattered stumps of the winches and the boats wallowed as the river took hold of their hulls once again. Dani loosed another couple of shafts at any wrecker who came near them, although drawing the boats nearer was evidently the last thing they wanted right now.

'Ach, leave them,' called Thorgrim. 'They are only river scum, not worth a light!'

De Guillac chuckled. 'Not even one of Volker's. That was a timely piece of conjuring, my young friend. What other demons haunt your satchel?'

Volker grinned. 'No demons – only what can be extracted from salt. Split it into its parts with a spell like the one I used, and you get that choking air, and a strange stuff – like a white soft metal, but lively. Heat it in water and it explodes and burns – and that spell isn't popular, because its reaction releases heat . . .'

'And fire that burns in water is no magic? Then I am no sorcerer. Come, my friend, we must celebrate your prowess. Perhaps a small liberation – ah, libation – from the hold? I have some skill with locks . . .'

'Be damned to this mist,' grumbled Thorgrim. 'As bad as those that hang about Britannia's coast, and promise shipwreck and sea-graves to good honest pirates!'

'The mist I wouldn't mind,' said Dani, 'if our dopey steersman could keep a straight line through it.'

'Could you do better?' said Volker. 'Or hadn't you heard that the rudder's jammed?'

Dani shrugged expressively. They had wasted the better part of an day nursing the badly-damaged *Walross* up the short, crudely built canal that linked the Regnitz and the Altmühl, a tributary of the Donau. That had seemed difficult enough, but now the barge struggled in the living grip of a turbulent current. Thorgrim's jury-rigged steering oar was all that stood between them and grounding or beaching at every bend, and the jammed rudder continually fought it. Now he and the merchants were arguing over the charts, to find somewhere they could land along this stretch of the river. 'Well, if you know a better hole, masters,' Volker heard him say, 'I suggest you go to it. But long before that, I am thinking, you will be at the bottom of the river, and there you may fare alone. Make your choice – we are almost upon it.'

Even as he spoke the mist-wall thinned to a ragged veil, and parted. Beyond it, landscape and clouds formed a puzzle-picture of shadow and silhouette. Steep crags stood purple and black against a darkling sky on either side of a deep, bowl-shaped valley. At the centre, rising from the river on a mist-wreathed crag, a rocky promontory stabbed upward out of the forest's clutching fingers towards the waning moon, glinting like a black gem in its light.

The current was drawing the barge to the centre of the stream, revealing what the rising ground had concealed. The rock spire was strangely formed.

'Gods!' muttered Dani, 'it's a *tower*!'

'Nebelstein,' muttered Joachim. 'I might have known it. Temple-fortress of the Teutonic Knights.' He scowled. 'May they rot in Tartarus.'

Volker gaped. Stage upon arcaded stage, each crowded with carved figures and gleaming with stained and painted glass, rose to a needle-slim summit crested with intricate pinnacles. Then, as they rounded a long curve in the river, he saw the eastern face of the tower.

It was eaten away like a broken tooth. At its crest, pinnacles and masonry alike stood out in jagged ruin; shattered windows gaped into blackness. Broken carvings took on an ominous, leering look, as if this was what they had really been meant to look like all along. Far below, massive walls rose seamlessly from the edge of the cliff.

De Guillac nodded, impressed. 'One might think them conjured from the rock itself.'

Thorgrim's eyes were half-closed. 'Such things are. But here I think . . . not. For castle-building the Knights have little need of magic.'

Dani scowled. 'I've heard otherwise. They have an evil name, those fighting monks.'

'The idle gossip of the low taverns you frequent,' remarked Thorgrim piously.

'And you *don't*?'

The Norseman shrugged imperturbably. 'What I have seen, that I believe. Their citadel at Vesterbjerg, for one . . .'

'You *saw—*!'

88

'A curious place. They are all built on much the same pattern, their castles. A tower, not so great as this, and long halls set about it like the spokes of a wheel; more timber than stone, which is scarce in those parts. The outer wall much as this one, a great circle roofed with red tiles. A few other religious houses, such as seek their protection in pagan lands, and a little town, to provide the odd temptation for the Knights to resist. Little else. Once new land is made safe, few choose to remain under the Knights' gloomy shadow.'

Volker frowned, staring upward like the others; but here, beneath the steepest part of the rock, it was hard to see anything. 'I can imagine. What on earth brought you there?'

Thorgrim looked uncomfortable. 'There was a man named – it does not matter. I worked for him. He had a long nose for rumour, an unhealthy taste for it. Like you, I guess, he had heard of virgins abused and children sacrificed, of demonic lusts and unnatural practices – the usual.'

'And?' said Guy, all ears.

'We found men. A little peculiar, to be sure. Their minds revolve chiefly upon fighting and hardship and other ways of proving themselves superior to other men – in their own eyes, at least. True barbarians; crashing bores. But as for evil . . . Their greatest sin is a weakness for their own – how do you say? – *aqua vitae. Akvavit.*'

Guy's eyes lit up with interest. 'They distil a spirit? *Schnapps?*'

'To clean their armour, they claim,' chuckled Thorgrim. 'But if I lived such a monastic life I also, I might take to drinking armour polish. There are worse crimes.'

'So why the stories?' said Volker.

Thorgrim stroked his beard thoughtfully. 'It is said that not all their sanctuaries are so innocent. Perhaps this is so, or perhaps not. But it is better to believe one's own eyes, not what others see at the end of a beer-horn.'

'Well, that's right enough, maybe,' said Joachim doubtfully. 'But why's so many of their castles in places no decent folk want to live? All out of the way, hid away, like here. Just a tiny little town about it, one or two mouldy old convents, half deserted, and people near as funny as the Knights themselves, they say. And they build on odd sites, sometimes, like here, too. They say there was a whatchmycallit, an oracle here once, in Old World days before the Romans came. Not a good one, neither.'

De Guillac chuckled. 'But that is superstition, surely. It is because the Knights, in their campaigns to conquer the heathen, chose to plant their altars where the old heathendom had ruled, both to borrow the aura of such a place and to show how the gods of Rome had over-come it. All the more so, when such places could be well fortified, as this can.'

'Ar,' said Landau. 'But look at yer tower there! Small wonder they say it's accursed. All fallen away like that!'

De Guillac waved an airy hand. 'Again this super-stition! This also I have seen before. Settlers were ready enough to live under the shadow of these chilly Knights while their protection was needed; but once the land was pacified, naturally they settled elsewhere. Accursed, indeed!'

The cabin door banged open, and the merchants came out. None looked happy; all looked cold. Goldfüss was coddling himself in a fur-trimmed cloak, Haagen had covered his bald spot with a dark blue chaperon, Beck's hands were buried inside the sleeves of his gown, and Diderik was almost lost in the folds of a voluminous cloak. By now the *Walfisch* was deep in the shadow of the cliff, and wallowing clumsily towards a stone-built quay lit by guttering torches. Their red-gold light flick-ered across a row of warrior statues flanking the dock, eight or nine about lifesize flanked by two much larger, but otherwise all uniform, faceless in dull plain armour and surcoats.

The figures moved. Only the larger pair were actual statues, cast in weathered metal. But the others, stepping forward to the dockside with a soft chinking of mailrings, still looked disturbingly like them. 'Sanctuary guardsmen,' muttered Joachim, discreetly twisting his fingers into a sign against evil. As they came clattering down the dockside steps, still with clockwork efficiency, the shore breeze wafted out a curious smell. It mingled stale oil and metal polish with the distinct, foetid odour of woollen hose long overdue for laundering.

Dani wrinkled her nose. 'They *need* a vow of chastity?'

Guy grinned. 'You might call it the odour of sanctity. Bathing is considered to be a worldly pleasure, unmanly to indulge in more than once in a while. A *long* while.'

Thorgrim looked vaguely puzzled. Volker suddenly realised that the Norseman was blissfully unaware of the stink; perhaps his sensitive nose for magic had taken the place of much of his ordinary sense of smell. He wondered how the Knights themselves stood it. These sentries were an ugly-looking bunch; their high pot helmets framed sour, emotionless faces that seemed totally indifferent to the arrival of the two barges. Certainly none so much as moved to lend a hand when the mooring cables snaked out on to the cobbled quay, and grumbling crewmen leapt ashore to secure the barges. But behind them, up on the dockside, Volker noticed a figure differently dressed, in a hood and short cloak of shadow-black wool, pacing up and down on skinny legs. Beside him he heard Thorgrim catch his breath, and thought the smell had got through to him at last; but then he too saw the badge exposed on the dark-clad man's shoulder, a double-headed Imperial eagle and beneath it, much larger, the hand of Justitia with her scales.

'That one,' muttered Thorgrim, 'is as welcome as a swarm of bees in a sauna.'

Volker barely heard him. *A witchfinder. That's one coincidence too many . . .* He narrowed his eyes, trying to pierce the deep shadows that masked the man's features.

'Face like a weasel,' muttered Dani, frowning with concentration. 'Scar on the left cheek. And the Knights fear him. I can smell it even through the stink of their armour.'

Thorgrim started, and gave her a sideways look: 'You, I think, have a nose like a bloodhound; or a very fine imagination.'

'I'm a huntress, idiot.'

'So it would seem. And what of this one?'

He gestured towards the knight captain stepping on to the gangplank of the *Walfisch*. He was not especially tall, but in that massive helm and mail, with his stiff, military gait, he hardly looked human.

'Who are you?' The voice was harsh, and the helmet gave it strangely unpleasant resonances. 'By whose permission do you approach our citadel?'

Goldfüss puffed out his chest. 'Does your master welcome weary travellers with drawn weapons? He should send you instead to crush the pirates at his own back door!'

'The Master is a busy man, stranger. Newcomers must answer to me first, or be off about their business – if we permit them.'

'Come, come, Goldfüss,' cackled Diderik. 'It's a chilly night for arguments. Master Beck is our spokesman, after all.'

It was said that on one memorable occasion Beck had charmed a Bacchic priest out of his wine-cellar; but now his engaging smile was slightly marred by his chattering teeth. 'Sir, your pardon,' he said. 'We are but honest merchants who would not dream of intruding upon the, er, peace of your sanctuary, save that we have been most foully attacked by river pirates. We drove them off, but thought it best to hurry here and inform your Master of this insult to his rights over this stretch of river.' He indicated the obvious damage. 'And, of course, to claim but a little of the charity for which the Knights are renowned – in tending the damage, and our wounded men. We would defray the costs of such service—'

'They have a woman with them,' interrupted another, harsher voice. They turned back towards the quay and the shadowy figure of the witchfinder. 'Why? Women are forbidden this citadel.'

'Master Passmeyer,' growled the captain, with barely suppressed fury, 'the Master has acknowledged your Imperial license. Have the courtesy to respect his rights also!'

Thorgrim swore softly, and glanced in surprised apology at Dani. Beneath the witchfinder's hood the boat-lamps revealed exactly the face she had described: long and gaunt, with a lantern jaw and narrow, close-set eyes. 'Your remark is noted, Captain. My inquisition concerns anything and everything in this, mmnh, Sanctuary of yours.' Passmeyer smiled thinly. 'Even so, I have no wish to interfere with your duties. You may continue.'

With a barely stifled snort of irritation the captain turned back to Beck and the other merchants. 'Very well then.' Volker suspected that the thin man's objection had made the Knight more ready to admit them, if only to spite him. 'The woman will be escorted to a fit place. The rest of you will come with us. Bring those that are hurt.'

'And our boats?' Beck inquired gently.

'We have shipwrights. They will work on it at once. You must leave tomorrow.'

Beck blinked in dismay, and was about to protest

93

when Haagen answered blandly 'We would not dream of disturbing you further. After all,' he added in a whisper, 'would you want to stay any longer in this gods-forsaken place?'

The sentinels more or less marched the merchants' party towards the citadel. For Volker this was an extended torture. After much dithering he had decided not to leave the precious case in its hiding-place aboard, but now he was constantly aware of the witchfinder who stalked along with them. Passmeyer's eyes were invisible beneath the black hood, yet Volker seemed to *feel* their unblinking gaze, probing the concealing folds of his cloak. Even Thorgrim seemed uneasy, as though, despite Ulrich's web of woven spells around it, he too was half-aware of the horn.

A narrow stairway from the quay took them up the flank of the cliff, sheltered by towering walls of new-cut stone, to a squat gatehouse. Beyond a double portcullis and drawbridge lay the little town of Nebelstein itself.

It was not what Volker had expected.

Ruins lined the cracked and crumbling road, flanked by tumbled walls of brick and weather-beaten stone that took them in a long, gentle curve upward and around the rock. Higher up, the arches and columns of the early empire were clothed in the timber and roughcast of a newer time, like the skeletons of Old World creatures prisoned in stone by the gods who had destroyed them. They passed the towering façade of a Roman temple, half-engulfed in a new-made wall. The statues on its tympanum were limbless, shapeless husks, but the inscription beneath them stood clear and sharp, as if new-chiselled:

AD DEUM INCOGNITUM

To the god unknown. What god? And what kind of god?

'Nom de Saturne,' muttered Guy, 'but this place, it is a mausoleum!'

'Halts' maul!' growled one of the knights, turning to reveal a face that would have been quite at home around – or maybe inside – Mutzelbacher's rat-pit. Guy's hand slapped on his sword-hilt before Volker grabbed it, and the hidden case jarred against the Armorican's ribs. He pulled away with a start and a frown of puzzlement.

'No arguments,' said Volker quietly. 'Not here, and not now.'

Guy acknowledged the sense of this with a curt nod. He too had caught the unease that Volker sensed. *The knights are afraid. These ones, anyhow – maybe more afraid than ordinary people would be. They're not used to it – don't want to admit it . . .*

As the road climbed, the buildings became less ruinous, but the aura of decay was everywhere. There were houses here, tall, jettied houses with finely carved gables; but paint and plaster flaked from rotten timbers, and the bowing, neglected roofs were gap-toothed with broken and missing slates. Goldfüss shook his head. 'With a few tiles and timbers a man might make his fortune here.'

'If anyone could pay him,' growled Haagen. 'I've seen more wealth in a Nürnberg beggar's bowl. And where're the people?'

It was a reasonable question. The knights' footfalls rang through empty ways. At street level most windows were boarded; those above were blank, or closely shuttered. Here and there a chink threw a narrow fan of pallid light across the cobbles, or a white face peered out for a moment, then pulled back into the gloom. In a main square littered with filth and refuse, an abandoned cart stood rotting by a dried-up fountain. On three sides there were mostly simple two-storeyed houses; but across the fourth loomed the ugly block-like gatehouse of the fortress sanctuary.

'Well?' demanded the witchfinder.

The guard captain cursed under his breath, but audibly, and made a point of ignoring him. He led the way to a heavy oaken door at the angle of the square, and Volker heard Dani catch her breath. She was staring at the peculiar sign it bore, the scene of a stag beset by hounds beneath a sickle moon, in what looked like tarnished silver. On this the captain rapped his mailed gauntlet. 'Here the woman remains. The rest, to the citadel. All will be escorted back to the docks tomorrow.'

Volker hardly heard. He had noticed Dani's sharp little gasp, of shock, perhaps, or anger. And his eyes, like hers, were fixed on the narrow line of light where the door had opened, and on the woman he glimpsed beyond, white-robed, her face half-veiled by a waist-length curtain of fine, yellow hair. Guy, following his gaze, raised an eyebrow and swiftly doffed his hat and sank to one knee in a florid courtly bow.

'*Ma demoiselle*, your servant! A *Draconnier* is yours to command, if there is—'

He might as well have been invisible. The woman's eyes, large and shadowed, met Dani's. She made as if to step back, but the woman raised her hand slightly. 'No! We knew of you. You are expected, and welcome.'

The guards looked up, and flinched at a sudden sweeping whiteness. But the owl ignored them, gliding to its accustomed place on Dani's shoulder. The guards glared and mumbled, but the woman half-smiled, a strange upward quirk of the lips more like a ritual gesture than a human response. 'Both of you. All hunters honour the goddess. Come.'

Volker saw suddenly that Thorgrim's knuckles gripped white against the dark halberd shaft. As if he had sensed some hidden interplay of forces at work . . . His fingers moved in one of those battle signals, but when

Dani ignored it, he spoke aloud. 'Well, girl? Is this what you want?'

Dani made no answer. Her face was set with a strange blend of defiance and resignation. At last she stepped forward, her eyes fixed on the doorway and the dim hall beyond. Volker and the others might never have existed. The door closed with a heavy click which was somehow more daunting than any resounding slam, and there was the soft metallic slither of heavy bolts. Night and silence flooded into the empty square – but as he turned away he saw that the massive gates of the citadel stood open.

Their guards marched them through the gatehouse into a wedge-shaped courtyard. Within all was paved like a parade ground, except for the fountain that bubbled from the pouting lips of a stone *lorelei*, weathered and vastly ancient-looking, the water trickling in twin streams across her bare breasts and down her shapely tail. Volker heard the hooded man sniff in theatrical disgust. Beyond her rose the tower, and on either side two of Thorgrim's 'long-halls', *basilicas* of the Old Empire – tall, three-aisled, and barn-like. Ruined barns, roof timbers stark against the sky like the stripped bones of some Old World giant.

Haagen looked smug. 'What did I tell you? Business is bad.'

Thorgrim shrugged. 'So. Another night beneath the stars. Yet *Better ill welcome than no welcome*, as the bear said when it met the huntsman.'

'Follow me!' rapped the captain. 'And curb your tongue! A night alone in the lower city might be even less to your precious comfort.'

Volker upended the brown earthenware bowl to reach the last drops of the pottage. He wasn't too sure why. He was desperately hungry, but even that couldn't lend savour to this thin, cold, almost tasteless goo.

'And they call this a hostel!' muttered de Guillac. 'If they must give us river water for ale, at least they might take out the pond scum first. Is that your *aqua vitae*, my barbarian friend?'

'Save your grumbling, de Guillac. We live, we drink, we eat—'

'This exudation of a Minotaur I should not feed to a pig!'

Thorgrim grinned. 'In this place the pigs wear armour.' He shook his head sorrowfully at the cheerless, ramshackle hall. Huddled like a sparrow's nest at the foot of the central tower, the lower hostel was not exactly filthy, but showed every sign of having been hastily and grudgingly cleaned, by defaulters, de Guillac guessed. Little heaps of dust and cobweb had been piled up in unobtrusive corners, odd areas left uncleaned as nasty surprises for the unwary. And every time somebody slammed a door, which was the only way to shut them, little flakes of rotten timber and crumbling mortar came drifting down, and sometimes not so little. Volker half-smiled. 'We're the lucky ones, Thorgrim. Imagine Beck swapping light table talk with this Master?'

Joachim tapped his bread suspiciously, watching the dry crumbs in his bowl to see if any moved. Some did. 'In Regensburg they say the Master's armour is plated with gold and studded with jewels.'

Guy almost choked with laughter. '*Foi de Guillac*, they *will* have something to speak of. Beck would sell his soul to Tartarus for such a treasure!'

'I reckon not,' said Joachim. 'But he might be open to offers.'

The Norseman nodded absently. 'It is our sharp-eyed huntress I wonder about. How does she fare tonight?'

In the awkward silence that followed, Volker was half aware of a deep, throbbing vibration somewhere, faint but perceptible; it was shaking a faint continuous rain

of fine dust from the rafters overhead. Somewhere in
the shadows a more than usually desperate rat clawed
at the few thin scraps from their table and scuttled to
its hole as a door creaked open at the far end of the
hall. For a moment the witchfinder stood framed in the
doorway like a gargoyle that had stepped down from
the tower above. Volker could almost feel the hooded
eyes sweeping across the company, and the horn-case
tingled against his side. The ram-headed staff pointed
to Thorgrim.

'You. I know you.'

The Norseman nodded, and took another swig of ale.
'And I you. *Hvad saa?*'

'You were bodyguard to Inquisitor Joris Ingelbrechts
of Brabant, my colleague.'

'Briefly. Not briefly enough. But long enough to hear
about you. Still pricking pretty girls for witchmarks,
Passmeyer?'

'You will address me as befits my office, barbarian!'

'Don't tempt me!' muttered de Guillac.

But Thorgrim only shrugged. 'As you wish. What do
you want, witchfinder?'

'You have an unusual talent. I need it again.'

'Alas,' said Thorgrim, stony-faced, 'I am no longer
for hire.'

'I do not *ask* for your assistance. I am uncovering
black evils here. At such times I may require whatever
is necessary—'

'Require?' commented de Guillac grimly. 'That I have
heard before. When others of your kind were persecut-
ing a sect of harmless Christians in my land – Cathars,
you called them, and every foul name out of Tartarus.
You *required* gibbets then, stakes and fires were *necessary*. *Nom d'un chien dement*, what evils you uncovered!
Astonishing! Why, it was just as well that you tortured
confessions out of those poor Cathars, was it not? Or
it might have been thought you had dreamed it all up.'

Passmeyer threw back his hood. His eyes had narrowed to the merest slits. 'Evidently we failed to scour their heresies wholly from the land. But now, fool, this is no village witch-hunt, but a matter of the foulest Tartarism at work, the First Creation stirring within its shadows – the willing perdition of bodies and minds in the pursuit of worldly power – pagan heresies against the Imperial Cult, the fomenting of rebellions, necromancy, unholy sacrifices of blood – the gratification of unspeakable lusts – twisted desires, the pursuit of tainted riches – demons in human flesh drawing their sustenance from fearful perversions—' The thin man was trembling from head to foot, and looked ready to start foaming at the mouth at any second.

De Guillac scowled. 'And where are they, these demons? I see little sign of riches around here, tainted or otherwise. And if this—' He tipped out the yeasty dregs of his ale contemptuously, '—is how unspeakable lusts are gratified, most of us will adhere to what is strictly speakable, *non mais sans blagues*! You are sure these demons are not merely the first sign that egg upon your shoulders is becoming addled?'

'Are you blind?' growled Passmeyer. 'Did you see *nothing* as you passed through the town?'

And suddenly Volker began to understand the meaning of the closed shutters, the wretched, half-ruined houses, and the miasma of death and decay drifting down from the castle rock. Guy shut his mouth abruptly, cutting off his contemptuous rejoinder. Thorgrim lost his obstinate surliness, and lifted his head slowly and cast about, as if catching some faint scent on the draughts, as if Passmeyer had alerted him to some distant, uneasy undercurrent.

The thin man nodded with unpleasant satisfaction. 'Day by day the folk of this accursed place live in terror, lest that night be the one another vanishes. None is safe, man, woman, child, babe in arms. And none is free from suspicion! If I could, I would tear these very stones one from another to burn out the evil at their heart!'

'And tear out everyone's heart to find the one guilty?' inquired Volker quietly.

The witchfinder rounded on him. 'Yes! Even that! It would be worth it, to damn the ones responsible!'

Volker bristled. This was the way of thinking that might have been applied to him – and might yet. 'And the rest? The innocent? How would *they* feel about that? How would it be different from what's happening now?'

Passmeyer snorted. 'You understand nothing of these things, boy! Their souls would be saved! And I shall put this place to the trial, yet. When I first heard the rumours about it I obtained an Imperial license—'

'He is coming up in the world,' observed Thorgrim. 'Those are expensive luxuries for a witchfinder.'

'*Enough!* All I need is one shred of good evidence to convince the Imperial Service, and I will have a warrant to strip this place to its bones, whatever these arrogant Knights may say. And you, Norseman, you are the instrument sent to help me find it! And you shall, though Hecate Arianroda forbade it! As an Imperial licensee I therefore requisition and require, under pain of penalty, that you—'

'No,' said Volker. Whatever was happening here, the task Ulrich had given him came before all else. 'Thorgrim's services are already commanded by my master, a wealthy merchant who has some Imperial influence. Does the name Ulrich Tragelicht mean anything to you?'

Clearly it did. The witchfinder balked angrily, then subsided into a cold chuckle. 'Have it your own way, barbarian. And you, boy, though there is something strange about you, I feel. Something I may yet have occasion to look into. Volker Seefried's the name, is it not? Ah, yes. I shall remember it.' He turned away, but looked back and added, 'Provided I need to; for before long you may be wishing you'd thrown in your lot with me!'

The window of Volker's guest-room opened directly on to the courtyard beneath the gently sloping, tiled roofs of the main building. In the pallid starlight they were the colour of dried blood. He shivered, and closed the shutters. The rooms had been lay brothers' cells at some time in the past; now they were little more than bare boards and crumbling plaster, with a few poor remnants of their forgotten function. This one had nothing but a candle in a simple iron holder and a bed too thin even for bugs to inhabit. Chill draughts blew clouds of fine dust from cracks in the wall, keening through the slats of the wooden shutter, and the blanket smelled unpleasantly of previous occupants. Volker shuffled it aside, surprised it didn't walk off by itself, but his cloak was barely enough to keep him warm and the horn-case made an uneasy pillow.

Sleep came slowly. Again and again he found himself juggling the few, bare facts that chance had thrown his way. Passmeyer's suspicions were meaningless in themselves; witchfinders were usually frauds, fanatics, or, not unusually, both, quite capable of concocting or extracting evidence to justify their own self-righteous suspicions. Fanatic this one certainly was; and the hatred he had evidently conceived for the arrogant Knights blinded him to all else. Yet *something* was destroying Nebelstein – something that everyone, including the Knights themselves, had come to fear.

Joachim's oracle?

It made no sense. Oracles didn't eat people. An oracle answered questions, hardly a sinister activity. You went to the priests. You gave them your offering and your question, and the answer – a rushing wind, a whisper of leaves – would be interpreted for you. Then you left, usually a little poorer and none the wiser. He smiled wryly. At this precise moment guidance of almost any kind would be welcome. What should he do next? And how could he carry out the terrible task the dead mage had laid on his shoulders?

If there really was an oracle, I could use it right now . . .

Guy de Guillac mumbled in his uneasy sleep, and turned restlessly on the understuffed pallet that was his bed. The salty pottage had left him with a roaring thirst, and now he dreamed of distant lands, or barrels filled with slowly ripening wine, of stolen moments in sunlit vineyards . . .

Dani paused for a moment, checking her lantern, then turned to the Prioress for the last time.

'You aré sure it was here, Mother?'

The old woman nodded. 'Marva, Hildegunda, Geno-veva – all came this way while we others slept.'

'And never returned.'

'We even tried to bar the portal.'

Dani pushed open the door. It hung limply, and freshly broken timber grinned along the line of its hinges. 'There's nothing else you can tell me?'

'Nothing. But the choice is yours.'

'And my penance to the goddess—?'

'Is fulfilled. Hereafter, you are free. As free as you choose to be.'

'If I live.'

'My daughter—'

'I'm not entitled to . . .'

'Nonetheless. Go with the huntress' blessing.'

For a moment, Dani hesitated. Then, sliding her bow off her shoulder, she raised her lantern and stepped across the threshold into the darkness beyond.

Volker's eyes flickered open, but found nothing to focus on.

He stood in darkness, with no sound but the faint, throbbing vibration he had sensed before. Vague memories of a dream – a voice calling him, promising an answer – faded and died. He had no idea where he was, or how he had come here. He felt a brief rush of panic before he realized the horn-case was with him, clasped firmly in his arms. The air was damp, still as a sealed tomb and stinking of nitre and mould. Chill struck through the soles of his boots. Gingerly, he reached out his right hand. Cool stone crumbled into his upturned fingers.

Behind him, something moved. A ringing, scraping sound, like metal rasping against stone, echoed endlessly into infinity. With it came a pale, flickering light, dancing and bobbing across round-headed arches, monumental pillars, disturbing, intricately carved capitals – and something else. Like serried ranks of bombards . . . He fumbled for his knife, and stepped into the light.

'*Thorgrim!* What in the nine hells—?'

To his amazement a heavy hand was clapped over his mouth. '*Befamle mig baglæns,*' breathed the Norseman, 'will you hold your noise? *Look!*' He pointed to a silent, moving shadow just beyond the circle of lamplight. It was Guy de Guillac, and he appeared to have lost his wits.

'I don't believe it. He's emptying his costrel on the *floor!*'

'All night his snoring keeps me from sleep. Then he starts to mumble like a madman, and down he comes to this hole in the ground.'

'Why did you follow him?'

'I think he sleeps still. Also I think there is something evil in this *forbandede* place, besides that *svineskidt* Passmeyer.'

'I'm sure of it,' whispered Volker. 'It brought me here the same way, in my sleep. Could be that snoring did you a favour. If you hadn't woken me . . . Come to that, maybe we'd better wake *him*.'

The big Armorican seemed to be fumbling with one of the cannon, though his flint and steel were still in their pouch. Even so, Volker edged forward. The battle on the Regnitz had shown him the havoc that gunpowder could wreak. Thorgrim followed, and in the growing light they could see that Guy was fiddling with a metal fitment. The chuckling gurgle that followed was unmistakable, and so was the rich smell of aniseed that wafted towards them.

'*Akvavit*,' grunted Thorgrim. 'By all the gods, I swear that this one would split an iceberg if there was drink inside it.'

Volker hesitated as the big Armorican turned off the tap, raised the costrel to his lips, paused to inhale its rich aroma, then with an artistic flourish tipped it back . . .

Volker winced. The Armorican wheezed and coughed like an elderly and unhappy dog, clutched at his throat with both hands, and doubled up. Thorgrim's lantern showed his lips moving in what appeared to be a wide-ranging and comprehensive curse, but not a single sound emerged.

Thorgrim grinned. 'Ah, your self-control has *schnapped*?'

Guy turned a furious scarlet face on them. '*Bougre d'imbécile!*' he croaked. 'What miserable alchemy is this? I dream I am in the *caves* of my ancestors, about to carry out a necessary testing of the perfected vintage of the *Seins d'Aphrodite* – which we hide even from the gods lest they prefer it to nectar – and I am most rudely awakened in a dismal Teutonic dungeon with a throat full of armour polish and exposed to the idiot grins of two absolute and utter *crétins* – *ahuris macrocéphaliques* –

flaneurs foutiste – fils dénaturés des putains morbides – sales enculeurs des laies suragées—'

'Never mind that,' said Volker hastily. He understood Gallic better than Thorgrim. '*Something* brought us down here, both of us. Maybe Passmeyer's something. Perhaps this is how people disappear. Thorgrim?'

The Norseman frowned. 'There is no way to be sure. I have felt something since we landed, maybe before. Like an ache in my bones. But far off still, so far I can get no scent of its direction or nature at all. And yet—' He hesitated, grew tense. 'Yes! There is something else, something nearer at hand. Below us, further down the stair. Something that . . . reaches out with magic.' He swallowed slightly. 'As if it hunts.'

Instinctively they crowded together, facing out at the shadowy columns of the vault. 'Some *thing*?' inquired Guy unhappily.

'I cannot tell. It seems human . . . It may be . . . perhaps not entirely.'

'Passmeyer?'

Thorgrim shook his head. 'He has no magic. Yet there is something familiar . . . No. The power is too strong to be hers.'

'Hers?'

'Our huntress. Dani.'

Guy looked exactly like a man who needed a big drink. He sniffed dubiously at his flask, then sighed and sipped it, savoured it and smiled. 'Perhaps I have done the *frères guerriers* some injustice. The true water of life will surely have grapes or apples or even barley about it, and not aniseed. But this will assuredly do.'

'Sipped, not swigged,' said Thorgrim severely, and demonstrated. 'Though it lacks iced beer and pickled herring to go with it. Well, Volker? What shall we do?'

The abrupt shift took Volker aback. Then he realised the two had been posturing, establishing how cool they were, which probably meant they were scared stiff. And that done, they were looking to him for a decision. So he had the authority he'd wanted! But he might have enjoyed it more if he could think of anything to do with it. 'For a start,' he remarked, 'I could use a little of that armour polish.'

That at least gave him a moment to think. 'If there is any chance that's Dani down there—' *Damn the girl! Nothing but bloody trouble!* '—she could probably use some help. Or anyone else who's been lured down, for that matter. We'd better go on.' *Mission or no mission. Wonderful. But anything else, and they'd think it was because I'm scared. And gods, I am!*

'*Nombril de Vénus*, how much further?

De Guillac was irritable, although – or because – he had been sipping absentmindedly at the *schnapps* ever since their hunt had begun. Volker managed not to swear back at him, but the tension was telling on them all. Only the Norseman's talent had been able to guide them through the half-forgotten labyrinth beneath the citadel. Vault after arcaded vault, mouldy and damp, had passed in and out of the circle of lamplight, until now they stood at the head of a forgotten stairway leading down into darkness. A long-forgotten stair, by the looks of it, wear-dished and dripping with stalactites of nitre and sporing moulds; darkness that should have been undisturbed as a stagnant pool, but was filled with the low, vibrating roar they had felt from within the citadel. And more than that . . .

'See for yourself,' said Thorgrim. He pointed to a moving spot of light some forty feet below. 'We should follow quickly. What she seeks is close by, and I cannot tell if it is one or many.'

'She?' said Volker. 'You still think it's Dani?'

'I . . . cannot be sure. Maybe. But there is something strange around her, about her, if so . . . Perhaps there is someone with her; but it is all concentrated in her.'

'Hah!' grunted Guy. 'She has courage.'

'She's a pig-headed fool!' said Volker. 'Why in the name of Mercury's high-speed sandals did she come down here at all? And *alone*?'

The Norseman ignored him, barrelling forward down the stairs with an impatient wave to de Guillac. Volker had no choice but to follow.

Damn the woman! I should leave her to rot. If Thorgrim's right, she's risking all our necks. And if Passmeyer's right, we're walking straight into a nest of Tartarists. 'Here's a nice horn, sir. We thought you might like it . . .'

Further down, the staircase was more crudely built, and its stones were worn more heavily. It was as if they walked down the centuries into a forgotten past. Then, abruptly, there were no more stairs. Thorgrim's lantern light glanced back off the blue-green walls of a tunnel-like cave, lined with stalactites and stalagmites and throbbing with sound that pulsed upwards through their feet like a living heartbeat. It was like peering down the gullet of a stone dragon, but beyond it was only pallid phosphorescence, and amidst it the faint gleam of Dani's lantern. As Thorgrim strode on to catch her up, the light revealed strange, almost sculpted shapes on either side, but there was no time to look at them. Streams danced down the rocks from all sides. Ahead, the cave grew higher and wider, until at last Dani's light spread out and glittered against a tall water-curtain that crashed from a sharp rockface through the cave-floor to fall, roaring like a furious monster, into even greater chasms below. A reminder, thought Volker, that even this deep they still stood on a thin bridge above the Abyss. Screening the waterfall was a monumental barrier of stalactites and stalagmites, for all the world like a distorted copy of the temple façade in the lower city.

And before it, robed in black, stood its priest.

Thorgrim's eyes narrowed. He swore quietly, and thrust the lantern at Guy.

'*Merde alors*, what—?'

'Passmeyer! I should have known that *he*—'

'Quiet,' breathed Volker. 'Listen!'

'Who are you?' Beneath the cavern's natural dome, Dani's voice echoed as clearly as a priest's in the Pantheon at Worms.

'I am a servant of truth,' said Passmeyer calmly, throwing back his hood. 'My quest is the same as yours.'

Dani's bow remained levelled at his narrow chest. 'Funny. You don't *look* like a priestess.'

'Both of us went to find a power. It is here. Long ago, before the Romans came to trouble the ancestral forests, there were great shrines within them to the elder gods of the earth and sky, whose names none now remember. And one there was that held an oracle, that to our Teutonic ancestors was a name as potent as Delphi and Didyma to the ancient Greeks. Always it answered truly, but never easily. And always there was a price to be paid.' The witchfinder bared his teeth in the mockery of a smile; there was a drawn look about his face that Volker seemed to recognize.

Yes! Like poor old Strauben, not long before he . . .

'When the Romans came, with their more comfortable gods, the people around that shrine grew foolish. They ceased to pay its price, and when the priests threatened them with a higher wrath they murdered them, sealed up this well and threw down the shrine. And over its rubble they erected shrines to those comfortable gods, raised tall temples and convents, and built a town around them, hoping to settle and civilize this part of the wild land. In time they all but forgot anything had ever dwelt on this site before them. But even in sleep its anger was potent. That town grew weak and stunted, the forests were never cleared; those temples withered and crumbled, the convents dwindled, till today only one lingers, under the doubtful shield of the warrior brethren. And even they grow tainted from within. For now the power can waken again, its long wounds healed; waken and gather strength, and call men to it once more. Those with the strongest magic hear it first, in their dreams, and are drawn. Only a few at first, very carefully, and never more than one at a time. For sustenance – and to draw in others in their wake. So I found it. I came to investigate yet another case of evil among the Knights, rumours of Tartarus stirring – and instead I uncovered . . . this. Old beyond measuring, beyond good and beyond evil. It is – wisdom. Knowledge. Infinite truth. What choice did I have?'

'I'm not here to answer riddles.'

'That is exactly why you are here.'

'I choose for myself, witchfinder.'

'There is no choice, only necessity. Duty compels our roles. Mine is to serve truth, though I find it within the gates of Tartarus. To give myself over to it, body and soul. To be its aid and helper, its acolyte, to bring it what it needs and be repaid. Richly.' His cold eyes gleamed wetly, and a trickle drooled from one corner of his twitching mouth. 'And yours—'

'Well?'

He smiled. 'Yours, my dear, is to be the precious price of truth. Yours is to offer up your life.'

Dani's lantern swung wildly, scattering shadows of confusion. She loosed even as he pounced; but he was too close. He must have crept up on her, been stopped only at the last moment. The arrow sang harmlessly into his billowing robes, and he was on her. She dropped the bow, swept out her long knife; but he was twice her weight, with a long spidery reach, and all too used to subduing struggling prisoners. A precisely brutal stomach punch left her paralysed and gasping; the lamp dropped and shattered, and the knife clattered away

110

among its shards. But as Passmeyer stooped over her a swift step grated on the stones, and behind it a snarling laugh and a singing hiss of metal. He glanced up and froze, as well he might. Thorgrim's face was a grim mask as he strode forward, halberd levelled, and behind him Guy's moustaches twisted into a tigerish smile, his sabre bared in his hand. Even Volker felt a surge of sudden, confident anger; spells leaped unbidden to his mind. Yet Passmeyer seemed unmoved. Pinioning Dani's wrists with his left hand he raised the other in a commanding gesture.

'Stop! All of you! Or learn the true meaning of pain!'

Thorgrim grinned. *'Naa? The mayfly threatens the trout?'*

Passmeyer's body, pressed against the stalagmite at his back, seemed to tremble with suppressed energy. His mouth twisted into a curious shape. His lips parted. Before Volker could react, a hideous noise hammered through his skull, as though the roar of the waterfall had become the shrieking cry of a beast in torment. Unthinkingly he clapped his hands over his ears, and the precious case crashed to the ground. Thorgrim sprang forward, but as the sound hit him he staggered and lost his footing on the damp limestone. He grabbed at one of the stalagmites, missed, and collapsed in a tangle of limbs. Guy gasped as though poleaxed, and sank to his knees like a drunken reveller at prayer, weaving and moaning. The lamp slid from his shaking fingers and fell over. For a moment the flame wavered in the chill draught from the waterfall. Then it flickered, and went out.

The waterfall! He's controlling the roar of it – changing it!

A hunting screech cut through the thunder. The great owl swooped overhead – and a rising wall of sound swatted it down in a disorderly flutter. But the attack had brought a precious interruption in the noise. One croak from Guy brought a blinding, sizzling ball of light

111

that raised answering, blue-green reflections all around the cave, and revealed Thorgrim, on his knees, with the halberd balanced javelin-like in his hand.

'Passmeyer!'

The witchfinder had dragged his victim to the very brink of the abyss. Her wrists were still locked behind her back, but the crippling barrage of sound had done little to quiet her, and Guy's soaring magelight had distracted her captor. Perhaps there was also the will of her silent sister priestesses above; they had sent her into these depths because she was better able to avenge their lost companions, but she was not unshielded. Her prisoned fingers clutched sharply backward like claws, and Volker winced as they clamped together with surgical precision. Passmeyer doubled up with a strangled, high-pitched scream as his captive twisted out of his arms, pirouetted neatly on one leg, and swung the other in a sweeping arc to connect with the retching witchfinder's jaw. His head snapped sharply back with an ugly cracking sound. He slumped at the edge of the chasm, teetered for a moment on the brink, then slithered slowly backward and vanished from sight.

Volker watched the owl land a little clumsily on Dani's shoulder, rocking unsteadily from one foot to the other and shaking its head.

Funny. I never thought birds could cross their eyes . . .

'Well?' said Dani. 'Who in Tartarus was *that*? And what in the name of the Huntress did he think he was doing? And while we're about it, how 'bout *you* guys?'

'This was a wolf in shape of a man,' said Thorgrim, climbing warily to his feet. 'One that loved to bring pain and fear to others in the name of duty.'

'Like all bad musicians,' muttered the Armorican, fingering the thin black wool of the witchfinder's fallen cloak. A distant splash sounded, far below, and a loud echoing rumble. 'His tailor, perhaps, should also hang. No, there was more to it than that. His witchfinding had given way to a new madness. He had come to believe that some Old World oracle still lingered here. He thought himself under its spell, heard its voice inside his skull giving him orders, telling him secrets, in return for the victims he brought it. A common enough kind of delusion—'

'We could use a little more light,' said Dani.

'*Mille excuses!* I shall—'

The rumble grew louder, and then, as if in answer, the noise from the waterfall redoubled to a mind-numbing roar. Pain lanced through Volker's ears and temples and stabbed into his eyes. His teeth clamped sharply on his tongue, filling his mouth with the warm, salty taste of blood. Every muscle in his body seemed to jerk and twitch in uncontrollable spasm. All around him blue-green calcite trembled, cracked and fell away in broken fragments; and the very bones within his body shuddered in response, tearing at the muscles and ligaments that bound them till his legs buckled beneath him. Through a haze of pain he saw stalagmites and stalactites quiver and shatter, revealing what centuries of accretion had hidden from sight.

The shrine! The shrine of the oracle . . . !

They staggered round like exhausted dancers, sick and giddy, retching in their pain. Pillars and capitals broke free as if some supernatural sculptor were shaping them from the living rock. Crudely carved figures fought their way to the light – a crowned king, a priest, a bound and helpless victim. The sculpted smile of a goddess burst from its nitrous shell, and as an answering agony tore through his skull he heard a high-pitched, rising scream ripped from his own throat.

The oracle . . . is the cave . . . and it's alive!

His toe stubbed against something hard and sharp-edged. In the chaos he'd forgotten the horn-case.

This torment, this death, this was sound. And this horn, its power must also be in its sound; that was why

Ulrich had found people to play it. Musicians – so the sound should be directed somehow. There must be something to its music. Even if it was only a bold discord, like the owl's screech, it might break this jarring confusion long enough to let them escape. He fumbled clumsily with the catches, but even the simplest motion demanded unbelievable concentration. It seemed an age before the cold metal mouthpiece touched his mouth. He could barely think, and there was no more time. Pursing lis lips, he pressed the horn against them, slid shaking fingers over the icy silver keys and blew for his life.

The scaly surface of the horn seemed to shiver beneath his fingers, like the flank of a living animal. The sound rang clear, but the note sliced through the chaos around them like a shriek out of Tartarus. A discord, jarring, uncontrolled as Volker's fingers skidded – but a massive one, a great singing wind that stung their cheeks and streamed out their hair. De Guillac snatched wildly at his hat, Dani grabbed her bow as it was blown along the floor. For a moment Volker felt himself struggling with another will, as if the horn itself were twisting in his hands, but the half-familiar pattern of the keys guided his fingers. He guessed at the pitch of that torturing vibration from the waterfall, and blew again, harder. For one awful instant the jarring conflict of the two sounds set up standing waves that rattled the brain in his skull like a pea in a whistle. Desperately he shifted the pattern – and again—

Then, suddenly, there was harmony.

The pain stopped. The vibration stopped. For the first time Volker heard the clink and patter of calcite fragments falling all around them, and the deeper, cracking concussion of fractured and tormented rock from the tunnel beyond. In the dim phosphorescence he could just see the nearest stalagmite, riven with multiple cracks . . .

114

'Thorgrim! Where is it? What's attacking us?'

'Not Passmeyer. He's gone; he was only a puppet, a lure. That pit there. Something – in the rock . . . like part of the *mountain*!'

It was unbelievable, but it had to be true. The oracle was living rock, or something like it, that heard, felt, perhaps even saw everything that was happening on it, in it, or around it. Long ago, before the Knights, it had traded knowledge for food. When the old city died, it had slept. And now it was awake, howling, throat agape for human flesh. Unless they could silence it . . .

As if his thought had summoned it, the sound began again, this time at a lower frequency that shook every bone in his body, then slid up to an ear-drilling shriek and back, faster than any human could respond to it. Guy, nearest the fall, reeled helpless into its grasp, gesturing frantically to Volker. He swung the horn up and blew, hard; but the result was appalling. It caught something in that awful roar and matched it. The whole air seemed to bend and sing like taut metal, and the flinty floor beneath Guy's feet cracked like glass; caught in the terrible interplay of forces, the big man was physically lifted from the ground. Volker choked off the horn, and Guy collapsed in a heap.

'I can't control it!' gasped Volker, as they ran to help him. 'I don't know how to use it! Gods know what I might do next time! I need something else—' He cast about. That sudden burst of confidence, that had been part of the lure. But one of those spells it had summoned up . . .

A party trick, like the light from salt. But if he could only increase the potential it should still work, with so much raw magic in the air . . .

'Guy! The costrel! Give me the costrel!'

Guy bled from nose and ears, and his eyes were bright red. 'Hnh? Keep y'r hands off, boy!'

'Thorgrim! Help me!' The Norseman ducked a wild,

swinging blow from the groggy Armorican, tore the half-empty costrel from his hand, and threw it at Dani. 'Into the hole with it!' screamed Volker, as the noise soared louder and higher. '*Now!*'

Dani's face was a question mark, but she caught the costrel in mid-flight, paused for a moment to weigh and balance it, then hurled it into a soaring upward arc with a vigorous overarm throw. Gleaming in the lamplight, Guy's treasured vessel tumbled end over end between the pillars of the ancient shrine and down into the unknown spaces below.

Reflexive fury sent the Armorican's hand to his sabre hilt. Thorgrim, horror-struck, dived forward but the blade was already free of the scabbard. The basket hilt caught the Norseman's jaw like a cudgel and sent him sprawling to the ground as his halberd rattled across the stones and out of his reach. With a raucous yell Dani launched the owl, but even her voice was drowned by the echoes of Volker's furious invocation:

Aquae cadentes! Aqua vitae transfundatus erat, ergo in aquae vitissima omnia fluvia transfigurate!

His clear voice echoed under the cavern roof. The light changed from a pallid green to a deep, saffron yellow. The note of the falling water seemed to change. The owl, swooping at Guy's face, swerved violently away from the waterfall spray. A weird sickly smell filled the air. Volker gaped at the spray that pooled in his outstretched hand. It looked oily; it felt slightly . . . sticky.

I don't believe it. I've turned the whole waterfall into . . .

The rumbling roar of the oracle faltered, bubbled, made a horrible sound, full of sloppings and splashings and rasping noises like a mammoth retching. No, a herd of them. In unison. Volker boggled, trying to imagine what hundreds of gallons of aqua vitae would do to a gigantic, living throat . . .

'*Run for your lives!*' he screamed.

He was barely in time. A howling updraught roared through the cave, billowing out Volker's cloak like a flag and filling the air with the pungent scent of aniseed. Guy took a deep, contented sniff, like a cook savouring rare spices, then staggered across to the half-stunned Norseman and hauled him upright. Moments later a rumbling concussion shook the ground beneath their feet. The cavern floor shuddered, and black pitchy stuff came spraying up through the crack. A horrible stink drowned out the aniseed. The stonework of the shrine trembled; then, with a despairing groan, the whole structure folded in on itself like a pile of wooden blocks struck down by an impatient child. Cracks gaped above the wreckage, spouting infant waterfalls (or were they *schnapps*-falls?) and whirlpools opened like hungry mouths among the rushing turmoil at their feet. A splash hit Volker's shoe, and turned a patch white. Whatever Guy had found, it might be good for armour, but Volker was damned if he'd risk swimming in it.

'The staircase!' he yelled. 'And *quickly*!'

He slammed the horn back into its case and snatched up the halberd, struggling to keep his balance as the floor bucked and heaved beneath him, praying to all the gods he knew that he could avoid tripping over hidden obstacles or catching his foot in a newly opened fissure. All around them, the strangely shaped stalactites he had seen before were cracking open, tumbling bones, skulls, and desiccated, half-mummified corpses in their path. No need to imagine what had happened to the victims of the oracle. Ahead, Dani leapt from rock to rock with enviable ease, but Guy, supporting the half-conscious Thorgrim, was trailing far behind; the blind drunk leading the blond, thought Volker crazily. A series of ominous ripples suggested the floor of the cave was about to look for a better neighbourhood. With a muttered curse Volker grabbed the Norseman's other arm, and together he and Guy half-dragged and half-carried him to the stairs. Dani had already disappeared.

Damn the woman! She might have tried to help . . .

The staircase was crumbling before their eyes. A fine rain of mortar drifted down from the flights above, and cracks were already opening between the stones. As the three of them stumbled upward Volker felt rather than heard individual blocks drop away behind them, and twice he felt a sickening wrench as the entire structure moved beneath his feet.

I've had nightmares like this . . .

Thorgrim's eyes blinked open, looked blearily to either side, and widened in horror. At the same moment something lashed at Volker's ankles, and his hand went automatically to his knife-hilt.

'It's a rope, idiot,' said a voice from above. 'Don't stab it – grab it. And throw me the halberd.'

'*Darde d'Endymion!*' grunted Guy. 'Well thought on, that one!'

Without warning the floor dropped out from under them. Volker snatched desperately at the rope, but his grip was poor and it slid through his hands, tearing off the skin of his palms. As he struggled to climb higher, one of Thorgrim's boots caught him a ringing blow on the forehead. Only sheer reflex kept him holding on, vaguely aware that the rope was moving. By the time he had unscrambled his brains, friendly hands were reaching down to drag him to safety.

Guy looked down, reshaping his bedraggled moustaches. 'I demand of myself what that one is going to feel like in the morning!' He reached to his belt, and sighed. 'Well, Master Volker? Where shall I find such another costrel? Hmm?'

118

Thorgrim grinned. 'Did he not stop the mouth of that *forfaerdelig uhyre*, my friend?'

'Those were a couple of neat tricks, right,' said Dani. 'That *horn*! Where'd you ever get *that*?'

'I'll – uh – explain about the horn,' said Volker. 'Elsewhere. Later. Somewhere safe. But while we're about it, where'd *you* come from?'

Dani looked down, scuffed a foot on the floor. 'The votaresses of Diana, they'd been losing sisters too. But they're kind of inexperienced; hunting's one thing, but this? They needed someone with a bit of rough and tumble behind her to see what was going on. Someone they could trust, who was still one of them.' She smiled cynically. 'And with a convenient penance to work off, as motivation.'

'Well, you've done it now,' said Volker brightly. 'So . . . you'll be wanting to go back to them now, I suppose. Here, or back at Nürnberg.' That ought to feel like a great relief. He was surprised that it didn't – not quite, not altogether.

Dani kept on scuffing the floor. 'You want me to? Just can't wait, huh?'

Thorgrim looked appalled. 'Back to lock yourself away again? *Frigga*, they call us barbarians, but at least we do not shut our women away till they spoil!'

'The hairy one is correct,' rumbled de Guillac. 'With those bloodless beauties you have no place. Besides, would you blight the life of this most promising young fellow here?'

Volker ground his teeth. How could he tell this Gallic oaf that he couldn't stand the girl, or she him? That would only make him worse. Guy had long ago studied every nuance of tact, and decided he wanted nothing to do with it. But to his surprise Dani didn't seem to react. 'Well, I put my foot right in it last time. Maybe I'd better wait before I go back, see a bit more of the world before I go getting myself caged again. In any way.'

'I think,' Volker said with careful casualness, 'that the first thing we'd better do is talk to the Master. He ought to be told what's in his cellar.'

'Perhaps he could spare us some of it,' said Guy. 'And something to carry it in . . . Though I suspect the waterfall will have changed only briefly. *Dommage!* One thing puzzles me, though. Passmeyer was trying to tell the fair one here that she was alone, that this thing summoned its victims only one at a time. Certainly that was the safe way, to avoid discovery. Yet all of us were called, and that was its undoing. Why? Why us, why not our employers or the other bravos? What is there so special about us, or our mission, that a force of Tartarus risks so much to destroy us?'

Dani and Thorgrim looked at each other, and at Volker; he could only shrug helplessly, hefting the horn in his arms. They all had more than their share of sharp wits, these three, and they weren't what you might call trusting souls. It wouldn't take them long to draw a straight line between two very awkward questions. He was going to have to play more than the horn very cleverly soon.

Guy clapped him on the back with explosive force. 'Ach, no need to look so long-faced for now! One thing is certain, *mon gars* – in you, Master Ulrich has chosen well. And he'll have an account of that from our own lips, you may be sure, when we get to Regensburg!'

Volker managed to smile. It was quite an achievement; his insides had turned to ice. *Regensburg! And when we get there – what then? What then?*

Chapter 3

In the tower of the Alte Schloss, high above the Etzel-brucke, a great bell tolled in the second quarter of the night. Volker, leaning on the stone parapet of Attila's Bridge, stared moodily down at the river flowing under his feet, oily black water dappled gold beneath the quayside lanterns and the bright inn windows. He shivered. He'd have been warmer within, with the rest; but he couldn't stand the strain. The moment they'd found neither Ulrich nor any word from him waiting on the wharfside at Regensburg, the party's buoyant mood drained away; and as the day wore on it got worse.

By now every man jack of them seemed to be suspicious of him, turning away and talking behind raised hands. Goldfüss and Haagen and their henchmen were the worst, but though Beck and Diderik had contented themselves with polite inquiries they came to much the same point. Till tomorrow morning, he could stall them so long and no longer; then, at the very least, they'd send to Nürnberg for word. At last, on the pretext of asking around, he'd fled out into the dark. Cold it might be, and by rumour alive with footpads and students – the distinction depended mostly on the time of night and the state of the drink kitty. Still, it would let him cudgel his brain in peace for the few hours he had left. He felt limp, helpless.

Plainly they were already wondering if he'd somehow made away with Ulrich; and if it came to trial he might have a hard job proving he hadn't, at that. He swore softly, and watched the oath swirl the haze into little coils. They'd dig out his links with poor old Strauben, too. Then the witchfinders would move in; and that, bar a little judicious maiming and scalding, would be that. He was trapped. What on earth was he supposed to *do*?

Step into Ulrich's shoes? Lead the expedition? Some hope of that, the way the others were looking at him now. Even Thorgrim and Guy had turned disturbingly quiet and watchful. He shivered again. If he could lure them away from Regensburg somehow . . . No. Without followers he could trust, he'd only be postponing the evil day. And how far would they trust him, right now? About as far as they could throw him. That would probably be the river; and he didn't blame them one little bit. Damn Ulrich! He'd dumped his whole burden squarely upon Volker's shoulders, without even a hint on how to get started. Unless . . .

His fingers drummed nervously, tracing complex and sinister characters on the dew-spangled stonework. It wasn't that hard to talk to the dead, of course, or some part of them. Perfectly possible, in fact. You just had to have the stomach to summon them up, always making sure it wasn't Something else, and bully them into answering questions . . .

He winced. You just had to be fundamentally sick, in other words. What kind of idea was that? That kind of trick led just one way, the way Strauben went. This river reek must be mouldering his brain. God knows what went into that water, flowing through the heart of the town, and some of its other organs. Across the bridge loomed the brooding spires of the university quarter; he was naturally drawn to it, and it should be fairly free of footpads. Robbing each other was against the students' code of honour, and hardly ever worth the trouble anyhow. A brisk stroll would keep his blood flowing, clear his mind of morbid ideas. And yet . . .

And yet. Without turning necromancer, there might still be a way. Back at the inn he'd said he was going to search for Ulrich, and maybe he was. If he could summon the dead man up in his imagination, try to build up that formidable personality he'd glimpsed in his own mind, imagine how *he* would have handled the situation. That might get him his answer, if there was any answer. He flapped his cloak to shed the mist droplets, and strode off across the bridge with a new determination. He saw nothing of the shadows that slipped noiselessly out of the deeper dark at the bridgehead, darting after him across the moist cobbles from one shadow to the next.

'You are sure?' A whisper, in an outrageous Gallic accent.

'There is one near him.' Concentration clamped fingers tight about the halberd shaft. 'Others, maybe, not so near.'

'So.' A softer whisper though lips hardly parted. 'What's he called up now?'

'Near him, I said; bound to him somehow. Yet I feel no power out of him.'

'Is it that he cloaks himself? He knows of your sense; and he is a mage. How powerful – that we are not yet sure.'

Large eyes lifted to the stars. 'Well, don't be too damn surprised if we find out!'

The backstreets and byways of the University of Regensburg contorted about one another like so much twisted logic. Volker let his feet guide themselves, and got lost mere minutes after he left the bridge, though it took a little longer to dawn on him. By then he was surrounded by a tangle of high, traceried walls capped with towers, turrets and decorative battlements, where twisted and monstrous gargoyles leaned out to leer. He shrugged. He felt quite at home, it was so like his quarter of Nürnberg; and, after all, where had he to go in any hurry? He thrust the thought aside and walked on, focusing his thoughts on Ulrich's bluff face, struggling to imagine the cool dark depths behind it, the mind of a master-craftsman of magic . . .

He stopped with a jolt. Something . . . something half-noticed, almost at the edge of sight. But not quite; and it shocked him rigid. What had he seen? He looked sharply around. Behind him and to one side a small street opened in the college wall, hardly more than an alley, black against blackness; and against it stirred something blacker yet. He stood stock still in the moonlight, heart pounding. The hair on his neck bristled, and he swallowed, unable to form words properly. Was he shuddering with fear – or hope? The shadow-shape flung up its cloak. Hiding its face? Or beckoning? Either. It whipped about and merged with the dark.

Volker plunged after it, wary as a wild beast, afraid: of ghosts, and of himself. Had he done this? Had fierce concentration summoned up some hidden force, some unconscious necromancy, from the deeps of his mind? He'd heard of such dangers, but only in the oldest and most potent mages, their minds silted up with too much arcane learning. The alley was empty now; but to his right a streak of grey showed where a small door stood ajar. So something solid had passed through, no spirit. He bit his lip. He should fetch help, maybe . . . but whose? And he certainly couldn't leave things hanging, not after his first glimpse of that face.

He sidled up to the door with cat-like care, Thorgrim's lesson live in his mind, and peered through the thread-thin gap at the hinges. Nothing stirred. Gingerly he pushed the door, and gasped. It opened smoothly and silently upon a stone-flagged cloister, smooth and empty in the moonlight, surrounding a cobbled square

124

and a central lawn; all around it tall walls rose, positively festooned with gargoyles. This had to be one of the famous university colleges, and a wealthy one at that. At its heart the brimming basin of an ornate fountain, stilled now for the night, mirrored the moon. Silhouetted above it was a ring of gargoyles, nonchalantly leaning and gaping like idling students, and above them the delicate statue of a naked girl, stooping gracefully to draw a small bow at a fleeing satyr, Diana, maybe, or Atalanta. Another time he might have had an eye for her, but he was going off statuary in general. Besides, she reminded him of Dani.

He stepped down. And there, at the far end of the cloister, was the figure, beckoning him with the same impatient gesture. It ducked into a open doorway and Volker followed, but warily, his boots booming hollowly off the flagstones. A little passage led him out into a much smaller, gloomier courtyard, where the moonlight barely managed to poke a stray beam in, blocked out by the immense belltower overhead. And in its deepest shadow, by a railed flight of sunken stairs, the figure waited expectantly. It beckoned again, and hurried down, but at the stairhead Volker stopped dead. Green he might be, but after Nebelstein he wasn't about to go rushing down into that pool of darkness without a good reason.

A heavy door creaked open a crack, and ruddy light shone out, pale as watered blood. The figure tossed its head slightly, and Volker shivered; the gesture was so characteristic . . . Then it threw back its hood.

Volker clapped a hand to one eye and blinked the other furiously, the usual test for magical hallucination; but the man did not seem to waver or shift. 'Gmm . . .' He swallowed hard and tried again. *'Master?* Master Ulrich? Then—' It occurred to him it might be a little tactless, not to say idiotic, to remind a powerful mage that he ought to be dead.

'Here! And quick!' hissed Ulrich. 'So I can ward this door! Tartarus is abroad, and hunts on your heels!'

Volker staggered down the steps, his boots skidding on the stone, dished and slippery with years of wear and water. The mere sound of that voice set his legs quivering with relief and astonishment. He should have known Ulrich wouldn't leave him in the lurch like that! The mage must just have meant him to look after the party till—

Oh no, he didn't!

Inescapable certainty boiled up in Volker's brain, and all the alarm bells clanged. But Ulrich extended a hand, and so commanding was his courtesy that Volker instinctively reached out in answer. Their fingers touched, closed—

Volker yelled aloud in a spasm of fright and horror. He whipped like a snake against the unbreakable, horrible grip, hot, clammy, slimy – inhuman.

Out went the light with a hollow pop. As if his cry had awoken it, the darkness boiled. The shadows seemed to grow a hundred hands, wire-strong, sharp-clawed, wholly unhuman; they plucked, snatched, snared him by arm or leg, clothes, hair, ears, anywhere they could, hauled him this way, that way, never letting go. The stench that rolled over him beat anything the river bubbled up, musky, rank and foetid as a midden; shrill voices cackled and gibbered in his ears. He choked, struggled, tried to lash out but was held helpless. Cold fingers clawed at his lips; he bit them, gagged violently at the taste, and had his jaws forced apart and a hank of sacking jammed in. It tasted a little better than the fingers, but not much. Stomach heaving, limbs pinioned, he felt himself hoisted into the air. Hinges creaked. Darkness boomed hollowly. Thrashing helpless as a hooked fish in that horrible grasp, he was swept away.

In their haste his chittering captors banged his head

and hands against the walls, and they came away covered in nitre and slime. From the turning and jolting he realized he was being carried down a spiral staircase, and wondered just what had hold of him – something less than man-high, beast-fingered, able to scuttle safely down lightless stairs . . . Come to think of it, he didn't really want to know. He had already guessed why, and that was more than enough. He'd fallen prey to Tartarus.

The hell-ride lasted only a few seconds. The stair ran suddenly straight, and his captors clattered down into a wider space, where the air streamed damp and chill around him and their excited squeals echoed oddly. Suddenly and roughly he was thrown down. He bounced painfully down a last step or so, and on to a floor of what felt like trodden earth, cold and unyielding. Gingerly, to a protesting chorus of bruises, he lifted himself up on his hands and blinked uncertainly about. He might as well have kept his eyes shut, for all he could see; but he would never have dared. He had seldom felt less alone. The darkness was stiff with presence.

Something – a breath, a rustle of cloth – alerted him. He looked around sharply, and screwed up his eyes as a red light flared in the dark. Blinking, he made out a shape behind it, and others further back . . . featureless, rustling, robed shapes. Before he could move, his aching arms were seized, he was dragged to his feet and flung into what felt like a large upholstered chair, heavy fabric, worn, clammy, greasy, like something left in a cellar too long. Dust puffed out, setting him coughing. The light shone in his face.

'So . . .' it began, then stopped abruptly. Shaken as he was, Volker was too scared to just sit. He tensed himself to jump up, to run, but evidently it showed. *'Hold him!'* barked the speaker, and figures came leaping out of the shadow, or was that loping?

Hunched, spidery shapes, they pinned Volker down with arms like crooked branches and about as solid, their hook-clawed fingers biting into his wrists as he struggled. Faces that might have been weathered out of dirty sandstone leered and sneered at him, and shook their flapping ears in aggressive mockery. They stank overpoweringly—

His mouth was very dry. Suddenly it seemed to him he had never really known what it was to be afraid. Not even alone with Ulrich's body, for then his fears had really been faint and far off, when compared with this. Gargoyles. Creatures of the Old World, lingerers from the Early Days before the empires of men, they had adapted better than most; like sparrows and foxes and rats, they had found new niches of their own within man's cities, haunting the high walls of temples and seats of learning, drawn, some said, by the musty stink of stale scholarship. For the most part they were harmless, provided one didn't stand directly underneath, and tolerated because they kept the pigeons and bats down. But every so often, it was rumoured, a group might mysteriously turn savage; the odd student or night-wandering scholar might disappear, and a pile of neatly picked bones be found days later and streets away. Whatever the truth of this, they were rarely hunted or driven away; many college authorities felt they added a touch of atmosphere. The nest above Volker's freshman garret back in Nürnberg certainly had, anyhow – a sort of combined midden and tannery ambiance, with just a nuance of chicken-run.

But adapted or not, they were Old Worlders, and so would share the – usually well-deserved – distrust and jealousy of man that made the Elder Peoples such a fertile recruiting ground for the Forces of Tartarus. It must be some of these who held him, and he could expect no mercy. But he was more afraid of the men they obeyed, because for men there was no such excuse.

Men *and* women, to be precise. For they were gathering close about him now, unshading and hanging up their lanterns and throwing back their hoods. About thirty of them, he reckoned, as his eyes grew accustomed to the light, and all people he'd have passed on the street without a second look. People neither old nor young, neither handsome nor ugly; just people, like himself. Their very normality was the most shocking thing about them. Even their dark robes looked more shabby than sinister, especially in what was neither the temple nor the dungeon he'd expected, but a very drab old cellar, its walls whitened with peeling limewash, its door set almost at the vaulted ceiling, with steps leading down. If Tartarists were as ordinary as this—

No. There must be a streak of corruption somewhere, deep inside, that let them serve the forces of Tartarus and made them enjoy its rewards, said to be . . . unusual, to put it mildly. He squirmed at the thought. More than a streak! *Gods, they're all as hollow as rotten trees!* He could see it in their eyes, glinting in that dull reddish light; it wasn't a way anyone normal would look at another human being, not even an enemy. They were gloating over him, but impersonally, as if he were just a piece of treasure, desirable but mindless, or some valuable beast at last caged. 'The horn!' shrilled one of the older women, slightly hysterical. 'Where's the horn? I don't see the horn!'

One of the men frowned. 'No! He's not carrying it.'

'Where is it, then?' she squealed. '*He* said he'd have it—' Fluffy, grey-haired and round as any well-fed citizen's wife, she swooped upon Volker, caught at his hair and jerked back his head. 'Where is it?' she hissed. 'What've you done with it, elf-brat?' Volker said nothing. She dug in her fingers and twisted till he gasped. 'Answer me, you little get of a dockside drab, you . . .' She jerked his head this way and that, spitting prim little obscenities in his ear. A trickle of saliva ran down the corner of her puffy mouth, and she bared her teeth at him like a dog. They were misshapen, discoloured, distorted in ulcerated gums, as if that inner corruption was eating its way outward. The others moved closer, chuckling quietly, exchanging whispers. After a minute a crook-backed old man pulled her anxiously away.

'That's enough, 'Stine. We agreed to wait for Him. Don't want to anger *Him*, do you?'

The woman straightened up sharply and looked around, licking her lips nervously. '*He* wouldn't blame me,' she muttered uncertainly. 'It's been so many years . . . *He*'d understand . . .' She rounded on Volker again, viciously, taking her fright out on him. 'Hear that, whore's brat? Till *He* comes, that's how long you've got! Just you wait till then! Just wait!' She spat in his face and turned away sharply. Some of the watchers laughed, chiefly the younger ones. The gargoyles blew out their cheeks and chittered in their own tongue.

'*He*'ll get answers, soon enough!' remarked a round-cheeked young man. 'If He has to wring them out of those long marrowbones! That should satisfy you, 'Stine!'

'If anything can!' drawled a dark young woman idly. The man waggled a finger in mock rebuke. Volker shuddered. The man was personable enough in a plump way, but the hand looked bloated and blotchy, its fingernails yellow and ridged. In fact, now that he was looking for it, there seemed to be something slightly wrong about most of them, except perhaps the youngest ones such as the dark girl. He should have expected it; he had read of the marks close contact with the forces of the Dark could leave on their worshippers, and these people, by Ulrich's account, were unusual even among cultists. No, when you gave them that second look, these were not ordinary people. They must cultivate that harmless air very carefully, thought Volker, to conceal so much. Why was the dark girl staring at him like that?

'He's very handsome,' she said idly, chewing on a finger. '*Very*. It's such a shame . . .'

An older man chuckled nastily. 'Maybe when Himself's done with him, then . . .'

The young man snorted. 'How much use d'you think this sprat'll be by then? To anybody! The Other might oblige, though – *if* you ask him nicely . . .' The others laughed coarsely, and the gargoyles bobbed their heads and brayed. The girl glared disdainfully and whirled away.

'Just you wait!' repeated the older woman, lost in a trance of anticipation now. 'He comes! He comes! *He comes!*'

The leather flask was tilted back . . . and back . . . and back, to the tune of slow gurgling, a deep, an endless swallow. The others watched in silent fascination, till at last it fell away, and the moustaches were carefully wrung out. '*Fort bien!*' A black cloak swirled close about him. 'Time, I think, that we make our entrance!'

Everyone jumped at the crash that shook the door, even the gargoyles who held Volker. As it ground open a crowd of their fellows came spilling in, lining the stairs like a guard of honour. A bulky shape filled the gap, swathed in a great dark cloak, and for a minute Volker thought he was seeing that deceiving image of Ulrich. But this one was stooped and twisted, hood low, limping painfully along on a staff as if its wearer must watch every faltering step. As the door closed behind it, though, it straightened up abruptly, the mantle falling in folds from its shoulders, and with it all appearance of weakness. Volker choked as he saw it rise up in the lanternlight, towering over the gargoyles, the hood brushing the ceiling. Not many men were taller than

131

himself, but this one was, easily, and far broader, a monstrous bulk of a man.

Metal gleamed. A gauntleted hand plucked at the neck of the robe; it fell away altogether, and was tossed to the gargoyles with the staff. Volker gaped in horror. Looming at the head of the stairs, stretching out limbs like a giant ape's and grunting with dour relief, stood a man clad from head to foot in armour, helm and all, and he could have been the model for the figure on the clock in Nürnberg, down to the black Knot of Odin on the coarse white surcoat he wore. It was a Teutonic Knight, not one of the rank and file from Nebelstein, not another young officer, but a full-fledged Knight of the Order, one of the warlords who headed its dreaded battle phalanx. Down the stairs he came, rattling and ringing faintly at every step, an ornate sword bouncing at his side, a huge black-bladed double axe slung across his back. His bulk should have shuddered the very stone, but he trod with the deadly lightness of a stalking tiger.

His armour was like none Volker had ever seen. It made the man look like an ancient castle, encrusted with so many centuries of battered fortification that its original outline was hidden. Remakes and repairs so encrusted the mingled mass of plate and ringmail that it had taken on new shapes, curling and recurving as if lashing back at the blows that had struck it. The peculiar textures pitting their surfaces might have been the work of time and weather, but not so the spatterings of arcane characters here and there, inlaid in silver, welded on in blued metal or simply gouged crudely into the metal. On all that huge frame there was only one speck of colour, a tiny flash of gold on the helmet's blank brow. The effect was sinister, fantastic yet still awesomely strong; the armour had lost all symmetry, so that the vast black shadow spreading across the entire cellar seemed more like a distorted demon's than a man's.

Volker drew a sharp, shocked breath. The gold was a crest, a mailed fist. The Knights were famous for forbidding any badge of rank, except to their highest officers; and they were secretive creatures who seldom showed themselves to the Order's rank and file, let alone any outsider, except in battle. This, though, must be one of them, a Master, perhaps even one of the Grand Masters. That was bad enough in itself; but as the Knight drew nearer and could be seen more clearly, Volker found himself beginning to shake uncontrollably.

The joints in that strange armour were every kind of flexible mail, from the complex interlocking chain that some called *Koboldwerk* to scale-mail and even loose rings; but in places it had been torn away and left to hang loose, as if its protection no longer mattered. Nor did it, for beneath, gleaming greenish-yellow in the light, were what looked like folds of heavy leather, mottled and scarred with a rash of horn-tipped pustules; and this leathery stuff swelled up around mail and rings to embed and hold them immovable. It had once been the skin of the wearer.

A mark of Tartarus, by far the worst of any here. The monstrous man loomed over him, and Volker shrank back. Not from fear – he could hardly be more afraid than he was. He just couldn't stand the smell. This creature stank worse than the entire contingent of Nebelstein *and* their stables, and no wonder, if his armour was a permanent fixture. The rancid oil on it contributed its part, too. It didn't seem to bother the cultists in the least; they crowded around this hulking menace, fawning on him, pawing him, devouring him with their eyes and hands as they might some spectacular hero. Which to their kind he probably was. For unmistakably this was one of the mighty warriors on the side of the

Dark, one of those votaries of its appalling Plutonian gods who had chosen to sacrifice a part of his humanity and receive in exchange vast strength, resistance to wounds and savage fighting skills, and perhaps also other, darker gifts. How long had it taken his skin to grow like that? Rumour told how legendary champions of the Knights from centuries past would suddenly reappear at times to fight alongside them; and Volker could well believe it. No wonder there was fear among the order, with creatures like this among its hidden rulers.

The huge man's face, if face was left him, was hidden. The helm left visible only his jaw, heavy and clean shaven, and his eyes, gazing down at Volker through its eye slits. They were a surprise, wide and brown, with a wild grief-stricken look in them like a maddened hawk's. But below the helm even the skin of the face was coarse and yellowish, the mouth no more than a cruel dark streak; Volker wondered if the helmet too had become impossible to remove. No surprise that such a monster had to walk Regensburg's streets in disguise! He was just the kind of leader Volker would have imagined for a Tartarist cult, the living image of brutal power. Small wonder they were so confident! Being brave was going to be a whole lot harder when this brute began tearing him slowly limb from limb.

But he was to be shocked still more. The Knight, absently brushing the dark girl aside, reached out and with casual brutality pinched Volker's jaw hard between metalled finger and thumb and shook him from side to side. 'So this is our new horn-thief! A boy! A squalling babe!' His teeth were horrible, fangs modelled in metal that turned his speech to a spitting growl; but had they also narrowed that tongue to a red ribbon like a dog's? 'No more sensible than his late master? Or maybe he still doesn't understand. Here, boy! Look upon your destiny!'

The huge man barked out a command, and the Tartarists scattered back as if themselves afraid of what he
had summoned. But the figure that picked itself up
from a corner didn't look too extraordinary. More
human than the gargoyles, in fact; except that—

Volker stiffened, appalled. It was the impossible
vision he had seen at the door. It was the living face of
Ulrich, eyes glittering, that glared down into his. Then
he shrank back against the greasy chair, trying to blink
his sight clear. But the blur was not in his eyes. Ulrich's
features relaxed, sagged, softened horribly as if decaying before Volker's eyes. Nose, lips, ears ran and
merged with the liquifying flesh. Hair and beard matted
into coarse patches, the eyes whitened, swelled and
flowed, and dissolved into the rest. Within the churning
skin outlined veins bulged out, tar-black against a
sudden swelling of white bone. The teeth stood out in
a tight mirthless grin. It was like seeing Ulrich's body
decay in the space of a second; and Volker, thinking
of the silent river depths, struggled to hold down his
imagination and his stomach. Then a swifter change
shimmered across that formless face, like the air on a
hot day, and it settled into something he took a moment
to recognize.

Fear slid down him like swallowed ice, as instant, as
sickening. He struggled and thrashed so hard that the
chair creaked and snapped beneath him, but he was
helpless against those horn-tipped fingers. That face –
worse, far worse than confronting Ulrich's! So familiar,
yet totally strange . . . nothing at all like looking in a
mirror. More like seeing your soul torn out. 'Well, boy?'
came the Knight's chill whisper. 'This is the Other. For
that is all the name he can ever have, now. Can you
guess the fate he stands for?'

Volker clamped his teeth hard to stop from screaming, or being sick, or losing his mind. Once this had
been a living man; now it was neither alive nor dead,

vampire-like yet less even than that, less than a ghost. The powers of Tartarus had dissolved its humanity, left it no identity of its own, save what it could steal from others, and to meet it in your shape meant terrible things. For it would begin by looking like you, but in the end it would become you, till neither mind nor memory was left you and it moved on to some other victim. The peasants who dreaded such things had named it well – *Doppelgänger*, the Walker in Likeness. Volker would far rather have faced a vampire; by comparison blood felt like something he could afford to lose.

'See!' cackled the older woman suddenly. 'See his eyes! He knows, all right!'

'He knows, all right!' mused the Teutonic Knight, his mail jangling as he nodded. 'Not quite the unlearned brat we thought, perhaps. As well we laid hands on him so soon. Well, boy? When we have done with you, you will be given to the Other, and he will wring you dry. Eventually he will walk in your shape, be able to go where you would go, know what you know. Unless, of course, you are reasonable, and save us so much trouble. Then our leader may be more merciful. But one way or another, we . . . *will* . . . have . . . that . . . horn!'

At each word a steel claw prodded Volker in the chest. He wasn't listening; his guts were turning over. Our *leader*? If this appalling monster wasn't their leader, who on earth could be? Who was this thing going to call *Führer*? Panic whispered in his ear; he didn't want to meet whoever – or whatever – it might be. Something steeped even more deeply in Tartarus, something like old Strauben's conjuration, perhaps. Something that would have him screaming his head off at the first sight of it, have him babbling out everything he knew. He could feel the sweat trickling down his back, pooling where it touched the chair. He wasn't brave enough for this sort of thing.

The claw hooked under his chin and jerked it back, heaving him half out of the chair. The steel mask was thrust straight into his. *'Think!'* hissed the huge man, wreathing Volker in cesspit breath. 'Before he gets here! You've minutes, if that! Tell *me—'*

The door quivered under a thunderous blow—

And burst open, crashing back on its hinges. The gargoyles at the stairhead ducked back squealing as two more seemed to soar in under the arch and plough through them. With a berserker's wolfhowl Thorgrim kicked the impaled bodies he'd used as a battering ram off the blade of his halberd and flung himself on their fellows. Evidently he hadn't seen the Knight, who dropped Volker and whirled about, snatching for his axe. Several of the cultists were fumbling among their robes for weapons. On the stairs a disarmed gargoyle rolled out of Thorgrim's path as if to flee, then snatched up a fallen dagger and sprang at his back, only to leap kicking out into space and crash down among the cultists. De Guillac, his sabre steaming with blood, reeled on to the steps with a cheery wave, hiccuped delicately, and swayed as if to jump down.

Volker surged up in his chair and yelled a warning. His guards forced him back, but de Guillac, almost too late, saw what was below. His eyes bulged. *'Con d'un dragon!'* he roared, and teetered drunkenly on the edge, frantically windmilling his arms to keep from falling right on to the monster. Axe in hand, the Knight charged for the stair. De Guillac spat out a single word of such strength that it sizzled through the air like a meteor, raced crackling across the ceiling and exploded in searing blue sparks against the wall. A cloud of nitre erupted from the ancient vaulting, stone shattered with an earsplitting crack, and without any more warning that whole end of the roof gave way. With a torrential roar a stream of blasted masonry came crashing down upon the Knight beneath, hurling him back against the stair, covering him even as he struggled, blotting him from sight.

Great clouds of dust boiled out, spreading choking confusion across the cellar floor. Through streaming eyes Volker saw Thorgrim come bounding down the heap of rubble, driving the shrilling gargoyles with great sweeps of Hlavisbana. *'Volker!'* yelled the Norseman. *'Where are you?'*

'Here—' yelled Volker, then choked as a gargoyle's dagger pressed across his windpipe. Thorgrim was forced back as a howling mob of cultists fell on him, swords slashing. He met them with a bellow of rage, hewing, thrusting, parrying, and kicked the foremost one in the stomach. They hesitated, some still hitching up their robes to disentangle weapons, others gesturing frantically to prepare spells, only to hop like startled rabbits and lose the thread, dodging arrows that sang down at them from the stair. Volker's guard glanced up in alarm, the dagger dropped a little . . . and with all his strength Volker tore a hand free and seized the leathery wrist. Its owner jerked it away and Volker, instead of resisting, yanked with him. With a meaty slicing sound it jabbed the other gargoyle's chest. It yammered in pain, Volker's hand was free, and with no great skill but a lot of feeling he smacked it straight into the dagger-wielder's ribbed snout.

The gargoyle went over backwards and Volker hurled himself from that hateful chair, sprang on to the wounded one and hammered its head on the floor. Above the roar of more masonry falling he heard the rising screech of an incantation, and threw himself aside. Barely in time; the fallen gargoyle convulsed, and a flood of white maggots erupted from its mouth. Revolted at the sending meant for him, Volker snatched up the stained chair and brought it crashing down on the spellworker's head. Its worn plush was caked with dull brown stains, that was why it felt so greasy. How many had died in that seat?

He hurled the ghastly thing from him. More of the roof crumbled. Lanterns fell or choked among the rising mirk. All around him it rang with coughs and shouts, brief panicky clashes of sword on sword. Here and there it bloomed into a sudden glare of ghastly green or lightning blue as some clever cultist managed to kindle magelight, only to regret it. One went off just behind Volker; he jumped as Thorgrim's halberd hissed within a finger's breadth of him. There was a shriek, and the light went out. This close the Norseman's magical sense must have pinpoint accuracy – or halberd-point, anyhow.

He grabbed Volker's arm. *'Drakener! Dani!* I have him!'

From somewhere among the swirling dust came a slurred roar of *'Eh! Du culot, hein, mon p'tit gars!'* tailing off into an explosive bout of coughing and the clash of sword on sword. Volker and Thorgrim flung themselves apart. A gargoyle reeled between them, clutching at its leathery belly as if to hold in its umbels. It failed, and collapsed messily on to the floor. Volker, swallowing, snatched up the jagged sword it had dropped, just in time. De Guillac backed out of the fog, hotly engaged with two or three cultists. One saw Volker, broke away and charged on him . . . the young man with the malformed hand. Instinctively Volker caught the blade against his own, dodged a vicious kick at his groin, then without thinking lunged in his turn. The impact surprised him, and his opponent too, briefly.

'Volker!' That was Dani's voice. *'Volker! Where in Chaos are you – oh, there!'* The dust swirled suddenly. He saw her across the dim room, bow on one shoulder and a short falchion gleaming in her fist. But she was looking the other way. She darted forward and grabbed someone's sleeve. *'Come on, dummy! Don't just stand there!'*

He opened his mouth to shout—

And for one crazy moment seemed to be standing outside himself, head whirling, watching himself be rescued. Then he hurled himself after them as they made for the stairs. Dani, alert for pursuing footsteps, whirled about and grabbed for her bow. Then she saw Volker. Her grim-set jaw sagged so completely that he almost shouted with laughter. 'Ward yourself, girl!' he yelled, shouldering her aside, and lunged at his living image. Suddenly feral, it snatched his arm with that inhuman strength and sprang snarling at his throat. Together they fell sprawling, rolling over and over the rubble-strewn floor, the Other with a hand crushing Volker's wrist and another over his face. Its strength was appalling. The blade was flung out of his numbed fingers; but with his own ferocity he scrabbled at its eyes. It flinched, and he went for its throat. Somewhere he heard Dani burbling 'Who – who -', for all the world like her own owl. As if she really was calling it, it swished down through the dusty air and shrieked its wrath at the Other.

'The bird knows!' cried Thorgrim, and jammed his halberd down into the *Doppelgänger*'s back. But even as he struck, the thing twisted like a snake, twined around the haft and hauled. The startled Norseman staggered; but Volker, free now, snatched the falchion out of Dani's nerveless hand. All the force of his loathing weighted the blow, and he yelled in horror as the dull impact jarred his arm, and his own head flew back on shreds of tendon, half-severed. But the blood was tarry black and smoking, and the face was changing, melting even as it fell, its skin heaving like a stream of lava, erupting into meaningless shapes and colours as its life ebbed. By the time it hit the floor it looked like nothing Volker wanted to remember, though he was afraid he was going to.

'*Hé!*' roared Guy, hopping up atop the mounds of rubble at the base of the stair. 'You have him? Then why stand yourselves around like the stuffed mummies? *Esquivons-nous!* Look to him, Dani! *Mais filez donc* – and fast!'

They ran. But despite Guy's assumption it was Dani who needed help. She stood shaking like a storm-struck tree, unable to take her eyes off the dissolving thing she'd tried to rescue. Volker pulled her, she struggled feebly and in desperation he slung her bodily over his shoulder like a sack of meal – not easy for a man of his height – and stumbled after the rest, praying the owl wouldn't misunderstand his intentions. Guy stood holding the rubble like a bridgehead, waving Volker past on to the stairs with his reddened sabre. *'Passez donc!* Have no fear . . . the Draconnier holds the way till the end!'

The mound heaved under him. He went over on his back with his high boots waving in the air, and a shout of *'Tonnerre de Brest!'*

The rubble erupted and avalanched away. Out of it, still buried up to the waist, a monstrous shape reared up and cast about. Its gaze lit on Guy as he scrambled up. A bellow of manic rage shook the unstable ceiling, and out of the fall, clutched in arms strong enough to withstand a ton of falling stone and dig free afterwards, exploded the huge black axe. It hewed at Guy with horrifying force. If he had tried to parry it he would have been cut in two; instead he skipped like a startled gazelle. It sang past his head, and with a clang like the hammer of Donar (or Jupiter-Tanarus-Sucellus, to keep these things official) it smashed into the already over-strained wall.

An instant of wincing silence ended in an even more shattering report. Long jagged cracks snaked out between the stones and up, up into the gaping hole in the roof. The wall quivered, then with something like an exhausted sigh the tormented stonework bulged out at the bottom and began to crumble inward. Yells and screams erupted all around the cellar.

At startling speed Guy shot up the stair past the others, and out of the door. *'Sauve qui peut*, my little lambs!' the voice trailed back. 'The end . . . that was it!'

They clattered up the spiral stair at his heels, over the corpses of discreetly silenced gargoyle sentinels, heading for the upper door. 'Put me down!' yelled Dani, kicking and drumming her fists on Volker's kidneys. 'I'm all right, put me *down*, curse you!'

'Don't think . . . I'm daft enough . . . to stand still . . . that long . . . do you?' panted Volker, taking a firmer grip on her belt. By the top he was almost on all fours and wheezing, but the crackle and rumble of collapsing masonry was a strong incentive to keep going. At the upper door he and Dani collapsed in an unlikely tangle of limbs.

'This is no time for showing you are grateful!' protested Thorgrim, hauling them apart. 'Run for your lives!'

Limp was about the best any of them could do, on the slippery courtyard cobbles; Guy managed a fast hobble. Before they reached the gate the cellar stairs were spewing out a stream of very dusty gargoyles and cultists; but none of them seemed at all interested in stopping to argue. They scattered in all directions, the gargoyles squealing and snapping at each other like hysterical rats. In the echoing corridors of the college doors were slamming, voices shouting. One elderly figure in a nightshirt tottered out and raised a tentative hand, then dived back with surprising agility as Guy came barrelling straight at him. Out into the cloisters they burst, and straight across the lawn. Volker noticed, without stopping to think, that there weren't any gargoyles on the fountain statue now.

Lights flickered up in the quadrangle windows, casements were flung back and heads thrust out, gaping

astonished at shrilling gargoyles and black-robed cultists scuttling this way and that across the lawn like so
many headless chickens. There was no sign of the
Knight, who would have been hard to miss. Students,
angry or uproarious, came spilling down into the cloisters and collided with the intruders; running fights
broke out. Volker and his friends, ahead of the rest,
dived for the side gate and spilled gratefully out into
the street, where the uproar was already attracting
attention; lights were going on in neighbouring colleges, people appearing on doorsteps and idlers gathering to gawp. Volker and company were just trying to
stroll away unobtrusively when behind them sounded
the deep chime of a bell; then another, and another, in
a strange swaying rhythm.

They stopped, unwillingly, turned and looked at each
other then up at the tower. The same awful thought
sprang into all their minds. Pale and austere against the
dignified college skyline the spire-crowned bell-tower
loomed, no hint in its serene aspect of what had been
lurking at its roots. It held the pose one instant longer;
then it seemed to slump slightly, like a tired sentry,
and a great crack jolted up its flank like some vast
shoot growing between the stones. The swaying bells
clattered in metallic panic. Across the town other bells
clanged tentatively in answer, as if wondering what the
noise was about. The row of fighting faltered; everything paused, time stood still. Then, in an eruption of
dust and fragments the stonework split apart, the spire
sagged and fell straight through, and with glacial slowness, a demented clangour of bells, and a yawning
rumble and crash that shook the street beneath them,
the whole tower caved inward and collapsed. Out of
the wicket-gate exploded a puff of dust like a bombard-
shot.

'Er . . . yes . . .' said Volker. 'Well . . .'

'*Bougre de basilisque!*' exclaimed Guy, considerably

sobered. 'They will have a hard time laughing *that* off to their landlord!'

The great main doors of the college flew wide open, and a panicky mob burst out, looking like so many spooks in their dusty nightshirts. A few cultists surged up briefly in the mass, still trying to escape from their student tormentors. Other students, whooping with excitement, came charging over to join in. Onlookers and idlers began to laugh and jeer, and were immediately included in the mêlée; more fights broke out. Older men, tutors and professors, tried to break them up, stopped a punch or two and either fell back or began hitting out in their turn. Soon elderly and respectable scholarly types were punching noses and hacking each other's scrawny shins with the best of them.

'It is good to see,' remarked Thorgrim solemnly, 'that men of letters can still enjoy themselves like ordinary folk.'

Dani clutched at the back of her neck. 'We'd better push off before they start enjoying themselves with us!'

'But shouldn't we explain—?' That was as far as Volker got before he was scooped up and swept bodily off. Above them the owl shrieked a warning, and they shrank back against the wall as a group of rowdy young men, more like apprentices than students by their dress, rounded the corner, saw the uproar and, raising a drunken cheer, ran to join in. 'That's all we need!' he groaned, as they dodged around the corner and away. 'Town against Gown, just like back home. It'll be all over the place in an hour!'

Dani called, and the white bird sailed silently back to her shoulder. 'That was how we found you!' said Guy. 'A bird that can follow like a hound, is that not an object most singular?'

Dani sniffed. 'No worse than a wineskin that walks like a man!'

The Gallian showed signs of swelling up. 'All in the

144

cause of magic, of course!' Volker added tactfully. 'And that was a master-stroke you unleashed! Thank you – thank you all. More than I can ever say. Or repay! But . . . why were you following me in the first place?'

To his surprise they all fell silent. De Guillac gave one of his vastly expressive and utterly meaningless shrugs; Thorgrim looked positively sheepish. Dani he could not see, her face turned away into the shadows. 'To speak truth . . .' began Thorgrim, then broke off to brandish the halberd at a shouting student. 'These strange attacks,' he said lamely, 'and this business with Ulrich . . . We had grown suspicious, there is no denying it.'

'They all had,' put in Guy, 'the merchants and the rest. As no doubt you knew. The theory most favoured was that you'd slain Ulrich and tipped him into the canal, and were using us to flee justice. Some were for having you taken up by the Watch, others for putting you to the question without such formalities. But happily there was one spoke up for you.'

'Thanks again!' said Volker.

'Oh, it was not I, *mon gars*. Nor the Hairy One here. It shames me to say it, but we did not know what to think. It was this fair lady who denied you could be a malefactor.'

'Dani?' demanded Volker, amazed. 'You?' He saw the glint of her hair, but the shadows were silent.

'*Mais certes*. She denied you had anything of guilt about you, only trouble of the spirit; and undertook most vociferously to prove it! When you fled the inn thus, we thought to follow unseen and discover what you were about. But for ages, *peste*, you stand on the bridge, you mope, and all we who lurk below learn is what curious things the folk of this town throw in their rivers. Then suddenly the Hairy One here scents something . . .'

'A stink worse than any in the river,' put in Thorgrim.

'I know the taint of black magic, none better, and this is it on legs. Near you it comes, and nearer, till we fear you are really in league with it somehow. But then you stalk away, and it follows.'

'The *Doppelgänger!*' spat Volker. 'They set it to decoy me, but walking here just seemed like my own idea!'

'Well, it would, wouldn't it?' muttered Dani sharply.

'Ah!' exclaimed de Guillac. 'And so hastily she sets her owl upon your track. And though it does not speak, this bird, somehow she sees and hears as from above, and with a night-hunter's senses. So, we know you are seized against your will, and held where there are many voices to be heard. What then? Seek help? Colleges are privileged, even the Watch cannot enter their walls without leave. Anyway, there is little time. Dash in and out, surprise – that is our best hope. So, summoning up our highest courage and greatest ingenuity—'

'He means, stopping for a few drinks first!' said Dani.

'Just as well you did!' said Volker. 'If you'd come any sooner that Knight would've been *behind* you!'

De Guillac went unusually silent at that. Thorgrim nodded. 'It was he who came in disguise? I had thought as much, for that one stank of magic. But I am thinking he will not burrow free as easily as he entered. What was he?'

'An enemy of Ulrich's,' said Volker, thinking fast. 'I can't tell you more now; there isn't time. Listen, you've helped me so much – but I need more!'

Guy raised his eyebrows. 'I think we have earned some answers from you, Master Volker – but if it is so important, well, we have gone this far with you—' He shrugged again. 'Command us!'

The uproar behind them seemed to be spreading rather than slackening, and they quickened their pace, heading back through the sidestreets to the river. Once or twice they ran into bands of boozy youths looking for trouble, but one sight of their well-reddened weapons had a remarkably civilizing influence. Before long they saw the river glistening between the houses below, and made their way back across the bridge. Its stones boomed hollowly with hurrying feet, and they stepped politely aside as a column of watchmen came hurrying past. Lanterns swayed from their pikestaffs and long clubs swung at their belts as they ran, urged on by a fat man on horseback. As Volker and the others hurried back over the slippery cobbles to the wharves they saw lights going on in the windows of all the riverside inns.

'You there! Ulrich's men!' That was Goldfüss, leaning out of his window wrapped in a heavy silken nightshirt, an embroidered nightcap askew on his blond hair. 'What in the name of Jupiter's all that row in the town?'

'The students are revolting!' shouted Volker, thinking it was true enough. 'And the apprentices with them! It's organized! They're shouting things—'

'What things?' demanded Beck, popping out of an upstairs window with a dishevelled-looking chambermaid beside him.

'Oh, *Down with the capitalists!* And *Property's theft!* That sort of thing—'

'*Les marchands aux lampadaires!*' contributed Guy. 'Did you not hear the bells?'

'And the shops being pulled down?' cried Dani. 'They're cleaning out the countinghouses, chanting about distributing wealth to the people—'

'Soon they will come to the warehouses,' intoned Thorgrim in his most doom-laden voice. Cries of horror arose from the windows around; in these riverside inns almost every guest would be some kind of trader.

'You mean they're heading this way?' cried Haagen from the floor above, looking distinctly green.

'*Men dog*, no need for panic!' trumpeted Thorgrim. 'Not for a good half-hour yet, I am sure—'

'*Eek!*' exclaimed Beck, vanishing as swiftly as he had

appeared. Goldfüss plunged back inside, and his powerful voice could be heard shouting orders through the inn. All above them windows were crashing open and shut, women shrieking, feet running about. Hidden in the inn doorway Thorgrim and Guy sank down, holding their sides, and Dani, to Volker's astonishment, collapsed hysterical with laughter against him.

'I would not sell my part in this sport for a pension of thousands to be paid from the Emperor!' whooped de Guillac. Even the owl, landing on the inn-sign above, hooted and flapped its wings.

The door flew open and Goldfüss barrelled out, his elegant nightshirt flapping around his shanks, bare save for a pair of riding boots; behind him padded Haagen, his nightshirt tucked into his hose, chivvying a couple of yawning ostlers with their baggage. 'Well, don't just stand there!' roared Goldfüss. 'Get your gear! Off to the boats! You there, Norseman, come with me as guard – you others, run on and roust out the crews! Search the inns on the way! Any we can't get aboard, we leave without them!'

Panic spread ahead of them to the wharfside, fuelled by the tumult drifting down from the town, and the sight of a squadron of cavalry from the castle cantering across the bridge. A great press was streaming out of the inns, headed for their precious boats. 'We may be doing them a favour, at that!' chuckled Dani. 'This burg breeds a nice line in sneak-thieves and second-storey men – all that education, I guess. With the watch busy they'll be out casing the fat-cat inns.'

'You seem to know a lot about them,' remarked Volker thoughtfully, clambering carefully down into the *Walross* with the horn-case and the rest of his baggage.

'Oh, I do, Master Alchemist,' she muttered. 'Believe you me, I do . . .'

'You speak true, my little cabbage,' said de Guillac, his eyes bloodshot with dust. He kicked back the foc'sle hatch with a crash and went clattering down it to roust out the crew. A chorus of hungover groans and moans greeted him. 'Up, slugabeds! Up, my little *arracheurs de pailles*, up before they steal the boat beneath you! Expel the lead from your *culottes*, or verily I will come heat it up for you!'

The idea made Volker shudder. 'They'd something of the sort in mind for me,' he said. 'Would have done it, too, if you hadn't brought the others. Thanks for sticking up for me, Dani. Thanks for getting me out.'

She did him a very elegant curtsey, pure court style. 'La, sir. But I guess I should thank you for getting *me* out.' She leaned against the mast, and suddenly her face showed the shock of the memory. 'That thing . . . and I thought it was you . . . Ach, I should've stuck to ratcatching! They were right, that's all I'm good for!'

'Never say that!' said Volker indignantly. Then he froze as somebody, or so it seemed, drove a fistful of needles into his scalp. Gasping, he forced his watering eyes open, and found himself trading beady glares with the owl, its quizzical face upside down as it peered from its perch on top of his head.

'Aaah!' crooned Dani. 'How 'bout that? He likes you!'

Before Volker could get any breath back, Thorgrim's powerful voice bellowed at the wharfside crowds to clear, and the merchants came thumping and complaining down on to the deck. The owl hopped back to Dani's shoulder. 'Cast off, all!' shouted Haagen.

'We are not ready!' roared Guy from the other deck. But at that moment a mounted detachment of the Countess's Guard came thundering up across the bridge, and the crewmen needed no more encouragement. The mooring lines came booming down from the bollards, oars were reversed to thrust against the quayside, and the *Walross* swung slowly out into the current.

'Here!' said Beck suddenly. 'Where's Master Diderik?'

'This is what I am trying to tell you!' snarled Guy, leaping the gap from the *Walfisch*, still tethered to its companion. 'He is still ashore somewhere, and so are three of your men, Master Haagen!'

'And two of yours, Master Goldfüss!' grunted Thorgrim. 'They must have slipped out of the area after drink or women—'

'Look there!' cried Dani. Along the wharfside above came old Diderik, hobbling along at what for him was a remarkable pace, waving his stick over his head and whacking it at the backs of the crowd in his path. He looked to be almost gibbering with fury. When he spotted the boats swinging out into the river he leaped in the air and practically did a little dance of rage. With a grunt of annoyance Thorgrim sprang up on the rail and leaped the yard-wide gap to the steps, raced up them and, more or less tucking the little old man under his arm, he took a run and sprang right off the quay's edge. He hit the deck with a ringing crash, too fast; his feet skidded under him, he slid forward and next moment his burden was dangling over the far rail, his skinny feet dancing inches from the noisome surface of the river.

They rushed to haul the two of them back, the old man so purple in the face he was nearly apoplectic. 'What's this, you miserable whoreson dogs?' he screamed at his fellow merchants, as soon as he could make sense. 'Can't a man slip out to the jakes of a night without his so-called partners scuttling off to pull the rug out from under him?'

'He's nodded off again, I'll wager!' grunted Haagen. 'Been out there for hours, probably—'

'Nodded off?' raved Diderik. '*Nodded off*? Why, you unlicked cur—'

Haagen dodged the futile blows. 'Because you'd have heard the row if you hadn't!' he shouted. 'There's a riot abroad!'

'A riot?' Diderik simmered down at once. 'Are all the lads all right? And the boats? And the cargo, eh?'

'All of it,' said Beck, 'and all of us who matter, now you're here. Your trunk, too; the ostlers must have packed it with the rest. Just a few of the men missing, no more.'

Diderik blinked. 'Missing? Well, shouldn't we wait for them? And what about Master Ul—'

'Wharf-rats and guttersnipes all,' said Thorgrim firmly. 'Their kind will come to little harm in a riot; more likely they will join it, take such profit as they can. It will go better here without them. *To your oars, all!*' He turned to the merchants. 'Out of the town, I think, *mine herre*, before the water grows as crowded as the wharves. We shall find a safer mooring to finish our sleep.'

Nobody argued, not with the tumult from the quay and the distant row in the streets. The merchants trudged off to their cabins, yawning, while Thorgrim manoeuvred the two boats, still linked, out into the current. Oars clashed and rattled as the sleepy rowers lost their stroke, but soon they were making slow, if erratic progress. *Walross* and *Walfisch* were almost the only boats under way; many others were all but drifting downstream, confused and barely under control, and there were some unnerving moments avoiding them. But it was not many minutes before they were gliding smoothly down the black river once more, the quickening current of the Danube plucking at their hull and the hubbub of the wharves dying away behind them. Volker moved to the stern beside Thorgrim. He looked back past *Walfisch*'s naked mast at the steep-peaked rooftops and the college spires brooding behind them, and thought of the evil that laired beneath. Was Regensburg its home, or had it followed him all the way from Nürnberg?

Both, perhaps. From what Ulrich had said, a Tartarist

151

cult could have adherents all over the Empire, under common masters. Such as the Teutonic Knight, perhaps, and his mysterious superior; that would explain why they weren't already in the cellar. They'd just given the local group its orders, then stayed out of sight till he was safely caught. All of which meant that, whatever had happened to the Regensburg group, the Knight even, there could be others following them still. Following; or . . .

'Volker?' It was Dani, and she sounded odd. He turned, and saw her standing behind him, a trace too far back. To his right Thorgrim was leaning on the tiller, blocking that way, and to his left Guy was idling up. Idling, but very purposefully, fencing him in. And they were all three of them watching him very intently.

It was Guy who spoke first: 'Well, my esteemed young sir? The night has grown clearer now, and a great deal quieter. Save for those who grunt upon their benches below, we are alone; and they will not be able to hear. It occurs to me that we have gone a very considerable distance upon your account, and that a good hour for settlement is here.'

'We want those answers you promised, Volker,' said Dani flatly, still watching him.

When he was only a day younger those stares might have unnerved him. These were three formidable creatures he faced, in their separate ways. But now he found the very strength of them almost reassuring. He nodded. 'I'll tell you. As you say, it's a good time. I might have sooner, but I still didn't know who to trust. If anybody. You three . . . well, you might just be playing some fantastic bluff, but I've got to risk that. Anyway, the secret's not safe if I'm the only one who knows it. I need someone else, badly. It's too important . . . and too involved.'

'The riddle game is good playing when a man must stay wakeful,' said Thorgrim, fingering his hammer-amulet thoughtfully. 'You tell, and we shall be the unravellers.'

Volker nodded, and swallowed. 'So be it, then. But be careful. The last time this was spoken, I saw the speaker die.'

Volker awoke with a start. His eyes fluttered open, and then, as he took in the grey light and the silence and stillness around him, he relaxed and snuggled back into his blankets, though he was not really cold. He had grown used to dawn mists coming up out of the river. Besides, this far south they had little chill in them, and seldom lingered; they might well herald a hot clear day. He hugged himself happily, and listened to the faint lappings of the water, the rustle of the reeds against the hull, that were the loudest sounds apart from Thorgrim's occasional thunderous snores. The previous night they had moored some miles from the town, among lands uncultivated yet not entirely wild, in a little crook of the river well screened by tall whispering elms and waving reedbeds. By then he had told his tale, and after it he seemed to have slept peacefully, more peacefully than he ever had since Ulrich laid the burden on him. The relief of finding someone to share it was enormous. It was the first night since he could remember that he had not dreamed of Ulrich, or old Strauben, or anything else disturbing. So what had woken him so suddenly? Just as the thought came to him he heard it again, a slight, hesitant scrape and scrabble, an oddly animal sound. He turned his head a little, but amid the swirling mist he could see barely a few plank-widths away, and make out nothing except the tall shadowy strands of some bank foliage, swaying gently. Most likely it was some little creature of the river, an otter curious about the boat, a watershrew tracking down someone's abandoned apple-core. Anyway, if it was anything more serious the lookouts would hear it, and call.

153

There it was again! Only louder, with a strange slight snoring sound to it, not at all like Thorgrim. Puzzled, he sat up and looked about more carefully; *Walfisch* was only a dim outline, but he could make out its bows. No lookout there, anyhow. Volker sighed; something was disturbing him, something that wouldn't let him be. He clambered blearily to his feet, still clutching his blankets around him, and went shuffling forward. The usual lookout's spot by the rail was empty. Off investigating the noise, maybe . . . Nobody up the mast either. Nothing stirring but those peacefully waving fronds.

Waving? In a still mist, what was making them wave?

He took another step, gulped, and shouted at the top of his voice – shouted without words. There were no easy ones for what he saw. As if he'd slept a year, not a night, and found the boat half-smothered with lush green growth. Except that this greenness was not growing but climbing, great fronds of slimy green crawling over the rail in a dozen places, crawling with the twisted, relentless energy of a lamed man straining to run, reaching the deck with the riverwater still pouring out of it. And except, also, that at the heart of it, suspended clear of the deck so that only one kicking heel scraped faintly along it, writhed the figure of the hapless lookout, snared in a hundred straining hands of green. Volker cast about frantically, seized a boathook from its rack and hacked and slashed at the clinging strands; the hook bounced back without making any impression. The man's back arched, his fingers clenching on nothing; his face was already blackening. Volker caught hold of the tangle of stems, meaning to tear them loose, but yelled in horror and disgust as the slimy things wormed and wriggled in his grip.

Then suddenly he was the gripped one. A flat ribbon whipcracked about his wrists. He yelled again and threw himself back as another looped out, trying to drop about his head, and fell half over the rail. He had one brief glimpse of some shapeless form just below the misty water, some slime-shrouded thing in which all the stems that rose were rooted, and at its near end a watery globule, dark-centred, fixed upon him like a blank inhuman eye. Then the rail thrummed under a resounding blow; he toppled back into the boat, his wrists skinned but free. Above him Goldfüss the merchant, still in his nightshirt, stared in queasy horror at the pallid pinkish jelly dripping from the blade of his boataxe. Behind him, others on both boats were chopping and hacking at the stuff, Guy and Thorgrim among them, but it was barely possible to cut unless it could be nipped between the blade and some hard surface. A sword lay unclaimed upon the deck; Volker snatched it up and set to with the rest, but the fronds were coming up faster now all around the riverward side of the boats, as if a single mind controlled them all.

'This is worthless!' Thorgrim shouted. Hlavisbana intercepted a taut front that went suddenly limp beneath the blow, then as swiftly snapped tight and flung the halberd back in his face. 'There is need of spells here!'

'There's none I could use!' yelled Dani. 'If I had dung from a sacred ox—'

'Those organic spells are no good!' interrupted Volker. 'That'll slow plant growth, not stop it. Besides, is this Hel-spawn thing a plant or an animal or what?' He dodged the vicious sweep of a frond. 'Where's Guy? His spells don't need so many props!'

'At this hour?' yelled the Armorican. 'And sober? Without even my breakfast?'

'*We* will be breakfast if you don't stop babbling and do something!' puffed Beck. 'If you know any magic, Gallian, for Flora's sake use it!'

Guy threw up his hands, slammed his sabre back into its sheath and stepped back with hands bunched under his nose, concentrating hard. Then suddenly he stooped to the deck, seized a dry beechleaf that had blown along it and, stretching it between steepled hands, brought it to his mouth, muttered a sibilant word and blew. A high, plangent singing sound swelled out, and with it a light glimmered faintly between his fingers, a strange sickly shade. He swung to face the heart of the overhanging fronds, and blew harder. The light burst out from between his hands. The dawn air was suddenly the colour of a sunless glade, gloomy and dank, the shade of moss upon a shadowed wall. The air filled with a stench of rot. The fronds jerked, arose, curled and snapped forward. Like a reflecting mirror they hurled that mouldering light back at Guy. With a roar of alarm he flung himself flat, and the light glared upon the mainstay of the mast and the rail beyond. The line parted with a strange soggy snap, and an instant later a chunk of the rail sagged, crumbled and fell in like a decaying log. The mast lurched sideways in its socket, the boom swung free. As Guy sat up with a whistle of relief it clouted him neatly on the head and crashed down over him, hiding him from sight.

The deck lurched beneath Volker as he swung up from the companionway. The moment he'd seen Guy's spell reflected he'd ducked below. That meant strong magic set against them; they needed stronger, and there was only one source to hand. The horn felt leaden in his fingers, the silver mouthpiece icy against his lips. He hesitated, trying to remember how it had sounded in the echoing vault, the pitch of that first key, those reverberating harmonics . . .

He pursed his lips, swung the bell to face the thickest of the fronds, and blew, very softly. Sound awoke. The air shuddered around him, and the fronds seemed to riffle and twist as if a stiff breeze was rising; the wind whined through their stems . . . F sharp, that was the note! If he tried a discord – with G major, to start with . . .

First key; so to raise it another fifth, his fingers slid along and pressed. He blew louder; and the horn seemed to shiver against his lips. Was that right? Near enough, anyhow. Sliding, guessing, for the third note, he stabbed at a key. What came out was not G major or anything he could put a name to, a weird, ghastly jarring sound, thin and needling on the ear. In a burst of desperate panic he realized that the horrible thing wasn't tuned in semitone intervals – or in any kind of regular intervals at all. As if its logic was as wrung and tormented as its blackened coils—

Then he saw what was happening to the fronds. They hung frozen in the air, shivering to the soft cutting note. He blew harder, but they didn't fall back, only stayed and vibrated even harder. When he ran out of breath—

But this far he'd achieved something. Time to go for broke. He shifted one finger on to the next key, and blew harder. Just enough to produce a clear audible note . . .

The horn blatted, juddered, then suddenly erupted between his fingers, a long clear note, startlingly pure, shatteringly loud. To Volker it seemed to shine through him like a blazing light, so strong that in his mind he saw himself fading to the merest glimmering outline against it. The hairs on his neck stood on end and a wild, cold shiver ran through his limbs, like a breeze stirring a forest. He wanted to leap high in the air. He blew harder, and awoke the harmonics, ranging up and down them in a wild, bugling call as if he held a keyless hunting horn.

It shivered the clinging mists apart like a knife, blasted them back in a great rolling sweep across river and bank. The light of a clear, bright dawn blazed down upon the deck, and as it touched the fronds they stiffened, blackened, withered and smoked as if seared by a tongue of flame. The body of the lookout, wrenched

157

and twisted, dropped with a thud on to the planking, and the deck lurched the other way as something monstrous plunged out from under the boats, seeking shelter in the deep water. But for one instant the gelid back broke the swirling surface, and at once it too blackened and smoked; the whole bulk convulsed, writhed and thrashed into the light. A great bubble of foulness billowed out, then the dying thing was caught by the current and borne away downstream, still heaving and twisting, with only a fading streak of rainbow slime to mark its passing.

Volker's breath gave out, and he sank down gasping, his mind half lost in the wild, weird music he had unleashed. He clutched the horn to his chest as if it was trying to wriggle free. What called him back to himself was a sudden explosion of oaths; the main sources were Thorgrim, chivvying crewmen to stay the sagging mast, and Guy, sitting on a hatchcover and complaining loudly and fluently in several languages as Dani tried to apply healing spells to the back of his head. 'There is little in the way with him,' remarked Thorgrim as Volker staggered towards up, 'or he would not be so loud about it. How is it with you? No hurt? Good; that was a mighty music, that, fit for Heimdall's horn. *Sa*, we have lost our two lookouts, and another has fared ill . . .'

Just beyond the fallen boom a small figure lay slumped against the coachroof, with the merchants gathered around him. Volker ducked under the half-unfurled sail and sank to his knees beside him.

'Master Diderik!'

The wrinkled face was grey, the nails bluish on his outstretched hand; but the hand waved, and he cackled faintly. 'Don't you fret for me, boy! Just a bit tired, you know. Gave that nasty thing a good taste of my cane, I did! But I've taken my potions and I'll be right as rain in no time. Just overdoing it a bit, that's all . . .'

'You'll be right if you act your age, for a change!' said Goldfüss with genial scorn. 'You just lie there quiet now. We want a word with Master Volker here.'

Volker became aware that the ring of master merchants was suddenly centred on him, with Joachim and other tough retainers at their backs. And all of the faces were grim.

Goldfüss took Volker's arm to help him up, and did not let go of it. 'Well,' he said heavily. 'No doubt we owe you thanks for getting us out of this latest mess. However it was you did it . . .' He eyed the horn uneasily, but without any particular recognition that Volker could see. 'Trouble is, it raises a few good questions. Like, how'd we get into the mess in the first place? Where're all these attacks coming from?'

'Bribed officials,' said Beck. 'Persistent river pirates . . . the usual minor incidents. Weird goings-on at Nebelstein, those are not wholly unknown. Those we might have swallowed. Even a city in riot; competitors might stretch so far to steal a march in something so profitable. But now this!'

'And where's Ulrich?' interrupted Haagen icily. 'That's what I'd most like to know! Convenient, wasn't it, that we had to flee without waiting for him—'

'And run straight into a full-fledged sorcerous attack!' rumbled Beck, his normally merry face suffused with red. 'What black sorcerer'd waste such power on a pack of harmless merchants, with no more on their mind than this venture of Ulrich's? For that was a creature of Tartarus if ever I saw one!' He also eyed the horn with unease but no apparent interest.

Goldfüss nodded. 'And it seems a full-fledged sorcerer met it. That sticks in my craw, too. It's gone far enough, lad; we want some answers, and we want them now.' His grip tightened. '*Now*, d'you hear?'

Volker, rather to his own suprise, shook his arm free. 'All right!' he said, and saw heads lift at the tone of his voice. He'd had enough of skulking and running. A full-fledged sorcerer, eh? 'Answers you shall have!' He looked them up and down. 'But they may not be to your liking. Where's Ulrich, you ask? This was not the first sorcerous attack upon us. The first struck against Ulrich and myself; and Ulrich is dead. You cannot wish more than I do that he was not.'

There was a moment of awful silence, and then the three merchants burst out all at once.

'Dead? By sorcery?'

'But this is Ulrich's venture – always had been—'

'How dare you entice us—'

'How can we hope – without him—'

'We must turn back—'

'I'm not going on—'

Volker raised a hand, but the tide was hardly stemmed. In desperation he brandished the horn; the silence that followed was startling. 'Ulrich's venture, you say? Always you lean upon him. But little you know what his true venture was. He was a merchant, true, but first and foremost he was a mage of great power and a good man. He had more than one venture afoot, and this, though real, was not the prime one. He meant to keep his pledge to you, yes. He would have led you through to Syracusa, yes, to grow rich; but on the way he meant to turn aside a while, upon concerns that are not yours. For that purpose you were to be his cloak. He did not tell you; but he told *me*! And in the very grip of death he pledged me to carry through his plan. If it fails, more is at risk than you can guess, enough to make your profits meaningless, maybe even your lives. There is no turning back from that, even if you safely could. I guess that now this party is marked, any who left it would soon be seized, wrung dry of the least scrap of knowledge they might possess, then quietly disposed of. You have gone too far to back out now.'

Haagen was the first to recover, and he did not speak

at first, but gestured to his retainers, who shouldered their way through the press. 'But what of you, young sorcerer? Suppose it was you we ousted, and left to fulfil this mysterious mission of yours alone. Would we not be left to go our way unmolested? I think we would! And since you tricked us—'

He stopped dead, his eyes bulging, his shoulders held at an awkward angle. A sweat broke out on his high forehead, and he stammered for words.

Thorgrim nodded, and twisted Hlavisbana a little against his kidneys. 'You were saying, Master Haagen?' The retainers rounded on him, only to jump back as the crowd parted before de Guillac's sabre. From behind them an owl screamed, and Dani drew her bow to her chin.

Volker, seizing his advantage, sprang up on the coachroof. 'Nothing has changed!' he cried. 'I have Ulrich's map, his directions – and his confidence. I doubted myself, but he told me I could do it. Otherwise I'd never have brought you this far! I mean to fulfil Ulrich's deeper purpose, yes – but the best way to do that is by fulfilling yours. I will do both, or die trying. These others are with me. You have seen what we can do. You're all seasoned merchants, men of courage; when you came on this journey you balanced the risks you faced against the money you might make. Do so again! Fight us or go along with us! Which will profit you better? Work it out!'

The silence that followed was split by a huge cackle of laughter. 'A lad of spirit! Now who said there weren't any, any more!' Old Diderik, his colour restored, was picking himself up and dusting off his robes. 'Got you all gaping and goggling like a herd of bullocks, he has! And bullocks you must be, not a ball between you! Course I'll go along with you, laddie! Why, he reminds me of myself at that age!'

'Somebody shut him up!' groaned Goldfüss. But he

looked up at Volker, and nodded. 'Very well, boy. Those are answers, all right. You said I wouldn't like them, and I don't! But I reckon I've less to lose by going along, right enough. And I think that'll go for us all . . . eh, gentles?'

The nods were unwilling, the looks cold, but Beck and Haagen agreed. The others relaxed visibly. Slowly, watchfully, his own followers lowered their weapons, but nobody gave them the least sign of a challenge.

'Well,' grinned Thorgrim, 'now you command us, *kaptajn*. Hands to breakfast, and then on our way?'

Volker sagged. 'Hands to breakfast, it is,' he sighed. 'I think we've earned it.'

Chapter 4

Guy de Guillac brushed the rain out of his eyes, gathered his sodden cloak tightly around his shoulders, and glowered at the world in general. 'This,' he grumbled, 'would be beneath the dignity of a brothel-keeper—'

'Good,' said Thorgrim. 'Then it will not trouble *you*. *Odin og Frigg*, will you stop your complaining and—'

'*Quiet*, both of you!' said Dani, through a thin mask of rain-soaked hair. 'The horses don't like it, either – and they're the ones pulling the barge.'

Joachim Landau shouldered his massive, iron-bound arquebus and whispered something into the ear of the leading horse. It quieted a little, but even Volker, who had little experience of animals, could sense their nervousness.

For two days the dearly bought horses had helped them tow the barges against an ever-stronger current out of Alpina Tartara, following the course of the river Gastein between ever-higher peaks that rose snow-capped and savage above the cloaking green darkness of the forests. The river was a swift-flowing ribbon cutting through a narrow belt of swampy grassland bounded by the twin walls of the forest. Once, long ago, men had lived here: there were clearings in the woods, charcoal-burners' hovels, and a dozen or more abandoned mine-workings. None lived here now, and the towpath had dwindled to a ribbon of mud between the scented darkness of the pines and the swift-flowing waters of the river. In itself that might have been tolerable – but after an hour of torrential rain, with thunder and lightning to match, tempers were running very short.

'Get 'em to some decent shelter,' said Joachim, 'and the beasts'll cease their fretting. Doing their best, they are.'

'They seem none too eager,' muttered Thorgrim.

'I don't blame them,' said Volker. 'This is where Ulrich told us to go, but I'll be damned to Tartarus if I know *why*. Would you believe he calls this place "the Singing Mountains"?'

'Hnh,' grunted Guy. 'I hear nothing but the weather gods – and these stupid animals.' He added a string of colourful oaths as the reluctant barge horses balked at the narrowest part of the path.

Dani frowned. 'There's something wrong—'

'And it is these *dromadaires déguisée*! I think that we have snatched them from the slaughter-house.'

'It is poor horseflesh,' agreed Thorgrim. 'Not like my little Skeggi, back home. He could put all of these to flight with a single hoofstroke. When I fought him against that moth-eaten Hvitserk of Arnulf's—'

A withering look from Dani cut him short. 'Will you *listen*? I'm telling you something's wrong. I can almost *smell* it—'

Thorgrim shrugged. 'I think your nose has lived too long in these stinking imperial cities. There is no magic here, no—'

'Girl's right,' rumbled Joachim, unshipping his arquebus. The weapon was luggable rather than portable, and barely reliable at the best of times, but no one could persuade him to part with it. 'Thought I saw summat moving in them there trees.'

Volker narrowed his eyes. It was true – there *was* something between the trees, half-hidden among the shadows . . .

'That's what I'm trying to tell you,' said Dani. 'In

164

Vulcan's name, Joachim, will you put that thing away before you blow someone's head off?' The grizzled bombardier nodded amiably, and continued priming his weapon, carefully shielding the pan from the driving rain. *'Joachim, will you please—?'*

A livid white lightning flash exploded out of the darkness overhead, followed by a deep, rumbling roar that echoed and re-echoed among the surrounding mountains. Volker saw an answering gleam of metal among the trees – but before he could open his mouth there was another deafening concussion, and the bell of Joachim's arquebus spat out a yard-long red-gold flame. 'Got the bugger!' he roared happily as the recoil threw him flat on his back. Volker, ears still ringing with the blast, bent down to help him – just as something huge, wet and smelly rammed against his buttocks and propelled him face-first into the mud. Instinctively he curled into a foetal ball as hooves thudded all around him. Then Guy, sabre in hand, was dragging him to his feet. Through veils of smoke and rain Volker could vaguely see a gap blasted between the trees, and broken shapes that glinted strangely, but there were other, more urgent problems—

'The tow-ropes!' he gurgled. The ringing still hadn't stopped; it was like shouting inside a gigantic bell. *'Cut the tow-ropes!'*

'I *have* cut them!' roared Guy. 'Of all the worthless—!'

'You damn *fool!*' yelled Dani, straight into Joachim's grinning face. 'You've just blasted a rock – a goddamned *rock*! And for that you lose the horses—!'

'Forget the horses!' roared Thorgrim. *'Odin og Frigg,* look at the *trees!*'

Guy froze in mid-oath, mouth open and jaw slack. Dani's eyes widened to the size of new-minted thalers. Volker tried to shout a warning to the barges, but nothing came out.

The forest was moving.

As if in a dream, Volker saw the crests of a dozen trees rise and fall like waves on a windblown lake, as though an army of pines was marching down the hillside. He had read stories like this, stories of forests lingering on from the First Creation that tolerated no intrusion, stories of trees that walked like giants, destroying anything and anyone in their path—

'They're *falling*!' hissed Dani. 'Like there's something pushing them down—!'

In the gap that Joachim's arquebus had cleared, a shattered tree-bole twisted and toppled, its roots scattering earth as they were torn out of the ground. Behind it a majestic pine groaned and fell as the soil at its base boiled like a witch's cauldron. On either side, other trees were swaying, their branches rattling one against another as they tumbled pell-mell down the slope towards the barges. But even through the driving veils of rain Volker could see darker shapes among the chaos – shapes that seemed to explode out of the earth itself, dripping with mud and slime, and rumble down the hillside in a chaos of shattered timber.

'*Hel og haglbyge,*' grunted Thorgrim, with what sounded like mild annoyance, '*Ogsaa her, disse jammerlige jaetter?*' With brutal swiftness he snatched at his amulet, scattering broken links from the chain as he hefted it, paused, and hurled it towards the nearest of the shapes. Volker saw what might have been a head turning pallid, green-glowing eyes towards the Norseman; then there was an echoing crack, and the green light was gone. Something whirred through the air like the wings of Dani's owl.

Volker blinked. The hammer was back in Thorgrim's hand, as if it had never been anywhere else.

I don't understand. He has *no magic. Unless the hammer itself is*—

With a wordless cry Volker thrust de Guillac to one side as a vast, lumpish shape rolled towards them.

Again Thorgrim's movement was almost too quick to see – and again, seconds later, the hammer was in his hand while his target crumbled into a strangely glittering pile of rubble.

'*Bougre de Brest*!' roared Guy, 'what in the name of Saturn *are they*?'

Joachim shrugged, and continued the appallingly slow business of reloading his arquebus, but Thorgrim gave the Armorican a pitying look. 'This one, I think was never young!' The Norseman dodged nimbly aside as a family-sized boulder lashed a club-like arm in his general direction. Chuckling, he darted behind it and crowned it with a ringing hammerblow that split it neatly in two. There were glistening striations along each half. '*Loke's lem*, did you never hunt for stone-trolls when you were a little *drakener*?'

Guy's eyes lit with sudden understanding, then widened in horror. Dani's shouted warning came a moment too late: the flying pebble they had both seen took Thorgrim neatly on the chin. For three heartbeats the Norseman stood tipsily upright, swaying like a shallow-rooted tree in a northerly gale Then he folded at the knees and crumpled into the grass.

'Dani!' yelled Volker. 'The hammer! Get the—!'

Another pebble whistled past his ear. The trolls had discovered a new game. Guy snatched up the fallen Norseman's halberd, swinging it in an elaborate series of flourishes to fend off a small hailstorm of stones, pebbles and rocks. Joachim, muttering darkly, retreated towards the barges, powder-horn in hand. Dani was crawling on her belly towards Thorgrim while the owl circled overhead, hooting disconsolately. Volker ducked behind the pile of rubble that had been Thorgrim's first victim as two of the larger trolls trundled randomly in his general direction. There seemed to be no malice in it, just a vague, meaningless panic, like a flock of startled sheep. The only difference was that these sheep happened to like grazing on rock, about thirty feet under-ground – unless mad gunners started firing artillery pieces at their food. Volker looked around, but Joachim was well beyond glaring range – and so was the offending arquebus. And these things weren't sheep; they were rocks, heavy rocks, and anything that got in their way was going to finish up crushed to a pulp.

How in all the seven levels of Tartarus do you stop a stampeding avalanche?

You couldn't. But there might be other options . . .

'Dani!' yelled Volker, 'We've got to turn them!'

'In Juno's name, *how*?'

'The hammer! Throw the hammer!'

'But I've never—'

'Then I suggest you *try*!' roared de Guillac. He was retreating, slowly and unwillingly, keeping his eyes on the boulder-like troll rolling steadily towards him, its mouth agape and spitting pebbles the size of small tombstones. But behind him—

'Guy! look out!'

A dozen trolls were thumping and bouncing across the turf towards the Armorican's back, the sound of their progress drowned by the clatter of rock against rock all around them. But these were moving faster than the rest, almost as if something was pushing them. At the last moment Guy heard them, and turned to face them, just in time to realize that he was trapped.

'Dani!' yelled Volker.

'I see them!' The hammer was already in her hand. She paused a moment, testing its balance and its weight, trying to understand how Thorgrim had used it, but there was no more time. A creature of nightmare burst through the line of trolls, a thing like the ball-flower capital of a temple column, except that this had a head, four legs, and a racing dog's turn of speed. It ran with its mouth open, baring impressively sharp teeth that glittered like precious stones, and its eyes seemed to be fixed on Guy. It drove the trolls aside like a wolf scattering sheep. De Guillac lowered the halberd, but the creature's hide was like panelled stonework. Volker grimaced. First the sheep, now the sheepdog; and he had no chance at all of stopping it, unless—

Dani rose to a crouch, swung the hammer twice in a whirling circle, and hurled it. The blow struck the creature full in what passed for its chest, and a spider's web of cracks and fractures snaked out from the point of impact. It raised a lumpish leg, opened its mouth for a single, soundless cry – and fell apart in a glittering heap of fractured rock.

Volker groaned. The hammer had not returned to Dani's hand, and now it was buried somewhere in the rubble. To his left, Guy was once again surrounded by a living, and slowly contracting, stone circle that would crush him to death in minutes. Thorgrim lay where he had fallen – and Joachim was still loading his arquebus.

Which leaves me. And the horn.

For a moment he hesitated. The horn was both powerful and unpredictable – and in the wild lands at the edge of the mountains there were other creatures that might be drawn to its magic. But he had run out of time. He put the horn to his lips, fumbled for a moment with the keys, and blew for all their lives.

Afterwards he could never remember exactly what he had played, and perhaps it was just as well. For a moment – just a moment – he struggled to think of something that might shatter rock. Ulrich had used frost, to devastating effect, but there was another, far more powerful force that Volker could call upon . . .

Probably. If his guess was right. And if he was wrong, none of them would live to complain about it.

His fingers found the same pattern of keys he had used to dispel the mists over the river, but his lips were slacker, and this time the note was deep, thunderous, shaking the ground beneath his feet. Guy and Dani staggered, and the trolls froze in their tracks. The trees and grasses of the forest fringe bowed before the blast as before a north wind – and then sudden inspiration guided him through a series of eardrum-snapping arpeggios that cut the air like a knife. Dani and Guy crumpled to the ground, clutching their hands against their heads to shut out the sound. To Volker it seemed that the world was closing in on him like a mailed fist, as if some mad god were thrusting down the vault of heaven itself to crush the whole of the Second Creation—

Light blinded him. An explosion of sound deafened him. Ribbons of brilliance tore across his sight, hammering deep into the earth and rebounding against the collapsing sky. He saw one of the trolls explode into white-hot fragments that burned the earth where they fell, while searing gobbets of liquid metal sprayed out to all sides. Volker was standing at the centre of a ring of lightning that seemed to flicker continuously between earth and sky, while an endless, echoing roll of thunder answered the swirling melody of his music. He blew till his head rang and his ribs were cracking with the strain and when, at last, he took the horn from his lips, there was nothing to see but broken rock, fallen trees, and mud. On the barges, dazed-looking crewmen picked themselves up off the deck.

Volker's guess had been right. The trolls were fleshed like the rocks they fed on, with a good admixture of metallic ore. His horn-call had done no more than summon the storm. After that, the gods of thunder and lightning had taken charge, grounding their terrible energies through the nearest convenient sources of metal. Volker devoutly hoped that he would never again find himself caught up in such an awesome display of power—

Then he froze. The mud was moving . . .

With a volley of unlikely oaths, Guy de Guillac hauled

himself – and Dani – out of the clayey quagmire that Volker's impromptu thunderstorm had made of the riverbank. 'Jupiter Teutates!' she yelled, 'can't you *control* that thing?'

'You had a better idea?' said Volker icily.

'*Mais sans question*!' growled Guy. 'I had only to—'

'Yes?'

Guy no longer seemed interested in talking. He was staring very hard at something just behind Volker's head. Dani turned to look, too. Her mouth dropped open and stayed that way. Volker hesitated. He didn't want to turn round, but he was going to have to . . .

Apparently, one of the trolls had survived. Certainly *something* scarcely human was walking – or rather staggering – along the towpath, dripping slime and ooze . . .

Dani started to giggle. Guy snorted, and then roared with laughter.

Thorgrim was almost unrecognizable. Thick mud, richly encrusted with weeds and rubbish, cocooned his body. His face was the leafy mask of an ettin; a dozen vine-like strands of vegetation had entwined themselves lovingly in his hair, and three more were investigating his mouth and nose.

'Come,' chuckled Guy. 'Let us unwrap the Hairy One before his own beard chokes him.'

Volker and Dani rushed to help, but the Norseman was effectively bound hand and foot, and the clinging plants seemed to be rooted fast in the mud that coated him from top to toe. Dani was the first to discover that some of them, at least, had thorns.

'*Damn* that horn. Can't we just lose it somewhere?'

'Like you lost the hammer?' snarled Volker.

'Muh hmhah!' mumbled Thorgrim through a mouthful of muck and assorted foliage. 'Whut ha – urgh!' His words degenerated into a magnificent volley of coughs and splutters, followed by a thunderous sneeze. It seemed to rebound from peak to peak, crossing and recrossing the mountain bowl that surrounded them, changing its pitch and intensity, its sound transmuted into a half-formed, whistling melody. To Volker it felt as though the mountains were talking to each other, channelling the winds through caves and hollows to create a strange and chaotic music. Dani's right hand hovered indecisively over the panpipes at her belt, as if she meant to answer the distorted echoes with a wild harmony of her own. Thorgrim, his fury forgotten, stood transfixed with amazement.

'And what *diablerie*,' Guy muttered fervently, 'was *that*?'

Volker glanced back towards the barges. The crewmen were staring wildly around them while Haagen, Beck and the other merchants boiled out from the aft cabin of the *Walfisch* as if they'd called up a more than usually noxious demon. Joachim and three of his cronies had recaptured the horses, and now seemed likely to lose them again as the startled animals reared in panic, lashing out with their hooves at anyone who tried to get near them. 'You! Gottfried and Manfred!' yelled Volker, sending another batch of echoes rolling among the mountains, 'Don't just stand there! Get those barges moored for the night! What's the matter? Never heard an echo before?'

'Not like that,' said Dani quietly. 'I think we've found your Singing Mountains, Volker.'

'Now perhaps you find my hammer,' growled Thorgrim.

'No need to sulk,' said Dani. 'It's there, under that rockpile that used to be a troll. And since when did *you* have a magic weapon?'

'There is no magic,' muttered the Norseman, scrabbling among the pitiful remains of the rock-creature. 'I have the trick of throwing it, is all. My nephew Steinthor, from his cradle he could make a better throw than yours.'

Dani shrugged. 'So next time I'll bring a cradle.'

The big man had found his hammer. It was broken in two, but he hardly seemed to have noticed – in fact he was staring very hard at something on the ground in front of him. 'Maybe,' he said, 'just maybe, you throw better than I thought.'

'What is it?' asked Volker. 'What have you found?'

'Perhaps nothing,' said Thorgrim, scraping something against one of the rocks, 'and then again, perhaps . . . something.' He looked cautiously around him, and then held up a small crystal. It glittered in the fading light.

'Rock salt?' said Guy.

Thorgrim shook his head. 'I think—' He turned the broken hammer-shaft upside down, showing the ruby at its base, hesitated for a moment, then ran the crystal in his other hand across its surface. 'I think not.'

'The stone!' gasped Dani. 'You've scratched it!'

'No matter,' grinned the Norseman. 'I have found a better.'

'Here's another one,' said Dani. 'And I think there's another over there—'

'Enough!' said Thorgrim. 'You want those wharf-rats to know there are diamonds here? You have won them, and you shall keep them – but say nothing, and trust no one!'

'For myself,' growled Thorgrim, 'I have no doubts. One of us is a traitor. Always they know what we do – the place, the time, to attack.' He glanced sourly round at the thirty-odd figures huddled near their dying camp-fires. The faint, flickering light turned the gnarled and twisted trees at the edge of the clearing into a haunted shadow-play. Each group, including their own, had weapons and firewood close at hand; after their close

173

encounter with the trolls, no one felt inclined to wander in the cold and the dark. Only Dani slept sound, curled in a tight ball near the fire and wrapped in her grubby woollen blanket. Volker stared at her absently. 'If there *is* a traitor, it could be anyone. Anyone at all.'

De Guillac leaned closer to the fire, pulling his cloak tightly about his shoulders. 'I cannot believe it. All have fought well – remarkably well, for the street-sweepings they are.'

Thorgrim shrugged. 'You think so? But a Tartarist, he will fight like any other man to keep the steel out of his belly. One we think of as a hero may in truth by the worst of *nithings*.'

'*Couilles de Cyclops*,' muttered de Guillac. 'You north-men! Everywhere you see treachery—'

'And so we live a little longer, my friend. Trust no ice till it is crossed, no man till he is buried, no wife till she is widowed—'

'And no doorway till you've checked it,' said Volker with a grin. 'But there's nothing to check. Nothing's happening. There've *been* no attacks since we killed the riverbeast—'

'Aside,' said de Guillac, 'from a few stone-trolls.'

Thorgrim shook his head. 'Because we were clumsy, my friend. In the bull's pen, be wary of horns.'

Volker started. 'That's it! The horn! The first time anyone besides us knew about it was back there, after I'd used it against the beast!'

'*Hel og haglbyge*, you are right!' said Thorgrim. 'But if our traitor knows of the horn, why does he make no move to take it back?'

'Perhaps,' said Guy grimly, 'because we seek its companion. So are we not doing as he wishes – taking it to the very place he would take it himself?'

Volker sighed. 'In that case we'd better find him, and fast. If he knows where we're going he knows more than me. I've followed Ulrich's notes to the letter, but as far as I can see the river simply gets narrower, faster and steeper. Even the horses won't get us much farther. And after that – well, look at the map.'

He took the cracked and stained vellum from his scrip, holding it in the light from the fire as the two men leaned closer to see. Ulrich's map was the work of a master mage, deceptive in its simplicity. A closer look revealed hidden traps and deceptions – cabalistic symbols scattered along and around the writhing line that marked their course, interrupting it, turning it, changing its meaning. Thorgrim, with the practised eye of a navigator, quickly found the outthrust line that marked the river Gastein, and whistled softly as he looked along it. 'That, I think, must be the mother of all waterfalls.'

Guy narrowed his eyes, peering at the cryptic marks near Thorgrim's pointing finger. 'These symbols – there is a portage, perhaps?'

'Or perhaps not.' Thorgrim seemed grimly amused. 'See how the land rises here, and here? I think that Yngvi the Ox himself could not carry these whale-fish barges across such a country.'

'Yngvi the Ox?' Volker's face was a question mark.

'My great-grandfather on my mother's side. He was the son of Eystein Fiddle, and the grandson of Rolf Goatsbreath, who was second cousin to—'

Guy gripped the Norseman's wrist. 'Enough! Save your sagas and your Goatsbreath for one of your northern nights. I have not the stomach!'

'As you wish. They say that Yngvi took twelve longships from Reykjavik to Old Miklagard through the land of the Varangians – and when the rivers denied them passage, he lifted the ships one by one and carried them on his own head.'

'And was henceforth known as Yngvi the Flathead, no doubt,' muttered Guy. 'A condition he passed on to his descendants.'

'They say also that no one should believe what is said

of his ancestors. Volker, what of these symbols? Do you know their meaning?'

'It's like a key. Ulrich couldn't afford to make it too easy – there was always the chance these notes could fall into the wrong hands. But as for *this* place – nothing. Nothing but runes and riddles.' He saw their doubtful glances, and felt a moment's resentment. 'Look, I *can* read them. Ulrich would hardly have—'

'Even so,' said Thorgrim quietly. 'My people have some skill with puzzles. Let me see.'

Reluctantly, Volker took the second vellum roll from his scrip and handed it to the Norseman. Thorgrim opened it confidently enough, goggled for a moment at its contents, then leaned forward with a frown of concentration, stroking his beard.

'*Naa* . . . Here.' He pointed to a line of cursive script mixed with runes and marked by a Hebrew character. 'Gimel, no? – what the Greeks call Gamma.'

'That's the place. The first bit's clear enough.'

'*Naa ja*. "Take the river Salzach south and west, and the Gastein southward from there. The current flows swift and strong against you from Alpina Tartara – good horses at Schwarzbad." '

Guy muttered a dark oath and prodded the fire as though it had done him a personal injury. Thorgrim smiled. 'I had reckoned Master Ulrich a better judge of horseflesh. *Saa*, here are your runes, Volker . . .'

'Well?'

'Not so hasty.' He chose a stick from among the kindling, took out his knife, and started to scratch a series of symbols there, for all the world like a clerk with a tally-stick.

'Hmm . . . *Jasaa* . . .'

'Well?' said Guy at last.

'A moment, my thirsty friend, a moment.' He scratched two final symbols, sighed, and smiled. 'It says "The gates of the Singing Mountains will be opened to you. Do there as you are done by. Beware: evil haunts the bridge at the giant's knife." And if this is a riddle, I for one cannot fathom it.'

'No,' said Volker, trying not to look smug. 'Neither could I. But if it *isn't* a riddle, what in all the seven levels of Tartarus does it—?'

'Quiet,' said Thorgrim in an altogether different voice. 'Maybe we find out now.' He reached gingerly for a crossbow, signalling to de Guillac with his free hand. The Armorican nodded and drew his sabre. Volker, bewildered, saw nothing suspicious, and heard nothing except leaves rustling in the faint breeze from the mountains. But one tree seemed to sway more than the rest – and in it, dark against palely moonlit clouds, he could just make out a shadowy silhouette. The head moved queerly, too big for the shrunken body that supported it. The arms, wide spread among the branches, were monstrous clubs. The legs were stubby and skeletal—

With a wordless cry he struck aside Thorgrim's crossbow. The bolt thunked solidly into the tree, and Dani's owl soared upwards into the night in a flurry of wings. At the same moment a shadowy figure crashed away through the bushes to the right. Disturbed by the noise, Dani moaned and turned over in her sleep. To Volker's surprise, Thorgrim reached across and covered her with the blanket. 'A creature of Tartarus,' he muttered, 'darker even than this dark place.'

Volker reddened. 'I'm sorry. All I saw was the bird.'

'No matter. I think my bolt would not have harmed it – or your blade, my fire-bellied friend.'

Guy grinned. 'No? At all events, it is gone, and she sleeps still.' He drew Dani's blanket a little closer around her.

'It is well we did not wake her,' said Thorgrim. 'When that one dreams, the Mother commands it . . .'

She was soaring, free as the night-wind that bore her, wings spread to catch the bellying updraught from secret valleys far below, watching for the tiny movements of her unwitting prey. Far ahead, the distant peaks had torn a gap in the clouds, and the mountain snows sparkled grey and silver like sunlit water in a winter breeze. A sudden gust fluttered her breast feathers, and she cupped her wings to meet it with firm, rhythmic strokes, oaring her way up the cloud-limned sky as if to strike at the very moon . . .

A shadow flicked across the snow-field; without time for thought, driven by instinct and the memory of a thousand moonlit hunts, she cupped her wings and dropped, talons outstretched, like the spear of a vengeful god. A spinning, silver world was rushing up to meet her, purified and hallowed by the ice and snow of the high passes . . .

With a cry and a thunderclap of wings she swooped up, away, beating the air with heavy strokes, fury rising within her. There was power here, power that had shattered the peace of the land, torn rock from rock, warped mountain and valley into alien shapes, ravaged their woods and their forests, poisoned their streams and their rivers . . .

'I think,' said Thorgrim quietly, 'that today you are not a popular man, Volker.'

After a restless, uncomfortable night they had left the campsite soon after dawn. Dani, the only one of them who had slept all night, seemed troubled, talking to no one and keeping herself apart from the others. Now, with the best part of the day already gone, they had covered little more than six miles. The river banks had degenerated into ledges of rock and gravel beneath ever-steepening, tree-capped cliffs that now rose some fifty feet on either side. The current, true to Ulrich's warning, was fast and furious, and they could barely make headway against it. For the last hour everyone, regardless of rank or station, had been lending their weight to the tow-ropes. The only exception was Diderik, who sat astride the bombard at the prow of the *Walross* and made a great show of directing operations. Fortunately no one could hear him. Beck, now grubby, red-faced and sweating, glared back at Volker.

'A fine idea – this one! Madness! Sheer madness!'

'You have maybe a better?' said Thorgrim.

Beck clearly did, but he had run out of breath. Diderik, however, had not, and although his words were lost, the way he was capering about on the foredeck suggested something unusual ahead.

'What in the name of Bacchus has got into the old goat?' muttered Haagen.

'Mad,' gasped Beck. 'Quite mad.'

'Not quite,' said Volker. 'Look!'

As they rounded a jutting crag the view that Diderik had seen opened out in front of them – and for a moment it seemed that the cliffs on either side were alive, and turning towards them—

'They're . . . they're faces!' said Goldfüss. He sounded as uncertain as Volker felt.

'If that is a face,' muttered Thorgrim, 'then I pity its owner.'

'Whatever it is,' said Haagen, 'someone made it – and I could do good business with them. In Frisia they'll pay a count's ransom for a well-chipped rock . . .'

Volker could barely believe it. The wavering shadows of the trees on the opposite clifftop added the final illusion of motion to a vast, mask-like sculpture, a sculpture so inhuman that it seemed like an intruder from another world. The jaw jutted like the ramming prow of a galley, splaying blunt, many-faceted teeth that all but concealed the lower lip. The nose had gone: all that remained were two hair-like slits where the nostrils

179

might have been. The eyes were narrow and deep-set beneath a forehead that sloped steeply backward.

How long's it been here? Who made it? And why?

Volker had been so intent on the carving that he had seen the rest without taking it in. Now, slowly, he began to understand what he was looking at. Beneath the lowering glare of the face, the cliff itself had been chiselled away on either side to create two broad, paved towpaths guarded by sinister looking castellated turrets. And beyond the turrets Volker could just see the winding gear for the enormous sluice gates that spanned the full width of the gorge.

The gates of the Singing Mountains. This has *to be the place that Ulrich meant.*

Haagen glanced back at Volker with a mixture of admiration and suspicion. 'If you knew of this, boy, why did you not tell us? Beck here's been swearing blind you'd lost your way, and I was half-minded to believe him.'

'And that,' snarled Beck, 'is why you said as much yourself!'

Volker smiled, and thought fast. 'I kept silence to confound our enemies, Master Haagen. If I showed lack of trust, I'm sorry.'

'Hm. Well. Should know who your friends are, my lad.'

Yes. I wish I did . . .

'Volker,' said Dani, 'there's something wrong about those turrets. I don't like the smell of them.'

Thorgrim nodded. 'There is a darkness about them.'

'And I,' said Guy, 'I mislike those arrow-slits.'

'Not to mention the furnishings,' said Volker, eyeing a line of exotic gape-jawed monsters just below the castellations. 'I think they're toll-gates – with a sting in the tail for anyone who balks at the price.' He looked pointedly at Goldfüss, whose face was now as long as

180

a tombstone. 'You can't expect a high road across the mountains for nothing, Master Goldfüss.'

'And exactly what *is* the price?' demanded Haagen.

Volker grinned. 'How are you at haggling?'

'Better than Beck, if those thrice-damned horses are anything to go by. *Ho there! You in the tower!*'

His rasping voice echoed down the gorge, rebounding from the knife-edged crags and overhangs that threatened them on either side. But there was no answer.

'Now *there* is matter for debate,' said Thorgrim thoughtfully. 'Such work as this, and no man to guard it.'

Volker was puzzled, too, but this was no time to sow doubt in the merchants' minds. 'If there's no one here we'll help ourselves,' he said. 'Goldfüss, I'll need four of your men to open the sluice gates, and a scratch crew on the barges while we take them through. The rest can watch the cliffs for uninvited guests.'

Beck snorted contemptuously. 'Are we to stand here all day, Master Volker?'

'No. Thorgrim, Guy and Dani are coming with me to take a look at those turrets. Perhaps you'd care to join us.'

'I? Do you think I have nothing better to do?'

Volker smiled disarmingly. 'Oh, I'm sure you'll find *something*, Master Beck.'

'I think,' said Thorgrim, 'that this is the most damn peculiar castle I ever see in my life.'

Volker nodded agreement. The gateway was surrounded by a carved band of intricately twined snakes and dragons. Beyond it was a portcullis, and beyond that a dog-leg passage vanished into darkness. Above, heavy bombards commanded the river and the gorge; but the portcullis was raised, and the shadows inside betrayed no slightest sign of life.

With a shrug, Volker strode forward into darkness. Beyond the dog-leg the only light came from murder-holes overhead. A door hung open at a crazy angle, the staircase beyond it a deeper darkness in the depths of shadow. Volker reached out a hand to feel his way – the stone was rough beneath his fingers, with an odd, half-finished texture. The steps, too, were strangely made, and he stumbled more than once as he followed their long, slow arc upward beneath a second portcullis and past another archway opening on a broad, circular chamber. It was lit by arrow-slits so close to the floor that a normal man would scarcely be able to use them. Beyond the arch was a half-open door, so low that even Diderik would have had to bow his head to enter it. Now, too, Volker could understand his difficulty with the steps: the broad treads and shallow risers might have been made for a child.

'We'd best go up,' said Volker, with a confidence he did not feel. 'If there's anyone above, they could—'

Dani's arrow was nocked and drawn back just a heart-beat before Volker saw the monstrous shape slithering down the central column. His hand leapt to the knife at his belt as de Guillac's sabre rasped out of its scabbard and Thorgrim's halberd swung to the guard . . .

Dani muttered something unrepeatable and lowered her bow. De Guillac chuckled, and sheathed his blade. Thorgrim, with a wry grin, prodded the stone monster with his halberd. 'I think, my *drakener* friend, that here is an enemy to blunt your blade.'

'And I, *mon ami*, I think that we have fallen among folk who gnaw stone and expel sculpture.'

Volker nodded silent agreement. As his eyes grew used to the murk he saw that what he had taken for rough, unworked stone was a mass of intricate carving that seemed to cover every surface – walls, archways, vaults and columns alike. But there was no consistency about the work, no overall design – it was as though

182

an army of sculptors had amused themselves here for half a century or so, each pursuing some private project, each so intent on his own ideas that he paid no heed to those of his fellows. Here a caricatured huldra princess with the ears and nose of a pig was half-eclipsed by a ramping bear in low relief, so skilfully carved that it seemed ready to tear itself free of the wall. There a gaggle of water-nixies struggled in a complicated and unlikely looking involvement with two ettins. And everywhere heads, arms, legs and tails peeped out from foliage, ruined buildings, trees and cave mouths.

Dani shivered. 'I don't like this place.'

'You have stinks in your nose again?' suggested Guy.

'She is right,' said Thorgrim, running his fingers absentmindedly over the nipples of a stone nixie. 'It is like the slime after the snail has passed. Something out of Hel has been here.' He kicked morosely at the half-open door, and bit off a sharp cry of pain.

'*Cornes d'aurochs*, what is it?' roared Guy, half-drawing his sabre.

Thorgrim seemed unwilling to speak. He simply pointed at the door and clutched his foot. Frowning, Guy pushed at the door – and pushed again, harder.

'Well, Volker,' he growled, 'you will stand there all day in the fashion of a decorative *espalier*, or you will perhaps help?'

With a puzzled shrug, Volker put his shoulder against the door as well. Even their combined weight was barely enough to move it, but the results were disappointing. Beyond the low-slung lintel was nothing but abandoned furniture, carved with the same obsessive attention to detail as the sculptures in the hallway: strange, squat-looking chairs in the form of chained huldrafolk, a chart table concealed in the spiky shell of a bandy-legged armoured dragon, and a snarling harpy, her body split down the midriff to form the doors of an empty cupboard. At the far end of the room were two further doors, also ajar. And everywhere – on every surface – was a thick layer of dust.

'That's odd,' said Dani.

Volker rubbed his shoulder. It felt bruised. 'What, the door?'

'No, the dust. It smells strange. I can't—'

'Once,' said Thorgrim, still massaging his foot, 'that dust lived and breathed. Or so it seems to me.'

Volker grimaced. 'The magic you felt – it's here?'

'It has *been* here – in this very place. So tread warily, as the mouse said to the stone-troll when they crossed the ice.'

Volker's skin was tingling, as if the power that Thorgrim had sensed was somehow touching him as well. Even his eyes were betraying him: it seemed, in the dim light, that some unknown force had leached the colour out of the room. Dani reached out to brush the dust from the harpy's gaping belly, and frowned.

'Volker—'

'Mm?'

'It isn't just the light, you know. Everything here – everything in this room – is made of stone.'

'Is true,' said Thorgrim. 'The door, also.'

Guy drew a warding sigil in the dust on the chart-table. 'They say the Medusa and her Gorgon sisters died long ago and far away. I think it is possible these reports are greatly exaggerated.'

Dani shuddered. 'Is *that* what you feel, Grim?'

The Norseman shook his head. 'I have tasted this power before. Last night, in the wood. But here it is stronger. And almost I am thinking it is—'

'Petrefaction,' muttered Volker, testing the pivoted, shell-like doors of the chart table. 'My old master had a spell that would turn living tissues to stone—' He stopped, aware that Guy was staring at him. 'Well it *would* explain the door. And the furniture. But there's too much else that doesn't—'

'*Down!*' roared Thorgrim, and thrust Volker sideways with a force that sent him sprawling face-first into the dust. A blinding light filled the squat archway that led to the outer hall. Volker was vaguely aware of Dani reaching for an arrow and Guy raising his hands – but Thorgrim barely had time to raise his halberd before a savage bolt of power struck the upturned blade and a dazzling, silent explosion of light leached the shadows from the room. For a moment Thorgrim's flesh burned with a writhing inner fire that cast bone-shadows against his skin and left his face a death's-head of twisting flame. He stumbled and fell against the chart-table, and the gaping stone jaws crumbled to dust at his touch. Then the halbord was in his hand, pulsing with the same supernatural energy, and Guy was roaring the rubric of a counterspell, and a line of green fire arced from Dani's bow—

And the archway trembled, and teetered, and collapsed in a smoking ruin of stone.

Numb with horror, Volker crawled to the fallen Norseman's side – but as he touched Thorgrim's hand a jolt of pure energy pulsed through his arm and hammered into his brain. For a moment the room around him was transformed: his companions were faint and insubstantial wraiths, and all that remained was the stone of walls, floor, vault and furnishings, in a rainbow of vivid, pulsing colours. Then the vision was gone.

'That,' said Thorgrim, 'you might have spared yourself.' Red spots of colour rose and vanished in his cheeks, but the translucent, flame-like flesh of his arms was solid once again.

'We – destroyed it?'

'Perhaps.'

'What *was* it?'

'A sending. The same that came to us in the woods. Or its first cousin.'

Volker shook his head. 'But what did it *want*? What was it trying to do?'

'I felt . . . fear.' Thorgrim seemed hesitant. 'But not of us. It is gone, but not through any work of ours. I think that it was starving – that it saw what it thought of as food, and spent its last energy to take it.'

Dani stared at the shattered chart-table and frowned in bafflement. 'I don't understand. Even the backwash of its power was enough to melt stone – but you're still here.'

Volker laughed hollowly. 'I took the last jolt myself, and all it did was cross my eyes for me.' He shivered, remembering the wraith-like images of his companions – and then, suddenly, he began to understand. 'It didn't want *us*. Maybe it never saw us. All it saw was that table, moving . . .'

A creature that feeds on living stone . . . ?

Dani threw him a withering glance. 'So now we have to find another way out, because you like to mess with other people's furnishings.'

Guy shook his head unhappily. 'But the sending? From where did it come? And this *phantasmagorie*, who makes it?'

'That,' Volker, 'is just what I'd like to know. And I'd also like to know why Ulrich didn't *tell* us who.'

'Curiosity put the bear in the cage,' said Thorgrim, peering curiously out through a waist-high crossbow port. He chuckled. 'Here. Come see this.'

Outside, Diderik was bounding along the top of the sluice gates like an elderly grasshopper, yelling inaudible instructions to anyone in sight. The *Walross* and the *Walfisch*, below, looked uncomfortably small this close to the gates, and from this high vantage point it was easy to see the maze of bypass channels and temporary storage tanks that drained the first lock and slowed the force of the main current. The whole construction was

186

a small miracle of engineering, but it stood deserted, haunted by dark magic.

Who built all this? And what happened to them? Did they die here? And if they did, is whoever or whatever killed them waiting for us, further up and further in? Is that what Ulrich was warning us about?

'Mille millions de magots microcéphalique!' muttered Guy, as if reading his thoughts. 'I wish we might close up these towers and post a garrison.'

'Not enough men,' said Volker. 'Besides, it'd be like crawling into a wine-bottle and pulling the cork in after us.'

The Armorican licked his lips. 'That idea also,' he said thoughtfully, 'is not without its attractions.'

After the strain of the past few days, the journey up the gorge was almost ridiculously easy. At any point where the current threatened to become too strong, sluice gates or winches had been built. The oaks and ashes on the clifftops gave way to ranks of pine trees. The cliffs themselves grew higher, plunging the gorge into deep shadow relieved by an hour or so of sunlight at midday. The air grew colder – and at the same time the towpaths on either side acquired a strange coating of tar and crushed stones that gave a better foothold to horses and men alike. Thorgrim was uneasy, but found only lingering traces of the dark magic they had seen at the gates. By the evening of the second day even Haagen had to admit that Volker had found a way across the mountains, but there was still no sign of the elusive engineers. At evening and morning, as winds swept up or down the valley, they heard the strange, whistling harmonies that gave the mountains their name, but there was no other sign of life, and no sign of habitation.

Then, on the third day, Volker's luck ran out.

After an early start, they had spent the morning negotiating a series of difficult zig-zag bends, each with its own lock. Their progress had been painfully slow and the engineering, for some reason, was less efficient. The mechanisms seemed to be the work of a different and rather more erratic talent, with designs that looked like working trials for the more successful installations further downstream. When the winding gear on one set of sluice gates jammed, it took the combined efforts of most of the crew to free it. The exuberant decoration of the lower levels had also vanished. There were a few curt inscriptions in a rune-like script, and one crudely carved frieze, some ten feet high, that seemed to show a savage battle between armies of dwarves. Then, shortly after noon, a scout reported that the canal came to a dead end barely half a mile upstream. It seemed impossible, but when Volker, his comrades, and the merchants reached the spot they found that the gorge ended at the foot of a roaring wall of water some hundred and fifty feet high. It churned the pool at its base into a witch's cauldron of eddies, swirls and currents, flinging up a mist of fine spray that rainbowed in the light of the midday sun. Even the last set of sluice gates could barely contain its force.

Haagen's grim face had taken on the semblance of an inquisitor about to pass sentence of death. Goldfüss was scowling at Volker, while Diderik repeated the words 'Most remiss, most remiss,' over and over to himself in a penetrating tone he obviously thought of as a whisper. Beck, as usual, was talkative.

'Totally irresponsible, boy. You said you knew every detail of Ulrich's plan – and now this!'

'If you've any excuses,' growled Goldfüss. 'I'd like to hear them. Now.'

'I have no excuses,' said Volker firmly. 'But this is where Ulrich told us to go, so there has to be a way forward. Anyway, no one builds something like this without a reason!'

'Which doesn't get us up this waterfall,' grumbled Haagen. 'Never mind the theories, lad – what are we going to *do*?'

'*Look behind you!*' said a voice that seemed to come from the cliff itself, echoing between the narrow canyon walls like the outcry of some demented ghost from the abandoned gatehouse. Instinctively Thorgrim swung into a defensive crouch, halberd at the ready as he whirled round to face the unknown. But the path behind was empty, except for the laughter that echoed from every side.

'*Up here, barbarian ape!*'

Volker's eyes raked the clifftop, but there was nothing to see. Except . . .

'It seems,' said Thorgrim conversationally, 'that pine trees grow ringmail in these parts.'

Volker nodded slowly. It was difficult to guess just how many archers and crossbowmen were lined up along the cliff, but there had to be at least a hundred on either side – and the gorge offered not one single scrap of cover.

'So,' said Haagen grimly, 'you were right, Master Volker. There *was* a purpose to all this.'

'Aye,' nodded Goldfüss. 'Robbery and murder.'

'What do you want?' yelled Volker, ignoring all of them. 'We'll pay a fair toll – but only when we reach the Flumina Adigia!'

Diderik stared at him and tapped a finger to his slowly shaking head. 'Boy's insane. River Adigia indeed. Never heard such nonsense.'

'*Toll, is it?*' stormed the voice from the cliff. '*What's the toll for murder in your stinking burg?*'

'We've murdered no one!' cried Volker.

'*You have too, you vugging coprolite!*'

'*Turned my poor Phacops into a pile of flinders, they did.*' yelled another, higher voice.

'*Oh, Phacops, was it.*' The first voice sounded dismiss-

189

ive now. 'He'll be small loss. Near took my leg off, that one.'

'He never did. Just a few chippings out of your arse.'

'*Never mind that!*' said the exasperated first voice. '*They've taken our animals – eaten 'em, too, like as not. You can't fool us, thief! We saw your leavings!*'

'Enough!' said Volker. 'We've taken no animals, nor killed any – but we're willing to pay for our passage! What's your price!'

There was no answer.

'*I should have spoken,*' grumbled Haagen. 'If there's haggling to be done, then I'm the one who—'

'*Quiet!*' said Volker sharply. 'Listen . . .'

'I hear nothing,' said Thorgrim.

'That's just it.'

Slowly, unbelievingly, they turned and looked behind them. The waterfall had gone. The turbulent pool at its foot was still – and beyond it was a high-arched tunnel, half-natural, half-sculpted from the living rock. On either side of the entrance stood massive watch-turrets with loaded catapults peering between the battlements.

'*All right, filth! Bring your barges through. We'll see about your Flumina Adigia!*'

'I've told you we mean no harm,' said Volker, for what seemed the fifteenth time, 'and we can pay for our passage. D'you treat *all* your customers like this?'

The heavily armed creatures packing the aft cabin jeered noisily, and several stamped their feet till the decking trembled underfoot. Volker had been cursing himself for a blind fool ever since the first of them had thundered up the gangplank. Their faces, as he should have expected, were like the giant face they had seen at the head of the canal. Their bodies, as he might have guessed at the fortress, were dwarf-like, squat and solidly built. And their flesh – the flesh that the creature

190

in the guardroom had hungered for – was like the flesh of their herd animals, the trolls. These were kobolds, and it seemed there was little difference between them and the rocks in which they lived.

The kobold leader was taller than the rest, and his elaborate half-mask helmet, crested with a golden bear emblem, made him taller yet. It had been formed from plates of black iron decorated with silver intaglio, and it was held together in a steel cage trimmed with silver wire. His ringmail armour glinted and flickered in the unsteady light from the cabin lantern, and so did the long beard that gave him his name – Eisenbardt, the iron-beard. Volker suspected it was more a description than a nickname.

'*Customers*, are you?' Eisenbardt made it sound like a dirty word. 'I'll give you customers!' He banged a stubby fist on the oaken chart-table, and splinters flew as the silver torcs on his wrists jangled in answer. 'What about Skirvi then? And Finn? And Yngvi?'

Volker felt anger surge up inside him, but this was no place for it. The *Walfisch*, crewed now by Eisenbardt's kobolds, was still being poled through the underground tunnel: although the cabin curtains were drawn, Volker could smell the pine torches that lit the towpath on either side. Thorgrim and Guy were imprisoned below decks, with the rest of the crew. The merchants were on the other barge. Dani he had not seen; the kobolds seemed to be keeping her as a hostage. It was a time for diplomacy – which was going to be difficult . . .

'I say we kill him, the way we'd kill any Helspawn enchanter,' said a long-faced, reddish-coloured cutthroat who seemed to be gnawing a lump of coal. 'I say we chip the skin off the stinking elf piece by piece and hang him in the waterfall till he's smoothed to a pebble.'

'Quiet, Skeldi,' growled Eisenbardt. 'Eisenbardt Kungri is the Brynjesson; I say what happens to the elf, not you.'

Volker sighed. Useless to tell them he wasn't an elf; they could all but smell his father's blood, and that made him automatically suspect. His only hope was to reason with them.

'I've told you once. I'll tell you again. We didn't know your trolls were there. They stampeded, and we had to protect ourselves.'

'And I suppose the petrocane tried to rip out your throat, hey?'

'Petrocane?' Volker was genuinely baffled.

'*Petrus canis*,' said Eisenbardt, in mock-scholarly tones. 'A rockhound, you ignorant troll's byblow.'

Volker bridled. 'Look, none of us had ever *seen* a what-d'you-call it – petrocane – and you must admit, he certainly had teeth. You may have noticed we're a good deal softer than you.'

'Hah! Revolting bags of filthy water, killing harmless animals—'

'Look, we've already agreed a price for the petrocane. We have other things to talk about!'

'Yes. We do.' The kobold thrust its chisel-like face aggressively into Volker's. '*Like where your friends are*!'

'Friends?'

'Don't play the innocent, you schist-head. Your assassins. Your little army. You'd better tell me, unless you want your friend with the long grass on her head fed to the petrocanes!'

It was too much for Volker. 'So *that*'s your game, you pebble-brained moron! Well, we haven't seen your missing thugs – but if they're anything like you they're probably out robbing a couple of unarmed cripples.'

To his amazement Eisenbardt began to chuckle, revealing a set of hideously splayed crystalline teeth. Before long the kobold leader was literally shaking with laughter, his breath emerging in hoarse, croaking gasps that soon infected most of his followers.

So that's *what Ulrich meant – 'Do there as you are done by'!*

'So,' said Eisenbardt, wiping a sticky looking tear from his eye. 'So, you waterfall of troll's-piss, you have a tongue after all.'

'Perhaps,' remarked Skeldi, 'we should chisel it down to size – a piece at a time.'

'Let's try it with yours first,' Volker riposted, warming to his theme. 'Pluto knows it's long enough.'

'Listen, elf-get,' said Eisenbardt. 'Never mind the fine talk. We all know why you're here – you *and* the rest. Rich enough to take good food and *burn* it to warm your slimy bodies.'

So they do *eat coal . . .*

'Or maybe it's the cutstones you're after. Years to train the beasts, months to find a vein, weeks to dig it out – and all your wet-arsed females can think to do with them is stick them on their fingers.'

They eat diamonds, too? For one glorious moment Volker had a vision of trolls tearing through solid rock like truffle-hounds on the scent – and grubbing out diamonds for a kobold's feast. He laughed. 'You're a fine one to accuse *us* of robbery. A rockbrain like you could never have built this canal. I reckon you stole it from a *real* engineer.'

This shaft was less successful, producing a stony silence. Obviously he had much to learn about kobold diplomacy; either that or he'd hit on the truth. Eisenbardt's metallic beard crackled with fury as he gripped his huge double-headed tomahawk in both hands and thrust its steel-spiked tip towards Volker, emphasizing each word with a vicious jab at his midriff. '*I am the true Brynjesson, you point-eared huldra-whore's bastard*!'

'Meaning,' said Volker, with more courage than he felt, 'that you *killed* the true Brynjesson?'

'It was a fair contest,' hissed Eisenbardt. 'And he was a fool. Him and his *democratia*! Kobolds want a strong leader, not a talking shop. Such a great Brynjesson, who would not be king! Such a great general, who would rather barter than fight! Such a great engineer, who could not finish the Bridge!'

Volker's brain was spinning. Obviously 'Brynjesson' was some kind of hereditary title, and his lucky guess had been right – Eisenbardt *had* killed the last Brynjesson, and taken his place. It was clear that *this* Brynjesson had no plans whatsoever to trade with anyone he could fight. Ulrich's plan had gone badly awry.

Got to think of something . . .

Yes. That gibe about engineering had hit a weak spot. Perhaps, after all, the worst work was the most recent. In which case Eisenbardt had stolen the title, but not the skill, of his rival . . .

'I'm better than he ever was,' raved Eisenbardt. 'Forgotten more than he ever knew!'

Sideways looks between the kobolds suggested this might be rather to one side of the truth. Eisenbardt stopped in mid-sentence, suddenly aware of how much he had given away. His wide, steel-grey eyes fixed on Volker with a predatory stare. 'You're a sly little rat, elf-get – but we don't hold with sly in these parts. If you're so clever, tell me how come you're here. There's none knows about Brynje's Bridge but the kobolds!'

'What about—?' He bit his lip. He'd been about to mention Ulrich, but he didn't trust Eisenbardt further than he could throw him – him or any other very large rock. Was he simply an ambitious kobold? Or was he more than that – perhaps, even, an agent of Tartarus? 'What about that spell on your outer defences?'

With a growl, Eisenbardt shot from his creaking chair, grabbed Volker's doublet, and thrust his stone-chill, protruding chin into the young man's face.

'*What do you know about that?*'

The time had come to stretch the truth a little. 'I

know it was there, and I know it's gone – because we destroyed it.'

For a moment Skeldi looked startled. Then, almost at once, he looked furiously angry. 'Ten of us,' he rumbled. '*Ten* of us turned to *dust*! Lifted it, did you, elf-get? Cast it, more like! I say we kill him, Kungri – *now*!'

Here goes nothing. Let's hope Ulrich got this much right . . .

'Do that and you'll never finish the Bridge,' said Volker levelly. 'You've had a lot of trouble – and we're the only chance you've got to stop it.'

Eisenbardt opened his mouth, closed it again, and narrowed his eyes. 'We guard our secrets well, elf-get, and you know more than you've any right to know . . .'

'Maybe I have – well, let's say "other helpers".'

The kobold nodded slowly. 'And there we have you, troll-turd! I *knew* there were more of you!'

Volker made a creditable attempt to look annoyed. 'Very well. I won't say it isn't true. And I think you'll agree it puts things in another light. We don't want much for our trouble – we aren't mercenaries. Get us across the mountains, and we'll get rid of your curse.'

'So,' rumbled Eisenbardt, 'you want to cross the Riesenmesser, eh? And then you'll get rid of the curse, which you probably laid, anyway. Thing is, petrocane-breath, we don't care for magic here, and I don't trust you.'

'It's mutual,' said Volker. 'So we'd better talk terms, hadn't we?'

'You made terms? With *them*?'

'Dani, there was nothing else I could do.'

She gestured angrily at the landscape around them, as if that in itself explained her fury, and the owl fluttered its wings in annoyance. Following the sweep of her arm, Volker still found the view almost impossible

195

to take in, although the *Walross* and the *Walfisch* had now been crossing the lake for nearly two hours.

Behind them, half-screened by yet another giant lock, lay the tunnel exit. Far above it Volker could just see the sequence of locks and channels that funnelled water from the high peaks into a holding reservoir. From there an elaborate control system fed the artificial waterfall at the northern entrance. To the left and right the fangs of the Singing Mountains stood sentinel, their shadowed faces brooding and dark like crouching dragons. To the south, a grandiose sequence of locks climbed towards a saddle-shaped peak known as Reginn's Seat. Beyond it, still blue with distance, was a ridge the kobolds called the Giant's Knife, the one Ulrich had mentioned in his cryptic note.

It was well named – an all but vertical wall of rock, thousands of feet high, linking two gigantic peaks called the Riesenfäuste, the Giant's Fists. Against such a back-drop even the mightiest engineering work should have looked insignificant, but the kobolds had built on a scale that matched the challenge, making each structure a grotesque work of art. The landscape was littered with giants, dragons, hybrids and monsters, frozen in stone and half-concealing the winches, sluice gates, cranes and water wheels that made up Brynje's Bridge.

'You know what they *did* to me?' asked Dani.

'You told me. Iron chains. Not exactly subtle. But they didn't torture you – they just *told* me that they had. I don't think they're as tough as they want me to believe.'

'They're . . . They've . . . This is . . . It's obscene!' She glared at him with fanatical intensity. 'What they've done here is an outrage against the Mother . . . against Flora . . . against all that's proper and right!'

'I can see how it might offend you, but—'

'*Offend*! Use your eyes, Volker!'

'I *am* using them.'

At this height the mountains were featureless slabs of rock; heaps of loose scree all around the lake showed where they were slowly sliding into the water. Here and there he could see darker gashes where the kobolds had quarried rock for building, or cut mines to retrieve metal ores. Dotted about the lakeside were a series of foundries and workshops, each belching its own cloud of coloured smoke. There were few trees, and those he could see were stunted, their leaves strangely tinted. Even the grass was thin and yellow. It was not an attractive place, but . . .

'I'm sorry,' said Dani, still struggling to control her anger. 'I'd forgotten you can't see it as I do. Close your eyes a moment.'

'What?'

'Trust me. Concentrate on what you've seen.'

'I don't—'

Cool fingers touched his eyelids as she stepped behind him, and the owl's wings brushed his hair. No point in protesting – besides, she was standing pleasantly close. Concentrate on what he had seen? Why not . . . ?

He gasped in astonishment. It was just like looking at a painting, but this was a moving painting in three dimensions, complete with the sounds and smells of the original subject. He was in the midst of a small lake, glittering in the westering sun, its waters so clear that he could all but count the pebbles on the bottom. Birdsong and the plash of falling water echoed all around. Dark against the fleecy clouds, an eagle watching for fish circled lazily on a rising spiral of warm air. On every side, scented pine forests climbed towards hardshadowed peaks . . .

The hands withdrew. The vision vanished. As he opened his eyes he seemed to feel a pang of loss.

'*Now* do you understand?' she whispered. 'That is

what was – what should have been. They've made it a desert. And you're going to *help them!*'

He nodded slowly. 'Yes. Because otherwise we'll never cross the mountains. We don't have time to hesitate or turn back. If we do, we might as well go back to Regensburg and give those Tartarist animals the horn.'

'There has to be another way across!'

'I doubt that very much.'

'You trust these kobolds?'

'Not an inch – and the feeling's mutual. Thorgrim reckons they're planning some kind of invasion; they seem to think that anyone who burns coal must have more wealth than they know what to do with—'

'Why?'

'Apparently they *eat* coal – and these days they need diamonds to dig it out. Thorgrim's taken a hate to them, but that doesn't mean he's wrong. He keeps saying he can feel magic – which is strange, because Eisenbardt keeps telling me the only kind of magic a kobold likes to use is something called *el gibber*. Something from the far south, he said – Araby, perhaps.'

'What about the merchants?'

'Goldfüss and Beck are worried about the price of the crossing, but my imaginary army should make a good bargaining counter. Haagen's wondering if I handled things properly, but he wasn't there, and I was. And whatever's really going on, only the kobolds can get us across the Knife. So I have to stand by the bargain. They help us, we help them. By all the gods, I hope we can!'

Dani's shrug as she turned away and leaned on the gunwale was all too expressive. He felt as lonely as he had in the cabin, confronted with a mob of angry kobolds. But that was part of the burden that Ulrich had laid on him, part of being a leader.

Which didn't make it any easier.

198

It took another day to bring the barges to the crest of Reginn's Seat, and every hour increased Volker's unwilling admiration for the kobold engineers. Each lock, each lift, demonstrated their mastery of some new skill. The folded arms of a sculpted giant opened outwards, revealing that the robes themselves were sluicegates. Two hideous trolls, frozen in the act of a somersault, became counterweights, rolling down a steep slope to haul the barges to the next level. A chimera concealed huge water-driven winches controlling three cables, one in each of its serpentine heads. Eisenbardt took pleasure in explaining these devices, though it was soon clear that he knew less about them than he pretended. But while he remained grimly on his dignity, some of his followers began to relax a little. Although Dani insisted on staying below, Thorgrim seemed to be dropping his guard, and Guy was soon swapping drinks, dirty stories and imaginative insults with the kobolds. Joachim, too, was delighted to find an audience for the kind of tall tales that only engineers could appreciate. Volker had seen little of the merchants, but it seemed that only Haagen and Goldfüss were equipped for the verbal duelling involved in normal kobold conversation. Beck had refused to be drawn, and Diderik had retired to his cabin muttering something about fat-headed midgets.

But it was only when they crested the first ridge that Volker realised just how much the kobolds had already achieved.

The deeply shadowed chasm that separated Reginn's Seat from the Riesenmesser – the Giant's Knife – seemed to plunge down into the very roots of the mountain. Volker grew dizzy simply looking at it, his eyes drawn irresistibly downwards by dozens of ribboning, rainbowed waterfalls. The river far below was all but lost in their spray, and the gorge echoed with the tumult of their fall. Yet across this crack in the world stretched a slender thread of silver some three feet wide, glittering with reflected light . . .

He shook his head, trying to understand what he was seeing. Only water could throw back light in that peculiar way, water brushed by a gentle breeze. He felt his skin prickle with fear. Was that the secret the kobolds were so anxious to protect? Some vast enchantment to make a twenty-foot wide canal hang unsupported in mid-air? And this from a race that had no truck with magic? He glanced towards Thorgrim, but the Norseman's face showed the same dumbfounded amazement as his own.

Volker looked again, muttering the usual charms for clear sight. The ribbon of silver was still there – it was not an illusion. But now he saw other things that his ignorance and the rising mist had concealed. On either side of the water was a slender stone rail. Rising from that rail was a series of black cords, cords that grew into gigantic wrought-iron chains as they passed above his head to embed themselves deep in the rock of Reginn's Seat. And below the canal, on the far side, he could see part of a massive stone arch rooted in the wall of the gorge, and writhing with the elaborate sculpture that was the hallmark of kobold craftsmanship.

'You are honoured, troll-dropping,' said Eisenbardt. 'You are the first human in fifty generations to see Brynje's Bridge.'

Volker said nothing. True, the bridge carried the canal clear across the gorge – but the far end came to an abrupt halt a thousand feet or more below the Knife's jagged summit, deep in the shadow of the ridge. There must be a tunnel, then . . .

No. Not a tunnel. Something else, something half-concealed by the mist and the lowering shadow of the Giant's Knife above. The Armorican seemed riveted to the eyepiece of his telescope.

'What *is* that?' muttered Volker.

By way of an answer, de Guillac handed him the telescope. For a moment Volker could see nothing – the focus was wrong for him. He fumbled with the brass tubes, catching blurred images of wheel-like structures and massive cables. Then, quite clearly, he made out the silhouette of a kobold against one of the wheels, like a busy ant, and behind the kobold, the shimmering silver curtain of a waterfall, apparently inside the cliff. Nothing made sense. Every movement of the telescope produced a new image that seemed to have no connection with anything else he had seen. There were two huge wheels, each with a waterfall behind it. Above them was a crouching hydra with cables emerging from its nine gape-jawed heads. Below the hydra was a metal basket. And inside the basket was a forty-foot barge, moving slowly upwards.

Eisenbardt grinned. 'That, elf-get, is Eisenbardt's Lift. The Bridge may be Brynje's. But the Lift – the Lift is mine!'

Thorgrim raised his eyes towards the seemingly inattentive gods, and there were one or two murmurs from Eisenbardt's own kobolds. De Guillac smiled faintly. 'It reflects your engaging personality. But what exactly do you hope to accomplish with it?'

'Accomplish?' growled Eisenbardt. '*Accomplish*, you wine-soused halfwit? I show you the heart of my kingdom and the wonder of the world, and you ask what I will *accomplish* with it?'

'Exactly,' said the Armorican, and for a moment Eisenbardt seemed at a loss for words.

'It's a fine work,' said a familiar voice at Volker's back.

'Joachim? You know about this?'

'I've 'eard a thing or two, Master Volker.' Eisenbardt gave the bombardier's waist a look that should have set his hose alight, but Joachim was unstoppable. 'You understand, sir, that all the easiest coal seams – nearest the surface, that is – are long gone. Our friends here have dug so deep that the tunnels'd fill with water if they weren't pumped – and those great wheels there, they drive the pumps.'

'So why the Bridge – or the Lift, come to that?'

'The coal's little use where it is, Master Volker. It must be taken to—'

'*Take that foul-smelling waterbug away*!' roared Eisenbardt. 'I want the names of all who spoke to him! I'll see them *pulverized*! And as for *you* elf-get – remember the terms of our bargain!'

Volker engineered a smile. 'You don't seem too keen on bargains, Eisenbardt. After all, your people built the Bridge so they could trade with the Empire—'

Eisenbardt laughed. 'Sell the work of fifty generations? I think not. The kobolds will hold their own – and *take* what they need!'

'You cannot hold even your own gates,' growled Thorgrim, looking strangely pale.

'But you,' said Skeldi silkily, 'you can hold your tongue – or we shall see if you manage better without it.'

The Norseman did not seem to hear him. Beads of sweat were standing out on his brow. Puzzled, Volker glanced down, and immediately wished he hadn't. The *Walross* was passing through the sluice gates at the head of Brynje's Bridge, with the *Walfisch* close behind. That much was comforting and familiar – but now, gliding out across the bridge, the near side of the chasm seemed to drop away and down into the mists of eternity.

'Feeling sick, Grim?'

The Norseman shook his head. 'There is something near,' he muttered. 'I feel it.'

What had Ulrich said? *Beware – evil haunts the bridge at the Giant's Knife*. Volker glanced swiftly around, but what he saw now drove all other thoughts out of his mind. Below the bridge, to right and left, a vista was unfolding, a sprawling complex of ditches, abutments, fortifications, and stone-carvings. It seemed like the product of a dozen different intelligences, each trying – and spectacularly failing – to tackle the same problem. As the barges slid gently into the shadow of the Riesen-messer, and the glare of reflected sunlight from the water grew less, Volker began to make out the individual designs. There was an early version of Eisen-bardt's lift, half-ruined, its wrought-iron basket lying at a crazy angle on a shelf some five hundred feet down the cliff. An elaborate series of stepped locks, dry and empty now, zig-zagged down the cliff to the left, ending abruptly in mid-air on the brink of a crumbling wall of rock. He found his unwilling eyes drawn downward, past jagged outcrops and shattered blocks of masonry, into the shadowed depths of the gorge . . .

There was something down there – no, several things. In the mist and darkness it was difficult to see them, but Volker had a good idea what they might be, and the very thought turned his stomach. The merchants had noticed them as well – he could see them gesturing and arguing on the foredeck of the *Walfisch*. And Eisenbardt looked even more uncomfortable than Volker felt. After all, it was hardly an advertisement for kobold engineering.

'Eisenbardt . . . What *is* that?'

'Old workings,' snapped the kobold. 'Not important.'

'If they're not important, tell me about the wrecked barges at the bottom of the gorge.'

'Experiments,' said the kobold evasively.

'Ulrich was right,' growled Thorgrim. 'Your *Heljadomt* bridge is cursed!'

'Ulrich!' roared Eisenbardt. '*Ulrich*? What do you know of Ulrich?'

Volker glared at Thorgrim, but the damage was already done. 'Ulrich told us of the Bridge,' he said. 'As he told many others. Your secret is out, Eisenbardt.'

'They are tricksters, Eisenbardt,' said Skeldi, 'tricksters and renegades. I saw this Ulrich, and he is like all his kind – greedy and self-seeking. If they have stolen his knowledge, be sure they have kept it for themselves, as he did.'

Volker moved across to the rail to win a few seconds to think, but the gunwale of the *Walross* was high enough to conceal the balustrade of the Bridge, and he found himself looking straight down into the dizzying depths of the gorge. It was like standing at the edge of the world. He shut his eyes, trying to concentrate.

'Well, elf-get?'

'We have stolen nothing. Ulrich sent us himself, because he knew your need – and knew that we could meet it.'

'So,' said Eisenbardt, 'if this is true, you tell *me* what happened down there.' He gestured towards the abandoned workings.

Volker opened his mouth, but Thorgrim was there first: 'A thing comes out of Tartarus. It moves the ground, like an earthquake. It destroys your work. Not once – many times.'

Several kobolds nodded, and Volker gave a silent cheer. Either Thorgrim's talent was working overtime or the Norseman, like Joachim, had been talking to renegade kobolds. Eisenbardt, however, did not seem impressed. 'You have good spies, elf-get. Or maybe you sent the earthquake beast yourself?'

'We knew nothing of it till now,' said Volker.

'Then you are liars, orc-dung,' sneered Skeldi. 'If Ulrich had truly sent you, he would have spoken of it.'

'He knew only of a danger to the Bridge. He wasn't sure what it was.'

Eisenbardt nodded. 'So much is true. I was there. The Brynjesson told him nothing.'

'Stubborn fool that he was,' added Skeldi.

Volker thought fast. 'And now you're going to make

the same mistake,' he said. 'If you don't tell us more, we can't help you.'

'Why tell you anything, elf-get?' growled Eisenbardt. 'We know well enough that you come only to take the little wealth we have. And we have only your word that you *can* help us.'

'You don't have to trust me,' said Volker. 'You have my companions as hostages.'

Eisenbardt frowned. 'We speak more of this later. You, the hairball and the wine-keg, into the cabin now. Hervi, get the owl-brain girl from the hold. She should stay with the other offal.'

'They are magicians!' protested Skeldi. 'We must keep them here, on deck, where we can see them!'

'Into the cabin, I said! Skeldi, you forget your place. You, elf-get, we take your barges over the Knife. That is our bargain. After that, you will do your part, and we will see if you speak truth. If you fail, then army or no army, you and your friends will die.'

'And here,' said de Guillac, 'is another fine mess you've got us into, my hairy friend.' His voice was a little slurred. The merchant's cabin had an excellent wine rack, and Guy had done it somewhat more than justice. Thorgrim, concentrating on the view, said nothing. While the *Walfisch* waited its turn, the *Walross* was being manoeuvred around an artificial pool the size of a market square cantilevered out from the face of the Riesenmesser like a scholar's bookshelf. To their left, Brynje's Bridge stretched its thread of silver across the gorge, its suspension chains soaring high above their heads to their fixing points in the cliff face. To their right the winch-house towered above them, with the massive drive wheels deep in the shadows on either side. The iron cradle had already been lowered to carry the barge on the next stage of its journey – a thousand feet straight up.

'*Espèce d'escargot*,' muttered Guy darkly, still glaring at Thorgrim. '*Cochon. Merde du pape*'

'Leave him alone,' said Volker. 'It doesn't help. Thorgrim, you are *sure* of this?'

The Norseman bowed his head. 'There is much discontent. The old Brynjesson promised a new order – trade with the Empire, and profits for all his people.'

'So what happened?'

'Eisenbardt and the army feared for their wealth and privileges. So they toppled the Brynjesson – over the Bridge, most likely – and set Eisenbardt in his place. Skeldi was his lieutenant, and now he is chief inquisitor.'

'And the gates? What happened there?'

'What you saw. Deep, dark sorcery – and such power as only Tartarus can summon. To make a living creature that preys on the stone-folk . . .'

'Who could do that?'

'I cannot say. But there *is* such power – here, in this place, now.'

'Meaning?'

'There is a mage here . . . and he is a kobold.'

'A *kobold*? But . . .'

'*Ja*, they say that they have no magic. This one, he has magic.'

Anja frowned. 'If you're right, then this kobold mage of yours set a monster to prey on his own people . . .'

'Exactly,' said Volker. 'To keep them away from the gate. To stop them trading with the Empire. To keep the power he'd stolen. It *has* to be Eisenbardt! Thorgrim, surely you can . . . ?'

'*Naeh*. I cannot tell. They stay too close together.'

'But this mage – he is on board?'

'*Ja*.'

'In that case . . . A sudden lurch cut short Volker's words, and thoughts. The landscape was moving down past the windows in a series of uneven spasms. It was not an encouraging sight, even from inside the cabin.

'If our enemy is here,' said Dani, apparently unconcerned, 'then he must act soon. He knows Thorgrim can sniff him out, and he knows we have magic of our own. That makes us a threat.'

'Then we should move now,' said Volker, 'and start the party ourselves.'

'We're already thirty feet up,' Dani reminded him, 'and the door happens to be locked.'

'The boy is right,' said Thorgrim. 'The *Heljadomt* mage is calling for help.'

Volker gulped. 'What kind of help?'

'Not a demon.'

'The gods be praised—'

'Something worse.'

Dani's eyebrows arched upwards. '*Worse*?'

'*Ja*. The thing I spoke of. The earthquake beast.'

'You feel it?' said Volker.

'*You* feel it,' replied Thorgrim.

'What do you mean . . . ?' Volker's words died in his throat. It was true. There was a trembling in the deck beneath his feet that had nothing to do with the lurching ascent of the cradle, as though someone on the other side of the ridge were playing a deep bass note on an organ the size of a mountain. From the chorus of yells and shouts outside, it was clear that the kobolds had noticed it, too.

''Shtime to leave the party,' said Guy, moving his hands in a series of rapid passes. Nothing happened. He looked questioning at his own hands, shrugged, kicked open the door, and stumbled out, followed by Dani and Thorgrim. As Volker reached the door he heard a roar of surprise and anger from the kobolds – and then, with a violent lurch, the jerky upward motion of the cradle came to a full stop, throwing Eisenbardt and a dozen others to the deck. In the stillness that

207

followed, Volker could hear the steel cables above his head vibrating with a deep, thrumming note that seemed to penetrate his very bones.

'What—?' he began.

'The beast,' said Thorgrim. 'For good or ill it is here, Volker. Now you must do your part.'

'But—'

'*You!*' roared Skeldi, pointing a trembling hand at Volker. 'You are the mage! You have summoned the beast! Kill him!'

Volker found himself surrounded by a forest of drawn weapons – and at the same moment there was a deafening crash from below, and the barge trembled in its cradle as cries of alarm echoed across the gorge. De Guillac took advantage of the distraction to grab a hammer from one of the kobolds.

'*Foi de Guillac*, but thish – this ish none of our doing! Anyone comes closer, I make him shorter by a – shorter than he is already!'

The cradle lurched again, and this time there was an echoing crack somewhere above their heads as one of the cables parted under the strain. A whiplash of steel flicked across the deck, cutting one of the crewmen cleanly in two and slicing a kobold's head from its body. Blood and ichor streamed down the deck as the *Walross*'s bows seemed to drop away into the abyss. The remaining cables took the strain with a savage jolt that left the barge tilted at a crazy angle, nose down. Thorgrim, taking advantage of the moment, dived head-first towards the deck, flipped, somersaulted, and struck Skeldi squarely in the midriff – but the impact cost him his control, and he tumbled helplessly into the bows in a tangle of arms and legs. Dani, thrown forward in the same way, grabbed at a rope, swung sideways with her legs outstretched, and toppled two kobolds who were threatening Volker. De Guillac, roaring lustily, clung to the mast with one hand while the

hammer, flaring now with a bright yellow flame, outlined the pattern of his guard in a web of blinding light.
Volker, caught by surprise like everyone else, clung to
the open door. Far below he could see the rocks and
boulders that the beast had dislodged hurtling down
on to the *Walfisch* – and then bouncing and tumbling
out and down into the chasm beyond. The sight was
mesmerizing. He seemed to feel himself falling with
them, down, ever downward, for all eternity . . .

Something struck his cheek with painful force, and
the taste of blood filled his mouth. The shock made him
lose his grip, and he rolled head over heels down the
deck after Thorgrim. Dani grabbed for him, but his
fingers slipped through hers. Other, hostile hands
clutched at him as he slithered past, and one found the
strap of his horn-case. For a moment it held him, and
a hedge of hammers and blades flashed towards him;
then, with a groaning crack, the strap gave way, and
he tumbled helter-skelter into the bows, bruising his
ribs against the bombard before he slid past it, down,
and clean over the rail into the abyss. He yelled in
terror, and yelled again as a steely grip fastened itself
around his ankle. A torrent of stone was falling up and
away from him, while high above tiny inverted figures
ran and fell, cascades of water showered towards him
to fall back up into the clouds, and a child's toy barge
drifted upside down across the sky until it was hidden
by a jutting outcrop.

'Not so fast,' growled Thorgrim, grabbing his other
ankle. 'You leave too soon, you spoil the fun for us.'

'Not . . . my idea . . . of fun,' gasped Volker. 'All the
gods . . . Grim . . . *get me up*!'

'The horn. Use it!'

'*I've lost it*!'

'I think maybe I drop you.'

'Don't . . . even . . . joke about it,' groaned Volker
as the Norseman dragged him back into the shelter

of the bombard. The cradle was trembling even more violently, and to Volker's scattered wits it seemed that the whole world was trembling with it. 'Is our kobold-mage doing that?'

'*Ja* – but I am not sure which he is.' Casually Thorgrim picked one of the small cannonballs from the racking next to them and hurled it at a kobold trying to climb down towards them. It hopped grotesquely backwards, clutching its foot with one hand and the rigging with the other while it screamed an unlikely series of allegations about the Norseman's ancestry, birth and sexual preferences.

'Not him,' said Thorgrim, reaching for another cannonball. Volker grinned, despite himself. 'My wager's still on Eisenbardt,' he said.

'Not mine. I try for the horn now.'

'How?'

'Like so.' Thorgrim hefted the cannonball, sighted carefully, and let fly. He was rewarded with a yell of pain, but nothing else; the kobold clung obstinately to the horn-case, howling inventive insults at the Norseman. Luckily he was too preoccupied to notice the warning shouts from his companions as Dani let go of her rope and slid ungracefully down the deck, snatching the case as she passed. She hit the bombard with a sickening thump and swore feelingly.

'Lucky you wear leather hose,' remarked Volker, catching the horn.

'And well padded,' smirked Thorgrim.

By now several of the kobolds were making their way down towards the prow, urged on by Eisenbardt. Skeldi clung to a windlass, glaring down at them. De Guillac was still fending off three opponents, though none seemed anxious to engage him – they simply hung on to any convenient hold and bombarded him with highly coloured language. Dani's owl was perched in the rigging, sulking over its interrupted sleep.

'Volker,' said Dani, discouraging a persistent kobold with a well-aimed marlin spike, 'if you're going to use the horn, now would be a good time.'

He nodded, raising it to his lips – and then the blood seemed to freeze in his veins. The shouts around him, the creaking of the over-stressed cables, the crash and rumble of falling rock from below, all slowed to a deep, throbbing pulse almost below the threshold of hearing. Muscles and tendons grated and locked as if transmuted into marble – even the slightest movement was beyond him, and his cry of warning froze on his lips. To his left, Thorgrim moved with glacial slowness, seemingly unaware of what had happened; to his right, Dani was a living statue. The kobolds, too, looked like figures from a carnival wax museum, their movements barely perceptible. Skeldi, balanced against the windlass, seemed petrified, his eyes fixed on Volker, his hands twisted in a curious, stabbing gesture . . .

Abruptly, as though a shutter had been drawn across his sight and suddenly withdrawn, his senses flooded back in a rush of conflicting, confusing images. It was as though a minute had been neatly cut out of his life, and in that minute everything had changed. The deck was pitched at an even more hair-raising angle, and trembled like a whale in torment. Skeldi was clutching desperately at the gunwale, his wildly sliding feet leaving a long black stain on the planking. Dani was struggling with one of the kobolds; the rest were hanging on for dear life. Thorgrim was still throwing ammunition, mostly at Skeldi, and yelling, 'It is him, the spellcaster! Stop him!'

'I *have* stopped him, *espèce d'idiot*,' roared Guy. 'Volker is free!'

Volker shook his head: strange after-images were still drifting across his vision, though he could guess now what had happened. The kobold-mage, too, had known a petrefaction spell – and Volker, unlike the kobolds, had not been born to feed on coal. Luckily Guy had seen what was happening, but now Volker had his own battle to fight. He reached for the horn.

It had gone.

In that lost minute someone had snatched it from his nerveless hand – or perhaps it had slipped, fallen to join the rocks and stones still cascading down the face of the Knife as the earthquake beast obeyed Skeldi's commands. But there was no time to think of that now. A foul-smelling black liquid dribbled from Skeldi's lips, followed by a ribbon of flame that flared into a blinding conflagration. At the same moment a sudden darkness enveloped the *Walross*.

'It's raining!' yelled Eisenbardt in a voice of pure disbelief.

It was true. Skeldi's fireball fizzled and died as a miniature cloudburst scoured the barge's deck and swept two of the kobolds from their precarious handholds to tumble headlong into the gorge. As Volker once again blinked away violet and green after-images he could see Guy's hands still moving in a measured series of passes. In this duel of magic his drink-enhanced speed and power was at least the equal of Skeldi's; indeed, he seemed to find it all highly amusing, though the fusillade of raindrops all but drowned his laughter – and Dani's despairing cry.

'Volker! Volker, you mush-brained elf, stop watching the show and help me! He's got the horn!'

Thorgrim raised his eyebrows and grinned hugely. 'Not one word,' said Volker reprovingly, scrambling up past the bombard. Dani and her kobold opponent were wrestling furiously as each tried to break the other's grip on the ammunition racking. Neither saw Volker, and as luck would have it Dani kicked him squarely in the face as she struggled for a new foothold. Bleeding – and half-stunned – he still managed to grab her opponent's leg and pull it just as the priestess shattered the kobold's fingers with one of the cannonballs. The creature howled in agony, and the horn-case clattered past Volker's outstretched hand, clanged against the bombard, and bounced up into the air.

'Hel's *teeth*!' yelled Volker, and slipped his hold, sliding down the deck in a shower of spray and doubling up his legs. With a desperate effort he kicked against the bombard, using the force of his fall to catapult himself up and after the case, only to feel it slip through his fingers as he tumbled towards the bow. This time, though, he was ready. He snatched at the rail, felt one hand slide on the wet, polished wood, and gripped hard with the other, almost wrenching his arm from its socket as it took the full weight of his body. Gingerly he pulled himself back on board, favouring his right arm. Guy's magical rainstorm was still in full spate, but the Armorican was in trouble. Three of the kobolds were clambering up the port and starboard rails like demented spiders, screaming and swinging their hammers. From Skeldi's laughter it was clear they were under his control, and equally clear that Guy had no wish to harm them.

'Here,' said Thorgrim, throwing Volker the horn-case.

'You . . . you . . .'

'Use it! Later we talk!'

With no time even to think, Volker wrenched open the case, put the horn to his lips and sounded it – a long, low note, in tingling counterpoint to the shuddering vibration of the earthquake beast. Cables thrummed in answer like the strings of a giant's cittern, holding that first sound as Volker blew the second and third notes of a thundering arpeggio that reverberated up and down the gorge. The echoes seemed to grow and redouble, creating a monstrous chord that held the very mountain in thrall. Its power swept away Skeldi's controlling magic like powdered snow on a glacier. The kobold-mage whirled round to face him, gaping in amazement, sticky black liquid trailing from his mouth as he drew breath for a second, devastating fireball. Volker could see the mail-clad chest heave, expand – and freeze. Skeldi's eyes widened in horror. Dark, smoking froth bubbled from his nose and the corners of his eyes. His chest seemed immovable as the mountain – and then, quite slowly, the brutal, chisel-shaped face seemed to fold in upon itself, and the body beneath it warped and twisted like a child's wax doll on a bonfire. The mouth stretched into a mirthless, slit-like grin – and Skeldi's head disappeared in a hissing, leaping explosion of flame as he slumped sideways and over the rail with Guy's hammer buried to the shaft in his back.

Volker barely noticed. The chord he had created was growing still, with a life of its own, echoing and re-echoing across the chasm until the sky rang with its power, and kobolds and humans alike were clamping their hands over their ears to shut it out. Even the cliff-face behind them seemed to shiver at the sound—

With a doomsday roar the face of the rock burst open, and a writhing, dark-stained shape thrust itself into the light. Its head seemed to grow outward like an opening flower, revealing a blinding red glow from within – and against it the falling silhouette of Skeldi's shattered body. The flower snapped shut, and with a discordant howl that almost shook the barge from its cradle the earthquake beast slid back inside the mountain, down to the punishing, eternal fires from which it had come.

For a dozen heartbeats Guy stared blankly at the blackened, empty hole below – and then sagged to his knees. Thorgrim, moving to help him, stepped on the dark stain that was Skeldi's last memorial, slipped, and sat down heavily. 'What is this *forbandede* stuff?'

Guy smiled weakly. '*Akvavit* for kobolds. *Petrum oleum*, or as you would call it—'

214

'Stone oil. I also have some learning. You are saying—?'

'The kobold-mage, he was like myself. But stronger. If it had not been for Volker—'

Thorgrim grinned wolfishly. 'Stronger?' he said. 'Not so. You, I think, have a better head for your drink.'

The sun was sinking above the Riesenfäuste before a kobold repair crew completed the awesome task of recabling the dangling cradle and hauling the *Walross* the rest of the way up the Knife. The *Walfisch*, still waiting in the holding tank at the end of Brynje's Bridge, had suffered some damage – and three casualties – during the attack of the earthquake beast, but the kobolds worked hard and fast, and it reached the clifftop just as the sun was setting.

The atmosphere on board was strained and mostly silent. Volker had fondly imagined that Eisenbardt's kobolds would see what he had done to them, and oust him on the spot. Clearly he and Skeldi had worked together, barring the gateway to the empire with a grisly sending. The earthquake beast which Skeldi controlled had served as a universal threat to unite the kobolds under Eisenbardt's rule – and to provide them with a never-ending source of work. But the wily Eisenbardt had been the first to attack his co-conspirator – and Skeldi was in no position to defend himself.

'And now,' growled Eisenbardt, 'there is the matter of reparations.'

Volker opened his mouth, but nothing much seemed to come out. He could hardly have been more surprised if the kobold leader had transformed himself into a hippogriff, but before he could say anything at all Dani was on the attack.

'*Reparations*, you miserable Helspawn midget? For destroying an enchanter you were too stupid to see standing right next to you? For getting rid of the earthquake beast? For breaking the spells on your fortress? *Reparations*! You should get down on your knees . . . !'

'Your woman talks too much,' said Eisenbardt flatly. 'You should control her. We have excellent devices to silence unruly females. Now, you beardless mage-brat, what reparations do you give for the killing of my men?'

This time Dani was left speechless – there were too many things she wanted to say. Only Thorgrim seemed unsurprised, plunging into the awkward silence with careless confidence.

'You wish *weregelt*? That is good, that you care for your kin. But we, too, we care for our people – and we have lost good men. What reparation for them, when it was one you took as your own who killed them?'

'You speak of the mage?'

'I speak of your henchman, you *nithing*!'

It was one insult too many. Eisenbardt roared with fury and swung his axe at the Norseman. Somehow Hlavisbana was there to meet it, with a clattering crash and a cascade of sparks. Then, suddenly, there were axes, swords and hammers everywhere.

'*Volker*!' cried Dani, 'you have to stop them!'

Volker ducked the backswing from Thorgrim's halberd, stumbled, and recovered just in time to avoid a kobold axe. 'What did you have in mind?' he asked.

'The horn! Use the horn!'

'Get him!' yelled Eisenbardt. 'Take that horn, you mother-futtering trolls'-gets!' He might have saved his breath. Volker could already see four of the kobolds rushing towards him with drawn weapons: there would be no time to wind the horn, and there was no Guy to defend him. The Armorican was in the after cabin nursing the mother and father of all hangovers. That left him to take four axes simultaneously with a single swordblade – pretty fancy footwork for someone who wasn't even a swordsman . . .

And then the four kobolds were falling in a tumbling,

clattering heap of weapons, rock and ringmail, with Thorgrim's halberd somewhere in the middle of it.

'*Now* use the horn,' he bellowed.

Volker grinned. Footwork. That was it.

As a musician, Volker usually did best in private. Now, in the middle of a battle, he discovered a new talent. He had always enjoyed the Gallian peasant dances favoured by town bands all through the Empire. The tunes were racy, vigorous, and simple. To his delight, he found that one in particular came readily to mind, and his fingers made their own dance up and down the keys. He had no time even to look at the effect of his playing; the notes came so thick and fast that they demanded his full concentration. Only when he had played through all four measures and started his first repeat did he even glance up, and when he did he all but laughed into his instrument.

The kobolds were dancing. It was not something that came naturally to them, and they were doing it very badly and very unwillingly; yet somehow, despite themselves, their feet – and bodies – were going through the motions of a vigorous *bransle*. Unconsciously, perhaps, he had chosen the washerwomen's *bransle*, where the steps caricatured an argument between a dissatisfied customer and a sharp-tongued laundress. And now a dozen heavily armed kobolds in jingling ringmail were stamping their feet, slapping their thighs, wagging their fingers at each other, and dancing in a ring, with all the effortless grace of pigs in a wallow. It was only his own helpless laughter that brought the lunacy to an end.

Eisenbardt was scowling, but made no effort to repeat his orders. 'Well, elf-get? What bargain do you offer?'

'I reckon things just about balance out,' said Volker. 'You lost one man when the cable snapped, two when Guy started his rainstorm to counter Skeldi's fireball, and three more below when the earthquake beast started that rockfall. We lost one man to the cable, one during the fight, and three more on the *Walfisch* – and then there's the damage to our vessels.'

'One thing you have forgotten, elf-get! Your *vessels* rest at the top of the Knife. They have not yet reached the end of the Bridge—'

'And they won't unless we pay. Is that how you honour a bargain?'

'*Your* way killed my men,' snarled the kobold, 'and threatened the Bridge and the Lift both! You can pay, or you can leave your worthless hulks to rot where they lie!'

'You must be mad!' said Goldfüss. '*How much*?'

'You heard,' said Volker.

'Incredible,' muttered Beck, 'simply incredible. You have a weapon that can drive away something like that . . . that beast . . . and you let them—'

'Yes,' said Volker, 'I let them blackmail us, and for a very good reason. One day we'll want to go home, and unless you're planning a new Bridge, they control the only way back across Alpina Tartara!'

'That's a tenth part of the cargo!' growled Haagen. '*I* could have done—'

'Nothing!' Dani cut in sharply. 'Volker's the only one they'll talk to!'

'*Equipage d'un eunuque*!' growled de Guillac, 'but you should have let them cut the throats of these windbags, and spared us their noise.'

Beck paled. 'Cut – cut our throats? What do you mean?'

Thorgrim chuckled. 'He means that the kobolds had four hostages – you. They also had our barges. I am thinking that a tithe of the cargo was a small price to pay.'

Volker spent as long as he dared enjoying the horrified looks on the merchants' faces, and their noisy protests, before he held up his hands for silence.

'Don't worry. I got a better deal.'

'*Well*?' growled Beck.

'They want something we have in abundance; something that's a great rarity for them.'

Haagen frowned in bafflement. 'By all the gods, what is it?'

'They use it the way we use fine spirits. They say it keeps them warm and makes them happy. Some of them think it's a nostrum against many kinds of sickness.'

'Come along,' chuckled Diderik, 'don't keep us all in suspense, my boy. Tell us what they want.'

'Something we'll never have a use for. A black, foulsmelling, poisonous liquid that chokes the life out of all it touches. *They* value it so highly they will even pay for it in diamonds. They want stone oil – *petrum oleum*. And by Jupiter Teutates, they're welcome to it!'

Chapter Five

'Are you sure we can trust this one?' demanded Haagen, for possibly the tenth time.

Volker eyes the castle uneasily. It looked more like a rookery than any hall of men, a great sprawling nest piled up against the flank of the mountain like some distorted outgrowth from the dense green woodland on the valley floor. 'No,' he answered, very patiently, 'I'm not. All I know is what Ulrich meant to do.'

'Which was?'

'To contact this warlord – who's currently the boss of the whole Transalpine region – and buy his protection for the trip down to the Mare Adriatica. It makes sense – but Ulrich would've found himself in just the same spot as us.'

Haagen sniffed, and his meagre face twitched. 'But why risk attracting attention at all? Aren't we just walking blindfold into a bandit's lair? Because if that isn't a bandit's—'

'That,' interrupted Volker, fuming,' is the palace, seat of government and garrison of the only semblance of law and order in this part of the world – and now we're in earshot you'd better start talking about it that way pretty damn quick. Remember, it was this prince Oberto's victories last year that cleared the region of Rus barbarian bandits and malevolent Old Worlders and the gods know what else.' *And a lot of Tartarist influence among them, you can bet.* 'It's only thanks to him our journey's possible at all!'

Haagen sniffed again, as if right now he wasn't too grateful for that.

'All right,' Volker persisted, 'so he went on and cleared out most of his rival lords, too. I suppose that's only natural.'

'Sure,' shrugged Thorgrim. 'That is how we do it in our country, all the time.' Haagen shuddered.

'Anyway,' said Volker, 'at least it means we're not dealing with just any brigand. The more ambitious he is, the more he's going to want to encourage trade, not bleed it.' *Here's hoping*, he added, but only to himself. The more he looked at that awful lair, the more he felt that Haagen had a point. It looked no better the closer they came. He hoped devoutly that the things dangling from the outer walls weren't what they looked like.

Thorgrim was whistling tunelessly through his teeth, and it came to Volker suddenly that he was nervous, too. 'I wish we could have ridden here,' he said. 'To arrive on foot, that will always make less of us before men of this kind.'

'We've come by river!' Volker protested. 'They won't expect—'

'It makes no difference. They will not think in that way. Best we carry ourselves well, make much of our weapons, walk proudly.'

'I've got blisters!' grumbled Haagen.

Thorgrim looked at him. 'Better feet that hurt than no feet.'

Haagen bridled, then nodded reluctantly. 'You know barbarians best, I suppose.' He managed to turn his limp into a stiff-legged stalk, and turned his temper on their escort of nine men, slouching footsore down the slope. 'You men there! Straighten your backs! Stride, damn you, don't shuffle!'

Volker's feet hurt too, after weeks on the boats and then the sudden exercise of portage, but he'd almost forgotten that. At first he'd been enjoying himself too much to care, with his first sight of ancient Italia. These southern mountainsides were unlike any he'd ever seen before, rich but dry, carpeted thickly with tangled scrub of a hundred kinds, willow and myrtle and rock-rose, filling the hot afternoon air with their heady scent. The forest, by contrast, looked shady, almost gloomy, as if the sun never entered there. Far down the valley below there were little patchwork farms, among what looked like cultivated groves. They were probably fruit trees, or those olive things he'd tasted once or twice. It was much like what he had heard of southern Gallia – not surprising, as it was just across the mountains. Once, under the old Empire, this might have been a land to grow lazy in, a land where tomorrow was soon enough for most things; now it was a debatable borderland, protected by neither realm, a prime target for the barbarians and the dark forces of anarchy and disorder that whipped them on, driving a wedge between the Northern and Southern Empires. He looked with interest at the vineyards stretched out along the valley slopes below the castle, and wondered what the local vintages were like. With luck they might be offered some . . .

With luck. Now he was too nervous to care much about them, or his blisters. He held up his head, though the sun was dazzling, and tried to walk with something of Guy's swagger. He wished they could have brought him along, but somebody had to keep an eye on the remaining merchants and crew. And they'd had to leave Dani behind, of course; Oberto enjoyed the nickname *Pecudalitere*, literally Oxbreeder or Stockholder, because of the huge harem he maintained and rapaciously increased. No sense in tempting fate.

Volker swallowed. They might be doing that, anyway. Those damned things along the walls were *exactly* what he'd thought. A fair selection of the nastier breeds of Old World creatures hung there, twisted and

222

withered by the scorching sun till their limbs contorted in a horrid parody of their last dance. There were a good few human heads, too, towards the top. 'It shows a poor taste in ornament, but it is a message one does not need many languages to read,' commented Thorgrim. 'What manner of man is this Oberto, anyhow?'

Volker shrugged. 'I couldn't say. Ulrich wrote only the bare details, so what I know I gleaned from river gossip . . .' Oberto's career had certainly been chequered. His birthplace was unknown, but he had started as a quack doctor in the Southern city of Tarentum, offering cures for the Gallic pox and other exotic diseases. He'd then branched out as an Oriental fortuneteller, unlicensed witchhunter and freelance exorcist. After a particularly frenzied investigation of a school for young ladies, he had fled to these wild lands, as did many Italians outlawed, adventurous or simply poor. There, skilfully exploiting his quasi-magical skills, he had served a number of lords, and eventually led a coup against one, beginning his present rise to power.

Certainly his stronghold was as eccentric as his beginnings. The closer they got the weirder it appeared. Somewhere at the heart of it there might once have been a smallish Roman villa of yellow stone, with some ramshackle farm buildings round the back. Somebody had added a rough wall and towers of the yellowish local stone, and a later owner earthworks and an outward defence, so the original walls became a central keep after the Northern fashion. After that, anything seemed to go till the result was the size of a small town centre, a crazy riot of walls, barracks, gates, barns and sheds. Low stone walls had been built up almost to the toppling point with a jumbled mixture of crude blockwork and meticulous dry-stone walling; in places the blocks were carefully sculpted, edge to edge, in others they were plastered with mortar, or even lead poured between the joints. Along the front the wall had been built still higher by adding a palisade of hefty wooden stakes, and behind it, dominating the whole wide compound, an extraordinary-looking tower. Its builders appeared to have patched it together from every scrap of used timber they could lay hands on, nailed into fantastic shapes and patterns, shored up, propped up or even just stacked into what looked like a series of lean-tos, each resting on the other; let one collapse, and very likely the rest would follow. Planks already painted seemed to have been left that way, others splashed with blazing colours, creating a riotous jumbled pattern across which heraldic symbols and hex signs were scrawled, often in thick gilt. There were odd bulges and curves in parts of the walls . . . 'Boats!' said Haagen, aghast. 'They've built it out of stripped-down boats!'

The others gaped. The merchant was undoubtedly right. 'Patched it up, more like,' grunted Thorgrim. 'From captured barbarian boats too wrecked for use. Let us hope he has no plans for home extensions right now. But why should a man use timber so niggardly with a whole forest at his feet?'

'That I can tell you,' said Volker decisively. 'He wouldn't cut those trees – least of all to build with their wood. Ulrich warned against that forest in his notes; he says it's an uncanny place, a home of living legends.'

'A wonder this Oberto hasn't cleared it out by now, like the rest of the country.'

'It may be so with him that he likes the dryads,' grinned the Norseman through his beard. 'It is said that, provided one takes care over such matters as splinters—'

'And leaf-rot, no doubt,' said Volker dryly. 'Ulrich said it's kept as one of his castle's defences – no surprise attackers would get through there. Anyway, we won't have to worry; this path skirts it to the outer wall. There must be a gate in it somewhere.'

224

Strictly speaking, he was wrong. There was no breach in the palisade itself; the gate was in a tunnel sloping down beneath it, and over the stone arch at its entrance hung the fleshless skull and leathery wings of a manticore.

They were challenged from the rampart above, as they'd expected. Without any undue haste Thorgrim lifted the halberd from his shoulder and grounded the point, and Volker raised his open hand. 'Travellers from the North,' he called out, 'come on a great and hazardous journey to seek honourable audience of the renowned Prince Oberto! Is peace said between us?'

'Shoah,' answered a laconic voice from the wall. 'But y'all may hafta wait. Oberto's having his self a siesta right now – and if it's with his ladies he'll likely take anuthah lil'ol lie-down justa catch his brayth, if'n y'all take muh meanin', haw! Don't go 'way now, y'hear?'

'What kind of accent's that?' demanded Volker, as they halted in the shadow of the gate.

'Ach, some southerner or other,' said Haagen. 'They get riff-raff from the most improbable places here, I've heard.'

Without warning the metal-sheathed slab that blocked the tunnel began to rumble and creak upward, and the same voice called down. 'Oberto, he says peace is say-ed, and if'n y'all jus'step in, why, he'll be right on down!'

Somewhat nervously, but with their heads held high, the little company marched in beneath the gate. In the shade behind a group of guards lounged expertly, scratching themselves under their armour; but their weapons were held ready for instant action. In this land, guessed Volker, that might be a survival habit. One of them languidly detached himself, negligently dangling his helmet by its chinstrap; although his only distinguishing mark was a chin bonier and bluer than anyone else's, he announced himself in rough Latin as the commander and looked them up and down. He seemed as unimpressed as Thorgrim predicted until Haagen let a silver coin drop into the helmet, where-upon he beamed alarmingly and without front teeth, and ushered them across the courtyard to the base of the crazy tower. This close, it looked a lot more impress-ive. Some very old stonework made a foundation two or three stories high before the wooden superstructure began, and even that seemed less ramshackle close to. The doorway was an ancient arch, dark and heavily carved in time-worn swirls.

'So?' carolled a cheerful voice, in fluent but fractured Burgundian. 'You like my new tower, huh? Gotta big-gest in the country, now!' Volker tried to hide his sur-prise at the figure who strode to meet them. Oberto was an unusually tall man, as tall as Volker, and not so much older, though it was hard to tell through the black beard, trimmed, curled and matted with perfumes and unguents, that covered most of his face; his moustaches were twirled into waxed spirals that made Guy's look modest. He wore the latest and sharpest Napoli fashions, a white ruffled shirt, carelessly fastened, with a coat of bottle-green velvet draped over one shoulder, tight scarlet hose, and a gigantic silver-gilt metal cod-piece studded with cornucopia. Only a second look caught the yellowed, bleary eyes, the pouchy lines of long debauchery about the nose, and the spreading wine gut contained behind a scarlet sash.

Volker's interest in the stonework put Oberto in fine expansive mood. Evidently he was very proud of his citadel, and flattered by what Volker could tell him concerning the old masonry. 'Is so old? *E vero*?'

'Old Imperial, I'd guess – before the Emperor came back to Syracusa. But maybe it was older than that – non-human work. Those are huge blocks, like what the Greeks call Kyklopean . . .'

'Kyclops? Could be. Was every goddam kind of thing

out of the *Mondo Vecchio* here once. Now I clean them all out – *poof, presto! Tutto disparato!* Except in that forest of mine . . .'

'Or it might have been the mountain kobolds. They'd know, anyway. We could ask them on our way back . . .'

Oberto's interest was captured at once. 'Kobolds, huh?' He scratched his curly beard with cheerful amazement, came across something, cracked it between his large white teeth and threw it away. '*Che meraviglio!* You friends with those little stinkers? *Madre mio,* I'm a-glad to meet you! Listen, you tell 'em, we make a deal, huh? I want to buy stone, I want-a stonewrights, make this place the best, the strongest, the prettiest in all Italia! *Bene,* you offer—'

'One moment, *mio principe,*' said Volker apologetically. 'You must tell me this later, when we have reached our destination and can return. Then we will be happy to act as your agents to them. But first, we stand in need of some help from you.'

The temperature sank noticeably. 'Help, huh? What-a kind?'

'We would of course be willing to admit a reasonable *honorarium,*' put in Haagen smoothly.

'*Hon* – ah, you mean-a you pay?' The temperature soared again. 'Ah, *molto bene, molto bene,* you come in, you no stand around and fry your asses inna hot sun! *Sandor! Ovè sai?* Give their men a drink! *Lucasta! Vino per tutti!* Come in, come in!'

The darkness inside was much cooler, but so laden with stenches that Volker began to long for the sun again. The floor was trodden earth – well, trodden, anyhow; Volker suspected it owed rather a lot to the innumerable dogs padding about, pausing only to snarl at the strangers, and the even larger numbers of small children. However, the wine a lushly pretty young woman served them was definitely drinkable, cool as a deep cellar and slightly fizzy on the tongue. By the second glass even Haagen had mellowed, and steered the conversation on to hard business with surprising tact, complimenting Oberto on his prowess and expressing polite hopes for the future peace and expansion of his realm. 'Which would of course open up immense new trade possibilities,' he added expansively. 'A whole new route between the two Empires – with your realm astride it.' Oberto froze with his wine cup to his lips.

'Of course,' oiled Haagen, 'the heavy responsibility of maintaining such frequent trade would inevitably fall on you. Establishing guard posts, with hostelries, at regular intervals. Providing escorts. Setting and collecting tolls. Harbourage. Provisioning. Enforcing fair weights and measures.' As he checked off every money-making possibility Oberto leaned forward, hanging wide-eyed on the master merchant's every word. 'Perhaps even a system of banking credits, with your own currency as the standard – quite a responsibility. Why, in effect yours would be the hand on the pulse of mercantile prosperity of North and South alike. I wonder any man could be induced to assume such a burden . . .'

Oberto clutched at his breast with an air of high drama. 'Ah, *caro mio signore*, you understand what it is to be a king! But, *per Bacco*, such a weight of troubles I take on gladly – for the sake of my people, *si*! And you—' His teeth flashed like a shark's. 'You have come to begin this trading?'

Haagen made a cautious gesture. 'A voyage of reconnaissance, a trip to the market as it were. To find out what there is to buy and what we should bring along to sell.' Volker approved; Haagen was being cautious. That might save them getting bushwhacked now or taxed to death on their way back. The merchant moved deftly into the question of passage for the caravan on its way southward, and hiring warriors to guard it. Oberto nodded vigorously, asked a few questions as to their route and requirements, and began to scrawl figures on his slates, while his entourage clustered around admiringly. Literacy was so rare in these parts that it enhanced his uncanny reputation, and he never missed a chance to show off.

'Alle flumine,' he muttered. *'Dunque cavaliere* – horse-guards, no? I spare you a guard easy. With remounts – allowances for detached service, *si*? Bonus for unusual duties if required, portaging boats and so forth – battle bonus for attacks of twenty men or above – all provisions to be found by you—' At length he passed over the slates. *'Eccola,* a bargain!'

Haagen's eyes glazed over as he scanned the slates. *'Excellenzia!'* He took a deep breath, and continued smoothly. 'You take too much care of your guests! We are only poor merchants, we cannot afford two full squadrons of cavalry. I had in mind a simple guard, a few soldiers only whom we could accommodate on the boats themselves.'

'So few I do not send out,' interrupted Oberto curtly, 'or maybe none at all come back. You neither. She is not so wild, this country, as she is made out, not now I clean her out nicely; but nor is she nice green pastures. Bandits, *corpo di Bacco*, is always bandits like bugs inna mattress. And in the mountains still much of the Old World stirs; sometimes they strike down into the plain and are gone. Maybe my guards catch them soon, maybe later. But by then you is maybe *rigatone*, huh?'

Oberto sounded sincere; and after all he was the expert. But you could practically hear the wheels turning in Haagen's mind, nasty suspicious wheels; he was sure he was being lumbered with unnecessary soldiery. Thorgrim caught Volker's eye anxiously; evidently he didn't agree. That put Volker on the spot; nominal leader he might be, but it was still the merchants who held the purse-strings in matters of this kind. And he didn't dare use up Ulrich's gold, not yet. 'Perhaps a merchant of your experience,' he oiled, 'could find ways to reduce the cost – ways,' he added hastily, 'which would suit both the Prince and ourselves?'

Haagen could certainly take a hint, though the way Oberto slid a long thin dagger from his sleeve and began paring his nails might also have helped. The sour-faced merchant was a first-class shaper of deals, ready to spot a sore point before the prince did, always sliding out from under a blank refusal and finding some new angle. Oberto never got more than mildly irritated. They ended up agreeing on a squadron and a half of cavalry, buying its provisions from Oberto's own farms, at discount, which would also save a bit on their own. But all the same, Haagen had had the sense to be generous; Volker was glad, but surprised. Oberto still seemed doubtful. 'Seventy-five men, *pfui*! Is not much, to guard two big boats. Still, *tuo damno, maestro borghese*! I see you on your way home – maybe!'

It was noon the following day before they arrived back at the boats, with their cavalry escort in tow. Once across the pass, the descent had proved remarkably easy; the southern slopes of the mountains, though rugged, were less steep, and portaging the boats past rapids and falls had not been hard with the help of kobold winches, even though trees large enough for rollers grew scarcer as they descended; they had had to take some with them, floating them behind the *Walfisch* like a raft. Now the boats rocked gently in a little lake, tied up at the quay of the stockaded settlement that had directed them to Oberto, while the tired rowers rested from the portages; it had been hard labour, but their last for a while. On this river the current would be with them, not against, and the barges would be sailing most of the way. Rest or no rest, though, in these lands the watch stayed alert; long before the train of horsemen reached the settlement the merchants were already bustling along the quay, and came popping out of the stockade's narrow gate to greet them.

'What's this? What's this?' rumbled Beck genially, breathing the fumes of country beer. 'Hired us half an army, then, Haagen – eh?'

'Going to set up as a prince yourself?' cackled Diderik. 'Don't blame you. Fat land, in these valleys. Good trade. Nice plump wenches—'

'And Old Worlder ghouls to sing you to sleep!' chuckled Goldfüss. 'Though you'd not mind, would you, old fellow? Long as they're female. You're so shrivelled up yourself—' He dodged the swipe of the old merchant's cane. But their good humour evaporated swiftly when they found out just how much they'd have to pay.

'What?'

'Whatever possessed you—'

'Must be mad—'

'—and with your share of the profits, not with mine—'

'So many—'

'Think we're made of bloody money?'

Volker listened, discouraged, as angry recriminations flew back and forth across the little cabin. Haagen was defending himself stoutly enough, but he felt he should help. 'Listen, it's worth it. Master Haagen got you all a bargain! For Thunor's sake, look at what's hit us so far! And this country's supposed to be worse!'

They all rounded on him. 'You and your mission—'

'After the trouble you made for us with those stinking kobolds—'

'Of course we need guards—but so *many*?'

Diderik thumped his cane on the floor. 'Masters, masters! The boy's right, leave him be! And you too, Haagen. They may be too many or they may not, but we can't go affronting this rogue warlord, can we? Not when we seek passage through his territory!' The old man had authority when he wanted it; the row subsided.

'Well . . .' mused Goldfüss, stroking his heavy chin. He and Diderik exchanged significant glances. 'No? No. When you put it like that, no. But there might be other ways – decidedly there might . . . We'll talk it over another time, masters.' And that was all, much to Volker's annoyance. 'Another time' would mean when he wasn't there. Not for the first time, he was left thinking that for sharp, successful businessmen these merchants could be numbingly stupid.

'What d'you expect?' commented Dani acidly. 'They're just greed on legs, merchants. Money's all the fools care about.'

'Not so,' Guy objected. 'Fools do not so easily succeed in commerce. But to succeed they must narrow their vision to their eventual goal. All too often these practical men become too sure, too narrow, refusing to believe any unlike themselves can be wise. They become less accustomed to being questioned. Then in their confidence they do something a child would find imbecilic. And, *foi de Guillac*, that is not confined to merchants.'

Volker nodded, thinking of old Strauben. 'That's true; but it doesn't make me feel any better. Now they'll probably try something without telling us, something lunatic – and just what is it going to be?'

But when he found out, it was far too late.

They set out at dawn the next morning, the low sun bright on the spread sails of the barges, winking on the armour of the horsemen who came trotting along the banks beside them. They were a rough-looking bunch, swarthy-faced with heavy beards or long drooping moustaches, but very well equipped. Their armour and weapons were a blend of every style and type Volker could imagine: mail, scale and plate, mace and spear and sword. Some even bore the turbanned helmets and curved scimitars of Libya Major, far distant beyond the

232

Middle Sea, and others a curious blade, apparently of local design, with a vicious downward kink at the tip. About half of them bore lances, tipped with two or three savage prongs. Short bows of horn bounced at their backs, sheaves of long arrows in wicker quivers at their saddlebows. Only scarves of the same scarlet hue as their scruffy banner gave them any uniform appearance, but they moved in disciplined files under the vigilant eye of their captain, the blue-chinned thug who had met them at the gate. He shone like a peacock in heavily embroidered cloak and hose and tall fur cap, but Volker found reason to suspect he had not bathed for a good year past. He also spoke an appallingly ancient Latin dialect, larded with barbarian words and an accent as rough as that of Kiev. Even so, the merchants treated him with respect, and on the first night out treated him to dinner in their cabin. Volker was conspicuously not invited; he did not know whether to be relieved or chagrined. But it was not till the middle of the third day that he noticed anything amiss.

By now the portaging was done, and they had moved out from among the hill slopes into lands that were less steep and more rolling. Volker was leaning on the port rail of the *Walfisch*, watching the column of Oberto's riders flow across a low hill.

Thorgrim, dozing in the sun nearby, sprang up at his startled exclamation. 'There is something the matter?'

'Shut up, I'm trying to count – no, it's impossible . . .'

'You know how we make it easier in my country? No? Count the legs and divide into a fourth!' He laughed uproariously.

Volker sighed; evidently old jokes knew no frontiers. 'It's not funny, Thorgrim. I could swear there aren't as many riders as when we started.'

The Norseman shrugged. 'One or two might be thrown, go sick, have a horse lamed –'

233

'They have remounts. And this is more than one or two.'

Thorgrim squinted and stared. Slowly his eyes relaxed, but deep furrows remained in his brow. 'Naa ja. I begin to see what you mean. Perhaps a scouting party? If so, they will return by nightfall. And until we make camp we can do nothing.'

The barges pulled in later than usual that evening, to a calm little nook of the bank, well sheltered for the horsemen. They arrived in cheerful disorder some time later, having been detailed into separate patrols to sweep the area around. But Volker and his followers were unobtrusively counting them as they arrived, and soon found that their tallies matched all too closely. 'Master Beck!' said Volker sharply as the merchant came bustling over from the *Walfisch*. 'Have you noticed anything about our escort?'

'Only when the breeze blows this way, lad. Why?'

'Because instead of the squadron and a half you're paying for, we have less than a squadron.'

Beck shrugged. 'Oh, what of it? Probably half of them are still out on patrol – or wenching, perhaps.'

Dani snorted. 'In this land? After dark? Most won't even leave the campfires unless they have to! They're not stupid! Volker's right – there's less of them about, and they're doing their best to hide it from us.'

'Well?' demanded Goldfüss, who had come up behind them silently. 'What of it? Even if you're right we can't very well go to Captain Dumnonicic and demand to count his men!'

'After all,' said Haagen, gliding out of the darkness, 'There are still plenty to protect us, aren't there? I did say all along that we could get by with fewer.'

Volker stared. 'But you're paying for . . . Oh.' In the space of a word he saw it, and yet he could hardly take it in. 'You. You've planned this, haven't you? All of you—'

'Ahhh,' breathed Guy. *'Mes compliments, messires.*
What a truly brilliant stroke of business,' he added bit-
terly.

Dani stared at Volker. *'What* have they planned?'

'They never wanted all these troops. Oberto advised
them, but they know better, don't they? He's just the
yokel on the spot, and they're sharp Imperial businessmen. So work out what they'll save if half the force
don't need food or pay – then lay out a fraction of that
to bribe our gallant Captain Dumbo-whatsisname. He
sends his best men off for a couple of weeks' unofficial
leave, and we get stuck with the dregs. Oberto doesn't
know, we don't know. Simple, isn't it?'

'Yes!' said Goldfüss rebelliously. 'It is! You and your
precious master, you never consulted us about this
lunatic quest of yours! You were just using us! We don't
answer to you, not in law nor justice neither!'

'That's right!' grunted Beck. 'We've a right to make
our own decisions, lad; we're not bound to come crawling to you at every step and turn!'

'I am thinking,' said Thorgrim coldly, 'that you sang
quite another tune on the far side of the mountains.'

'That's right!' Dani burst out. 'How far'd you ever
have got without him?'

'Without him we wouldn't have had the troubles
we've had!' spat Haagen.

Diderik had hobbled over to see what the fuss was.
But even he shook his wizened head and sighed. 'It's
what we think against what you think, lad. And after
all, it's our money making this possible, isn't it?'

'Yes!' agreed Volker harshly, feeling his spine stiffen,
his fists clench. 'And the profits will be yours, too. But
without Ulrich's idea you'd never even have started.
Isn't that reason enough to do things his way?'

'His way, maybe!' grunted Goldfüss. 'He was a seasoned man of affairs, and now you tell us a learned
mage as well. Him we might have heeded – though not

235

slavishly, mind! But he's not here to listen to, is he? All we've got is you. And what are you? An unlicked pup!'

'Better a wise pup, perhaps, than a sleek hound who has never before strayed from his kennel?' suggested Guy sardonically. There was a thoroughly nasty glint in his eye. 'I trust you would not call me a pup, *messire*, nor these my friends. We have grown accustomed to heeding this young man, and we most earnestly suggest you do the same!' Thorgrim and Dani said nothing; but they moved forward to stand on either side of him.

Goldfüss's narrow eyes darted about in alarm; evidently it had not occurred to him or the other merchants that they were alone with this trio, capable of swabbing the deck with any of their own bodyguards. Equally evidently he didn't relish the idea of confronting them; but nor was he easily cowed. 'That's as may be,' he said shortly. 'But for this matter of the troops, what's done is done. They can't be recalled. So – what exactly are you going to do about it?'

Volker looked the merchant up and down, solidly, arrogantly sure he was right, and from him to the others. 'Nothing,' he said coolly. Anger wouldn't impress these men. 'As you say, there's nothing we can do, not now. But for your sake as well as ours, let's hope no one else takes the chance you've given them!' He turned on his heel and stalked away into the darkness.

In the days that followed it seemed that nobody would. They were peaceful, drifting days for the most part, yet there were always reminders that this was not a peaceable land. The two barges glided smoothly on through the deep Transalpine vales; often the rugged valley walls sloped so steeply that the trees and bushes grew out, not up, and overhung the river like banners, and their depleted escort had to pick their way carefully along ways that were little better than deer-paths. Yet paths they were, and every so often some presence of men – a hut, a farm, orchards or vineyards, small towns, sometimes even a craggy castle looming over a defensible narrows. They were not like the palatial castles of the Northern empire, many-towered, vast and impregnable, townlets behind their walls; these were single towers for the most part, windowless and isolated keeps without cheer of colour, only strength. Some, clearly, had not been strong enough; they were no more than ruined shells. The occupied ones flew unpleasant banners, strings of misshapen skulls or monster-skins, sometimes sewn back together and inflated. One tiny farm boasted two huge troll skeletons flanking its narrow door, their fleshless hands wired up into a warning gesture. The message was always the same: *Stay away! Keep moving!* These were not Oberto's men, though this was still land he claimed to control; they were outlivers, fiercely independent, following only the laws they made for themselves. But at the sight of his banner many gates were opened, and the travellers given a warm welcome; and even where they were not, no man dared stand in its way.

Others, however, did. Predators of every kind laired in the rugged terrain of the upper valleys, humans not the least; brigands, bandits, cannibals, freedom fighters and anti-Oberto partisans – the exact name usually depended on who happened to be butchering whom. Smaller bands were scared off by the very look of the escort, but two larger ones laid ambushes, one cleverly, at a point where boat and escort were well out of each other's sight. Both attacks, luckily, were held off by the deafening blast of *Walross*'s bombard until the horsemen came roaring up in answer. Unhuman enemies were more trouble. The wildlife of the Empire was bizarre enough, but here, where the forces of Tartarus seemed to have held sway for centuries, it was so much stronger that every stir and rustle on the bank had to be watched. Wolves and bears were no great danger, but there was worse around. Twice the escort flushed small packs of medium-sized satyrs, who might or might not have been lying in wait near the river, and locals spoke of larger packs on the move inland; the captain despatched men to bear word back to Oberto.

Not far from cultivated fields, there was an uproar when the lookouts saw bushes part on the far bank ahead and a huge flattened head, long-jawed, saw-toothed and carunculated, thrust through to the water. It made no attempt to enter it, however, but began to drink in great gulps that shook its long barrel body, as long as a rowing skiff; it seemed not to hear the shouting and commotion, but as the boats passed it raised its head and launched a hissing bellow at them. *'Teufel-schwanz!'* exclaimed Goldfüss. 'That's a pretty brute! What in the name of Hela-Proserpina is it?'

'It will be some kind of *ormr,*' suggested Thorgrim. *'Vurm,* you would say, or *draco.* Such as infested the Northlands before the days of old King Sigefrith the Wormslayer.'

'Draco be damned!' roared Guy, coming up from the stern. 'You think the hereditary Draconnier of all the lands north of Morbihan does not recognize his lawful prey in all its guises? Even if admittedly they have been in slightly short supply in these recent decadent generations? That is a mere impostor, a corkindrill, a beast that dwells in the Libyan streams where it does fearful battle with the riverhorses, and produces a dung much valued in the making of unguents and perfumes, or so the bestiaries report. Mind you,' he added some-what feebly, 'you might as well look to find a corkindrill in the Northlands as in Italy. How in the name of all the deified Emperors' buttocks carved in marble did such a brute come here?'

Volker thought for a moment. 'The Old Empire ship-ped across hundreds of animals every year from Libya and Africa Minor—'

'Ah!' said Guy, with sudden understanding, 'the games!'

'Exactly. Maybe a few of the younger ones escaped through the *cloacae*, the great sewers. Even bred there. And we've seen how long the shadow of Tartarus can be in these lands – long enough to draw in creatures like that one. Not that it's evil in itself, but evil can always make use of *predatores*.'

'Well, if it looks like an *ormr* and smells like an *ormr* and bites like an *ormr*,' said Thorgrim, nettled, 'then an *ormr* it is. So we say in my country, and it is a wise saying. Although this one, I admit, breathes no fire. Perhaps a *kaltsormr* – a cold-drake. We have books that tell of such things . . .'

'Dragons?' sneered Goldfüss. 'With a head at each end, I suppose! Ach, come on! You can read anything in books! Especially barbarian books! You're not taking that tripe seriously, are you?'

The Norseman frowned. 'This is a land like my own, close to the edge of civilization, where the Old World is still strong. In such places a wise man is less ready to laugh at strange things, lest he find them snapping at his heels.' He looked sourly at Goldfüsss. 'And why should it not have a head where its arse should be, when some men have an—'

Goldfüss growled and turned away. Volker sighed, and glared at Thorgrim. The Norseman shrugged. Volker knew there was no use saying anything. Ever since the episode of the escort relations had grown more strained between his party and the merchants, and he could guess why. They'd suffered his leadership only because they needed him to get them across the mountains. Now they needed him no longer, or so they thought. They might even be right. Soon the barges would reach the confluence with the Flumina Poiana, and from there it looked like relatively plain sailing all the way to Sicilia. When he wanted to turn aside – well, he had better be ready for trouble.

Meanwhile there were problems enough, even after they emerged from the steep valleys and out among low rolling hills less suited to brigandage. One of Goldfüss's followers, a stolid Rus swordsman called Yaroslavl, vanished into a bush to relieve himself one morning, and never came out. Half a hour later, when they went to look for him, they found him entangled in a small, very green tree, and very green himself – not only dead, but apparently half putrefied. It was only when the tree branches whipped out at Joachim as he strayed too close that they understood; this was one of those disgusting things called *gebludtbaume*, or Freya's Mantrap, a foul hybrid of plant and animal that entangled, then swiftly digested its victims. Hack at its rubbery limbs as they might, there was no way of freeing the corpse without risking another victim; so they threw fire on the revolting thing and left it to burn. The next few days were entirely peaceful; but nobody seemed as eager to stretch their legs ashore as they had been, and any plant that entangled an ankle was likely to be hewn and stamped flat into the mud.

Soon the hills, too, were passing, and they saw opening out before them the wide flat expanse of the river floodplains that would eventually lead down to the Mare Adriatica. 'Doesn't seem so very bad, this place, does it?' remarked Beck one mild evening, as the boats rode at anchor in the river. He swatted. 'Apart from the gnats, I mean; and they're worse in southern Gallia. Why, it's just as Master Reiner was saying at dinner just now – we had more trouble in the Empire, all told, than we've had down in these lawless parts.'

Dani, sitting behind him, grimaced at Volker; the merchants were getting over-confident, all right. 'We didn't have an escort back home,' Volker reminded him. 'And their banner happens to terrify everyone and everything that lives here. Besides, we haven't got through. Not yet.'

'Tu l'as dit, that we have not!' agreed Guy lazily. 'And until now the homes of men have never been distant. But these plains ahead, nobody farms them. Yet they are richer and more fertile even than the lands around the Garonne, or my own dear Loire and Blavet, and they lie bleak and desert. You have not wondered why?'

Beck deflated visibly, and his piggy eyes lost their good humour; the fat merchant began to glance around nervously at the shadowed banks. 'Not exactly . . .'

Guy swung his boots off the rail. '*Bien*, I will show you!' He took the merchant's shoulders and swung him irresistibly around to face the extreme east. The moon had just appeared in the sky, and against its pale gleam a dark line became visible, a faint irregularity on the horizon greater than the swaying of tips of reed and sedge could account for. 'You do not know what that is? My good sir, you look your first upon the highest summits of the eastern mountains, Alpina Carnatica. Do you know what lies beyond, held back as by a dam? Dalmatia – Dacia – Macedon – once Roman lands, now full of fierce barbarians, thirsting for Imperial land and gold, and more fearful monstrosities of the Old World than even Ulysses ever ran into. And beyond them the great steppes of the Rus lands, stretching far and flat to fierce Kiev, ruled by the close relations of my esteemed hairy friend here in their own inimitable manner, who have even more determined designs upon Imperial borders, north or south. And among them all, whispering of dark ambitions and dark powers, bought with fire and blood and sacrifice, move the agents of Tartarus. You look upon the summit of the dam – but the dam is crumbling, leaky, under such pressure and spills over constantly. We have but one protection, *mon ami*, and that is the forest that lies across those foothills like a cloak of darkness.'

'F-forest?'

'*Vraiment!* And *such* a forest! In its shadows are all the sports and monsters of the First Creation – and all the ghosts of the Old Empire that was. But day by day, hour by hour, the old forest dies. Maybe late, maybe soon, maybe tomorrow, the dam will break – and what lies beyond will roll over these fields like a flood of dark water, shot with blood . . . Tell me, master merchant, does the land look so peaceful now?'

Beck, white as a sheet, mumbled something and tore loose from the Armorican's grasp. He was about to scuttle off back to the stern cabin when he started suddenly and squeaked like a startled mouseling. He had excuse; the uproar on shore startled everyone, and brought them to their feet, grabbing for weapons. Horses were neighing, men shouting, weapons clinking; merchants and crewmen came boiling out of cabin and foc'sle, shouting contradictory orders. But before Thorgrim could override the merchants long enough to warp the *Walross* with its bombard in towards the shore, the row had died down, and the escort captain was hailing them. A group of his pickets, it appeared had laid hold of some monstrous creature sneaking around the edge of the camp, and they were dealing with it now. Volker shouted to them to wait until he had seen it; but it was too late. When he got ashore, he took one look at what was left and turned away in sick revulsion. Flayed, the carcass looked shockingly human, except about the feet; more than that, the creature had worn harness and weapons, and fought with fierce cunning. But the head and skin, nailed to a tree, could have belonged to some great goatlike thing, savagely horned and tusked. When Volker protested, the captain only rasped a thumb through his stubble and shrugged; he was not accustomed to wasting his time talking to *minotauri*, as he named the thing. Why was it sneaking around the camp? Who cared? After a meal, most likely.

Spying? The captain laughed. What was there left to spy for, this side of the Carnaticas? Volker went back on board, and back to his bed, in a terrible mood. Only next evening did one of the riders let slip to de Guillac, over the inevitable dice, that there had been other watchers they hadn't caught.

For all Volker's fears, though, the flat lands in their turn rolled away as peaceably as the rest, though not nearly as pleasantly. Too much of the riverside country, though warm, was damp and fenny, breeding mists and miasmas and every kind of midge and stinging fly. The plant life was dull and uniform, dark brown, dull green, dotted with clumps of low trees, but few flowers to lend touches of colour. Once in a while, though, it would appear to go mad, and some writhing tendrilly monstrosity would sprout high above the mire. 'Some ancient contamination in the soil, that shows,' nodded Thorgrim as they passed by perhaps the hundredth of the things. 'Strange, that we should have things the same in my cool land. They say there it is *seidr*, ill magic spilled in the conflict of the gods with the giants – or the Titans, as the Armorican says they are named in these parts. Maybe it washes down from *there*.' He inclined his head towards the darkness on the horizon, that had grown swiftly to jagged teeth.

'Perhaps,' said Volker. 'But don't you think we're seeing the things more often?'

The Norseman shrugged. 'Perhaps. What of it? Mostly they are harmless, unless one tries to eat fruit or roots.'

'Nothing, I suppose. Only . . .' Volker tapped the folded chart. 'We're not far from the confluence, you know. Four or five days' sail, by my reckoning; no more.'

'*Saa*. The joining of rivers. And it is there you wish to turn aside?'

Volker glanced instinctively around, but the merchants were all out of earshot. 'Right. Then make ready for ructions!'

He was right; but not as he thought. It was on the afternoon of the fourth day that they saw the river curve and widen some way ahead, and more distant still, the white patch of turbulent rapids where the two strong currents met.

'We won't be there before nightfall,' remarked Haagen. 'And I for one don't fancy steering around it in the dark.'

'True,' agreed Thorgrim stolidly, leaning on the tiller. 'But nor do I think we should anchor in this current. Keep a lookout for some fitting place on the bank. The horsemen can check it.'

The light was already failing and the usual mist gathering before they came upon what seemed a suitable anchorage, a deep shingle spit near the mouth of a reed-filled oxbow where the river had changed its course. A rare stand of trees and thick bushes gave the place an unusually sheltered feeling; however, trusting nothing, the travellers had the cavalry search the whole bank up and down. After much stamping and clanking in the bushes, a couple of cavalrymen hailed the barges and came trotting up between marshy patches to draw them along to a dry spot. Volker and one of Haagen's bodyguards stepped up to the bows to hurl them the bowlines; but even as the ropes snaked through the heavy air and the riders reached up to catch and fasten them to their saddlebows, there came a faint flicker like distant lightning.

Everything changed.

Patches of green marsh-grass beside the riders suddenly appeared to boil up and erupt, strange shapes burst upwards in a shower of mud and roots and swirling mist, and other hands snatched at the falling ropes. One rider tried to pull his horse around, but there was a sudden flurry, a flicker of metal, and his horse screamed, reared, and toppled, rolling on him in its agony. The other rider stabbed out with his three-pronged lance and spurred his horse away, but was seized by one foot, hauled bodily from the saddle and hewn even as he fell. The bowlines went stiff as strong hands hauled them in. Guy shouted, swept his sabre from his belt and rushed at the lines, but too late; the keel touched, the boat ground and lurched in the sandy clay, the *Walfisch* behind nudged hard against the stern, and he and all the others were thrown back, skidding in a heap along the tilting deck. Grapnels came falling out of the mist and thudded into the deck, were snatched back by the ropes and dug in. One caught the carriage of the bombard and hauled it over on its side with a crash. Over the gunwale arrows rained, driving back Thorgrim as he struggled on hands and knees towards the nearest grapnel. 'It is no good!' he shouted. 'They have us!'

Some way along the bank their escort, just dismounting, took one look and sprang as one man back into their saddles. But a deep warhorn bellowed across the marshland, and even as they formed their ragged column and came charging back along the bank another long line of figures raced out of the mist. Right across the fen before them they stretched, black figures manlike in shape, yet unlike in the way they moved, all afoot, hopping, bounding, leaping with terrible energy across country that would mire a man. Weapons glinted in their hands, helm and breastplate gleamed dully about them, and between their mailed shoulders shone the helms of a second line, with a third behind that.

'There's hundreds of them!' choked Dani. The owl lifted from her shoulder with a screech. 'A thousand, easily! An army—'

'But no army of men!' muttered Guy between clenched teeth. 'Those beastmen things and some less human yet, the things that lurked in the mud. I have read of something of the kind – from Dalmatia, I fancy – now what were they called? And who, I wonder, is so able to direct such monsters?'

All too quickly that question was answered. Above the grim lines of Tartarus the grey mists thickened and swirled like spectral banners. Then they parted, and Dani screamed. 'It can't be!'

Thorgrim's steely fingers seized Volker's arm. 'Half-Elf! Is this the *glam*-sight on my eyes?'

Grimly Volker shook his head. 'No. I see it also.'

'I see!' breathed Guy. 'But I do not believe . . .'

'See what?' shouted Goldfüss, gripping the rail. 'What is . . . that thing?'

Behind the lines of Tartarus, whipping along the fearful creatures as a herdsman might drive his cattle, a single vast figure loomed up in the mists, as if darkness grew solid. Upon a fitting mount he rode, a horse by its shape and high-stepping gait but larger than any horse of common kind, and so enmeshed and encrusted in fantastic armour that it seemed more machine than living beast, save for the breath that steamed about its champing jaws. So also its rider; for there was no mistaking that form, huge and hunched in its warty carapace of armour, its misshapen helmet set low over a clenched jaw. They had not forgotten him, though they had not thought to see him ever again.

'They are strong, yes, the hall-troops of Loki,' protested Thorgrim, 'but are they immortal?'

'It can't be – not him! Not the same one!' cried Dani. 'The whole tower fell on him—'

'It's him, all right,' ground Volker. 'He dug himself free the first time – gods, maybe he could do it again! I'd believe anything of that monster!'

'Then my work was ill done!' muttered Guy. 'See!'

The horsemen had turned away to face the new threat. They had no choice; they could not ride on to help the boats or the onrushing lines would come crashing into their rear. Volker saw the captain signal frantically; the horsemen swung about suddenly and formed ranks, lancers to the fore. Horses bridled and plunged, a horn sang, then gradually they began to move forward, straggling and parting over the uneven ground but hanging together, walking at first, then breaking into a trot, a canter, gathering momentum until at last they were galloping. At the forefront of the charge the ragged banner lifted, there was a wild whoop of war-horns and the lances dipped in an uneven wave. The ranks of Tartarus ahead brandished weapons, and raised a baying, bestial mockery of a cheer, hungry and howling. The Master of the Teutonic Knights lifted his hand; something hissed through the air like a meteor and burst in spattering sulphurous flame among the second rank of horsemen. With a dull roar and clangour of metal the two forces met. 'They're far too few!' raged Dani. 'They'll be torn apart!'

'This is your doing!' raged Haagen. 'Get us out of here! Get moving!'

'You *nothing*, do you not see we are pinned down?' bellowed Thorgrim. 'They hold us with grapnels till the guard is busy – then they attack—;

'Get up there and cut them, then, damn you!'

'You try, and see how long you live!'

'You've got us into this!' roared Goldfüss, shaking his huge fist in Volker's face. 'You and your bloody plans – and your swindling moron of a boss Ulrich – you've sold out the lot of us—'

To his own utter astonishment Volker slammed his fist straight into Goldfüss's ham face, no hard blow, but it made the big man stagger and fall back. Beck and Haagen fielded him, raging at Volker. 'Get back aft!' he ordered, rubbing his stinging knuckles. 'If you can't do anything more useful, lock yourselves in! Aft, damn you! You too, Master Diderik—' But they were already dragging Goldfüss back to the cabin, and after him

Diderik, shouting and expostulating. Volker dived below, feet scrabbling on the tilted stairway, and swung his way through to the cabin. The horn had slid back under the bunk, and he knocked his head hard in reaching down for it. With the black case in his arms he swung giddily back to the deck, and as he emerged he tripped on the stairhead and went sprawling. He landed in the scuppers, but on something soft and writhing. It felt not at all bad. He found himself staring down into Dani's face; she was staring back at him. It struck him suddenly how pretty she looked like that, wide-eyed and startled, panting a little. She smelt nice, too, a warm smell like sun on the grass. Before he quite knew what he was doing, he'd reached down and kissed her. That, too, felt not at all bad. Curiously unlike kissing the tavern girls he'd made his first clumsy experiments with, on the rare occasions he could afford to. Somehow they hadn't seemed quite so . . . yielding. No – not that – so . . . mobile. She was sliding under him like an eel, making little noises . . .

Then something else struck him, right in the back of the neck, and he rolled free and sprang up, remembering where he was, grabbing furiously at the case. Dani sprang up to face him, her face flashing. 'Will you let me *breathe*, you bastard!' she shouted. Then she looked down. She was holding the horn-case. Volker was holding her bow.

'*Give me that!*' they shouted in unison, and grabbed. Naturally they collided again, and froze. The message from both their bodies was instant and unmistakable, but at that moment a stronger instinct took over, and they yelped and dived apart as the shower of arrows whirred over their heads. A bevy of misshapen things in jangling armour swarmed across the bows. Man-high or larger, ape-armed, bandy-legged and heavy, they clattered down on to the deck with long tails lashing. Guy yelled, struck out, and the first one folded over and toppled over the gunwale with a splash. Another flicked its tail and sent him sprawling, only to stagger grotesquely and slide after the other as Hlavisbana hissed in a great arc. Its head bounced along the scuppers to Volker's feet, a hairy caricature of humanity, squat, gnarled and chinless, wide pale blue wolf-eyes staring and blue tongue lolling between the tusks in its heavy jaws.

'*Laistrygons!*' yelled Guy, kicking another in the stomach and trading great slashing strokes with the one behind. 'I who forget nothing should have remembered sooner! The description is precise, in the *Bestiaire Infernale de Belami*—'

'For your scholarship I shall be indebted to you for as long as you live!' panted Thorgrim, jabbing one through with Hlavisbana and kicking the one Guy had kicked as it tried to get up. Two others set on him and he flailed the halberd about. 'Although given how long that now seems likely to be – *hah!*' – one creature failed to dodge fast enough, and sprawled messily on the deck '—the interest will be light.'

One teetered on the rail, gargling over the arrow in its throat, and fell heavily on to its much-kicked kinsman. 'Well,' yelled Dani, 'would you kindly tell a mere priestess *what in the name of all stuck-up male knowalls they happen to be?*'

'Old World ogres,' rumbled Guy, slashing his opponent's arm off. 'From Dalmatia, indeed. Eaters of men – when you can lay hands on one, *eh, mon coco*?' He ducked under the embrace of another monster and swept the legs from under it. It rolled over, shrieking, and knocked the kicked one down again. Thorgrim staved one off the rails with his halberd-butt, then sprang up after it, caught a trailing rope and swung across the deck, scything the long blade in a deadly arc that reaped down four of the creatures. The rest scattered, squealing like pigs, and Dani's arrows hissed

249

among them. Volker, still fumbling frantically with the horn-case, found one of them bearing down on him with an arrow in its back, roaring with pain and fury. Desperately he swung up the heavy case and clubbed the ogre right in its fangs; it staggered back, right into the path of Thorgrim's return swing. The Norseman's feet caught it right in the face and swept it over the rail with a crash; Volker grabbed Thorgrim just in time to stop him following it, and dropped the horn-case on his foot. Guy, facing a Laistrygon with a great two-bladed axe, was dodging from side to side, without trying to parry. Once, twice, the axe crashed into the deck; then he seemed to falter. With a triumphant howl the ogre slashed out at waist height – and Guy jumped up and back on to the coach-roof. The axe wielder was swung around by the force of his own blow. Behind him the kicked one sat up groggily, straight in the path of the runaway axe. With an impatient roar the wielder swung back to shatter his opponent. But by now Guy's sword was coming the other way. The creature fell heavily on the deck, and Volker, one fingernail torn and bleeding, at last managed to get the case open, grabbed at the horn and put it to his lips, letting the case drop.

His fingers caressed the keys, he took a deep breath – and then a huge shadow swung up in front of him, and Dani screamed. A mockery of a face, pale eyes glaring, tusks agape, a spiked mace swinging to smash him flat . . .

With the shock his lips faltered, his fingers clenched and he blew a horrible blatting discord, virtually into his attacker's stomach. The sound seemed to swell and fill the air around him, stiffening it into something almost solid, jabbing at his eardrums with tormenting spikes. Then, like the breaking of a steel blade, it snapped back. The mist billowed and vanished as if a fist had been punched through it, the monstrous face distorted and crumpled like an image mirrored in thin foil. He heard the crash of the mace dropping to the deck; then the mists swirled back around him, his breath failed, and he found himself on one knee, gasping. Beside him Dani was scrambling shakily up, and her owl, perched on the companionway, was flapping its wings and screeching. Further along the deck Guy, Thorgrim and various pale-faced crewmen were also picking themselves up; one heaved himself over the rail and retched, others shook their heads dazedly. At Volker's feet lay a shattered, shapeless thing, steaming faintly in the mist as its dark blood trickled down into the scuppers.

'The others are fled,' wheezed Thorgrim, 'back to the bushes – and small wonder!'

De Guillac nodded jerkily, then clutched his head. His moustaches had half unravelled, and his hair was standing out in great wisps. *'Enfer*, yes! That was a bold stroke, *mon gars*, that little lilt of yours. But I would be most especially desperate before I used it again! Now let us get that brute overboard ere it poison us all—'

A screech from behind spun them around, in time to see Goldfüss's burly back disappear over the after rail. With a chest of some kind clutched under his arm, he sprang the short distance to the *Walfisch*. After him Haagen leaped, swinging a heavy bag in front of him, and three or four of their followers and crew. Beck was already bustling along the deck, shouting orders to the rest, and the oars were beginning to thrash. Along its side hung severed grapnel lines. Evidently some cool head, far enough behind that horn-blast, had taken advantage of its aftermath to cut free. The screech had come from Diderik, left hopping with fury in the door of the tilted cabin as fleeing rowers and bodyguards barged past him. *'Come back! Come back here, you cowardly unwiped scuts, you! You mother-futtering sons of shag-arsed satyrs, stand and fight like men!'*

Volker stared, took one uncertain step. A blade gleamed in the mist, and the line between the two craft twanged, parted and splashed down. Men were still leaping the gap, but one fell short and splashed into the river, clutching frantically at the *Walfisch*'s rudder. The rowers behind him hesitated; De Guillac cursed luridly and pushed past, sabre in hand, only to throw himself down as Haagen whipped his arquebus to his shoulder and fired. All the others fell flat as the ill-aimed charge of shot smashed into the planking around them – and Volker yelled in horror as the horn slipped out of his hands, skidded down the deck and bounced through the open scupper and over the side. A soft splash sounded from overside. He hurled himself after it, but a hand caught his ankle and he measured his considerable length on the deck. *'Let me go, damn you! I've got to—'*

'Not just yet, laddie!' said Dani, and pointed. From the rail where Volker had been about to leap at least five arrows stood out like quills. The remaining crewmen yelled in panic and dashed below. 'It's in shallow water – we can delve it up in minutes. Just so long's we stay alive that long!'

Volker nodded jerkily, cold fury in his heart as he glared at the *Walfisch*, now out in the current and hoisting sail, heading swiftly towards the confluence and escape. The merchants had chosen to abandon half their cargo, not to mention one of their number and the rest of the crew, to avoid the consequences of their own stupid stinginess – just the kind of selfish, spur of the moment opportunity that would seem very clever to them, a stroke of good business. Well, it might be, at that; it wasn't far from here to the Adriatic, and relative safety. And no doubt they could recoup their losses from the part of Ulrich's and Diderik's goods that were aboard the *Walfisch*. Volker ground his teeth. Much as he hated violence, he'd give a lot to have a good long word with those three; and if somehow he escaped all this and met them in Sicilia, they'd better beware.

But the noise from the marsh claimed his attention again, as the battle milled and swirled back their way, the embattled riders careering this way and that to avoid being encircled. 'We've got to try for the horn, at least!' he protested. 'It's our best weapon! Those riders over there won't last ten minutes!'

There was a resounding crash from the after cabin, and Thorgrim came running forward, ducking and weaving to avoid the arrows that sang at him. After him scuttled Diderik. Both carried armfuls of flasks. 'Ten minutes, you say?' called Thorgrim. '*Saa*, hereditary hounder of mere dragons – can such a wizard of wineskins as yourself get a skinful in five?'

De Guillac's eyes widened, and he scratched his head, staring at the rows of bottles Thorgrim had torn from the merchants' abandoned stores. 'A man might try . . .'

He reached out, selected a dark flask of Armorican apple brandy, then regretfully tucked it in his pocket and chose another, of a very pale amber. He twisted the cork out with his teeth, took a huge swallow and coughed violently. Volker recognized the aroma of a fierce spirit imported through Bremen from distant Britannia, reported to be distilled somewhere in the glens of wild Valentia; it was rare, expensive and occasionally fatal.

Diderik sneered. 'Fine wizards you are! Can't control your own damned spells without daft paraphernalia – horns, drink, I don't know what mages are coming to! Why, when I was young I knew men who could make a spark of true lightning by just twanging two bits of bent wire!' A grumble of thunder in the distance lent weight to his words.

Guy ground his teeth. '*Mais faites-le taire, quelqu'un!* Or verily I shall twang *him*, bent that he is . . .' He took another swig of the spirit, gagged, wheezed, and abruptly he rounded on Volker. 'You, *musicien* – that cittern of yours, with what do you tune it? A pitch-pipe? Or a forking-tune – *ah, merde!*'

'A tuning-fork? No. I tune the centre string from my hautbois, then the rest relative. Sorry.'

Guy released him with a snarl, casting about; then suddenly he glanced overside, and snapped his fingers. 'Give me a moment ashore! Dani, can you cover me?'

She picked up her longbow, and the owl hopped back to her arm; she tickled it beneath the beak a moment, then drew a deep breath. 'Come to that, a woman might try as well,' she said, and launched the owl like a falcon from her arm. Up towards the clouds it climbed, spiralling till it seemed to vanish from sight; her eyes, following it, grew mistier, vague. She leaned almost absently on her bow, without looking at it, and fumbled like a blind man for an arrow. 'There . . .' she murmured, 'and there . . .' Then with startling speed she sprang to her feet, drew, aimed and loosed, and while the arrow was still in the air she drew and loosed another, lower and to the right. The low branches of a tree vibrated suddenly, there was a fearful screech, and a bulky form toppled crashing down into the bushes. To the right another rolled clanking out of the undergrowth. The arrow through the chest turned it over with a thump and sent it bouncing down the bank into the water.

Guy seized the spirit flask, swung himself over the rail and dropped lightly to earth. He ran, squelching in the soft mud, to where some of the riders had fallen in the first ambush, and plucked up a long trident lance from a dead hand. Another of Dani's arrows sang, and almost above his head a body slumped and swung head down out of a tree. He hardly seemed to notice, but struck the long prongs with his fingers, listened, and whooped with triumph. He was just turning back to the boat when the battle flared again beyond the

254

bushes, and a knot of ogres burst through. Dani felled one, but swore; many of the others were carrying long shields, and raised them against her as they rounded on Guy. *'Une baiser d'Armorique!'* he roared, and reversing the lance in his hands he swept the heavy butt-end at them, braining the nearest and staggering the others.

Then they staggered the other way as Thorgrim, with a truly barbarian battle-yell, launched himself boots first off the rail right on to one of the raised shields, and stomped its bearer face down into the mud. Skipping lightly free, he raised one edge of the shield with Hlavisbana's tip, shrugged, let it fall and faced the rest as they fell on him en masse. Volker grabbed a boathook and, reaching out over their heads, caught one's collar and tipped him struggling under the feet of the others, tripping several. Hlavisbana hissed among them, and as they fell back Volker hooked another by the shield; Dani sprang to help him, laying the shaft of the hook across the rail. Volker caught her meaning and together they threw their weight on it. The hapless ogre swung kicking into the air and dropped on the heads of his fellows. Thorgrim, snarling, plunged Hlavisbana once, twice into the throng and turned to call. 'Come, Armorican, the way is . . .'

His voice tailed off. The mists swirled where Guy had been. He hesitated, peering around. But the remaining ogres were scrambling up, snarling and champing. *'Leave him, Thorgrim!* called Dani. *'Get yourself back, at least!'* It was good advice, but as the Norseman turned to take it one of the creatures snatched up its spear and flung it. With a whirling twist of his halberd Thorgrim parried. The spear boomed against the boat's flank, raising a frightened yell from the skulking crewmen, and he lunged forward in a straight-armed thrust. The point skidded a bright scratch across the creature's crude breastplate, came to a joint and sank in. The ogre fell howling while the Norseman snatched up the spear as a pole and vaulted for the boat's railing.

Just at the apex of his leap the shaft sank into the mud with a satisfied slurp. Thorgrim hit the broad flank of the barge face first, arms and legs akimbo like a bearskin rug, and slid down into the slime. As Volker and Dani leaned over, a dripping figure arose with great dignity and flicked off a small amount of the gooey river clay that covered it from head to foot. 'You know,' Volker remarked in an undertone as they reached down to it, 'there was this old rabbi who lectured at my college – he was always trying to make a *golem*, but I never thought I'd see one . . .'

His voice tailed off. Dani had stiffened suddenly, staring. At nothing, apparently; but her eyes, wherever they might be, were showing her something different. Volker strained his sight, but even elf-eyes are little use against the arch-deceiver mist. Then Thorgrim's grip tightened suddenly on his wrist, and he too froze, half-way up the side, glaring into emptiness; it was his magical instincts that had been triggered, picking up what none of them could see. But an instant later they could, far out on the plain, as the mists swirled apart again.

'Oh sh . . .' breathed Volker. 'Er, sorry, Dani . . .'

'Oh *shit*!' howled Dani.

'*Ej, skidt!*' bubbled Thorgrim. '*Og løg!*' Alerted, perhaps, by the blast of the horn or the sight of the fleeing *Walfisch*, the black bulk of the Teutonic Knight was smashing through the battle, in fear and fury lest his prize escape him. Trampling across friend and foe alike with heedless wrath, he turned at full tilt across the marsh, straight towards the boat. Nothing stood in his path; the Laistrygonians ululated and broke line, the cavalrymen reared and skittered away as his great horse, so encased in armour like his own that its colour could not be told, came charging through their ragged

256

lines. Dani nocked an arrow, but hesitated, shaking her head. 'Can't waste a shot! And even if I wait till I see the yellows of his goddamn eyes, I don't know any normal point's going to get through that armour!'

'Or his filthy hide beneath!' agreed Thorgrim, squelching over the rail. 'The bombard – no, that will take hours to remount. The powder, then! A barrel, with a fuse, if we could throw that—'

'*No!*' cried Dani and Volker together. 'Not after the last time!'

'Help me over!' insisted Volker. 'I might just find the horn!'

But Dani called out and pointed. The mist had blown thin for a moment, and out on the plain, right in the path of the approaching Knight, they saw Guy racing out past a clump of trees, waving a bottle and pouring out a stream of Gallic oaths.

'Well, he *looks* drunk enough . . .' mused Volker.

Thorgrim shook his head mournfully, shedding little flakes of clay. 'No. He is still running in a straight line.'

Guy raced back in the other direction, apparently leaping in the air with rage. 'I guess we might've overdone it,' said Dani, unhappily. 'It's gotten to him at last.'

Then he reappeared, running even faster because he was being towed along by the riderless horse he had been chasing. He had caught it, but only by the bridle, and he was being dragged along in great leaps, straining to grab the saddlebow without dropping his precious lance. As they watched, he made it, pulled himself clumsily up and grabbed the reins. The horse bucked and protested, but he kept his seat and turned it to his will. Then he tilted the bottle to his lips for a long swig, oblivious to what was bearing down on him. Dani shrieked. *'Guillac, you lousy sot! Look out!'*

She had a carrying shriek. De Guillac peered around, and choked in horror at the metal-cased monster bearing down on him, the marsh-mud thrown up in torrents by its driving hooves. The jangle and crash of its armour carried even over the confused row of battle behind. The bottle flew from his lips in a great spray of spirit; the startled horse shied under him and almost fell. With a mighty heave the Armorican sent the now empty flask arcing straight at the oncoming Knight. Expecting some sort of magical assault, the monstrous figure yanked on his rein, bringing his enormous warhorse into a skidding unstable wheel about as the bottle fell. It struck his elbow with a musical clank, fell and shattered under the great hooves. Tilting in his high saddle, the monstrous Knight peered down at the shards; the horse sniffed at them dubiously, gave the largest an experimental lick and sneezed. The Knight sat up furiously and wheeled his mount around once again. But even as he swung out to charge Guy lowered his trident-tipped lance to rest, and charged in his turn.

'No!' yelled Thorgrim. 'Not that! Cleft-wit, you cannot go tilting at such a thing! Your horse is too light! Your armour is elsewhere!'

The Master of Knights gathered in the chained flail he had used to whip on his beastmen, lifted his own vast lance from the socket by his saddle and lowered it to the ready. It looked like a small pine trunk, capable of driving in the very timbers of the hull itself, and that even without any magic upon it. But magic of some sort it would surely have; this time the Tartarist would know with whom he had to deal, and would take no chances. He looked like a moving castle now, or some black ship of battle racing to ram. Guy's dishevelled curls billowed in the wind as he gathered speed. 'He really has flipped!' gasped Dani.

Volker shook his head, full of a growing gleam of glee. 'I don't think so!'

'What?'

'He wanted a tuning-fork, remember?'

'Sure! Bits of metal to twang, like old Didi said – but how's even a hot spark going to hurt that thing?'

'It can't – but what sort of note did that armour sound when the bottle hit? About F#, maybe?'

Thorgrim goggled. 'I think you have hit your head once too often – and yet . . . there is magic building up around him, yes! He is saying a spell—'

'Too late!' yelled Dani. *'Here they come!'*

'And the tines of a lance are ten times larger than a tuning-fork!' shouted Volker. 'He's going to – *down*!' He hauled at the other two. There was a sudden dull clang, and—

Something that was more a blow than a sound hammered at their ears, shaking and rattling the deck beneath them. Their sight filled suddenly with dancing pink streaks, and the air with a sulphurous, tingling smell.

'—to throw a thunderbolt,' Volker concluded, though his own voice buzzed tinnily in his ear. 'F# it was.' Thorgrim's fervent reply he could not make out, but he saw what the Norseman meant. A rain of pieces was pattering down through the seething air, blackened and smoking, and there was a horrible stench of roasted meat spreading beneath the sulphur. Half the stand of trees were fallen or sagging, and along the bank the bouncing tails of a number of ogres were fast disappearing into the distance, somewhat singed. Out on the field the battle milled in sudden mutual panic. The horse Guy had ridden was galloping even faster in the opposite direction, with a great black stripe seared along its back, but of him or the Teutonic Knight there was no sign in the scorched circle of mud where they had met.

'Oh, good gods . . .' said Volker shakily, but then he saw something black stir in the mud. Slowly, painfully, it heaved itself up upon all fours.

'Who is it?' breathed Dani, leaning over Volker's

shoulder. 'It's him – it must be – we've got to help him!' Then the form reared up suddenly on its knees, and from its back it pulled an enormous sword.

'So!' said Thorgrim, very decisively, and hefting Hlavisbana in his hands he sprang up and over the rail. But he stopped dead as he landed, because the Teutonic Knight, without getting up, slashed wildly out at the scorched mud only some six feet away. What looked like a lump of it sprang up with understandable speed, brandishing the twisted stump of a lance. It ducked the blow, aimed a kick between the Teutonic Knight's legs, clutched its toe with a scream and went hopping away through the mire. After it, staggering just as much over the smouldering tussocks, came the Teutonic Knight, furiously hewing and slashing. Thorgrim bounded out after them, but the muddy front-runner waved him away with a shout.

'No! He is mine, this one! This time he has pushed me too far! *Get the horn!*'

Volker was already scrambling down the side. Thorgrim hesitated, shrugged and came stamping down the bank to help. 'It was just here!' panted Volker, splashing around thigh deep. 'It's hard sand, luckily – but it slopes down to the clay – try there!'

They ducked down, raking around the shallows beneath the hull. Thorgrim, with most of his clay washed off, glanced anxiously back over his shoulder. 'Let us hope the wineskin is right about his playmate! Sooner or later it will catch him – or its little friends will finish with the guards and come to help!' Even as he spoke the bushes burst apart, and de Guillac, slathered in mud, came staggering out on to the bank some hundred yards ahead. 'Beware, sheep-head!' yelled Thorgrim. 'It is pure marsh there!'

But an inhuman roar of rage drowned his words as the Teutonic Knight stumbled out of the undergrowth, hewed at de Guillac, missed him and fell flat on his face in the mud. De Guillac turned, swatted at him with the remains of his lance, missed as conclusively and slipped down on his backside. Up rose the Teutonic Knight and came stamping forward, only to find his sheer bulk sinking his feet into the mire, giving de Guillac time to scramble up and lurch away. On they came, slipping and falling almost by turns as each lost patience and lashed out at the other. Guy was mired to his shins, the Teutonic Knight wading to his knees, but for all his weight he was gaining, his huge legs driving inexorably through the bog as if it was deep water. In desperation Guy turned and hurled the lance at him, but the huge sword batted it aside and came on, unstoppable.

Guy fell again, and rose only to his knees, swaying. His sabre hung sheathed at his side, but he made no move to draw it. Out of his tunic he plucked what Volker recognized as the brandy flask, still miraculously intact, and raised it to his lips. The huge sword quivered, poised, advanced . . .

'Well, *messire*,' said Guy, striking a theatrical pose of noble resignation, 'I can run no further through this miserable *marais*! Permit me one last drink before the inevitable. You will, of course, join me?'

With sudden force he flung the bottle; the black sword shattered it in midair, and its contents sprayed out in the blundering monster's path and sank into the mud. Guy thrust out his hands and dug them deep into the mire, chanting:

Spiriti omni excellentissimum vinorum, audite, adiuve,
subvenite!
Esprits de bon Armagnac, à moi, à l'aide! Effervescendus
est!

Just in front of the Teutonic Knight, where the brandy had fallen, the marsh bubbled and belched. Then it blasted upwards in a single explosive, fountaining column, a great geyser of brownish-red that sent the huge man reeling back – once. He bowed his head and plunged straight through it, swinging back the sword with a triumphant, inhuman roar. The blued steel fangs that were part of his horrible helm glistened. De Guillac knelt where he was.

But the stroke faltered. The cry changed. The huge man had ceased to move. Suddenly he was sinking deeper; by now he was mired to the waist. He roared, plunged again, and moved half a step, at most. Only now the marsh was above his waist, rising to his chest, weltering and gurgling around him as the fountain bubbled inexhaustibly. They could smell it from the boat now, rich, heady fumes overpowering even the marsh fragrance, fragrant and dizzying. The Knight shook his ghastly head as if he was even more affected, his red tongue lolling; he struggled furiously, sending great gobbets of marsh flying, and sank still more, to his armpits. The great sword whistled within a hand's breadth of Guy's face, but the Armorican knelt unmoving, as if willing the marsh to spout up more and more wine. It was almost at the Knight's neck now, but only when some of it splashed into his gasping mouth did his true plight seem to dawn on him. He struggled no more, but spoke strange words in a loud metallic whisper, sweeping his hand in wide passes across the marsh. Beneath them it seethed, hissed and began to steam; Volker recognized a heating-spell, setting the particles of liquid shaking to boil away the new inflow. Clever – since it was alcohol, with a low boiling point, he might just manage before he boiled himself.

But it was what Guy had been waiting for. He scrambled up, hand to sabre. Unfortunately the wine fumes, plus what he'd already drunk, had got to him, and all he could do was stand and sway. The huge Master roared in triumph and swung a frenzied burst of slashes at him. Any one should have eviscerated him, but Guy just leaned back at a ridiculous angle, like a sapling in a storm, and they sang a finger's breadth past his muddy sash. He gave an irritating giggle, and wagged a cautionary finger at nowhere in particular; Volker suspected he was seeing several Knights. The real one snarled through his encrusted animal mask and aimed a tremendous slash at Guy's feet; it went into the marsh instead, and sent a great wall of winey muck splattering over the Armorican. He staggered, dripping horribly and spluttering with rage, wiping the stinging stuff out of his eyes – and stumbled within range of the sword. Volker and the others yelled a warning, but already the Knight, with a triumphant snarl, was bringing the blade crashing down in a blow that should by rights have split Guy from crown to ankle.

But in the same moment Guy's weapon left its scabbard. He could not have stopped that blow directly – no normal human could – but it glanced off his sabre at the hilt. It was the merest touch; but it was enough to turn the Knight's sword by its own force away from Guy, past him and beyond. It crashed like a shadow of dark iron into the muddy softness of the marsh, and the Knight, carried along by his own unstoppable strength, fell with it, face forward into the sullied marsh. An angry roar choked in bubbles – and Guy sprang. There was no doubt what he was seeing now; his boot landed right on the back of that frightening helm and ground it clear down beneath the muddy surface of the wine. Again the marsh erupted; the vast arms in their jagged armour flailed and scrabbled, the sword struck our blindly. Bubbles burst up around the Armorican's feet. Guy rocked and heaved like a boat at sea; any minute now he'd be overturned. But a minute was all he needed; this time, without fumbling, the sabre swept out, glittering above his head. Then, with all his strength, he hewed down hard into the churning bog at his feet.

The marsh erupted once again. He stumbled back. Then Dani screamed as, horrifyingly, the glaring beast-mask burst up leering through the surface, ready to leap for his throat. But it juddered, and bobbed, and fell aside. The growing pool shone with a sudden brighter, spreading red. The foul thing turned upside down and sank amid sticky bubbles.

'They should have warned that one,' remarked Thorgrim, 'how easily a man may lose his head in wine.'

Guy came skidding down the bank and collapsed face down into the river. Thorgrim ran to help him, but as Volker floundered after them he felt something bob against his ankle, like a nuzzling fish. He reached down and his fingers closed about the horn. With a yell he seized it, fell flat into the river but burst up, dripping and triumphant, and brandished it aloft. A great stream of water sluiced out of it and down onto his head, and a small crayfish struck him in the left ear. Up on the deck Dani was positively leaping with triumph and urgency. 'Sound it, Volker! We're almost out of time!'

Waist-deep in water as he was, he swung towards the land and raised the horn to his lips. But he hesitated. What should he play? Not that jarring, murderous blast again, nor anything like it. Too easy, too powerful; like almost any powerful force, this horn was more naturally destructive than creative. Ulrich could have played discords himself; but he wanted a musician. Someone who could make music speak . . .

He blew, and his fingers shaped a half-remembered call he had once heard echoing from castle walls at dawn, a rising call of triumphant challenge. Out it sang across the flat land, and the trees bent and quivered.

'Play it again, Volker!' called Dani encouragingly.

He splashed through the shallows to the bank, up and through the bushes, still playing the theme over and over, extending it, developing it till the horn was fairly whooping with excitement, and he felt the wild music shiver through his bones like a cold fresh wind. The trees lashed and rattled their leaves as if a gale had struck them and stripped away their leaves, the grasses hissed and bent humbly to the spongy earth. The brown pools lifted and quivered in strange patterns of vibrant ripples that did not die, but fed on the sound and grew stronger, clearer, diffracting the last low sunlight till it leaped from them in a forest of rainbows.

Out on the plain he saw the tight coil of battle untwine and break. Some of the beastmen were breaking off the fight, jumping, prancing, flailing their heads about wildly, as if goaded by stinging gnats. One or two ogres were even tearing off their helms and throwing down their weapons to claw at their malformed ears. Were the others hardier, or just tone-deaf? All too likely, among evil Old World breeds. He played on, fighting for breath, and saw some begin to break and run; yet the little knot of riders were still hugely outnumbered. It wasn't enough, but he couldn't think how to alter or heighten the call any further. He could hardly keep on playing. His mind was clouding with sheer effort, his ears playing tricks; he seemed to hear echoes where there was nothing to make them, his call coming back at him from the distance. His breath failed him. Red-hot bands snapped tight around chest and forehead, and he fell gasping to his knees. But over the roaring darkness in his mind he heard the horncall still, felt the horn he clutched vibrate in sympathy. Forcing himself to look up, he saw across the wide land a glint and sparkle of metal, and heard beneath the horncalls the faint rumble of many hooves. 'Scarlet banners!' shouted Dani, from the boat. 'I can see them!'

'And she does not even look that way!' said Thorgrim mildly, helping Volker to his feet, and helping him back towards the boat. 'But the eyes she uses have the right of it, I think. The prince Oberto comes, with all his *haerethmen*! And see those brutes begin to run!'

'But how . . . so soon . . .'

'Days past our noble captain sent riders back to tell of the satyrs; perhaps the Black One was troubled by what he heard. Or perhaps by other things that he heard: tales of the First Creation flocking to a new leader like ravens to a battlefield. Or perhaps,' added the Norseman as he heaved Volker up over the bows, 'perhaps he caught some rumour of our merchants' little bargain, and was already on our heels. I am thinking he will be ill content to play the fool. I am also thinking that we should not stay to find out.'

'Me too!' said Dani, hauling Volker in. 'At least not till we have some nice juicy trade goods to pay his tolls. Anyway, this is no place to hang around. Those beastmen'll get here before he does, and they'd just love a boat to haul ass in!'

Guy, slumped against the coach roof, detached a wine bottle from his lips long enough to grunt agreement; but nobody made a move. Volker realized with astonishment that all of them, even Diderik, were waiting for his word. 'Well, er, let's get moving!' he said. 'Thorgrim, could you possibly—'

But the Norseman was already barking orders. 'Volker, Dani, take the tiller! Guy, go and pole her off! Keep a weather eye open!' Volker might be their leader, but Thorgrim was the skipper. Guy swayed to his feet, seized a quantpole and walked the deck like a tightrope to the bows. Below their feet Thorgrim was kicking some spirit back into the terrified crew. 'Up and to your benches! If you are afraid, then fear *me*! I am *right here*!'

In seconds the oars were threshing. Guy leaned heavily on the pole, but with every sign of going to sleep right there. Dani ran to help him, and Volker hauled the tiller around. Slowly, grindingly, the *Walross* righted herself with a lurch that sent Guy staggering back across the deck, and began to slide like her namesake back across the gravel into the safety of the water. Guy fell down the companionway and stayed there, his boots sticking up into the air. Loud alcoholic snores drifted out of the well. With hoarse cries a group of beastmen burst out of the trees. Volker let go the tiller, seized the horn and blasted a single searing F straight at them. This close, the pure sound seemed to sting through the air like an arrow; they ducked, but one was caught and whirled around by the sheer force of it. Others came splashing out into the shallows; he blew notes like slingstones that whipped up little splashes of water among them. Louder and louder he blew, and the rowers pulled in time with him; little by little the *Walross* pulled free and away from shore. The current touched her, and she swung around; Dani, running back, caught the tiller, and the horizon swung wildly in front of Volker. But as it steadied, and the joining of the rivers opened out ahead, he seemed to hear more echoes of his horn, more distant, fainter, somehow subtly changed, as if their timbre had darkened. The boat swung slightly, and they vanished. He hardly knew then if he had actually heard them at all. *Albensohn!* he told himself contemptuously. *Elfsson, drunk on illusions! Always ready to conjure up what isn't there!*

But then Dani, unskilled with the helm, overcorrected its swing, and the landscape passed in front of his eyes again. He blew another blast. There *were* echoes there, as if waiting; but echoes from what, in this flat country? They seemed louder, stronger now that he was listening out for them; and they were coming from a particular direction . . .

From the land came the rumble of Oberto's approaching cavalry, the screams of ogres and beastmen being ridden down and spitted. Dani looked back once, then shut her eyes and looked away. A beastlike shape plunged into the water beside the *Walross* and was borne away in the quickening current, screaming unavailingly. They were safe now; but Volker hardly noticed.

He aimed and blew again, a questioning minor, and again the echoes came to him. There was no doubt of it; the horn was showing him a way. His way, to fulfil his charge. Across all this great space of flat land it was drawing some strange harmonic resonance to him, out of the dark forest boundaries of Alpina Carnatica. From the very lip and brink of the Empire, of human civilization itself, the second horn was calling.

Chapter 6

Volker stared mockingly down into Dani's face, watching her eyes slowly widen as she stared back. She was wriggling and sliding under him like an eel on a fishing hook, making small, meaningless sounds. She smelt warm, like earth baked under a hot sun. No mistaking his body's response . . .

'Let me go, you bastard!'

Her fists flailed, but one hand easily pinned her down, and he slapped her face sharply to quiet her. Her flash of anger and fear only whetted his desire. He chuckled at how easily his knife parted her doublet laces; a single contemptuous slash through her silk shift revealed her smooth, quivering belly . . .

Silk shift . . . ?

Something – an iron vice clamped around his arm – a terrier's jaws shaking a rat – something metallic, iron-cold, dripping warm mud – in his face a rancid stink he'd thought well buried in the marsh . . .

'Hel og haglbyge, what night-mare rides *your* shanks?'

Volker found himself staring stupidly into Thorgrim's face, still expecting to see the half-crushed, half-shattered horror that had once been the metal-fanged face of the Knight. The big Icelander's stare was not entirely friendly, but then he'd been sunk in Nordic gloom since the moment they entered the forest. 'It is your turn to watch. And it seems to me you should be drinking less of the *drakener's akvavit.*'

Volker lips shaped a twisted attempt at a smile. Fragments of dream still clung to his mind like river-leeches. 'You're right. I can't handle spirits in his quantities.'

Thorgrim's stare became pointed. *'Naa?* I think it is not spirits you have handled; but the cold, that will soon put you to rights. I go see what dreams this *ufor-dommelige* place can bring me.'

'Believe me,' said Volker, 'they couldn't be worse than mine.'

As he stood up the chill night air struck him like a body-blow. Quickly he thrust another log into the sinking embers of the fire and sat down again, wrapping his cloak more tightly around himself. The day had been hot and humid, and his face still tingled with sunburn, but nightfall had brought a marrow-chilling breeze that sighed among the forest leaves like the ghost of an abandoned lover.

Thorgrim was already asleep, his snores combining with Guy's in a grotesquely unmusical counterpoint. Dani was curled around her scrip on the other side of the fire, and its flames raised red-gold highlights in her hair. He remembered the feel of that hair between his fingers, the yielding warmth of her body, the taste of her lips like a carnival sweetmeat . . .

And the edge of her tongue, like a well-sharpened axe. Gods alive, I'm supposed to be keeping watch . . .

Sitting still was difficult. The ground was hard, the night breeze was whistling through the growing number of rips and tears in his cloak, and he longed to be moving. Each morning he sounded the horn, and each morning the ancient, half-forgotten landscape echoed and re-echoed with its sound, rousing the harmonies of its hidden companion. For three days they had travelled, halting only when night fell, and now Volker could feel the growing power of the second horn all about him. At first, like Thorgrim, he had felt hemmed in by the trees, as if they were closing ranks behind him, walling him off from the sun and the sky.

270

Now, though, he saw the forest with new and different eyes. Watching fans of sunlight cut through the rising mists of morning he had felt, for the first time, that this ancient landscape held a secret that was his for the taking. More than ever before, he was conscious of every tiniest detail of his surroundings: the dark, encircling trees, the lingering scent of their leaves, the soft, sibilant music of air moving among twigs and branches . . .

And something was missing; something important, something that altered the harmony, or lack of it, around him. He glanced quickly around the fire, counting heads. Dani was turning uneasily in her sleep, moving her hands as if to ward away an evil dream.

Me, perhaps.

Joachim lay in a protective huddle around his iron-bound arquebus, keeping his powder dry. Thorgrim was flat on his back and snoring lustily. The three crewmen lay where Volker had placed them, grouped around the provisions, but . . .

'Guy! Guy, where are you?

His yell roused the entire party. Thorgrim lurched awake, thrust aside his blanket, sprang up and tripped over his halberd. Dani groaned and flailed her arms as the owl pecked her out of her nightmare. Joachim, still half-asleep, began a lethal juggling act with his arquebus, his powder horn and a lighted fuse. Thorgrim grabbed a brand from the fire and swung it in a roaring circle, but there was nothing to see.

'Guy!' yelled Volker. *'Guy!'*

'Gone,' said Thorgrim decisively. 'But for how long?'

For a moment Volker made no reply. It was almost as if he could *hear* something, something far away among the trees like the last whisper of a magical wind, or a fading snore . . .

'Volker! The watch was yours! *How long?*'

Thorgrim's voice was urgent rather than angry, but

Volker bridled at the implication. 'He was here when you woke me, Alfvinnsson. I could hear him – loud and clear, the same as you.'

The Icelander shook his head. 'It is like the earth had swallowed him up. And there is – '

'I'd like to see it try. He'd make more than a mouthful for the earthquake beast. No, I'd swear that wherever he is, he can't have gone far. What we need now—'

'Is me,' said Dani quietly. 'Except that this time I can't help you. The owl is flying wherever she can, but it's almost like the trees are moving to block her sight.' She sniffed at the air. 'One thing I *can* tell you. The huldra were here.'

Thorgrim nodded. 'That would explain . . .'

'Huldra,' snarled Volker. 'I could have guessed that for myself. A sneak attack, at night, and unprovoked . . .'

'Unprovoked?' Dani's voice was cool. 'This is their land. We've got no right to be here.'

'Volker,' said Thorgrim, 'you should . . .'

Volker ignored him. 'So it's *our* fault they attacked us. Is that it?'

'Every morning you sound that horn, Volker. Every morning we, and everything else in the forest, can hear the response. They're frightened, that's all.'

'So what do *you* suggest? You want me to go ask them for our friend back?'

Dani's face hardened. 'You want me to do it for you?'

With an effort Volker bit back a furious retort. Long ago – almost longer than he could remember – he had made his decision never to seek out his father's people or to acknowledge, in any way, his blood-ties with the forest folk. But now . . . now, perhaps, Guy's life depended on whether or not Volker could swallow his pride.

'You have finished, you two?' said Thorgrim. 'Good. There is the taint of huldra magic about this clearing,

272

and it is stronger than any I have known before. It is little use to follow them through this murk, and a place so unchancy. Else we'll all be their prisoners before morning.'

'He's right, Dani,' said Volker. 'They know this forest – every leaf, every twig, every blade of grass in every clearing. If you or anyone else moves away from this fire, we might just as well bind you hand and foot and *give* you to them.'

'Then *do* that, Volker Seefried – if you can!'

With a deafening roar, the fire exploded into a searing, white-hot column of flame. Instinctively Volker covered his eyes, stumbling back from the blast and half-falling across his own scrip where it lay concealed in the grass. When he could see again, Dani had gone.

'That one,' chuckled Thorgrim, 'is a sly little vixen. I think she has more magic than all of us.'

'Then I wish to Hela Proserpine she'd use it to *help* us! Now I'll have to follow her, fetch her back—'

'*Naa?* Can she not take care of herself, the little ratcatcher?'

'Against *huldra*?'

The Icelander shrugged. 'She is a priestess of Diana Skadia, no? You think, perhaps, that you would be a better hunter?'

'I know huldra, Thorgrim – and whatever else she is, she's only human. Believe me, it isn't enough.'

'And the quest, my friend? What of that?'

'If I don't find Dani – or Guy – it's over anyway.'

'Then I come with you.'

'No. Stay here with the others, and stay alert. If you're awake, you'll feel huldra magic long before anyone can see them. And if you even *think* they're coming, don't wait. Run.'

Thorgrim scowled. 'Are they so terrible, these huldra?'

'Put it this way, Grim – if I had the choice between

273

a pit full of vipers and a pit full of huldra, I'd choose the vipers every time.'

The Icelander shrugged expressively. 'So when shall we meet?'

'I'll wind the horn at sunrise. Follow the sound, and be on your guard every step of the way.'

He closed his eyes for a moment, expecting the usual struggle to remember a charm for night vision; but now he could almost see Strauben's massive grimoire lying open before him on its monstrous bronze stand, its gilded characters gleaming in the flickering lamplight. The spell seemed to unreel before his eyes, changing sunlight to moonlight, candlelight to the flickering blaze of a pine-pitch torch. He opened his eyes on a different world, a grey and silver midnight world, leached of colour like the kobold fortress. It was like looking at sunlight through smoked glass, except that sunlit shadows never managed to look *quite* that threatening . . .

Thorgrim watched him go, sighed, turned to put another log on the fire – and froze. Somewhere close by he could hear a slow, rhythmic and distinctive sound that had become all too familiar over the last few weeks. . . .

'Du! Drakener! Din sagnagtig snorkegris, hvad i al Hel laver du der?!'

The appalling noise stopped, to be followed by two staccato snorts, a sigh, and a hacking cough. A placid, rather sleepy face peered round a tree at the edge of the clearing with an expression of mild curiosity.

'There is something wrong, *mon ami*!'

'You!' roared Thorgrim. '*You* are wrong. You should be a prisoner of the huldra! You should be wrapped in chains! You should—!'

'And you,' growled Guy, 'you should have excavated that bat-infested cavern you are pleased to dignify by the term "nose"! Every night I must flee to some haven beyond the reach of your glacier-grinding snores!'

At first Volker's unreasoning anger with Dani blinded him to everything but the faint trail he had set himself to follow. In his fury he had scarcely thought about the spell that had come to him so easily, but now he began to appreciate its true power. In the strange, single-coloured world around him Dani's footprints were a brilliant, flaring orange like the trail of a salamander, fading behind him to a dull, glowing red. A flittermouse swooped into his path, and for the first time he heard the shrill, pulsing whine of its hunting cry before it scuttered to one side with a crack of its leathery wings and panic-stricken chirrup. Since his childhood he had feared the forest, without knowing why. Now he seemed a part of it, and more: he felt a power and a confidence he had never really known before, as if some energy from the trees, or the earth itself, was surging into his body with every step. He looked at his own hand, and saw a pulsing, sparkling network of interconnected forces, shining through his flesh like sunshine through a leaf. As the jaws of the forest opened on a storm-swept clearing, he seemed to look up for ever – beyond the spheres of the sun, the moon and the planets, beyond the fixed stars themselves, to the silent and mysterious sphere beyond. He stopped, transfixed. Faintly, at the very edge of hearing, there was a sound like distant bells. He closed his eyes, struggling to concentrate, and once again an image from Strauben's elaboratory seemed to fill his mind.

High above his head, the painted bronze orrery glittered in the light from the dying fire like a jewelled crown, its miniature planets moving swift and sure on their gearwheel courses. But now each movement, each planetary rotation, each twist and turn of the mechanism, was part of a single, soaring sequence of complex and interlocking chords that wrung answering harmonics from the cittern in his hands, from the ancient harp in the far corner, from the crystal retorts and ramekins on the shelf, from the very flames in the fire. As his understanding grew, he realized that even the dustmotes dancing in the rising air were a part of that same, impossibly complex harmony – that the rhythm of the blood pulsing through his skull was simply one of a dozen counterpointed rhythms underlying the slow, stately dance of the planets and the stars . . .

He opened his eyes with a new understanding. Strauben had written about the music of the spheres, but he had come to music slowly and painfully, committing the rules of harmony to memory like an ignorant child learning its grammar. He had known as much as any man alive, but his understanding had always been that of a scholar. Volker had been *born* a musician; he, like Strauben, had learned his musical theory from books, but for him the rules of harmony were simply a framework, giving structure to something he already understood. And unlike Strauben, he knew instinctively how and why the rules could be broken. Strauben had never played an instrument, never learned that music was a living thing, growing and changing with time until the old strictures no longer applied.

And that's what I can hear. It's beyond all our petty rules, all our silly, mortal ideas of what's right and what isn't. I've been waiting to hear this all my life – and now I've heard it, I know it's been there all the time . . .

'Volker!'

The voice startled him abruptly out of his reverie. In the shock of discovery he had almost forgotten about Dani, but her voice was unmistakable.

Just like the woman. Run from you one minute, and the next—

'Volker! You going to stand there gawping all day?'

'Where in Tartarus are you?'

'Over here. I'm stuck.'

'You're *what*?'

'In Flora's name, Volker, *get me out of here*!'

He could see her now, a gold-edged, glowing figure half-hidden behind the gently pulsing shadow of a tree, struggling to free herself. Whatever she was trapped in had made some interesting rearrangements of her clothes, and she seemed to be embarrassed, angry and frightened in about equal measure. And yet there was something unreal about her, as if what he was seeing was no more than an image out of his nightmares—

'*Please*, Volker. It hurts!'

'All right, all right. Keep your hair on. I'm com—'

He stepped forward into nothingness. There was no time even to curse before the ground came up and hit him.

A noiseless shadow passed through the forest. A hunting wolf paused, sniffed the air, and went warily on its way. A dozen small creatures felt the same passing hint of danger without understanding its cause or its origin. At night, in this ancient forest, Dani was a wraith, disturbing nothing, leaving nothing but the fading warmth of her footprints to mark her passage.

The path she followed would have baffled even Volker's heightened senses, but to Dani, sharing the perceptions of her night-bird companion, the trail of bruised and broken grasses, bent twigs, and disturbed leaves was clear beyond all doubt. A heavy object had been dragged this way; and just ahead, at a bend in the path, something glinted among the litter of the forest floor.

It was an enamelled cap-badge, emblazoned with Guy de Guillac's family crest.

Dani shivered, glancing quickly about her, but the owl sensed nothing at all. It perched daintily on a tree branch overhead, swivelling its head in a discreet search for food. She smiled, sensing its hunger, and keenly aware that she had taken only the bare minimum of provisions for herself. But she, like the owl, was a huntress; and both of them needed to exercise their blunted skills. In the seclusion of the convent she had yielded to an illusion of peace and security. Now she had pierced the illusion but she could no longer fully trust her own abilities. At Nebelstein overconfidence had very nearly killed her, but here, now, she had the chance she needed to rediscover the full extent of her powers.

As if sensing her thought, the owl launched itself from its perch. Through its eyes, she saw the tiny movement in the bushes that had drawn its attention; and then, quite suddenly, there was darkness. At the clearing it had been nothing more than a shielding shadow, cloaking the wildwood from her sight. This was more, a stifling, midnight blackness that reached across the space between the bird's mind and her own, drawing her into endless silence. Only once in her life had she ever felt anything like it, at the moment when her first familiar had fallen prey to a mountain lynx . . .

And then, quite suddenly, she knew that death was coming for her.

There was no time to think, and barely enough to act. The owl was gone, with no way for her to know if it was alive or dead. She was already running when the first, terrible sound of pursuit came chittering down the wind. She could not tell what it was that sought her – even its scent was alien to her – but there was a smell of carrion about it. It made a sound like mad laughter, and it was moving faster than she could run.

The hunt had begun – and she was the quarry.

'The huldra are coming,' said Thorgrim. 'We must go from here.'

'Must?' rumbled Guy. 'We *must* run from a pack of effete wood-elves to whom straw in the hair is the height of fashion? We *must*—'

'That is what Volker told us to do.'

'Me, I don't run from nobody,' muttered Joachim. He hefted the arquebus awkwardly in the crook of his right arm, stumbling to one side as an iron ball slipped from his ammunition belt and cut a deep gash in the earth by his left foot. 'Let's see 'em argue with *this*.'

'*Des belles sentiments*, Master Joachim,' said Guy, drawing his sabre with a ringing flourish. '*Foi du Draconnier*, a civilized argument is none the worse for being expressed with a tongue of steel!'

'As well swing at a moonbeam,' said Thorgrim darkly. 'These are not the *alvar* of your woodland demesne, who have lived so long with humans that their own powers are forgotten. I feel their magic; it is dark and twisted, like the magic of the *fordomte* Tartarists. If we—'

For no apparent reason the big Icelander swung around, thrusting forward and upward with his halberd. A howling shadow dropped from the tree above, twisting desperately aside to escape the thrust, and at the same moment a pocket thunderclap erupted at his back, and the clearing exploded into momentary brilliance. The Norseman was already fending off two slim blades wielded by shadowy, half-visible opponents, and had no time to look behind him; but as he was forced to give ground he saw Joachim writhing on the ground in a swiftly spreading pool of blood. He could sense dark magic all around, magic tainted with the crawling horror of the First Creation. Shapes out of Tartarus leered out of the darkness, baring illusory fangs. The ground quaked beneath his feet, opening muddy, grass-bearded mouths to swallow him. The seasoned wood of his halberd-shaft changed beneath his fingers to a scaly, writhing mass of bone and muscle. He clenched his teeth against the illusion, ignoring the living blade that seemed to curl round and strike at his face. Instinct told him where it truly was, and he swung the long cutting edge in a scything arc that sent his opponents scattering for cover. In the swaying column of light from the fire he had a vague impression of lean, gaunt limbs, uncannily long, and savage, point-jawed faces with bulging, green-glittering eyes, but his training and experience kept his concentration on the edged weapons that surrounded him on all sides.

Guy had turned his back to Thorgrim at the first hint of attack, weaving a guarding net of steel with the blade of his sabre while he pulled his costrel from its pouch with his other hand. He wrenched the stopper free with his teeth, spat it out, and gulped down a triple mouthful of spirit just as two vine-covered trees stepped into the firelight, their branches lashing out towards his head.

Guy gave the costrel a stern look, hesitated for the briefest of moments, then roared a thunderous incantation.

In nomine Mercurio – in vino veritas!

Taking a second huge swig, he spat out a fine spray of liquid that kindled to a sheet of flame in the heat from the fire. Leaves withered at its touch, and a revolting scent of singed hair and burning rubbish drifted across the clearing. Blinking in disbelief, Guy found that the trees had apparently become two massive, bearded men dressed in a bizarre mixture of furs and vegetation and swinging clubs the size of major roof-beams. He grinned, and stepped back with a mocking bow.

'*Bonsoir, messieurs.*'

The new arrivals looked at Guy, and then at each other.

'*Affterooclode,*' said the first, pensively.

The second shook its head, studying the Gallian as if he were a rare and unusual specimen for a private collection. '*Affteroosirrill,*' it said, and then shook its head again. '*Orbucket – toogadir.*'

Without another word the creatures swung their clubs from the left and the right in a co-ordinated swing that should have crushed de Guillac's skull. Instead, with miraculous timing, they clanged together either side of Thorgrim's halberd blade, catching the weapon on its backswing. Guy ducked low and stabbed upward, spraying another blast of burning alcohol into his opponents' faces, just as Thorgrim, now completely off balance, fell heavily on top of him. The Gallian, taken by surprise, swallowed the remains of his mouthful of spirit, and curled up in a hacking, coughing ball.

The clearing rang with chittering laughter. Thorgrim, stumbling to his feet, discovered himself face to face with a hazel thicket that looked a little the worse for Hlavisbana's attentions. Guy was confronted by two merrily burning hawthorn trees.

'*Fumier fremissant du dragon dyspeptique*!' rasped Guy, in a voice like a rusty timber-saw. '*En tas*! Illusions! Illusions and trickery! And *you*, you addle-pated, stringy-limbed idiot of a Norseman, *you*—'

'Enough,' said Thorgrim. 'Not all was illusion, my friend.' He knelt by Joachim's side, but the grizzled bombardier was beyond all help. His face had been ripped apart, and his right arm was a mangled mass of charred flesh and splintered bone.

'*Enfer*, what *did* this to the unfortunate one?'

Thorgrim picked up the shattered remains of the arquebus. Its main bore was undamaged, but the powder-chamber at the back was a nightmare of twisted, broken metal. '*This* I should like to return to its maker – in a place where the sun does not shine.'

Guy nodded grimly, glancing about the clearing. There was no sign of their three companions. 'So, *mon gars*. It is you and I.'

Thorgrim dusted off his hose and frowned at a new tear in his jerkin. 'Bare is back without brother to guard it,' he said, with scarcely a hint of irony. 'But I should be happier with two. And perhaps a sister, also.'

'You may need them,' said Guy, with no irony at all, 'if *that* is not another illusion.'

Thorgrim squinted at the new arrival – a hulking shape poised to spring on the far side of the clearing – and frowned. 'It should be. But I think not.' He shrugged. 'No matter. The ale is good in Valhall.'

'Perhaps,' growled Guy, 'but the wine is poor. I suggest that we fight it.'

Dani ran. There was no time to think, and barely time to see where her feet were falling. On either side she heard the panic-stricken cries of birds and small animals caught, like her, in the tide of fear that was sweeping the wildwood. The trees around her rose from a twisted, intertwining network of roots that threw ribbed and branching wooden hawsers across every pathway. Above, tree-limbs meshed one with another to make a primeval canopy that shut out starlight and moonlight alike, trailing ropes of vine and creeper that brushed against her face like clutching fingers. The sounds of pursuit echoed bafflingly all around her, as if the chittering horror that filled her senses came from all directions at once, converging on her alone as its chosen prey. It sounded for all the world like a pack of marauding rats – which it just possibly might be, if some of her less guarded thoughts about Volker had angered the Mother. Even without the owl to help her, Dani could see detail in the darkness beneath the trees. On the whole, she would have preferred the darkness.

All around her, in a narrowing circle, the forest floor was coming to life. Leaf-mould writhed and scattered as the squealing, high-pitched cries grew louder. For a second she hesitated; then she grabbed one of the trailing creepers, tugged on it, and pulled it sharply off the tree. With a blistering oath she seized another and swarmed up it hand over hand, muttering a poignant prayer to the Mother as it, too, began to tear away from the branch overhead. She clung to it desperately, letting its pendulum swing carry her upward to the point where she could grab the branch and haul herself to safety. The damp bark stained the front of her jerkin a livid green. She hoped it would be good camouflage.

The old oak smelled warm and safe, like the hollow tree where she had sometimes hidden as a girl. She could feel small movements from inside the trunk – other creatures, taking shelter as she had done, chattering angrily at one another like respectable citizens grumbling about a declining neighbourhood. She crept along the branch, finding a place where the foliage gave her a clear view down into the darkness, and stared.

A thousand eyes were staring back.

The base of the oak seemed to explode, as if individual roots were tearing themselves out of the earth and leaping into the air. And then, at last, she understood what was happening. Once, long ago, Mother Hippolyta had told her of a skeleton that two novices had found in the forest. They gathered up the scattered bones with wondering reverence and brought them back to the Huntress's shrine, asking what could have killed a full-grown man so quickly, yet without leaving so much as a scrap of flesh on his bones. Mother Hippolyta had studied the bones carefully, measuring the tiny scratches that covered every surface . . .

Dani began to laugh. For the last hour she'd been running in terror, using all her woodcraft and all her natural skills, to escape from creatures that would probably have fled if she's so much as said 'boo' to them. She remembered Mother Hippolyta's face as she described summoning the two fidgeting novices to her private chapel and showing them the terrible monster they had discovered.

One of the creatures reared on to its hind legs, scrabbling at the roots of the tree, and Dani laughed again. There could be no doubt. She'd been treed by a pack of stoats.

'Hey!' she yelled. 'You down there! Run away! You want fresh meat, get someone else to kill it for you!'

She had expected the stoats to panic at her first shout, but the only response was another flurry of activity around the roots below her. It was almost as though the stupid little animals thought they could dig up the tree . . .

Something the size of a wolfhound leapt vertically towards her and snapped at the toe of her boot. She felt the wrench as its long teeth sank home, tearing at the soft leather. She felt the fangs grazing her toes – and then the stoat lost its hold and dropped back into the writhing mass of fur, teeth and claws below her. At the same moment she heard laughter like a mockery of her own, low, malicious laughter, without a trace of humanity in it.

It was coming from the tree, just above her head.

For a moment Volker seemed to hear mocking, sibilant laughter, but when he could open his eyes, he heard nothing but the call of some woodland animal. The fall, and the blow to his head, had done nothing to change the power of his night vision: he could still see the world around him in clear shades of grey, tinged with orange and red. But there was something missing . . .

'Dani? Dani, where are you?'

The Hel with it, she was here a minute ago . . .

A wave of dizzying nausea turned the world sideways for one gut-wrenching moment, and passed. He found it difficult to concentrate – the ground kept trying to kick him in the face, and the trees kept trying to fall on his head. Even so, he could see no slightest trace of Dani's footprints.

Been out a long time, then. Unless . . .

Unless he had been deliberately led astray.

Huldra. Their kind of trick. Split us up, lead us astray, play games with us. And that laughter . . .

His face darkened. He had little love for his father's folk, and none at all for the wildwood tribes. Once or twice he had seen them, tall, wire-limbed figures, eyes bright with power and malice, fiercely independent, yet inward looking, self-absorbed, and utterly hostile to strangers. And here, in this place . . .

Yes. What exactly is this place?

He seemed to have fallen headlong over a small cliff about twice his own height into a glorified ditch some four paces wide. A stream trickled over the stones and away into darkness. Various insects, disturbed by his movement, were crawling back into their hiding places. One of them looked as big as his hand, but then his eyes were still playing tricks with him. It might be possible to scramble out of the miniature valley, but it certainly wouldn't be easy.

Got to try. Got to find Dani's trail, if it isn't too cold to follow by now . . .

It took him three attempts, two broken fingernails and a set of bloodied knuckles to climb out of the trench. From the higher ground he could see it quite clearly, like a line through the forest – to his heightened senses there was even a faint difference in colour, as though the stream below glowed with some inner radiance of its own. His fingers still tingled where they had touched it. He could see the dying traces of his own footprints, wide-spaced where he had run to answer Dani's cry for help; but her tracks led away in the other direction, and by now their lingering warmth had faded to the very limit of his perception. He set out at a jogging run.

Damn the girl. If she didn't run so fast, I might have a chance of catching her up – and she's probably taking me clear away from the horn.

With his eyes fixed on the ground, watching for the

slightest change of colour, it was some time before he noticed the light ahead of him. He stopped for a moment, frowning and shielding his eyes. From his glimpses of the stars he knew that the night had many hours still to run, yet here was a brightness like sunrise, streaming through the trees and casting long, hard shadows ahead of it. And the shadows were moving in a rhythmic, swaying pattern that had nothing to do with the wind.

'I think,' said Thorgrim philosophically, 'that its mother was a wolf. The Fenris wolf, perhaps.'

'Something northern, at any rate,' grunted Guy. 'The hairiness is authentic.'

'In that case I shall take the left, and you can have the right of it.'

The creature – whatever it was – looked hungry. It also looked twice the size that any wolf had a right to be, with strangely muscled forelimbs, massive shoulders, and grotesque hindquarters. Its face, thick and heavy-jowled, was wary, following the movements of Thorgrim's halberd without quite losing track of Guy's drawn sabre. With no further word the two men stepped further apart, weapons at the ready, each trying to distract the creature's attention from the other. For a moment it seemed to hesitate; then the hind legs kicked out, and the jaws opened on a ravening nightmare of bristling fangs as it launched itself at Thorgrim.

The Icelander took three running steps forward, dropped to a crouch, rammed the butt of his halberd against the ground and drew it sharply upward to impale his attacker – but the creature leapt clear over his head, striking out with its tail in passing. Thorgrim ducked by sheer reflex as something like a small morningstar whistled past his left ear and shattered the trunk of a nearby tree.

'*Par Cerbère,*' chuckled Guy, 'but this one would make a fine guard dog!'

Thorgrim rolled sideways into a defensive crouch as he brought his halberd to bear a second time. '*Netop* – but first you must teach it not to wag its tail.'

Again the creature seemed to hesitate, wary of the halberd but unsure of the swordsman. When it leaped again Guy barely had time to slash at it with the sabre before its deadly tail clubbed at his outstretched hand. His reactions were a fraction too slow, and a numbing pain hammered down his arm as the hilts were struck from his grasp.

Seeing him fall, Thorgrim sprang forward, rammed the halberd-shaft into the ground ahead of him, kicked off, and polevaulted feet first at the creature's spine. He had meant to cripple it, or at least slow it down. Instead he landed squarely on its back. He grabbed desperately at its long ears as the enraged beast leapt and twisted in a frantic effort to throw off its unwanted passenger and crush him underfoot. The tail swished uselessly past Thorgrim's helmet, but there was no way the wolf-thing could harm an enemy astride its own back. With a final, despairing snarl it turned on its hind legs and bounded away into the depths of the forest.

Guy staggered to his feet, nursing his injured hand, and stared after it, shaking his head. '*Fieu,* but he should practise this *saltimbanque* trick with the halberd more carefully. Next I think he will spit himself on that eldritch *couperet* of a blade.' He dusted off his hose, recovered his sabre, and set off after Thorgrim at a loping run, grinning hugely. It seemed, after all, that the hairy Icelander had finally found a mount that suited him.

'*Arroliddergir.*'

The creature was still chuckling, a noise that Dani found disturbing, but it didn't look actively hostile. In fact a vague movement among the vines, creepers and foliage that passed for its clothes suggested it might be a little *too* friendly.

'Just keep back,' she said. 'Stay right where you are.'

The creature chuckled again, and stepped forward. It had no weapon except a long staff, but Dani knew from experience just how powerful a weapon that could be. She nocked an arrow to her bowstring and took a careful step back.

'*Wodyedotni?*'

'I said keep *back*!'

She drew the arrow back in a warning gesture. Somewhere among the leaves an opening like a mouth appeared, its corners turned down. The leaf-creature looked at the staff, looked at Dani . . . and threw the staff aside. Two heartbeats later she heard a furious chittering from the base of the tree.

'Look, friend, I've got worse things than *you* to worry about. How about leaving me alone?'

The creature spread its arms, opening six-fingered hands palm outward, and took another step forward. Dani drew the arrow back to her ear. 'Look, I am *not* fooling, you hear? One step closer, and—'

It took the step. She loosed, with a strident curse – and missed. The creature had moved faster than she imagined possible, grabbing the branch overhead with its outstretched arms and swinging sideways around and over it. Now it returned, feet first, before she could nock a second arrow, and struck the bow clean out of her hands. She swore again, savagely, and aimed a vicious kick between its legs – but again it was faster, grabbing at her foot and twisting it sharply. She responded as she'd been trained to do, by turning her whole body in the same direction, standing on her hands, and lashing out with her other foot. This time she connected with the creature's jaw, sending it stumbling backwards. Seen from upside-down its face was

288

surprisingly human-looking, apart from the flat nose, wide, hairy nostrils and protruding tusks. It looked like some kind of silvanian pig: an extremely male kind.

The pig-creature roared once, and pitched back into the fight, but this time Dani was ready for it. Ducking low, she aimed a series of swift, sharp punches at its kidneys, chopping savagely at its throat and neck as it doubled up in pain. Still roaring, it limped backwards along the branch. Its ardour looked to be cooling very fast indeed.

'Right. You stay there. I stay here. It's very simple.'

'*Liddrollpasskinfort!*'

The anger was unmistakable, and so was the injured male pride. But she couldn't fight this thing for ever . . . and the alternatives were unthinkable. She had to *stop* it, preferably without hurting it . . .

Far away, and echoing among the distant glades, she heard the sound of Volker's horn, and a mischievous grin lit up her face. There *was* a way, but it would need all the power, and all the concentration that she had.

Thorgrim Alfvinnsson had galloped stout-bellied, short-legged ponies across lava-fields and ice-floes. He had ridden bareback into a Rus charge with no more than a lance and his own wits to protect him. But nothing had prepared him for a wolfback ride through the wild-wood at dead of night. Low branches swung at him out of the dark, lashing him with leaves and trailing creepers. His mount bucked and twisted like an unschooled stallion, flailing at him with its club-tail, and with Hlavisbana still firmly in his grip, there was only one hand left for hanging on.

'*Skidt og sildemad!*' he roared, 'you will kill us both! Hold hard, *din ufordommelige uhyre!*'

The wolf was unimpressed, and reared up on its hind legs to prove it. The Icelander clung on grimly, goading the creature with his halberd till it dropped back on all fours and careered off through the forest in the latest of a dozen or so random directions. Thorgrim was vaguely aware of lights and music in a distant clearing, and a sound that might have been Volker's horn; then it was back to the dark, and the stinging slap of twigs, wet leaves, and anything foolish enough to bar their passage. A moth flew into his mouth, leaving a taste like foetid ale – bits and pieces of it caught in his beard as he spat it out. An owl appeared in front of his face and scuttered out of his way, hooting indignant reproaches in his wake. And then, at last, the wolf began to slow. He could hear its breath coming in long, hacking gasps, feel the pulse racing beneath its hairy hide . . .

'*Saa*,' he muttered. '*Saa*. Now you will do as *I* wish, *ja*?'

The creature sank back on its hind legs, but Thorgrim was too canny to loose his hold. 'Now, my little wolf, I wish to go find my friends . . . and as you have taken me so far out of my way, you shall help me.'

The wolf bowed its head, almost as if it understood him – and then reared up on its hind legs and all but threw him off its back.

'So,' roared the Icelander, 'you play leapfrog, hey? I show you! I . . .'

Inspiration struck. Leaning forward, still clinging to the wolf's ear with one hand, he struck it firmly on the nose with the flat of his halberd blade.

It sat down instantly, with a dismal howl.

'*Nice* wolf,' said Thorgrim insincerely. '*Good* wolf. Now you behave, yes?'

The wolf remained motionless, panting hard, its tongue lolling out of its mouth.

'Good,' said Thorgrim, after what seemed a decent interval. 'Enough rest. We go now.'

The wolf continued to sit and pant. Its breath was steamy in the chill night air, and would have smelt of rotting meat if Thorgrim had been able to smell it.

'We *go!*' said Thorgrim loudly.

The wolf clearly had other plans. Most of them seemed to involve sitting very still with its tongue hanging out.

'*Naa*. Now you play the mule. And so I shall treat you.' With an evil grin the Icelander reversed his halberd, and prodded the wolf just under its tail.

It was probably his worst mistake to date.

When he was next fully aware of what was going on, the forest seemed to be passing on either side a little faster than it would have done if he was an arrow newly loosed from a hundred and ten pound bow. He was hanging precariously on one side of the wolf while its shoulder rammed repeatedly into his chest like a blacksmith's hammer on a newly forged iron bar. Every so often stray bits of forest floor splattered into his face. Most were muddy. Some contained spikes. A few were still alive, and definitely not happy to meet him. With a desperate wrench, he pulled himself up on to the wolf's back.

He was just in time to see the tree-branch that curved low over the forest floor directly in the path of his unwilling mount.

Dani's attacker seemed to be in trouble.

It had begun confidently enough, rumbling its way into a towering rage and then making a menacing advance along the branch. Its problems had started when it tried to lift its right foot.

The foot refused to move. It seemed to have fallen in love with a particularly gnarled section of branch. In fact, it was just about rooted there.

Dani's grin broadened. The idea was simple enough, but her training – and her skills – made this kind of magic more than usually appropriate.

'*Geridofome!*'

The creature's improvised clothing had clearly taken

on a life of its own. Inquisitive shoots were burrowing into its nostrils, looking for somewhere pleasantly warm and wet for new seeds to germinate. Tendrils and creepers were discovering fascinating new bits and pieces to coil around and stick to . . . not all of them on their original host. As the vegetation that covered it burst into frantic growth, the creature was being helplessly trussed to the tree by its own body covering.

The principle was simple enough, but keeping the magic at the level she needed called for all Dani's skill and concentration. She could feel the energy draining out of her body as the spell drew on every ounce of her reserves, but at the same time she felt a fierce, almost savage joy. She could scarcely remember the last time a spell of this potency had worked for her . . .

Something heavy, moving very fast, passed immediately beneath the branch she was standing on. At the same moment a half-familiar figure cannoned into the living cocoon in front of her, ripping it free and hurling it outwards and downwards into the dark. From below came a furious medley of sounds like the arrival of a solitary female in a cage full of tom-cats. A strange looking wolf-like creature was chasing its own tail in ever-decreasing circles, trying to shake Dani's erstwhile attacker off its back. The remnants of her magic had apparently bound the wild man firmly to its shoulders, and there were other problems, too. The enraged stoats were mobbing both rider and ridden en masse, swarming over both of them like an army of agitated ants. Seconds later the entire collection had vanished into the forest, leaving nothing behind but the ever more distant and chaotic sound of their progress.

'*Befamle mig baglaens*, groaned a familiar voice, '*men det var dog en ordentlig tur.*'

'*Thorgrim!*' Dani's relief ran full tilt into her anger, and lost. This barnstorming fool of a Norseman had shattered the most wonderful, the most *powerful* piece of magic she had managed in years, and turned it from triumph to pure farce in a few seconds. 'What in the name of all the gods were you trying to do? Do you *know* what you . . . ?'

'*Dani, du kaere pigebarn!*' he roared, ignoring both her words and her fury and half-crushing her in an enthusiastic bearhug. 'Hel's hailstorms, I thought the *fordomte* huldra had you for sure! Such a time we have had of it, Guy and I! First we . . .'

'Guy and you?' A pang of fear thrust aside her anger. 'Then where's Volker? What's happened to him?'

'He followed you, *pigebarn*. You have not seen him?'

'No.' This was ridiculous. She had no business being this worried about Volker: with the horn in his hand he was a match for anything in the wildwood. And hadn't she . . . ? 'I heard the horn a little while ago . . . least, I think I did. Too far away to be sure. Hard to be sure of anything in these woods.'

'Hey, up there!' roared a familiar voice.

Thorgrim ignored it. 'I, too, I trust nothing in this place. I could swear I heard the voice of our winepaunch friend de Guillac – but then illusions are everywhere tonight.'

'And one is in your own head,' roared the voice. 'It is the illusion that you, my hairy friend, have a brain.'

Thorgrim raised both eyebrows and stared downward between his feet. 'You are here? Now? *Skidt og sildemad*, I think you have borrowed the sandals of Mercury!'

'What do you do in that tree, you two?'

'Nothing,' smirked the Icelander. 'This one, I think, has eyes only for Volker.'

Dani gave him a withering look. 'On the whole,' she said, 'I preferred the wood-pig.'

Thorgrim shrugged, jumped easily from the branch, and caught his foot in a trailing vine. He landed flat on his face at the Armorican's feet. Guy grinned, and helped him up. 'I am here, my fine athletic friend, because you and your Hel-horse have made circles around this wood for half the night. A dozen times I have seen you pass, and each time your face has been a little greener. But I did not think to find the huntress here, also.'

Dani jumped to the ground with all the grace that Thorgrim had failed to achieve, and Guy welcomed her with a bow that was only half-mocking. She ignored it and retrieved her bow.

'You look troubled, *ma belle sorcière*.'

'Yes. I've lost the owl. And yes, dammit, I'm worried about Volker!'

Music burst into Volker's mind like water from a kobold sluice-gate, sweeping every other thought aside, drawing him irresistibly towards the misty circle that was the huldra dance. He saw slim figures turning towards him, reaching out their hands to welcome him, and he felt the answering call of his own blood hammering through his veins. He had dreamed of women like this, tall, high-cheekboned and majestic, eyes glittering with power and desire, dressed in shimmering, translucent robes like woven mist that half-concealed and half-revealed lithe, taut-muscled limbs . . .

With an effort of will he stopped at the very edge of the circle, reaching for the horn. The pounding rhythm of the dance grew stronger, more insistent, and now it seemed that the eyes of every woman in the circle were fixed on him, drawing him inward, willing him to yield his body and his mind to the dance. He could feel his own limbs twitching in response as he raised the horn to his lips, drew a long, shuddering breath, and blew a single, ringing phrase that echoed around the clearing and reverberated among the trees beyond.

In an instant, everything changed. The shimmering elf-light vanished, and with it the glamour that had cloaked the huldra women. He saw them as they truly were: gaunt, vicious and hostile, with long-clawed hands and disturbingly sharp, close-set teeth. He saw the piper at the centre of the circle, and the fury in his face as the power of his music was shattered by the horn. Far away, at the edge of hearing, other, discordant notes seemed to answer him, tugging at the darker, hidden emotions of his nightmares, but the dance he was playing had a momentum of its own. In the mountains it had forced the clumsy kobolds to dance within an inch of their lives – but for huldra women, dancing was as natural as walking. They had lost the beauty and grace of illusion, but they had a wilder grace of their own that made the magical vision tawdry by comparison. Their sinuous, sensual movements seemed to feed back into the music he was playing, driving him to greater effort, challenging him to play ever faster and more complex measures. Each new ornament, each new improvisation, brought a new and even more dramatic response from the circle of dancers . . . even the far-away discords from the second horn became a part of the dance, as if they, like him, could see and hear far more than ordinary mortals.

Except Dani, perhaps. If they've hurt one hair on her head, I'll play them the dance of death . . .

The dance was reaching its end. His simple melody had run its course a dozen times, and there were no more variations or ornaments he could think of to make another measure. By now a dozen or so huldra women were throwing each other into the air by turns, whirling with outstretched arms to steady themselves, while the rest formed a stately outer ring spinning widdershins around them. He blew a final ringing waterfall of sound that brought the dance to a triumphant climax, then lowered the horn, and faced the enemy.

Two of the huldra women winked at him. Another gestured towards the bushes with an invitation known in all languages. A younger Volker might have been embarrassed; now the energy of his own playing, and the energy of the dance itself, seemed to tingle through his body. He had seen what their limbs could do, what his music had *made* them do . . . why not take the reward? Nothing he had ever imagined could match the promise of those long, slim, sleekly muscled thighs . . .

'Not bad, boy. Not bad – for a halfbreed.'

The drawling, nasal voice was pitched about half an octave above its proper register. Its owner was a tall figure crowned with a curiously carved wooden head-piece and carrying a staff that still sprouted living shoots. The *huldramann*'s inward-sloping eyebrows matched the lean angularity of a hard, unforgiving and ill-shaven face. He was chewing something that didn't seem to like the idea of being swallowed.

Volker's hormones suddenly found something better to do. This was an enemy . . . and probably a danger-ous one. But before he could answer the *huldramann* a tall, spidery figure detached itself from the shadows and shambled into the circle, grinning hugely. 'Aw, come on, pate – that was *music*, that was! Why, Lir'zel there was just about ready to . . .'

'*Quiet!*' roared the *huldramann*. 'Don' care what your ma says, Arges, you ain't no son of mine . . .'

'I am *too* . . .'

'. . . and *you*, stranger, you ain't welcome here – and it's Adranus, Emp'ror of the huldra, a-tellin' you. Understand?'

'You're the one who doesn't understand,' said Volker levelly. 'I've come for my companions . . . and I'm not leaving till you bring them to me. I warn you, not all my music is good to listen to.'

Adranus rubbed his nose and spat noisily. 'So we're all supposed to fall on our faces and kiss your mucking boots? Thing is, I ain't too keen on snot-nosed half-breeds playing trashy music in my forest.'

Volker grinned. A few days with the kobolds had

sharpened his wits for this kind of wordplay. 'Perhaps I should play something harder, to teach you a little hospitality.'

'*Yeah!*' said Arges eagerly. 'More music, more music!'

Adranus shrugged, and leaned nonchalantly on his staff to spit at a passing firefly. He hit it squarely amidships; to Volker's heightened perceptions the sound was like fat sizzling in a hot cauldron. 'Yeah. Do like Arges says – go right ahead. See how well you play with your arms pinned t'your body.'

Hel and hydra-shit. I should've got away while I had the chance. Now that Volker knew what to look for, the silhouettes of huldra archers were all too easy to spot, and all of them had arrows on the string. But to yield now, and lose face, would be worse than death, and they'd almost certainly kill him anyway. Arges' lopsided grin had vanished. Now the hulking creature simply looked ugly. 'What'samatter with him, pate? He don't play! I want him t'*play*!'

Adranus bared his pointed fangs. 'Well, stranger?'

So I'm dead if I try and dead if I don't. There has *to be something else* . . .

There was. It was a surprise even to him.

'What's up, halfbreed? Lost for words?'

Volker shook his head. 'Just don't believe in wasting them. You see, I didn't come alone.'

Adranus grinned. 'I know that, halfbreed – but you're alone *now*.'

Again, Volker shook his head. 'I don't think so.'

And here goes nothing. Half-closing his eyes, he remembered a mountain lake in Alpina Tartara . . . and smiled.

From the depths of the wildwood came a wind that shook the trees at the edge of the clearing and filled the air with the dancing patterns of fallen leaves. From every side blinding flashes of light heralded the earthshaking roar of multiple thunderclaps. But this thunder had a rhythm of its own, like the beating of gigantic wings . . .

Adranus stepped back, guarding himself with his staff, shielding his eyes against the multi-coloured lightnings that danced around the clearing to the rhythm of the storm. Archers loosed in a dozen different directions, beguiled by half-seen wraiths and baffling eruptions of light. And then, from the eye of the storm, came slow, massive wingbeats that seemed to drive the forest before them, and a gigantic bird that filled half the sky. It hovered above Volker like a god come to judgement, its savage, hooked beak held open, its cries echoing down forgotten glades, its claws unsheathed and outstretched to impale the enemies of its master.

'Well,' said Volker, loud enough for all the clearing to hear it, 'do you still defy my powers, Adranus?'

The *huldramann* scowled, but said nothing.

'Good,' said Volker. 'Then I'd like to see my companions. *Now*, Adranus – before the bird grows impatient.'

Arges suddenly seemed to wake up. 'Hey, pate, you gonna let him talk t'you like that? Pate?' Dimly, the hulking huldra became aware that everyone else in the clearing was staring at something above Volker's head; so he stared, too. Time passed. The thunder died away. The wind dropped to a faint, singing breeze. Only the bird remained, like a messenger from the upper world, light playing about its head like—

'Hey, pate,' said Arges, 'what's so all-fired scary 'bout a stupid owl?'

—like three circling fireflies.

Volker shut his eyes and mouthed the foulest curse he could think of. Unsurprisingly, it was one of Dani's. He had created a perfect illusion, just as Dani had done in the mountains, playing on the huldrafolk's finely-tuned senses. A breeze from the forest had become a storm out of Hades. The pallid lights of fireflies had become lightnings and supernatural haloes. And Dani's bewildered owl had become a sending from the gods themselves. But now the vision was shattered. All that remained was a gangling half-elf with a bird on his shoulder . . . a bewildered owl that looked about as awe-inspiring as a chicken pecking corn.

Adranus began to laugh. 'So the halfbreed knows the Art, hey? If he filed his teeth and got hisself a new face he'd almost pass for truefolk.'

A dozen or so of his followers moved forward, with their hands on their weapons, but Adranus waved them back. 'Awright, boys, that's enough. He's got the Art and he's got the Sight, and he knows how to use 'em.'

Volker managed a smile. Inwardly he was cursing himself. He had won the respect of these woodland bandits by using their own kind of magic against them, by calling on his huldra blood. And in doing *that* he'd sacrificed his self-respect.

'Your son,' he said dully. 'How did he . . . ?'

'Aw, don't pay *him* no never-mind. Arges don't have the Sight like the rest of us – which comes in useful now and again. So now you'd best tell me what you and those misbegotten humans are doing on my land.'

'They're here?'

Adranus shrugged. 'Weeell . . . Let's just say that I know where to lay hands on 'em.'

Something in the *huldramann*'s manner warned Volker that his test was not complete. Without thinking, he began a spell for clear sight – then hesitated.

Maybe I don't need it. Maybe I can just . . .

He narrowed his eyes like a short-sighted child squinting to see the leaves on a tree, and concentrated all his attention on what he saw. At first there was nothing unusual – only the moon – the firelit dance-glade, the double shadows of the huldra, and beyond them the darkness of the primeval forest. But the darkness had an edge . . . a shimmering border like a curtain ruffled by a forest breeze . . .

Concentrate, damn it!

A solid-seeming tree wavered, like a reflection in a rippling pond, and then it was gone. The buzzing of an insect changed to half-understandable human speech, but distorted, as though he were hearing it from the bottom of a deep well. It took him a while to realize that the voice was Dani's.

'*Yes, dammit, I'm worried about Volker!*'

'Then you can stop worrying,' he said.

Adranus shrugged. 'Cain't win 'em all, I guess.' His hand moved swiftly in a series of ritual gestures. A few of them looked obscene, and probably were, but the tattered remnants of the disguising curtain melted like morning mist.

'I see three of my companions,' said Volker icily. 'Where are the rest?'

'This is where they came, boy,' said the *huldramann* silkily. 'And if you get closer than this, you're some kind of crazy. That, or there's more magic in your little finger than the gods have got in the whole of the Upperworld.'

Volker narrowed his eyes, testing the limits of his newly discovered senses. He could almost *feel* the presence of the second horn, despite the distractions of the nightmare landscape around them. There were trees with monstrous, barrel-like trunks and crawling, tentacular limbs. There were thickets like bundles of pikes, defending their seed-cases with steel-sharp leaves the length of a man's arm. There were thistles the size of cannonballs, and grasses the length of dagger blades. And beyond the first circle of defences, the ground dropped away in a slow and gentle curve like the rim of a titan's drinking-bowl.

Idly, Thorgrim swung Hlavisbana at a giant thistle –

and stepped smartly back on to Guy's foot as the puff-ball burst open, peppering the undergrowth with razor-edged seedpods. Guy roared a colourful protest, then ducked in his turn as the sound dislodged a dozen dagger-like leaves from a tree just above their heads.

'I am thinking,' mused Thorgrim, 'that this place could use a gardener.' He looked meaningfully at Dani.

'Count me out. Flora herself couldn't tame this freak show for plants.' She shivered. 'Any ideas, Volker?'

'Not yet . . .'

The *huldramann* laughed spitefully. 'There's no entering the Green Chapel for mortal folk, *masters*. What it wants, it keeps.' He pointed to an area of trampled grass under one of the trees. Narrowing his eyes, Volker could just see a pile of yellow-white bones, with a few clinging fragments of flesh. The skull that belonged with them was lying some three feet away from the skeleton, cloven almost in two.

'Reckon your friends got a little greedy,' said Adranus smugly. 'Wanted a deal of their own. Pity, huh?'

Volker wasn't listening. The second corpse, close to the first, was already little more than a shapeless mound of fungus. The third was further in, one arm extended in a futile attempt to protect itself. Even at the limits of his powerful vision, he could see no safe path to the crater. But now he had other ways of looking . . .

The owl perched among the trees above the lip of the clearing. It was preening itself, holding back among the shadows, seeming half-aware of the blighted circle beyond. Something heavy moved among the lower branches, and the offended bird launched itself into the air. It circled restlessly, reluctant to fly any lower – the bowl-shaped valley below did strange things to the air. Besides, there were movements among its monstrous trees and plants suggesting creatures that could take an owl and its prey together, in a single bite. At the eastern rim a small stream entered from a shallow valley – and disappeared . . .

Volker opened his eyes. 'I know where to find the horn.'

Dani blinked. 'You *know*—?'

'Yes. What I don't know is how to reach it alive. So we'll do it together.'

Thorgrim blinked. 'This is a good plan?'

'It's the best I've got. Alone, none of us would survive. But there are four of us, and we all have our own talents. We can help each other, protect each other . . .'

'Die for each other,' suggested the *huldramann*. 'You go right ahead. Could be fun to watch.'

Thorgrim smiled dangerously. 'You, my friend, can have a seat among the *gothar*. Perhaps you should join us, just to be sure that your people try no more of their little jokes.'

'The Hel I will. My mother didn't raise no stupid children.'

'Leave him be,' said Volker. 'There's nothing he knows that can help us . . . and it's his own business what his people think of him.'

'You trying to . . . ?'

'Remember me to your womenfolk, Adranus.'

'What you saying, boy?'

'He is saying goodbye,' growled Thorgrim.

The *huldramann*'s laugh sounded forced. 'Goodbye it is. And don't expect no burial party, y'hear?'

Thorgrim stared at the stream dubiously. The water was oily, glinting with a disturbing rainbow sheen, and the bubbles that rose to its surface burst with an almost audible pop. 'This is water?'

'Not necessarily,' said Volker.

'*Zut alors*!' exclaimed Guy, 'there are things that walk themselves about in it!'

302

Dani nodded. 'Be grateful you can't see them as well as I can.'

'The bad news,' said Volker, 'is that this is the only way to the second horn.'

Dani laughed curtly. 'Then we'd best swim for it – fast. If we walk, those things'll have our feet for breakfast in about six paces.'

'We don't have to walk *in* the water, but keep an eye on it, all the same.'

'I think,' grumbled Guy, 'that this water, it keeps its eye on *us*.'

Volker shivered despite himself. Guy was right. The thick, rising bubbles with their rainbow patterns *did* look unpleasantly like bloodshot eyes, except that nothing he had seen or heard of had quite so many eyes, in quite such a random pattern. Dani was just opening her mouth when Thorgrim stabbed one of them with the tip of his halberd.

After that a great many things happened more or less at the same time.

The bubble popped unpleasantly. Dani and Volker both yelled a warning, so neither of them could be heard. A second bubble rose to the surface and kept on rising, turning this way and that to see what had disturbed it. Two arms tipped with lobster-like claws reached out of the water and seized Guy's left boot in a fond embrace. He struck out savagely with his sabre as a nest of jointed arms, each the size of a small sapling, blossomed out of the water and clasped themselves haphazardly around Thorgrim's halberd, tugging fiercely. The Icelander pulled the other way, beginning an impromptu and very one-sided tug-of-war. Then Volker put the horn to his lips, and blew.

There was a sound like the end of the world.

A dozen trees on either side of the stream burst apart, scattering rotten timber and startled insects. The water boiled around the creature in the stream, and Thorgrim swore in amazement as its arms withered and crumbled like twigs in a bonfire. A horde of maggots erupted from the rotting remnants and crawled up his halberd shaft. The claws clutching Guy's boots melted away to slime, leaving sticky black trails in their wake. A few moments later what was left of the corpse drifted slowly to the surface. All that remained was a tangled, steaming mass of slimy tubes and offal, already crawling with maggots. A dozen other mutilated corpses floated belly-up around it.

Guy retrieved his fallen sabre, hacking and coughing as he struggled not to vomit. He looked as though the spell had come close to turning him inside out as well. Thorgrim gave up the struggle, and threw up what was left of his supper. Dani, looking pale and frightened, struggled to control her voice. 'What *happened*, Volker? Why did you . . . ?'

He barely heard her. He was staring at the horn as if it had changed into something else, something utterly monstrous. 'I was beginning to understand it. But *that* . . . I never expected that. I never *wanted* that.'

'I think,' said Thorgrim, 'that you have more power than you realize, my young friend.'

Volker shook his head. 'I *know* what my powers are, even with this. There's something about the second horn . . .'

'Yes,' said Dani, 'or about the two of them together. Either way, another medley like that one could kill us all.'

'Think of something else,' then,' said Thorgrim. 'We have company again.'

Guy chuckled. 'You are frightened of a few flies?'

'Have you see *anything* here that is not dangerous, *din besnottede bagfjert*?'

Volker was still staring at the horn; he did not see the swarm until it was too close for his magic to help. There were so many that they cast an all but solid shadow, and within seconds they were biting at every tiniest morsel of exposed flesh they could find. Each bite burned like liquid fire, and there seemed to be no defence against them.

'Follow me!' yelled Volker and dived head first into the oily, corpse-laden waters of the stream.

Thorgrim jumped after him, apparently without a second thought. Dani held back until she saw Volker come up for air twenty yards downstream . . . then she followed him, with Guy close behind. Even in the water some of the insects clung fast, biting again and again until the current swept them away, and when the four companions struggled to shore again they looked like the victims of a plague of boils.

'One question,' said Dani. 'Is this damn horn worth the effort?'

Volker tried to smile, but his lips were too bitten to manage it. 'It had damn well better be,' he croaked. 'I never tasted water as foul as that in my life.'

Thorgrim brushed away a clinging, jelly-like creature that was trying to eat a hole in his hose. 'At least we are close to the rim.'

Guy poured several things with too many legs out of his boots, and shaded his eyes from the rising sun, trying to see what lay ahead. He scowled. 'There is a thicket. I think it grows in the water as well as out of it . . . and if it is like all else in this dismal domain, it will probably snap us up for the little breakfast!'

'Those plants we have seen before,' said Thorgrim. 'If we do not burst the seed-pods, all will be well with us.'

'There's another way,' said Volker, 'and it's safer, too. They all look pretty close together. I expect Dani could drop an arrow into . . .'

'I'll try it,' she said. 'The rest of you stay low.'

'Dani,' said Volker, in a voice full of sudden urgency, 'I think you should—'

Before he could finish his sentence an arrow was climbing towards the sun in a high, whistling arc. For a moment it seemed to hang against the sky – then it dropped clean into the middle of the thicket.

There was a quiet explosion, like a cork leaving a bottle. Guy licked his lips reflexively. Volker saw a dozen razor-edged seeds exploded from their pod . . . and those, in their turn, sliced open other pods. The outsized lynx he had noticed earlier darted desperately from side to side, twisting and turning to escape, but by now the air was filled with flying death. It staggered a few yards out of the thicket before it fell and lay still.

Guy nodded appreciatively. 'Two for the price of one. A good bargain, *chasseuresse*.'

Dani lowered her bow with a troubled frown. 'It was a bad way to die.'

'Show me a good way,' said Volker. 'Especially round here.' At the edge of the thicket he could already see carrion eaters scuttling out of the shadows, always alert for the scent of blood, and within moments the corpse of the lynx had vanished under a living cloak of insects and animals battling one another for its flesh. In the time it would have taken Volker to play four dance measures, the corpse had been utterly consumed. Already most of the surviving feeders were crawling away from the cracked and broken bones.

'Time we were moving,' said Volker quietly. 'Nothing in this place stays still for long.'

Dani nodded, nocking another arrow on her bowstring, and Thorgrim brought Hlavisbana to the forward-tilting guard position. Guy shrugged, and hefted his sabre. There was open ground between them and the thicket, but they had been surprised before.

'It's clear,' said Volker, unthinkingly. 'As far as the other side of the thicket, anyway.'

Dani gave him an old-fashioned look. 'How do *you* know that? That's the *second* time that you've . . .'

'I don't know how.' Volker felt embarrassed. Ever since their meeting in the huldra dance-glade, he had seen through the owl's eyes almost as easily as Dani did herself.

Guy had forged ahead, hacking through the remnants of the thicket with his sabre. Now he paused, shading his eyes, and called out to the others. 'This, *mes p'tits*, you should see for yourselves.'

Dani's expression said everything that needed to be said. Volker could almost feel himself reddening.

Thorgrim whistled softly. At the lip of the crater the stream became a rushing waterfall, rainbowed in the light of the morning sun . . . and cascading into a landscape from another world. The plants and grasses at the rim were pallid precursors of the twisted and distorted mutations that grew within the bowl, yet everything here was disturbingly familiar. It was as if a nightmare of the wildwood had come to life.

Guy stroked his beard thoughtfully. 'I have seen a ruin that was like this place, in that part of my country they call Provence. A great theatre of the Old Empire.'

'A theatre?' said Thorgrim. 'What kind of theatre is that, with plants and trees?'

'The kind, my honest hairy barbarian, where men, women and animals kill and mutilate one another to amuse the good citizens of the town.'

Thorgrim grinned. 'Then this, *min gamle sjuskat*, is a theatre for the gods. We shall hope they are amused, *ja*?'

It was late afternoon before they came close to the floor of the crater. By now they took it for granted that everything they saw was hostile; even some of the grasses were knife-sharp, and Guy was bemoaning the damage to his boots. Thorgrim was limping badly from a close encounter with a broken tree-stump. It had housed a small but vicious animal that had bitten a chunk out of

307

his thigh. The Icelander had taken it philosophically, trusting that the beast enjoyed its meal before choking on it. Dani's face was bleeding where a branch covered in iron-hard thorns had whiplashed against it. Volker's left palm was raw and bleeding, after he had touched the barbed and poisonous bark of an innocent looking tree. All of them were tired, muscles aching from the constant need to push aside heavy branches, cut down plants and trees that blocked their way, or fight off hostile wildlife.

Time after time Volker had found himself holding back. He dared not use the horn, and he would not use the raw, rising energy that came from his father's blood. Once already he had betrayed himself . . . he dared not let it happen again. And there was something sickening about the landscape around them, a perversity and horror that reminded him all too strongly of what had happened by the stream.

"Ware wildlife,' said Dani wearily.

Gods alive, what now?

'I think perhaps the rocks are walking,' said Thorgrim thoughtfully. 'But such trolls I never saw, even among the Rus of the north.'

Guy grabbed a rock and threw it at one of the newcomers. It bounced. 'Too many legs,' he growled. 'Every living thing in this *trou de peste* wears legs in plural this year, *c'est claire!*'

Volker agreed. The creatures swarming towards them looked like nothing so much as domed-up rocks surrounded by a curtain of legs. They reminded him of something he had seen in some other life, but the memory refused to surface, and at this particular moment there were other things to worry about. It worried him, for instance, that beyond the swarming newcomers the stream simply disappeared.

Thorgrim strode forward and prodded the first of the rock-beasts with his halberd. Hlavisbana made no impression at all, but the pincer-like claws that responded to it took another neat slice out of his hose. He stepped back smartly, with a muttered and unusually potent curse.

Volker still found it difficult to concentrate. They were standing almost at the bottom of the crater. The water had to go *somewhere* – barring magic of a remarkably high order, it couldn't just disappear . . .

Of course. Like the basin in Strauben's elaboratory. It's going down . . . Come to think of it, that's where . . .

'Thorgrim, I'll need Hlavisbana for a second.'

'*Hvad i Helved* . . . ?'

He snatched the halberd from the indignant Norseman, thrust its blade under the rim of the leading creature's shell, and flipped. With a thin squeal, it rolled helplessly on to its back, legs waving. The rest kept coming, but his companions were already hacking long branches from nearby trees, and soon all four of them were hard at work turning their attackers legs over carapace. It was weary work, but remarkably easy.

Dani wiped her forehead. 'Tell me . . . how did you know?'

'I thought of the woodlice I used to find in Strauben's basin. The rest was easy enough.' He grinned, and handed Hlavisbana back to Thorgrim. The Icelander studied the blade suspiciously.

'Any stick would have done,' he muttered. 'This is a noble blade – my father's father's father carried it at Stiklastad.'

'So?' Guy was intrigued. 'Did he win honour there?'

'The old fool broke it.'

'Doubtless it shattered on the helmets of his foes.'

'Doubtless he tripped over it when he was running away. Four generations it has taken to reforge it, and still the blade is too short to make a sword that a full-grown man may use.'

Volker steered a careful path past assorted legs and

pincers to the very centre of the crater. Close to, he could see the vapour rising from the waterfall where the stream disappeared, but its sound was strangely muted . . .

The stream funnelled down into a hole the size of a small chimney. The sides were slippery with moss and slime, and the bottom was invisible in the gloom. There was no way down.

Not here, anyway . . .

'Thorgrim?'

The Norseman broke off another of his inexhaustible family sagas with a reproachful look. 'What is it?'

'Can you . . . feel . . . the second horn?'

Thorgrim frowned. 'Yours I know, like a smooth shell echoing the sea. This other . . . It is not the same. It is like broken bones, sharp-edged, deformed. And the feel of a sound like stone cracking in a hard frost . . .'

'Where?'

The Norseman hesitated. 'Here. Below our feet . . .'

'*Damn* . . .'

'. . . but there is something else. Closer, I think.'

Guy looked around him with a puzzled frown. 'The huntress – where is she?'

Thorgrim looked startled and hurt in about equal measure. 'I thought that she listened to . . .'

'I'm over here,' said the distant voice. 'Come and see.'

The Icelander shrugged unconvincingly and stalked across to the bank where Dani was pulling up handfuls of grass. 'Look here,' she said, 'these stones! They're so damned old they're just about falling apart.'

Thorgrim nodded, his annoyance forgotten, and turned to Volker. '*Ja*, it is so. And there is magic here, a thing I have never known before.'

In which case we need a senior magician. 'Guy, could you . . .'

'No he couldn't,' said Dani decisively.

'But . . .'

'*Look.*'

Guy and Volker both bent down at the same time. When he stopped seeing stars, Volker saw that the stones formed a small circle. As his eyes quickly adjusted to the darkness beyond, he realized it was the entrance to a narrow, stone-lined tunnel. There was no trace of mortar; each stone had been painstakingly chiselled to fit the others around it. It curved slowly into the distance, but the curve was downward, towards the heart of the mystery that Adranus had called the Green Chapel. Here, if anywhere, was the way to the truth, but the tunnel was barely wide enough to take his shoulders.

And Guy's shoulders are half again the width of mine. Thorgrim could manage it – just – but . . . 'All right, Dani. It'll have to be you and me.'

'Then I'll go first . . . just in case you get stuck.'

Guy chuckled. 'You will need some . . .'

'Light.' She smiled. 'I can take care of that.'

Dani twisted her hand in a gesture that reminded him of Adranus. For a moment her fingers seemed to burn with a pallid supernatural flame, then he saw that her flesh was illuminated from the inside, like the stained-glass windows of a basilica in the light of the rising sun. She smiled again, and ducked into the passage. Volker followed her, forcing his way between the stones of the narrow entrance. He heard the owl flapping just outside the entrance, but it was almost as though something held it back.

Or maybe it knows something that we don't.

His mind touched the owl's just long enough to sense its fear.

Thorgrim watched gloomily as the younger man's feet disappeared into the dark. 'Saa. A day it has taken us, and blood and sweat enough, and now you and I

311

must stand here like doorkeepers while these two take the glory.'

There was no answer.

'*Odin og Frigg*, do you also not talk to me, you wine-paunch?'

Somewhere behind him, a very large cauldron boiled over, accompanied by a strangled shout from the Armorican.

'*Bougre de barbare*, cease mumbling and *aid me!*'

Thirty paces in, Volker was beginning to wish he had never started. The passage sloped ever more steeply downward, but showed no sign at all of widening. The horn case was increasingly difficult to manoeuvre, and he could only wonder how Dani was coping with her bow and quiver. The whole crater seemed to be sitting squarely on his spine, waiting for the right moment to crush him, and Dani's light, just ahead, seemed to grow fainter by the second. Confused sounds from outside reverberated around them – noises of wind and water, and distant voices distorted to a strange kind of melody by distance and echoes.

But there was no turning back.

If this damn passage runs out I won't even be able to turn round. And I'll never get out backwards.

And if I don't, neither will Dani . . .

Slowly, like the answer to his prayers, the passage began to open out. He saw the faint sheen of Dani's hair in the light from her hand, and the reflections from damp and polished stones on either side. Then, quite suddenly, she stopped.

'You won't believe this,' she said, 'but there's a *door*.'

'I see it,' he said. 'And you're right. I don't believe it.'

What he saw was clearly man-made, a massive door of thick oaken planks, bound together with elaborate ironwork. But there seemed no way to open it. The planking was embedded deep in the earth on all four sides. Dani traced out the scrolling pattern of the iron-work with her fingertips, eyes half-closed, as if its curves and its crudely-formed dragons' heads might tell her something of its maker. Then, very faintly, she smiled.

'*Well*?' said Volker, eventually.

'This door was never meant to be opened, and it was made a long time ago.'

'How long?'

'When this amount of iron would have bought a small kingdom.'

'*That* long. Uh . . . how do you know?'

'I can feel it. In the wood.'

'That's quite a trick.'

'Not for a . . . a true follower of the Mother.'

For 'true follower' read 'hands off, Volker'. The impli-cation annoyed him, as if she'd been spying on his dreams. 'So that's what you want to be, is it? Do you really think . . .'

'Not now, Volker. Please.' Perhaps she *could* read his mind; by the sound of it hers was as troubled as his. 'Just . . . just help me, will you?'

'Oh, whatever,' he growled. 'What d'you need?'

'We have to find out how this door was sealed.'

He chuckled despite himself. 'By the looks of it, with about five tons of earth.'

'I mean the *magical* seal – what Thorgrim could feel.'

'Sorry. Here, let me try.'

'No, *wait* . . .'

He realized his mistake as soon as he touched the ironwork. It pulsed under his fingers like a living thing . . .

And then the door grabbed him.

There was no other way to describe it. The ironwork seemed to reach out and wrap itself around him in a brutal, bone-cracking embrace. He could feel waves of power beating through it, like energy from the earth itself, primal energy, the very stuff of magic. A dragon's head reared in front of his face, jaws agape, spitting out glowing sparks of agony . . . but his arms were pinned to his sides, and there was nothing he could do to protect himself. Dani did nothing, said nothing; he wanted to scream at her for help, but a coil of living metal was closing round his throat, and the rising hum in his ears felt like the end of his personal universe. A tide of darkness swept over the world, and for a moment, on the edge of the abyss, he saw Strauben's gilded orrery gliding before him into nothingness, and heard the distant, singing harmony of the spheres . . .

Far above the earth shook, and a deep, throbbing vibration boomed out of the mouth of the tunnel. It sounded like the death-cry of a titan.

'*Odin og Frigg paa Helvejskryds*,' yelled Thorgrim, 'what is *happening* there!'

'Save your breath and help me!' roared Guy. 'We have troubles enough with *this*!'

'This' was green and yellow, scaly, and measured about thirty feet from the top of its flat, toothy head to the tip of its long and unpleasantly spiny tail. Its distant ancestors had probably been lizards seeking warmth on hot stones; this creature's slender, forked tongue was the length of ten or more good-sized ancestors, and was tightly wrapped around Guy de Guillac. The Armorican's sabre had little effect; it bounced off the improbably blue tongue like a child's toy.

Thorgrim hesitated, torn between Volker's unknown need and Guy's more obvious one. But the dragon – if it *was* a dragon – showed no sign of using its massive claws to disembowel its victim. In fact, it hardly seemed to have noticed Guy at all.

The big Icelander looked at the sun, looked very hard at the dragon, and laughed aloud. 'You are the *drakener*,' he shouted. '*You* deal with it!' With another bellowing laugh, he ducked into the tunnel-mouth and disappeared.

'*Poltron! Cretin! Hyène! Lâche!*' roared Guy. '*Fouteur des sale cochons! Barbare au fesses-poilu! Necrophile! Flatuosité de bison! Goinfrerique à la gomme*! And *enculeur des onagres lepreux*!'

The dragon tipped its head to one side, for all the world like a dove in a castle cot. It stared at its noisy captive as though he had just been conjured into existence by a third-rate necromancer. Then it rolled its tongue experimentally, spinning the Armorican like a whipping-top. His sabre slipped from his grasp, hurtled through the air and buried itself in a nearby tree, followed by a curious assortment of tools and weapons: the dagger from his left boot, the knives from his doublet, the wire picklock from his shirtcuff, a forgotten set of knuckledusters a louse-comb, his eating-knife, his crested pewter spoon, and finally his hat. A stray gust of wind carried it high into the air and dropped it neatly over the dragon's left eye.

The tongue unrolled. Guy dropped heavily to the ground, staggered to his feet, and groaned. The world was still spinning around him in dizzying circles – the cave-mouth, the tunnel, the dragon and the surrounding vegetation were a green and yellow blur that alternately hissed, bubbled and roared, and his supper was trying very hard to climb back up his throat. More by luck than judgement, his hand grasped the hilt of the sabre. He tugged experimentally. The tree bent a little, but the blade stayed exactly where it was. With methodical determination, he wedged his feet against the base of the tree, grabbed the hilt with both hands, and threw all his considerable weight into the task.

Nothing happened.

Behind him, his hat slipped from its precarious perch and flopped sideways on to a thorn-bush. The dragon suddenly noticed an unfamiliar creature doing something cruel and unusual to a tree. It lumbered across to investigate.

Guy, absorbed in his task, found help from an unexpected quarter. A long arm curled around his waist and tugged. The extra force was just enough to pull the sabre free.

The arm was blue and forked. It did not let go. Instead de Guillac found himself lifted bodily into the air, while the trembling tips of the fork investigated every part of his body in embarrassing and intimate detail.

'*Ventre de Venus!*' he roared.

The dragon brought him closer to one of its huge, unblinking, slit-like eyes and made a sound like a bucket of water hitting a smithy fire. Then it put the new discovery carefully into its mouth, and closed its jaws.

Volker opened his eyes.

Fragments of memory drifted back into his mind – Dani's voice, intoning a sequence of deep and solemn tones before . . .

He was surrounded by broken fragments of ironwork, and the wooden door had vanished without trace. A warm, flickering light showed the way ahead.

'Volker?'

He groaned theatrically, and she sighed with relief. 'You all right, Volker?'

'Not exactly,' he croaked. 'Feels like I had an argument with a hangman.'

'You nearly lost.'

He stared at her. 'Now wait just a Helbound heartbeat. I *did* lose. I could feel myself starting to die. It was *you*, wasn't it? What did you . . . ?'

'I don't know.' The denial was too quick to be convincing. 'Something just . . . well, came into my head.'

She helped him to his feet, wincing as she saw the livid blue bruise across his throat. 'Come on. Time we were moving.'

'Let's not, and say we did.' His forced laugh broke down into a hacking cough. 'All right, I'm with you. But afterwards you can tell me what *really* happened.'

She was already listening to something else. 'Do you hear water, Volker?'

He sighed. 'Yes. Better than you hear me, probably. Sounds like it's round the corner.'

'So we've reached the bottom of the waterfall . . .'

'By the scenic route. Come on.'

There was not very far to go. At the end of a long, slow curve the tunnel opened on an enormous cave lit by a slim shaft of light from above. Along that shaft the stream fell in a rainbowed column into a deep and turbulent pool. Close to, the sound was deafening . . . and strangely distorted.

Then he saw the horn.

It had been there a long time – perhaps for hundreds of years. Now it seemed almost a part of the rock on which it stood. The tumult of the waterfall echoed within it – echoed, and changed. Against the roar of the torrent, it sounded like a chorus of angry and conflicting voices. The path led directly up to the rock where it lay: there was nothing at all to bar their way.

'It can't be that easy,' said Dani. 'It just *can't*.'

Volker laughed. 'How many times did we face death to get here? How tough do you *want* it to be?'

She reddened. 'I just meant . . .'

'Maybe you'd like a titan or two. Would *that* make it hard enough?'

'All that . . . outside . . . that was *different*. The door-spell . . .'

'Oh yes, I'll grant you that was your big moment . . .'

'That's *enough*!' There was the hint of fire in her eyes, enough to remind him of the light spell she had used

317

at the tunnel-mouth. 'I don't know how those creatures and plants came to be made, any more than you do . . . but I *do* know that whoever made them had nothing to do with the door-spell.'

'And how in Hel do you know that?'

'*You* know it, Volker, if you'd only think about it! Those things outside are warped, evil, like Tartarist magic. The door-spell was different . . .'

'*That* I'll grant you . . . it was *primitive*. Who uses earth magic these days?'

She laughed. 'Women do, Volker . . . the women of my order. Because it's pure, it's powerful, and it's very, very old. No Tartarist would make a door like that one; they can't use elemental magic, any more than I could call on the First Creation.'

'So why should there be another spell . . . ?'

'Because the door was only a warning! Don't you see, Volker? It was simply telling us to keep out . . .'

'I *can't* believe that. Gods alive, if that was someone's idea of a warning, what would they do when they got serious?'

'Volker, it was *old*; I'd bet it used to stand in the open air! And the signs around it would have sent your ancestors running for the nearest cave. No, there *has* to be something else, something guarding the horn itself.'

'She is right,' said a voice neither of them expected to hear.

Volker climbed carefully back into his skin. 'Thorgrim? How in the name of Tartarus did you . . . ?'

'I heard you cry out. I felt great magic. So I came.' He forced a grin. 'I had not thought the passage so small. My halberd, I think, I should have left behind.'

Volker gaped. 'You crawled through there with . . . ? You must have bones like green saplings.'

'No,' said Thorgrim. 'Only bruises . . . purple and blue. But the huntress speaks truth, Volker – I feel a second warding spell, greater even than the first.'

'So why can't I see anything? Or *feel* anything?'

By way of an answer, Thorgrim picked up a stone and hurled it straight at the horn. It never reached its target.

The waterfall changed its note, plashing and spraying over an invisible *something* that surrounded the rock where nothing had stood before. Dazzling lines of light appeared, and where they met water they turned it to crackling, hissing droplets of vapour. Volker watched in wonder and horror as a network of fire wove itself around the horn, growing and branching like a living creature. It was elemental magic, as basic as the doorspell . . . but its power and sophistication staggered him. The tree was no mere artifice: it was real, and it was getting bigger. Leaf-like flames pulsed along its branches, and crimson, roseate fire-blooms flowered among the leaves, spreading and reforming into swelling globes of brilliance . . .

When he finally saw what was crawling up the path behind them, it was already far too late.

Thorgrim shrugged, and levelled his halberd. 'At least,' he remarked, to no one in particular, '*these* do not have too many legs.'

Guy de Guillac was not a happy man.

First and foremost, his dignity had suffered. He – Lord of Josselin and Pontivy, hereditary Draconnier of all the lands north of Morbihan, and Knight Commander of the Tributary Dukedom of Armorica – had been picked up like a child's toy and stuffed into the mouth of his rightful prey. It was an insult of such magnitude that in earlier ages his outraged relatives would have slaughtered anything remotely resembling a dragon, from the tiniest lizard to the mightiest firedrake, within twenty square miles. This was one reason why the Draconnier's rightful prey, along with most of the reptiles in Guillac, was virtually extinct. This had been small comfort to those of his ancestors whose last gasp had been tainted with the foul mixture of soot, burning garbage and rotten meat that is the true dragon's breath – and as two sets of teeth converged on his body Guy had a small moment of bafflement. The breath of *this* dragon was as sweet as that of a ten-thaler whore . . .

The teeth did not close. Instead, the creature's six-yard tongue prodded at him as gently as a mother settling her child into its cradle, and with much the same effect. The teeth surrounded him like the bars of a cot, denying all escape, while the tongue enfolded him like an unusually revolting coverlet. His barrage of colourful and imaginative insults went unheard, leaving the infuriated Armorican ample time to think up exotic tortures for Icelanders who abandoned their companions in the face of danger. Boiling in oil was predictable, and mercifully quick. Flaying alive was possible . . . as an experienced hunter, Guy had some idea how to go about it. Even so, he decided against it; before he had finished the Norseman would have bored him to death with wittily stoical remarks like 'See that my hide is well cured – it would not do to spoil it.'

Yet in the midst of this and other thoughts Guy was haunted by one inexplicable detail. Why had Thorgrim looked up at the sun before he turned away . . . ?

Foi du Draconnier, to so cold-bloodedly leave a man to die . . .

That was when Guy remembered the lizards in his father's vineyard. At midday they moved like green lightning, avoiding even the swiftest of clutching fingers. But in the morning, when the sun was low in the sky, *then* he could catch them—

This dragon-lizard lived at the bottom of a crater, and it had spent the whole morning in the shadow of the rim . . .

With a more than usually obscene curse, Guy wrestled his right arm free of the dragon's enfolding tongue and jabbed the tip of his sabre into the roof of its mouth.

For long moments nothing happened. He could almost believe the creature had no feeling in its mouth at all, that it could graze contentedly, like a goat, on anything and everything. And then, quite suddenly, the massive jaws opened, the tongue wrapped tight around him once again, and he was lifted up to stare straight into an unblinking, slit-like eye. Pinioned and helpless, he had no choice but to wait for the killing blow.

It never came.

Soundlessly, without any fuss, the tongue unravelled, and Guy de Guillac fell some fifteen feet into a cold, fast-flowing stream. When he surfaced, bubbling and spluttering, it was to see the dragon grazing contentedly on the high leaves of a nearby tree, oblivious to the massive thorns that protected them.

'*Bougre de Brest*, I should have guessed! Is it not that an eater of carrion has breath like its food?'

Struggling to the bank, Guy found that the current had already swept him several yards downstream of the dragon, but he felt no need to go back. There was little glory in hunting down a cold-blooded, leaf-eating reptilian snail that spent most of its life in a dazed, torpor, not when he had friends in danger. Though later, of course, there would be scores to settle with the Icelander . . .

To his amazement, he found himself once again at the lip of the crater. The seeming eternity he had spent in the dragon-lizard's mouth had been long enough for it to climb the slope where they had spent the whole morning, brushing aside every plant and every animal in its path. Looking down, he could see the trail of devastation it had left behind it – at least his second journey would be easier than his first. With another muttered string of oaths, he set off at a run . . .

. . . and skidded to a halt as the crater floor exploded upwards and outwards in a boiling hail of shattered rock, white-hot steam, and leaping, red-gold flame.

'I think,' said Volker, 'that I'd like them better if they had more legs.'

Thorgrim shook his head. 'They would move faster.'

'Yes – but they wouldn't leave that revolting slime all over the path. You should thank the gods you can't *smell* it.'

Once, a very long time ago, the creatures between them and the tunnel had been fish. They still had big, lustrous eyes, and fins on their backs and their tails. But they had been very ugly fish, and changing their front fins to stubby, five-clawed legs had not improved the basic design. It was difficult to tell where the skull-like head ended and the bloated body began . . . and the long, slim tail that trailed along behind was barbed and spiked like an ogre's club.

Whatever they were, they looked hungry.

Thorgrim took three steps forward and flourished his halberd in a neat figure of eight. Volker winced – he had seen for himself what the manoeuvre could do to an opponent – but the fish-things were unimpressed. They continued their advance at the same relentless pace, dragging their tails behind them.

'Volker . . .'

Dani's voice had both wonder and fear in it. Glancing over his shoulder, he could see why.

The fire-tree was still growing. Soon its branches would fill the upper part of the cave – and each branch carried the swelling globes of flame that were its fruit. Volker remembered the puffballs at the rim of the crater, and wished he hadn't. He ground his teeth in frustration. In his hand he held the most powerful source of magic he had ever seen or heard of, but he dared not use it here, even to save their lives. He could imagine, all too clearly, the effect a single blast on the horn would have on the fish-creatures and, in all probability, on Dani and Thorgrim. The risk was too great. But he had to do *something* . . .

Thorgrim did it instead. He lowered his halberd, sprinted forward, and thrust Hlavisbana straight between the gaping, tooth-filled jaws of the first fish-creature. Volker heard the blade rattle against the inside of its skull, to no effect. The jaws snapped shut in a blindingly fast reflex that almost severed shaft from blade.

'Stupid fish,' muttered Thorgrim. He thrust again, aiming for the eye this time, but the creature's left leg lashed out with baffling speed, kicking the blade aside and all but wrenching the shaft from his hand. Cursing, the Icelander retreated up the slope.

'Not so stupid fish,' said Volker, dodging an inquisitive branch of the fire-tree. In another few minutes he and the others would be forced into the serried rows of teeth on legs coming up the path; it was either that or burn. The light in the cavern was changed to glowing orange and blood-red as the tree grew to its full height. He couldn't help wondering if it was hot enough to burn the rock as well . . .

A ball of white-hot fire hit the ground a yard ahead of him and exploded in a blinding burst of sparks, leaving a small, steaming crater. Glancing up, he saw that the fruits of the fire-tree had ripened, and now they were falling, destroying anything and everything they touched. As a warding spell, it was horribly effective. Right now he would have been more than happy to run back down the path and up the tunnel . . . but that was no longer an option. It seemed the spellcasters had meant to block every possible avenue of escape.

Or did they? When this spell was cast, these walking teeth were probably ordinary catfish . . .

So who – or what – changed them?

'Huntress,' said Thorgrim quietly, 'you have a bow. There is work for it to do. Huntress?'

Dani did not answer, or even turn round. Her eyes were fixed on the fire-tree, and she seemed to be humming a slow chant under her breath. Volker touched her hand, but she was holding the bow in a rigid, unyielding grip.

'Dani,' said Volker, 'we need the bow. *Today*.' There was no response. She seemed to be entranced. 'She can't hear me. And that's a pity, because I'm right out of ideas.'

Thorgrim howled. There was no other word to describe the noise. The halberd whirled round and round his head in a lethal circle of flying steel as he ran forward down the path, leapt six feet in the air straight over the first of the startled creatures, and landed squarely in the middle of them.

Perhaps he had meant to kill them all, or die in the attempt. But he had reckoned without the slime they had left all over the path. His boots found no purchase at all; he simply slid, like a skater on a frozen pond, and kept on sliding, using the halberd for balance like a tightrope walker at a fair.

The first of his opponents died in seconds, gutted from stem to stern as the halberd blade swept past. With commendable presence of mind, Thorgrim swung the blade in a wide arc to open up his next victim's eye, and was rewarded with a faceful of pungent yellow liquid. A third creature stepped resolutely into his path, jaws agape, and was knocked teeth over tailfins into the water. Several others jumped after it, but one, with more courage, strode forward with jaws agape. The halberd blade caught it squarely in the face, forcing it back down the shallow slope at high speed. Several others, too slow to see what was happening, were bowled over like skittles in an alley – but the halberd was wedged fast, and the tunnel mouth was looming.

Thorgrim disappeared into the dark with a yell that might have been fury, horror, or sheer enthusiasm, and moments later a strange sound echoed through the cave, as if a bucketful of jellyfish had been dropped into an overcrowded smithy. It was followed by a volley of Nordic curses sprinkled with choice expressions from at least twelve other languages.

Well, at least he's alive. Thorgrim had already done all that his gift and his weapon could do. But Dani . . .

Dani had closed her eyes, holding her hands out palm up like a supplicant before her goddess. Her voice was rising slowly in a wordless, keening chant. Volker was suddenly and sharply aware of his own limits. There was more magic in the world than he would ever know, and far more than he could ever learn – yet what the huntress was doing seemed *right* in a way he was beginning to understand . . .

He *did* understand.

She was keeping her voice low in a desperate, continuing struggle to damp out the strange and discordant vibrations from the second horn – but her wordless music was reshaping the fire-tree. Already its branches stood taller and straighter than before, and the deadly fruits were rising with them, till they no longer stood overhead. But the concentration her magic demanded was ferocious. She was blissfully unaware of the creatures stalking up the path behind her.

Time for a little harmony. Wish I was a better singer . . .

Gently, beginning with a low, wordless hum, he began to build a subtle counterpoint to the simple series of notes that Dani was using to reshape the tree, changing the pitch and tenor of his singing by slow and careful degrees. One mistake could undo everything she had achieved, but he needed more than she had time or energy to give him . . .

Above his head, a single branch of the fire-tree swayed and drooped forward over the path, heavy with deadly fruit. The rotten-fish scent of the nearest creature was already filling his nostrils, but he fought his desperate need to cough or choke. A single lost note could shatter both Dani's spell and his own.

Slowly – very slowly – he brought in a gentle vibrato. The branch trembled above his head.

The creature lifted its leg to disembowel him . . .

. . . and he gritted his teeth in a series of sudden, staccato notes.

For a moment his would-be attacker stood blank-eyed at the heart of a fireball, then it was gone, leaving nothing but a sickly smell of burned and rotten fish as a line of white-hot fireballs scoured the path, destroying all that they touched.

Dani's voice had almost reached its limits. It was harsher now, and she was struggling for notes that lay at or beyond the bottom of her register. The tree had become a soaring yellow-orange column, surging with pulses of white as fire-fruits dropped from its branches. The second horn lay at the heart of an inferno, yet it was untouched and seemingly untouchable.

Volker groaned in frustration. He understood the source of Dani's magic, but he could only guess what she was trying to do.

A waterfall. A door in the earth. The fire-tree . . .

A sound far below finished the thought. From the heart of the world came the whistling howl of a rising wind.

Volker closed his eyes. In the forest he had *heard* the harmony that underlay the new creation, the harmony of the elements. Dani's purpose was simple: to unravel the elements of the warding spell, and return them to their natural state. Something within him, something hidden deep in his huldra ancestry, knew exactly what to do . . . but to reach it he would have to surrender his humanity.

Dani's voice faltered, and croaked. As she lost control

the swaying column of fire lashed out randomly from side to side, leaving white-hot trails of molten rock where it touched the cavern walls. Its hot breath seared the wool of his doublet. A blind rage forced all thought and all fear from his mind, and he roared his defiance to all the gods of the upperworld.

A door seemed to open in his mind.

Without thinking, without trying, without remembering, his voice took up Dani's chant . . . but lower, and more slowly. The wind from below encircled them both, lifting their hair and ruffling their clothes as it became one with the fire and the water above. And then, with a slow, grinding roar, the roof of the cavern began to crumble.

Rocks, boulders and stones fell all about them, but the whirlwind around them was like a shield, throwing off anything and everything that could harm them. Light flooded in – the clean, natural light of the westering sun – and the fire became a crimson globe, roaring upward to cleanse and scour everything in its path. Volker could feel the same fire within himself, burning out the doubts and fears of his human half, scouring out the vilenesses of Strauben's elaboratory, opening the passage to true power, and the fulfilment of true desire.

He wanted Dani – now, at this moment.

Her voice had failed, and his was silent, but the whirlwind around them still sang the harmony they had made together. When he held her and pressed his lips against hers she yielded willingly, gladly, caught up in the tumult that burned through his body. Her mouth tasted impossibly sweet, and as her body locked against his he felt a pulsing energy that linked them into a single, indissoluble whole . . .

The wind fell away. Pebbles rattled down the crater rim in a clattering fusillade, splashing noisily into the new lake at its base. Volker found himself at the bottom of a bare and rocky bowl that was slowly filling with water. All else had gone, swept away by the warding spell's apocalyptic fury.

He looked into Dani's eyes. She looked the way he felt . . . dazed, incredulous, and utterly caught up in the power that bound them together.

'I – I thought . . .'

He smiled. 'What did you think?'

'It all seemed so clear before. My punishment was over. I was free . . . for the first time, really free, and with everything I'd lost restored. I knew exactly what I was going to do . . .'

'And now?'

'I . . . I don't know. I think . . . I think I'd rather . . .'

He put an arm around her waist, drawing her with him up the path. A day ago, she would have pushed him away with a brisk insult or a casual joke, but now she accepted the touch without thinking. 'Come on,' he said. 'Let's see what this was all about.'

At the crest of the path, the horn sat mute on its rock, as it had done for hundreds, perhaps thousands of years, ever since the ancient loremasters had buried it here. The one he carried looked like an instrument – a strange one, but fashioned by human hands, polished and shaped within its cagework and its keys. This horn had clearly been torn from a living creature; it was dark, matt, and ridged, and for a moment he hesitated to touch it. The air above it looked troubled, almost turbulent . . .

In the forest he had stumbled on a ditch filled with mutated insects. Further on, they had found a stream-bed crawling with monsters. And finally they had battled their way down the waterfall, into a deep crater.

But what made the crater? And what changed ordinary plants and animals into the horrors we saw there?

His fingers touched the horn, and recoiled. It felt strange, almost twisted. In his mind he saw an image of a dark star falling out of the sky, skipping across the forest like a pebble on a pond before it struck the ground with an earth-shaking thunderclap . . .

Maybe the spellcasters didn't bury this thing at all. Maybe they just left it where it was, and sealed it there. Because they knew what it could do.

When he finally picked up the horn, his face was grim.

Chapter 7

'If I never see a forest again,' remarked Guy, 'It may be too soon, I think.'

Volker grinned. 'Suppose you were back in Armorica . . . in the forests of Guillac?'

'Ah, but they are *different*!' insisted Guy, so seriously that the others burst out laughing. He scratched his blunt nose thoughtfully. 'Though *voyons*, perhaps I am not in such a hurry to walk that way again. There is no place like my little *domaine* in all the world, you understand; but there is no denying it could be the slightest trace . . . well, dull. A tourney or two, a duel – one turnip-head knocking off another's. Now and again a plump peasant wench, and the rest of the time what is there to do? Just sit and watch the grapes ripen.'

'Come to the Northlands, then,' said Thorgrim gravely. 'Between the Ice as a neighbour and our own gentle customs, there are many ways for a man to pass his time. All winter long we squat around the fire close enough to gnaw the coal, telling over the list of murders and manslayings. And all summer long we go make that list a little longer.'

'Why?' asked Volker.

'Because, *min ven*, we must have new things to speak of for the next winter.'

'What about the seasons in between?' laughed Dani.

Thorgrim turned to her with an astonished look. 'Autumn and spring? They are for sowing and harvesting, of course. Also, you wash.'

'I can hardly wait,' grinned Volker. 'For me . . . I could use a little dullness, for a while, Give me a nice peaceful library, with wide airy windows. It seems ages since I could sit and study at peace.'

Dani nodded enthusiastic agreement. 'Me too. Rat-catching didn't exactly broaden my mind. Maybe the High Priestess in Nebelstein had something else planned for me. Trouble is, she never told me what.'

The debate broke out again in earnest. All the way down back from the crater they had been arguing, in the best of spirits. Volker in particular felt as if a great weight had been lifted off his shoulders. They had had some trouble, naturally; a rather half-hearted attempt at a surprise attack by some remaining huldrafolk, a night ambush by a gang of ogres, and the growing pangs of hunger. But by now he could almost take these things in his stride. The huldrafolk were understandably terrified of the horn, and fled incontinently when the first blast of it shook the trees, the more so as the other horn seemed to add some strange harmonic. The ogres, closer to the riverine marshes, had just plain and ordinary banditry in mind, plus the customary man-eating. They were wholly unprepared for the tune that sent them hopping and dancing away, an extremely dangerous way to act in the middle of a treacherous swamp, as most of them managed to demonstrate. As for the hunger, that was only annoying; after all, they had a shipload of supplies to look forward to. Volker hardly gave any of it a second thought. Against all odds he had actually achieved half of Ulrich's task . . . probably the more difficult half. Now, if he could just get the horns to Syracusa, he'd be free. The thought had him walking on air.

'We should come in sight of our *Walross* shortly,' remarked Thorgrim, when the argument slackened awhile. 'Unless the old coalbiter has chosen to slip cable and set off after his friends.'

331

'If he has we shall feed him to Dani's owl for a field-mouse!' chuckled Guy. 'But I doubt it. Say what you will of the old *rabougris*, he would not do such a thing lightly. He seemed to want us to succeed.'

Something, the tiniest fraction of unease, drifted across Volker's thoughts, as intangible and as disturbing as a fleck on the eye. But he could not focus on it, and a moment later he forgot it when they crested a ridge and saw, in the shallow vale below, the welcome shape of the *Walross* wallowing in mid-river. An immense relief flooded through him. 'That, at least, is there,' said Guy thankfully. 'Can anyone see a man on deck?'

It seemed quite natural to Volker to shade his eyes and stare. 'One by the tiller,' he said cheerfully. 'I think it's old Diderik, sunning himself.'

'And keeping watch, no doubt,' nodded Thorgrim. 'He is no fool, that old man. Well, let us go down. My belly calls for weregild for my cut throat!'

Volker chuckled with the rest – and only then did he realise what had just happened. At this distance only elf-eyes could be expected to make out men; in not asking him outright Guy had just been tactful. It had certainly had an effect, that tact. For a moment, just one unguarded moment, his own elvish blood had not bothered him. It did now, though, just as much as ever. An unguarded moment of real, unalloyed happiness. The implications of it shook him; he couldn't grasp them – half of him didn't want to. With his head in a whirl he trooped after the others. Long before they had raised the small boat and set off downstream, hunger had pushed less immediate worries well into the background.

When they hailed him from upstream, the old merchant sprang up with an energy that belied his years. 'So you're back, eh?' Diderik cried. 'Beginning to wonder, I was! Well, well, born to be hanged, the whole pack of you!' He himself caught the line they threw him, and spryly wrapped it around the stern cleats. 'Got what you were after, too, eh? I can see it by the smug look of you!' Volker climbed aboard first, ostensibly to protect the horns, actually to help Dani avoid Diderik's all too helpful hands; but though she didn't seem to mind Guy propelling her up by the seat of her hose, she shied away from Volker. That hurt and annoyed him, but he was too glad to be back aboard to dwell on it.

Guy pulled himself heavily over the rail, and looked around with a displeased air. 'Good day, old man! Nobody but you? Our industrious crew should surely be up and about!'

'A truth, sir,' agreed Diderik. He rapped his cane hard on the deck. 'Hoy, below there! Up and about, you lazy slugs! Our wandering lambs are back!'

The stirring below decks, the rumble of feet, sounded startlingly loud in the still air. Thorgrim, who had been stowing the oars, swung himself up by the backstay, but stopped with one knee over the rail by the tiller, puzzled. Volker stiffened. Loud, yes, for the few men left them.

Too loud . . .

But before he could voice the thought, the hold hatch and the foc'sle doors burst open as if on a tidal wave – and a wave of bodies came spilling and shrilling out across the deck. More swarmed out of the oar-ports, up and over the rail, and into the rigging. Dani's owl screeched and sprang from her shoulder. Volker, head swimming with hunger and shock, felt he had somehow landed upon the decks of that dark and doubtful pleasure-barge, where the foul masks could fall away and show him human faces; yet he knew they would not. These things were swarming in the rigging, scuttling and squirming like spilt filth across the deck – bent, loping bodies, leathery skins pale and green as cave-slime beneath the dirt, crumpled malicious faces like mummified apes, save for the yellow glitter of their eyes . . .

Gargoyles, Satyrs. Ogres. Smallish, mostly; none were the real Old World monsters, but all were as well-armed and vicious-looking as the taller shapes among them – swarthy-skinned, hard-faced men.

But the sight didn't freeze Volker, as it might have. Before his thoughts cleared he was already swinging the horn from his shoulders, almost as fast as Guy grabbed his sword-hilt and Dani her bow. But in the tumult before them there was uncanny order; instantly the air hissed, alive with arrows. Dani skipped back as one slapped into the deck between her feet, and Guy whirled about and sagged, cursing, as one transfixed his left sleeve, level with his heart. The horn bucked violently in Volker's grasp as another whined off it. They might have been cut down in that instant, save that Diderik, with a spitting sound of fury, brandished his cane – and the arrows stopped.

Guy drew a deep and painful breath, unbelieving. 'You?' It was hardly more than a whisper. The companions stared open-mouthed at the old man, momentarily unable to move.

The ancient merchant nodded sombrely. 'Myself.' He gestured calmly at the bows levelled on them, at least thirty already, with more archers scrambling up from below. His meaning was amply clear. Those were only warning shots. They were covered, all too literally. One move, one step out of turn would bring death inescapable winging down on them. 'No doubt you are shocked. But pray do nothing about it, my dear Draconnier, or your title will certainly lapse. The same for you, apprentice. Set down those horns, if you please. With care!'

Dani shook her head. 'I don't understand . . .' she stammered. 'How *can* it be him? He was in danger just as often as we were, from the wreckers . . . that thing in the river . . . the kobolds, the ogres, even the Knight! I can't believe it!'

Volker felt a great chill below his heart, as if something there had turned to wintry stone. 'But I can!' he said, with bitter bile. 'I can!' He punched the air, for lack of anything else. 'It fits, it bloody well fits! In Nürnberg; Hel-fire I should have seen it then! The Tartarists were waiting for their leader, and the merchants were all at the inn, all except *you*. Oh, you had your excuse ready, and you put on a good show, but—'

'Indeed!' spat de Guillac painfully, nursing his injured arm. 'So good you had to be rescued! And then, after the river beast attacked, we found you so exhausted, did we not? From the effort – but not of fighting it, no! Of raising it up!' Volker heard his teeth grind in anger, and knew how he felt: furious, helpless.

Dani's eyes narrowed. 'Yes! And the other attacks, they wouldn't have harmed you, would they? Not when you were commanding them . . .'

Diderik cackled cheerfully, and his prune face crinkled up into a beaming smile. 'Now there, my pretty one, you do me a grave injustice! The early attacks, yes! On young Volker here . . . we thought only to rob Ulrich of his chosen tool, never dreaming that he would throw away his precious life for him. And how truly fortunate I was, that we did not succeed!'

'I wish you bloody well had!' said Volker miserably.

Diderik flapped a withered hand. 'Ah, no, no, lad, never say that! Beyond price, you've been to me – beyond price! Not that I foresaw you would be, of course; I thought only of wresting the horn away from you. That I could have done in an eyeblink, if Ulrich's clever little charms hadn't shielded it from me. So we needed you alive to uncover it for us. And *that* meant either destroying your guardians, or luring you away from them. Hence the wreckers, and the oracle, and

335

the little surprise we prepared for you in Nürnberg. I was moving carefully, you see, just in case Ulrich was somehow still with us! But then, after Nürnberg, when I realized you had even escaped from the Master of Knights, ghastly brute though he was, when I actually saw you use the horn on my little waterbeast – why then, I confess, I was surprised. Perhaps you and your funny followers might amount to something, after all. In which case, why not leave you alone and let you try for the other horn? If you failed, you would at least have blazed some part of the trail. And if you succeeded . . .' He gestured around. 'It would be all the easier to trap you, still, and relieve you of both horns. And I am proved right, am I not?'

Volker frowned. 'But the kobold-mage . . . the Master . . . *they* didn't leave us alone!'

Diderik shrugged apologetically. 'Ah, when one recognizes the inevitable triumph of Tartarus, one must . . . shall we say, come to terms with the draw-backs. Such as the fact that one can't ever quite *trust* one's underlings. They grow restive, they're forever sneaking about, trying to steal a march on their betters. That little vermin and the Master, my strong right arm, had lately set their sights higher than the point of their own misshapen heads! Thinking I dithered! Thinking they could wrest the horn from you, and conveniently dispose of me at the same time! Ah, but they had not seen you in action, you four. You soon taught them the error of their ways! Saved me no end of trouble!' He waggled a gnarled finger. 'Though mind you, I did have to bale you out, now and again. As when I prompted you, my dear Draconnier, to remember the tuning-fork spell. I feared I was being too obvious.'

'You could have saved yourself the trouble, *messire*,' grunted Guy with bleak contempt. 'Your half-cooked spell slew only his horse; it was my brandy he drowned in!'

Diderik waved away the sally. 'Pah! What matters is that you took care of him for me, that's all! Except the last service, of course. Which is to require those horns of you, my dear young sir.' He saw Volker stiffen again, and added, quite mildly, 'I do most earnestly advise you to obey. I won't insult your intelligence with false promises; but at least you will live a *little* longer . . . and a little more comfortably. And that can only be to your advantage. Come now!' Volker noticed, as if in a dream, that Diderik's way of speaking had changed, become more florid and old-fashioned as he let his real self show through. He talked like somebody born in another century. And, Volker realized with a shudder, he very probably had been.

So many little puzzles about the old man were becoming glassy clear, now that he knew, now that it was too late. Ancient gods, what a weird object he really was! Even his appearance, wizened and wrinkled and bent, suddenly seemed less like age alone. It reminded Volker unpleasantly of the Tartarists and the deformities they all seemed to have developed. Whatever sickening process caused them might very well reduce a man to something like Diderik. Looking at him that way, his sprightliness, endearing before, became almost obscene, a horrible goblin capering. Even the faint musty smell that had always clung about him grew stronger, and carried with it the taint of corruption. The cackle in his voice sounded weird now, like the cawing of some carrion bird imitating human speech.

'Come now!' he repeated impatiently. 'The horn in your hand, the other at your back – set them down! Then stand away!'

'*Don't do it!*' hissed Dani frantically. 'He's scared to come too near you! If he dared, he wouldn't stop to ask!'

Diderik waggled his head, the earflaps of his ridiculous cap flying out like spaniel ears. 'Not so, not so, my dear!' There was a hunger in that dry, creaky voice that was horrible to hear. 'A dead hand will give them up, just as easily. If need be . . . *Now, sir!*'

The command cracked like a whip. If there was a spell in it, none was needed. Volker, aware of a slight soft scraping at his back, was thinking furiously. Dani was right, up to a point. Diderik was being careful to keep his distance. Perhaps he feared Volker; or perhaps he feared blocking the fire of his inhuman archers. Either way, it made little difference. One wrong move and Volker would die. If he pitched the horns overside, maybe even dived with them . . . no. He wouldn't have enough time, not if he was dodging arrows, and Diderik could soon fish them up. The old Tartarus wizard was right; he had no choice.

Except, perhaps, one.

At his back the scraping stopped, and something twanged softly, like a slackened lutestring. He shrugged, then simply opened his fingers and let the horn fall.

The silver mountings clattered on the deck, and the eccentric spiralling shape rolled crazily off towards the scuppers. '*Hoi!*' shrilled Diderik in startled outrage, and scuttled after it. All eyes followed him – as Volker had intended. He grabbed Dani and flung the pair of them bodily to the deck. With a bloodcurdling berserker yell, Thorgrim released the backstay that, as Volker's keen ears had detected, he had been carefully unshackling all this time. The mast swayed violently, the rigging sagged and jerked, and one or two of the archers lost their grip and smashed on to the deck, or overside into the river. Others, howling with fear, clung on for dear life as the mast swayed sickeningly; many dropped their bows in their fright. Not all, though. A swarm of arrows sang back towards the stern, but far too late. Dropping that horn had given Thorgrim the distraction he needed. He was over the rail and into the water before

Diderik's howl brought his creatures rushing back to the rail, overwhelming Guy as he tried to follow; horny fingers held Volker and Dani tight.

A yell went up as a head bobbed in the sun-blazing water. Arrows fishtailed down at it, there was a scream and a body rolled over and sprawled, face down, bowed limbs floating limp. It was one of the fallen archers. Another head . . . and they shot at it just as ferociously, not caring who they hit; a satyr yelled and thrashed. They waited, bowstrings taut, arrows swaying slowly this way and that – one breath, two, three. But no more heads appeared; nobody climbed out on shore. More breaths, longer than any man could have held his. No sound but the calm lapping of the river. One of the men said something to Diderik; Volker caught the word *noia* – drowned. He wasn't so sure; he remembered Thorgrim telling him how Norsemen cultivated endurance underwater as a means of showing off. Of course Thorgrim had been a long time away from home . . .

At last Diderik snorted. 'Well, whether he is drowned or not, he can do us no harm down there. To your posts, all! And guard these two . . .'

He stopped, glaring angrily down the length of the boat, to where a dark-robed figure was hunched over the bombard, ramming something home. 'You there!' he rapped. 'Did I not say leave that? It's dangerous, and we've no need of it n—' Again he cut off short. He had seen the trickle of bright blood that ran down the deck from the bow-rail, the spreading water stain, the bodies stuffed hastily beneath the thwart, the halberd against the tiller.

The figure straightened up, and its hood fell back to reveal one of the Norseman's wide bushy grins. '*Saa*?' said Thorgrim. 'And here am I, thinking that this is exactly what you need.' The slowmatch hissed as his tinderbox sparked it alight. The few gargoyles still at that end of the ship yelped and charged him; he

339

snatched up Hlavisbana and slashed at them. Heads and limbs flew, and the survivors scattered, howling and stumbling back, falling over each other to get away.

'Call them off, little man!' shouted the Norseman. 'Over the side with the whole filthy pack of you! Or I scatter you to the four winds!' The great gun creaked on its trunnion as he swung it around, and as its blunt mouth trained across the rigging the few remaining archers screeched and hurled themselves immediately into the water. Old World creatures had come to know and fear gunpowder weapons; survivors often complained that men were getting too far ahead of them with this sort of thing.

Diderik, too, had seen just what sort of death came spewing from the muzzle now trained upon him, but he simply leaned on his cane and shook his head. 'And scatter your friends also? Come, barbarian, be reasonable—'

'To Avernus with reason!' screamed Dani. 'Blast him, Thorgrim! We'll take our chances!' Guy growled agreement.

Diderik's walnut face convulsed into a horrible leer of fury. 'You will, will you? And just what chances are those? None at all! For see there, you barbarian idiot! See there, and despair!' He gestured furiously with his cane. Thorgrim did not turn, only clicked his flint threateningly, evidently suspecting a trick; but Guy, resting his injured arm against the rail, stood up with a muffled oath, and Dani and Volker scrambled up to see.

Volker's heart sank. Beyond the bend of the river some quarter of a mile behind them, the tip of a sail was drifting past the treetops, a flame of orange against the green. Out into the main river it glided, tacking across the breeze and bearing down on them fast, and Volker saw it was a heavy, high-hulled shape new to him, its crude-looking baggy sail slung from a long gaff

340

that was simply hung on the mast. The men who lined its sides looked strange and barbaric also, sallow men in flowing robes striped or patterned, just like the two on deck here. But there was nothing remotely primitive about the twin lion-snouted tubes projecting either side of the short bowsprit, like horns above the staring eyes painted on the timbers; they looked like small but functional bombards.

Thorgrim, seeing his friends react, risked a quick look. He whirled back with a lurid curse, and the berserker stare blazed into his blue eyes. *'Guderneskidt!'* he roared. 'Up yours first, wizard! *All of you . . . jump!'*

He was warning his friends, but they hardly had time to break the grips that held them before the Norseman's hand darted to the touchhole. Just as swiftly Diderik flung up his cane, twirling it in his gnarled fingers, shrilling a word in his high-pitched voice. The air in front of him seemed to gel and shimmer, iridescing like a brilliant bubble. Then the match hissed home.

Light burst in Volker's eyes as he leapt, but he heard no sound at all. What plucked him out of midair seemed too enormous, too all-enveloping, the flicked finger of some god Thorgrim had insulted. Deck, river, sky, vanished in that devouring flash, leaving him dangling against a searing radiance in which time and direction alike lost meaning, struggling to hold himself together against the forces that threatened to strip him apart, half from half. *Not now!* cried something within him. *Not like this!*

Then, abruptly, the light went out, and a dark mirror shattered over his head.

They fished Dani up at the end of a boathook, and dragged her over the carved gunwale that way, choking and spluttering. She had hit her head going into the water, and swallowed too much of it before she could gather her wits and start swimming. All she could do for an hour or more was sprawl face down upon the deck and heave, barely caring whose deck it was or why. Then, when she had coughed the last of the Poiana River out of her gullet, she began to sit up and take an interest. Beside her, head hanging, slumped what looked like a Libyan or a Nubian, jet black, with frizzy hair on end. '*Naa*,' it inquired in a listless whisper. 'Are you well enough now?'

She started, stared at him, then clapped her hand to her mouth to stifle what looked like a peal of wild laughter. 'Thorgrim! I didn't know you! I thought you were some southlander!' Quickly she looked around the figures crowding the deck, and her face fell. Then, between the crudely carved bars of the gunwale, she caught sight of the *Walross*, aground and heeling, with a splintered mess at the bows and a giant's mouthful bitten out of the stern cabin. Nothing moved but curling wisps of smoke. 'Thorgrim – what *happened*?'

He winced. 'The bombard exploded. Strange; I watched Joachim with all care. Perhaps it was the old devil's counterspell. Also, it was already loaded.' Dani groaned. '*Alligevel*, it exploded – mostly forward, or I would have woken up in many places, as most of the Chaos creatures did. I was blown up in the air, I think, and came down in the shallows. They hooked me up, like you.'

'And V–Volker? Guy?'

'They were not found. I do not know.' He gestured to the robed men milling about the deck. 'No more do these goblin-lovers; they hunt for them still. Perhaps they have escaped; I hope . . .' A harsh order rang across the deck. A thin-bladed spear jabbed him in the shoulder, and a swarthy face bent over them, a finger clapped to its drooping moustaches then drawn swiftly across the windpipe. A gap-toothed grin suggested the guard found the prospect funny. Thorgrim scowled,

342

but fell silent. He had noticed the hush falling across the whole deck, as if they were listening.

Dani jerked her head towards the high stern; Diderik was scuttling up with crab-like energy, Ulrich's horn swinging over his bent shoulders. He looked comical, but nobody laughed, and in the guards' grim faces Thorgrim read their fear of the old man. The wizard's head swung back and forth, peering with the beady malice of a snapping turtle; then he raised the horn, took a deep breath and blew. One flat, unsteady note emerged; but it was powerful enough to waken echoes from the hills around, and set the smoke-wraiths dancing over the *Walross*. Nothing else happened, but as Diderik lowered the horn he seemed to be listening, and the others with him. Thorgrim and Dani looked at each other in sudden, horrified understanding. The old mage was searching as they had searched, trying to awaken the strange sympathetic resonances of the other horn; only now, presumably, the other was wherever Volker might be. But the echoes died away without any change, and Dani hung her head. Diderik blew again, one note, then two, wavering between flat and sharp with a force that set the air shimmering and the echoes jangling; on the hills above a scree-slope slipped and went hissing and rumbling down among the pines, reminding Thorgrim of the great Norse avalanches. But there was still nothing new among the echoes, no resonance.

Or was there?

A very strange expression crossed Dani's face, and she began to squirm slightly; then suddenly Thorgrim felt something, some uneasy shiver that seemed to tickle the base of his spine. Nobody else seemed to notice, but then nobody else was sitting down . . .

He caught Dani's eye and glanced down. Mystified, she followed his gaze, then jerked bolt upright, squirming, as Diderik blew again. Diderik, too, had sensed something; he was muttering and glancing this way and that with wary malice, raising the horn again. He had to be distracted. Thorgrim set his lips and heaved himself to his knees. *'Befamle mig baglaens!'* he stormed, 'Slay me if you must, but spare me your crack-toned tortures! A bear breaking wind makes better music!' The flat of a scimitar rapped the side of his head and he subsided, but Dani's eyes sparkled . . . at least, until she saw Diderik make his way, more slowly than usual, down on to the deck again, and come stalking towards them.

'A sensitive barbarian,' he murmured. 'Very remarkable. I suppose you know nothing of your young friend's whereabouts? But then you hardly had the chance. Well, I fear your hastiness with that bombard has cost you two friends, and me half my prize. Of course, it cannot be so easily destroyed, but where it has got to . . .' He shrugged, as if casually, but Dani could see the shiver growing in his twisted limbs as his anger broke its bounds. 'Over many long leagues it answered its fellow, and from beneath the earth itself. All the magical barriers of old could not restrain it. It was forged in the fires of Tartarus – yet one little explosion, and now – *nothing!*' His mask of calm slipped, and his little eyes sparkled like specks of fire in rotten wood. 'Not even a tremor! Almost in my hand! And most of my creatures slain!' He glanced anxiously upstream, and Volker guessed why. 'And if I dally any longer that mutton-headed warlord Oberto will learn of my ship and come down on us!' He kicked Thorgrim, hard. 'Your doing! Yours! So now I have to flee, and leave my prize! But I'll be back, with twice the men and creatures to scour the countryside, dam the river if need be! And for your insolence I can promise you a fair reward! Oh yes! You'll be far more fitting than the usual frightened slaves!'

'Oh?' asked Dani with exaggerated interest, like a

hostess flattering a boring guest. 'Fitting for what, exactly?'

Diderik's bluish lips curled. 'Why, as offerings, of course. Burnt offerings! To One whom we serve, these men and I, as did our ancestors before us throughout all the long ages of His sleep—'

'If He has slept,' said Thorgrim idly, 'your labours have been small. From Him you should expect no tip . . .'

'Sounds kind of boring to me,' remarked Dani.

'Truth!' agreed Thorgrim. 'No wonder the little man has fallen from his waggon.'

'Like his ancestors before him,' added Dani.

Thorgrim nodded. 'They must have done, to produce him!'

'*Enough!*' spat Diderik. 'This bravado of yours, I would admire it more if you knew who and what you will face. But even to a half-witch like you, priestess, His name would mean nothing. It would not fill you with the terror it deserves. This alone I will tell you, you who opposed Him, you who hindered His return. He'll dance upon your squeaking ghosts! Dance, until all you have done is undone . . . or else forever!'

Thorgrim lifted a bored eyebrow. Dani shrugged and raised her eyes to the clouds. Diderik snorted impatiently and rounded on their guards with a flurry of orders in a harsh guttural tongue. They bowed low to him, crossing their arms as if to shield their heads. He nodded irritably and went shuffling away down the deck, calling orders to the sterncastle. Men ran to haul on ropes, blocks groaned, and the triangular sail began to creak up the mast. The guards kicked the prisoners to their feet, and began fitting manacles to their wrists. The anchor, a shapeless stone block, was hauled dripping to the deck, and the boat nosed slowly out into the current. Still tingling with that strange thrill, Thorgrim glanced back, half hoping, half fearing, at the wallowing hulk of the *Walross*, and the river and bank around it. Nothing moved but the reeds in the wind. Dani, too, was looking, and since their guards had not understood Burgundian he risked murmuring, 'Hope on! You have other eyes, priestess; what more do they tell you?'

The face she turned to him was pale. 'They're lost, too. I am more than blind.'

By the time Volker broke surface, and Guy beside him, the strange ship was disappearing beyond the trees. Even so, they waited a good while before they clambered, slimy and dripping, out of the reedbed; it offered little concealment, and anyone left behind would spot them at once. A horrible rasping growl made them jump violently, but Guy upended the horn he had taken from the mountainside, and tipped out, among a flood of mud and weedslime, a very small and panicky frog. 'Just a croak! But this horn . . . changed it somehow. And not for the better.'

Guy, resting his injured arm, looked up. 'As it did with our breath, when we took air through it. An ill tune that made! I was afraid they would hear us when they were searching the reeds. I myself, I would have gone deeper.'

'Then you couldn't have breathed at all,' remarked Volker.

'I have read of such feats.'

'You read lies. Deeper than our few inches the weight of water's too much; it presses on your chest, you can't draw enough air into your lungs.'

Guy grinned. '*Vrai*? Well, perhaps after all this philosophy of things physical is of some use.'

Volker grinned back. Worried as he was about the others and the horn, the relief of just being alive and in the open air was like fresh wine. 'Well, Diderik could have used some of it! The great necromancer . . . or whatever he thinks he is. The philosophy of sound,

346

especially, if he's going to monkey with musical magic.
I bet he felt sick when he got no answer to those horncalls of his – afraid Thorgrim had blown the thing to
bits, and us with it! He should have realized. Sound
can vibrate through solid matter and keep pretty much
its original pitch. But not in water! It answered its twin,
all right – but not so he could hear!'

'But we heard it! And felt it! Would it not have shaken
the hull?'

'Not enough for anyone to notice. Not through their
bootsoles, anyhow.'

Guy swept back his straggling curls and wrung out
his moustaches with a flourish. '*Magnifique, mon brave!*
Though where that boat came from they wear mostly
sandals, I believe!'

Volker sat up. 'You know it?'

'The type, but yes. They trade into Hispanic ports
quite regularly, and even to Bordeaux, from time to
time. A *dhow*, they call it, or some such word of Araby.
The boats are built in Libya, but they trade throughout
the Mediterranean. That one, with those painted eyes,
it must have come from Sicily, for all boats there bear
them—'

'All?' interrupted Volker. 'So it came from there?'

'Originally, beyond doubt.'

'So it's headed back there?'

'Probably, yes.'

'*Then we can follow!*'

'We must, yes! But . . .' Guy cocked a dubious eyebrow at the *Walross*. 'In that wreck . . . and neither of
us seamen?'

'What about that expensive education of yours? You
learned to sail, didn't you? And I've picked up plenty
from Thorgrim. As for the boat, it's still afloat, and it
was built as a sea-going vessel in the first place. Guy,
it's that way or none. Even if we survive wandering
overland, we'll be weeks behind! And Diderik could

347

slaughter Dani and Thorgrim out of hand, any time he wants to . . .'

Guy shook his head, sending water droplets flying. '*Courage, le mec*! We saw them fished living from the water. If they were for killing, would they not simply have been tossed back with throats cut, on the spot? For some reason they are being kept alive – even, perhaps, as bait for us, in case we still live. We must march carefully . . . but we may achieve much, if we are masters of the situation and not they.' He flexed the fingers of his injured arm in strangler's style, and winced. 'Let them only run aground, or delay themselves in some other way, and they will see what it is to rouse the wrath of a lord of Guillac! And', he added encouragingly, 'a young wizard of learning and power!'

'Some wizard!' Volker groaned, turning the rough horn in his fingers. 'This is all the magic I have left. And a strange sour-toned thing it is! I suppose it could be as powerful as the other – but I don't even know how to control it!'

'Then study, my friend, study! If our road is all the way to Iskandarya, you should have plenty of time! But first . . . bend your mind to boatmending!'

The damage was not the first thing they looked at, when they had splashed and struggled out to the *Walross*. It was well within Diderik's power to have left some spell-sprung boobytrap aboard, and there was no Thorgrim to sniff it out. They searched, and carefully. It was not a pleasant experience. There was no trace of the crewmen they had left aboard, and no clue to their fate; but it was not hard to guess. Driven deep into a bow-timber, they found Thorgrim's halberd; Hlavisbana's shaft was scorched and smoked but intact, and it was still a valuable weapon. According to Guy, the goblins had not been long aboard: below decks the cargo was virtually intact and unplundered, but the living space had been thoroughly befouled. Worse,

348

most of the stores had been devoured, and what remained was unfit for humans. 'It goes hard on a man already hungry, and condemned to labour!' growled Guy, mouthing past the nails he held in his teeth. They were busy patching up the shattered stern with the planks of the devastated cabin. 'And too sober to conjure up a feast! Later, maybe, we shall mislead innocent fish. But for now . . . we follow famished, or not at all!'

Dani blinked violently as she was led up into the sunshine. After days as a chained captive in those black and stinking bilges the blazing southern sun brutalized her as badly as her ogre guards. They pushed her roughly into the hands of Diderik's humans and went scuttling back below, where they liked it. Still fettered from neck and wrist to ankle, she staggered a little with the effort of standing straight. The deck seemed to be heaving more than usual beneath her; the motion made her feel queasy, and gratefully she took a deep breath of the clear air. Then she almost choked with surprise; it had a strange tang to it – and it was filled with eerie cries.

'That's right, my dear,' creaked Diderik's loathsome voice in her ear, making her jump. 'We've reached the sea.'

She turned sharply, and found herself eye to eye with him; he was standing on the quarterdeck steps to give himself height. Hastily she turned away again, and suddenly, looking out over the vast expanse of blue, she forgot her peril. Dani had never seen the sea, and only once or twice the wheeling white birds that made those cries, when bad weather had driven them far inland. The expanse of water before her seemed as infinite as the lighter blue they flew in; it drew her eye to the horizon and held it there in the haziness . . .

Diderik coughed in her ear.

'Not that way, my dear. You were not brought here

to gawk at that, nor for the good of your health. That hardly matters now, does it? But I wouldn't grudge you one small shred of satisfaction, at least . . . nor your barbarian friend,' he added politely as Thorgrim flew up out of the hatch. The Norseman landed on the deck with a crash and clank of fetters, roaring and cursing, still streaked and scorched with the soot of the explosion. Grinning human guards hauled him to his feet and dragged him over to the rail. Dani's guards propped the two of them against it, keeping firm hold to make sure they had no chance to jump overboard. It would be suicide in those fetters, of course; but evidently Diderik thought even that would be some kind of escape for them. She swallowed. He must really be planning something. 'Now!' he cackled. 'Look there!'

Anything Diderik wanted to show her, she'd sooner not see; but the hard hand of a guard clenched in her hair and turned her head. Thorgrim began to growl an insult – then stopped, and breathed a different, astonished curse. On the other side there was no great expanse of water; they were riding at anchor, still in the mouth of the Poiana river estuary. But now breakers burst against its banks, and wide flats of sandy mud opened on either side of the channel; she guessed they had been uncovered by the strange moon-magic called *tide*. And high up on the mudflats, beached high and dry, there was something: another ship. No, not a ship. A hulk, its superstructure stripped away from its bare ribs. And around it . . . Her stomach clenched again. Around it on the brown sand were sprawled the empty skeletons of men, still plucked and torn at by the gulls. Its hollowness looked every bit as horrible as theirs, as if it too had been a living thing. And strangely familiar . . .

'Seen it somewhere before, haven't we?' cawed Diderik. Thorgrim's fetters clinked sharply, and he cursed. Dani gasped in sudden horror. Was it the *Walross*? Had

Volker or Guy come after them, and been ambushed? Then she caught hold of her wits, and an icy wave of understanding slapped at her. This must have happened weeks ago. Not the *Walross*, then; the *Walfisch*. The merchants' boat. The cowards who had fled, and left them to die . . .

Only it seemed they'd run even faster towards their own deaths.

'Haagen – Goldfüss – the whole crew?' she whispered. She had been raging mad at them, she would have skewered any her arrows could have reached; but now she could only feel sorry for them. Poor fools! Little enough hope was left her, but she was still streets ahead of them. 'Are . . . they're . . . all dead?'

Diderik shrugged. 'How should I know? I count at least eleven skeletons. I'll waste no time looking for more.'

'But there may be survivors! Wounded, maybe, or wandering, starving . . .'

'Hah! Let 'em! Let 'em! Why'd I need 'em now? And Tartarus, but they were tiresome, with their endless squabbles and petty pedlars' greed!'

'You stinking old *trollkarl*!' said Thorgrim thickly, and spat copiously on the deck. 'They were your friends, man, or thought they were! Why do such a thing as this to them?'

'I?' Diderik's eyes sparkled. 'You malign me! Neither I nor my creatures had any hand in this. They ran into some ordinary pirates, I don't doubt, and were too few to cope with them; a hazard not unknown in the Mare Adriatica . . .'

Dani glared at him. 'Then why're you so keen to show this off to us?'

The sorcerer smiled. 'I am a generous man; I felt it a pity to grudge you this small satisfaction.'

'Satisfaction?' Dani's voice rasped in her throat. 'Is *that* supposed to give us satisfaction? I just feel sorry

351

for the poor stupid sons of bitches! And sick to my stomach being anywhere near you!'

Diderik let out a wheeze of malicious merriment, and she realized how avidly he had watched the play of expressions across her face. 'Just wanted to pleasure yourself, right?' she muttered. 'Getting off on watching me suffer! Come on, Thorgrim, let's get back to the bilges. It doesn't smell so bad there.'

Despite the pain of her hair she twisted her head as far aside as she could manage. She couldn't help one quick glance upriver, though she knew how stupid it was. If by some chance Volker and Guy were still alive, she hoped they were taking the second horn straight to Sicilia and this Temple rather than trailing after her; that was the best way of getting Diderik screwed. Even if she wasn't there to see it . . .

She shivered, and decided to be honest with herself. That was what she ought to hope. But for days now she'd caught herself praying he was coming to rescue her. Some selfless priestess! She'd made a better ratcatcher. In all her life she'd never felt so scared and so helpless. And what could she expect to see? He wouldn't come galloping up in full view! But she couldn't help looking, all the same.

And she might have known Diderik wouldn't miss it. 'Not that way, little one!' His clawed fingers pinched playfully at her thigh. 'You won't find any help coming, I fear. Even if by some miracle your young Volker were still in one piece, he should be scuttling back up north to Worms with that other horn, back to Ulrich's interfering colleagues at the college there. Bah! Let him! Let them puzzle over it! They would find it past their power to destroy, and so dither and delay, and meanwhile . . . our Brotherhood has its agents there also. Incompetent, like those fools of Nürnberg, but they would watch over it well enough and get word to him. In time we shall recover it, as we recovered this one!' He pinched again, harder, and she fought to keep the tears of pain from her eyes. 'Meanwhile we are bound another way altogether, one he has no reason in the world to come. We are going to Syracusa, greatest city of the southern world. I hardly think he would follow us there, do you?'

Dani blinked. No reason to go to Syracusa? But that was where Ulrich had *sent* him, to seek this Templa Volcana! Diderik couldn't have guessed. She struggled to keep the sudden blaze of hope out of her face. If Volker was alive, he'd be coming after her anyway.

But there was no deceiving Diderik's uncanny eyes. If he could not read thoughts, he could do almost as much. 'Now why should that excite you so?' he mused. 'D'you think you'll have a chance to get away in the big city, or cry for help? Don't deceive yourself. We'll have you well guarded . . . and nobody will lift a finger for you, not a woman and a foreigner to boot. Life's too cheap there. And I shan't be lingering. I'm going to hang this horn secure where it belongs, whence it was stolen, so long since, in the hidden Templa Volcana, to await the coming of its partner! And offering the pair of you up will make a nice climax to the rites of rededication! So if I were you, I'd contain my enthusiasm!'

He cackled happily at the sudden change in Dani's expression, and gestured to the guards to take them back below. For an instant she came face to face with Thorgrim, and saw her own confusion and dismay mirrored in his stolid features. The Templa Volcana? It couldn't be! Somehow, in some crazy way, everything had gone wrong. Volker was expecting to find a place where the horns could be destroyed; and instead he would be walking straight into the stronghold of his enemies. And how in all the world could they ever warn him?

*

353

'Here's the last of them!' Volker called. He made as if to touch the leathery bundle of sun-dried skin and bone among the sandgrass with his foot, then thought better of it.

'Who was it?' asked de Guillac quietly as he came up between the dunes.

'Goldfüss, I think. From the size of him. And that yellow hair . . .'

'Yes, Goldfüss. He was the strongest, he may have fought his way free and tried to run. They cut him down from behind. Then they stripped his clothes and left him lying for the birds and the beasts.'

'That little bastard Diderik!' grated Volker. Once sights like these would have left him sick and shaking; now his nausea was turning rapidly to a rage that startled even him. 'I'll tear him limb from limb if I ever get my hands on him!'

'May you do so . . . and I will hold your coat! But I do not think this is his work. It happened some time since, while we were in the forest. And what use would he have for the boat's cargo, rich as it was? But it has been removed, and swiftly. That is why the hull is so torn apart. Yet wonder of wonder, they have abandoned much of the plainer stores, taking only what was rich and rare. Old World creatures would not do that! This sounds more like pirates in haste, to me.'

Volker nodded. 'You're probably right. And there isn't much we can do about it, not after so long. Anyway, I've got more than enough reasons for going after Diderik's hide. What now? We've no time to bury them all; could we burn them in the hull?'

'A plume of smoke is seen from far, across the flat shorelands. If Diderik saw it he might guess there was someone on his tail! Or it might alert the good men who did this . . . and would we fare better than the merchants? Let us sink them in the deep water, these miserable bones, and be gone. At least now we will

354

have enough to eat, and need not delay to fish or forage.'

It took little time to salvage the remaining stores from the hulk, and less to sweep the beach of its sorry debris. Guy stared down at the swirling mud in pity and disdain. 'So it ends, all their petty bickering and squabbling! They would have done better to keep faith with us! But they were not bad men, as merchants go, and brave enough to attempt this voyage. Only not quite brave enough.'

'I wonder if I am,' said Volker moodily, as they turned away.

'You?' protested Guy, with a twist of his moustaches. 'You will serve, *mon enfant*! Definitely you will serve! Why, you might almost be the equal of the noblest blood of old Armorica, of I myself!'

'Thanks,' said Volker, trying to keep his smile straight. 'But right now I'm about as discouraged as I can get. On the river we might have caught that *dhow* thing . . . but on the Mare Adriatica? That's the *sea*! And we're going to cross it in an undermanned riverboat with a shaky superstructure? We'll be lucky if we make it to Sicilia, never mind catching up with Diderik. And even if we do, I've got no magical weapons to match his – not even this!' He turned the horn over and over in his hands. It felt strange somehow, without the silver cagework the other one had. Less wholesome. More disturbingly . . . alive.

He fingered some of the holes awkwardly, and blew gently into the huge mouthpiece, very softly, like a faint tremor of wind. The sound that emerged was weird, a sharp keening moan, wild and lonely as the gull cries but deeper, hollower, as if the very earth sang of the sorrows it bore. An infinite loneliness and misery settled on Volker like a chill mist, a deep confused yearning for something he had found and lost. Misery and depression clung to him, dragging him down. He did not want to love . . .

Guy turned a horrified face to him, echoing the same wrenching feelings, and hastily pulled the horn from his lips.

'You see?' groaned Volker. 'I still can't get the hang of the bloody thing! It's nothing like the other one, it's got some weird tuning of its own. Oh, I tinker with it, stop up holes here and there with wax and pitch; that changes it a little. But nothing like enough. If I could somehow narrow its bore . . . Anyway, what could we do to Diderik? Make him die laughing? We'd be lucky to get away ourselves, let alone rescue the others!'

'Lucky, you say?' Guy seemed about to tear out his hair, but settled for doing a little dance on the sand and waving his fists at the sky. '*Sacré dard d'un dragon*! After what we have survived this past half-year this infant still demands luck? My child, every minute I think I will find I have been dead for months and they were just breaking it to me gently! But what would you rather do? Abandon the chase? Leave our priestess and our hairy Norseman to the mercy of that little *rat bougri*? Take this horn home and tootle it on street corners? Hope is a luxury in our profession, *mon gars!*'

'And what profession's that?' grinned Volker. 'Whatever it is I'm still an apprentice.'

Guy grew strangely serious. 'There is no one name for it that I can think of, and no one training. There is no guild, no sign, and yet no brotherhood is stronger. From many lands, from all walks of life its members come, they may be lifelong friends or sworn foes, yet they bear a common stamp that never leaves them till their lives' end. Their hearts beat as one, their thoughts flow in the same channels, and ever their eyes move to the next bend in the road, to the misty distance behind the next ridge, to where the sun falls beyond the edge of the world. And for better or worse, Volker the Sorcerer,

Volker the Musician, in that profession you are no longer an apprentice! You have proved yourself. You are nothing if not a journeyman.'

After a moment's silence, fidgeting with the horn, Volker nodded. 'Then I'd better finish my journey. To Syracusa, whether or not we can catch Diderik. And once there, fulfil what I can of Ulrich's charge. Then we can tear the place apart till we find Diderik and the others. And Apollo Cernunnos grant we'll be in time!'

'*Parfaitement!*' Guy slammed his fist into his palm, then, mercurial as usual, turned sombre. 'Though tearing that place apart will not be so easy. I have read something of this Syracusa, long ago. A great, a beautiful metropolis, that makes our own Worms look stark and cold, that even approaches the nobility of Paris. But it is also a hive, a seething nest. Every kind and quality of men clusters there like moths to a lantern. Traders, thieves, sightseers, assassins, scholars, pirates, holy men and charlatans of all nations, races, colours, a great seething human stew. It will take some stirring, *pardi!*' He nodded sagely. 'But first, I agree, find this temple. Get one of the horns, at least, into safe hands. But how do you propose to find it? Every god you can think of is worshipped there, openly or in secret, and a hundred more you cannot! By all accounts there are more temples than jakes in the city! *Figurez-vous, mon cher*, one author claims that they even outnumber the *maisons de joie!*' Guy blew out his cheeks in horror. 'And that is only the known ones! What if this one is secret? To such arcane places one does not simply demand the way of a dragoman!'

'I've been thinking about that. I've read about Syracusa myself. They say that the ancient library of Alexandria, wonder of the world, kept getting burned. Then the fifth Constantinos moved it wholesale to Syracusa, to a magnificent new building, a kind of temple of culture – library and theatre and bath-house, all in one!

357

Books from every land, learning going back centuries! And open to any scholar! Think of it, Guy, all that knowledge, all that wisdom! *That's* where we'll find a clue to the temple!'

'*C'est juste!*' applauded Guy. 'But move with care! In this profession of no single name it pays to think as your foes do. Remember this: they know more than we. They may suspect you will look for this temple. And they may already know where it lies. In which case . . .'

Volker found himself shrugging; he was catching the habit. 'In which case we'll keep our eyes open. And keep trying . . .' His voice trailed off. For a moment he seemed to be looking beyond the horizon, across the seas to Dani, and Syracusa . . . Absentmindedly, he blew gently into the mouthpiece of the horn. His fingering had shifted, and the sound that came was different, dramatically different. Sharp, shrill, it stabbed straight through their agonized ears like hot needles; a command, not a feeling. The wind wailed in answer, bending the grasses and sending waves of dry sand hissing and rattling across the shallow slopes of the dunes towards the sea. From the shoreline the gulls leaped up in a cloud and wheeled screeching about the mast. But Volker, ignoring Guy's glare, found himself straining his ears for some other answer, however distant. None came; his head began to ache. He was about to get up and stow away the horn again, when a plummeting brown form burst abruptly through the wheeling ring of white overhead, and landed with a flurry and a scrape upon the sternpost.

'*Bougre de Bergerac!*' erupted Guy. 'It is Dani's!'

Wide-eyed and astonished, they stared at the owl; and beadily it stared back at them. Its plumage was ragged, and much of it was new growth; some scorch-marks were still visible on the rest. But it was unmistakably the same bird.

'It was the note she whistled!' said Volker, aston-

358

ished. 'I was thinking about her – and I just blew it – by accident!'

'*Ça alors!*' puffed Guy. 'Such accidents I do not believe in! But however that is, it may be that you have won us an aid of great value!' He turned to the owl. 'For you also wish greatly to win back your mistress, *hein*? And even if we cannot see with those eyes of yours, we may still use you to track her down for us, eh?' He waggled a fragment of raw fish in front of the owl's beak. '*Gentil hibou*! Eh? *Kilikilikili!*'

The owl leaned over and deftly took the fish. Then it bit him.

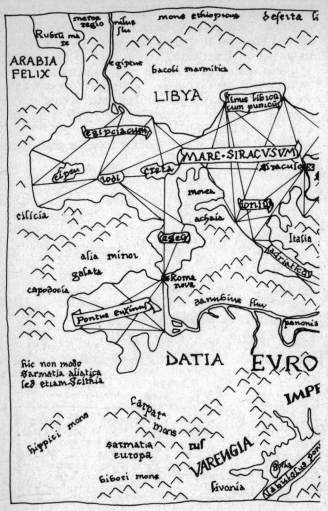

A map of the known world from the Codex Muntorum in the Philippian Library at Syracusa. The Codex survived at least three fires between the reigns of Manuel I and Marcangelo III – scholars believe that this map, drawn after Ptolemy by the northern cartographer Muntus, originally included more detail to the south.

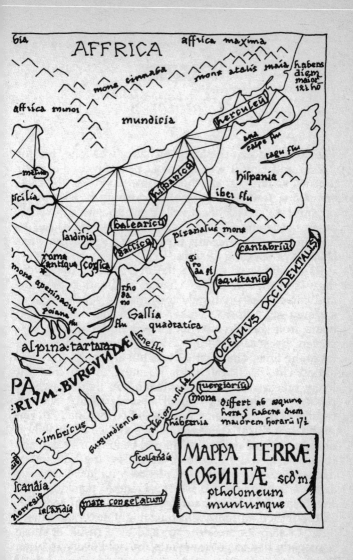

Chapter 8

The voyage down the Mare Adriatica was long, but for Volker and Guy it was the most peaceful time of their journey so far. Guy set their course parallel to the eastern shore, Dalmatia, but not so close as to risk shoals, or tempt some pack of starveling pirates with a rowboat, or any seagoing Old Worlders. Besides, the closer to the centre of the Adriatic they steered, the better their chances of spotting Diderik.

Its waters were not like the open ocean; they were more sheltered and less changeable, and both wind and currents ran naturally towards the south. Neither suffered seasickness, Volker because he was used to boats from his Bremen childhood and Guy, he suspected, because he found dry land just as unsteady a lot of the time. The weather was hot and mild, the skies almost cloudless, the winds no more than a constant lively breeze. They ran southward on light seas, and passed through one small thunderstorm without trouble. That came as a great relief. Ulrich had chosen his boats well, but there were limits to their adaptability, and the *Walross* had taken quite a beating. The damage to the bows was superficial, except for the hole in the deck where the bombard had taken its leave; but the superstructure was a mass of splintered planking, and the fallen mast was hard for just two men to raise. Without their mutual spells they might never have managed to step its broken end; and as a result of those somebody had to go down into the hold every so often to trim off the roots it kept putting out. Guy kept a beady eye on the masthead for any sign of leaves.

But the weather wasn't the only danger. Soon after they set off Volker, tipping overboard some scraps of smoked fish that even the owl turned up its beak at, was startled by the underwater arrow that arced up to seize them, its head snapping this way and that like a terrier after rats. Then he noticed the other sleek shapes gliding around and under the hull, but thought no more of them till next day he cast out his line and quickly hooked a huge fish, some four feet long, with rainbow scales and strangely barbed fins. He almost had the writhing monster to the side when a whole flight of arrows converged on it, thrashing, worrying, beating the water to a foam with their sharp back and tail fins. He cursed and struck out with the boathook he used as a gaff. He'd just managed to hook his catch when he noticed the larger – *much* larger – shape gliding lazily up from the green depths. There was a sudden flicker of movement, too fast for him to see, a fearful wrench which almost plucked him over the side, and he was left holding a slack line and the headless shaft of the hook.

The huge arrow had sheared it away almost without noticing, engulfing Volker's fish in a single bite. As Guy's feet thumped on the deck it wheeled lazily away, the lesser shadows darting after it to snap the very meat from its jaws. '*Mais quelle monstre!*' muttered the Armorican. 'Who was fishing for whom? I did not know they had tithe collectors in these parts!'

'It almost pulled me in!' said Volker shakily, gazing at the bloody flurry receding into the depths. 'I think we'd better forget about falling overboard here, Guy. There wouldn't be time to climb out . . .

'I do not know about that. *Foi de Guillac*, I would learn to fly!'

With only the two of them to man the boat they had to arrange hours of watches. When Volker not only offered to stand watch during the darkest hours of each night, but openly urged his special eyesight as the reason, Guy flashed him a startled look.

'It makes sense!' urged Volker. 'Otherwise we might easily sail by Diderik one dark night and never know it!'

'It makes supreme good sense,' agreed Guy, still weighing him up. Clearly he would have said more, but Volker gave him no chance. He knew he'd changed, these last few months, but just how was hard to say. It felt like a change for the better, but he couldn't be sure. He was afraid to think too much about it; that might stop the change, or it might speed it up, and he wasn't sure which scared him more. He felt torn apart enough as it was, between his duty to Ulrich and his fears for Dani – not to mention poor old Thorgrim. More doubts and divisions he didn't need.

But as he sat up through the long night watches, he found his thoughts straying more and more often along new paths. There was rarely much to do; he would sit by the long oarshaft they'd lashed to the rudder in place of the shattered tiller, gazing alertly at the horizon ahead, or scanning the white streak of shore through a wide spyglass. The lands on either side were arid and sun-scorched, but there were still deep, shady patches of cool-looking forest. From time to time Volker's spyglass would pick out points of light among the trees, sometimes singly, often sprinkled in close patterns that suggested camps or small towns. Probably these were just outlaws, ogres, ghouls or some of the other unpleasant breeds of Old Worlder that Ulrich's notes warned infested the region but they set Volker thinking of the Transalpine woods, and the eerie lights of the huldrafolk among the blackness of his northern trees. He might be accepted there, if he wished. What would it be like to walk there with them, to learn all the secrets of the forests and sing songs that were ancient before the first coming of men? Maybe even to make his way into the ancient huldra kingdoms that still endured, somewhere in the hidden heart of the northern hills?

It was a pretty weird idea. And yet it wasn't as weird or unpleasant as he'd once have found it, not so long ago. He stared over the rail and saw himself briefly mirrored in a patch of calm water. He realised now just how much like a *huldramann* he must look to those who knew, though he had lines of humanity in his face they usually lacked. He could even imagine himself striding along among those tall proud foresters he'd seen back home in Bremen long ago – his uncles or cousins or kinsmen, maybe? That really was weird. Like his father. Where *had* he gone, all those years ago?

Maybe I was wrong about him. Maybe he didn't get bored with us. Maybe something happened to him, something his kinfolk didn't know about – or wouldn't talk about.

But Volker, and perhaps his mother also, had believed the worst of him. Why? Because of their own feelings of shame and inferiority? Their own doubts about mingling with another kind?

There was no simple answer to that, and never would be. But meanwhile Volker was what he was, a bridge between two kinds. And he knew what happened to bridges; they got walked over. Why make it harder than it had to be? So bigots on either side wouldn't accept him . . . why do their job for them? Why not go all out for the advantages it gave him? And to Tartarus with the rest?

It took a lot of darkness and a lot of thinking to get that far. It was good to have the time to think, though, and darkness of itself had never bothered him, even as a child. His keen senses had always stripped shadows and strange noises of any terrors. And here he found it restful, after a day of sunlight like molten metal that seemed almost to overload his senses. Was that the *huldra* in him? If so, it might explain why even civilized *huldrafolk* stayed haughtily aloof from bustling humanity, why they disliked hard labour and lived so much for their rather arcane pleasures. If their senses were so keen, keener even than his, they must find rougher human things actively painful.

That made Volker lucky; he could enjoy the best of both worlds. He could bask in the noon sun as it beat down on the bright blue waters of the Gulf, but he was as much at home in the dark as Dani's owl, with whom he shared his watches. The owl tolerated Guy as long as he kept his fingers well away, but Volker could feed it by hand. Sometimes it would glide down and perch on the tiller, usually with its back to him; but after a while, if he left it alone and went on with whatever he was doing, he would look up and find the head had swivelled in its disconcerting way and the huge eyes were watching him. Sometimes he even found himself talking to it, sharing his worries about Dani with it, and also his doubts about himself, and it watched him with a look of such understanding that it alarmed him a little. But that was just the cast of an owl's face, he told himself; no wonder they were chosen as symbols of the goddess Verena Minerva, of wisdom. But it seemed to help him, all the same, setting out his doubts and fears before that calm unhostile gaze. The difference between man and *huldra* might not seem so enormous to an owl.

And as the nights passed, and Volker grew more and more reconciled to his own divided nature, he found something strange happening. At first it took him some time to spot other sails when they appeared, even in bright moonlight, and longer to make out whether they were likely to cross his course. Sometimes he had to wake Guy to help. But increasingly often he began to see those distant sails more clearly, even in the dim, deceptive light of nightfall and dawn. At first he decided he was just getting more experienced, more used to the conditions; but soon enough he knew there must be more to it than that.

With only two on board they had had to give a wide berth to every other sail they saw, even little fishing boats, in case they turned out to be gunwale-deep in bandits. Only when they saw the triangular *dhow* rig did they steer towards it, in case Diderik had somehow been held up; but it was never his. Once or twice, though, Volker had woken Guy to come look at a ship, and found the sharp-eyed Armorican couldn't even see it. And there was more. One night, when he'd steered in towards shore to avoid a dangerous looking *dhow* headed northward, he was surprised how loud and clear the distant breakers sounded. The pirate passed by, too far away for their own lookout to spot the *Walross* – but Volker, as he watched, found he could clearly hear voices jabbering in furious argument on its decks. Not loudly. They sounded tiny, as far away as they were, but clear, crystal clear. Impossibly clear.

Volker swallowed nervously. Shakily, he put his hands up to his ears, and felt them carefully. They didn't seem to be growing larger or more pointed than they already were, which was quite big enough, thank you very much. His eyes felt the same, too. He let out a weak moan of relief. At least he wasn't turning into an Elf or anything. After some of the things he'd seen on this trip he wouldn't have ruled it out. So if he wasn't changing physically, where were these keener senses coming from?

Had he always had them . . . and refused to believe them? Was that how he'd somehow escaped from so much? By warning himself in time? He glanced suspiciously around at the owl, perched in its favourite spot. It looked back at him, and let out a soft hoot of amusement. Amusement? How did he know that? A rapport with animals, wasn't that supposed to be *huldra*, as well? He sighed, and gave up. There was nobody here to ask but the owl. And he wasn't about to do that. He might get an answer, and then where would he be?

Volker sighed. If he was going to be a half-*huldra*, he'd better take the famous advice and lie back and enjoy it. And keep as sharp an eye as ever on the sea. So far they'd seen no sign of any *dhow* that could be Diderik's. He strained his new vision to its limits, but saw nothing more along the wide horizon. Not even elvish sight could reach beyond the curve of the world. But every night he kept on looking, and he was seldom in any hurry to wake Guy, even when the sky lightened with coming day; and that suited de Guillac very well indeed. That was how Volker came to see both the first sign that their long journey had succeeded, and the first distant sight of Sicilia, their destination.

It began fourteen days after their departure from the Poia river estuary and its grisly relics, when they had only the broadest idea where they were. Neither was a good enough navigator to work it out exactly from the stars, and they hadn't dared to ask any passing vessels. At last Guy reluctantly decided to tack across the open sea towards the western shore. If they left it too long they risked missing their turn southwards through the Straits of Otranto; but if they did it too early they would land in waters the Southern Empire didn't control. If rumour had the right of it there were more pirates than Imperial ships off the north Italian coast these days, and it was sometimes difficult to decide which was which.

Guy sat up with Volker for most of the crossing, but there was no sign of trouble, and after the first distant smudge of land appeared on the horizon in the early hours of the morning he went back to his bunk, yawning and stretching. Volker was sprawled out by the tiller, reading one of the surviving books; he could read by moonlight now, or the dim pre-dawn glow. But after a while he gave it up and went back, as he so often did these days, to tinkering with the horn.

The more he tried it, the less he liked the strange overtones it gave to even the faintest breath of sound, and the shivering harmonics when he blew any harder. He tried varying its bore and resonance by pouring in warm wax, with some success, but it would not coat thickly enough, and it deadened the resonance too much. Now he had melted pitch from the ship's stores over the bricklined galley fire, and was swilling it gently round the rough black mouthpiece as he poured. The ridged matt surface of the horn felt even odder under his fingers as it grew warmer; he kept wanting to drop it, afraid it would suddenly shiver and squirm in his grasp, like a snake or a slug. The other horn simply gave an impression of great power, neutral and undirected; what it did depended on the music you played on it, rather than anything in itself. But this one definitely had something *wrong* with it, something as vile as that filthy drip from old Strauben's ceiling, or the mouth of the oracle-thing – an essence, an epitome, an ultimate in wrongness, something he was learning to associate with the Old World at its worst. A plain C major on this would sound sinister, a little children's tune destructive and perverted, and powerfully so. Did Diderik want his horn for that corrupting strength? And the other one, perhaps, because it could counter it? In that case, each had the weapon the other wanted, but Diderik could still use the other horn. If Volker could change the tuning of this one, though – bring it nearer the other – he might be able to teach the old devil a new dance or two. Music was what would make it powerful; Ulrich had known that. With the horns equal, music would hold the balance of power between Diderik and himself. 'And if that wizened old creep has one real tune in his body,' said Volker to the owl with some relish, 'I personally am a satyr's uncle!'

He blew into the mouthpiece to harden the pitch; but the reek of it made him sneeze violently. There was no describing the sound that emerged; but it rattled the planking, sent the owl screeching for the masthead, and brought Guy bolting bleary-eyed up the companionway. '*Cul d'un centaure*!' he erupted when Volker explained. 'Well, we will not lack for a foghorn, should we . . .' He paused, glanced over Volker's shoulder, beyond the stern. '*Mais regardez-mois ça*!' was all he added.

Volker obeyed him and looked. There in their wake, where the ship had passed only moments before, several large fish were surfacing, belly-up and still. They both looked at each other, then down at the horn. 'May the gods be thanked you did not instead break wind!' remarked Guy. 'For my part – I am going back to bed.'

Volker put the horn down carefully, and gazed out at the land, now swelling into solidity in the first light. Whatever lay ahead, he had a weapon to face it with; but he hated the idea of using it. How could he test it? Point it into the empty air and blow a couple of notes? He shivered. The result could be anything from a lightning bolt to . . . his mind boggled. He stirred up the pitch, and was about to pour again when he registered something he'd hardly noticed, a dark smear against the grey-lit waters. He stared, hard, and suddenly it swam into focus, a long low shape churning through the waves towards them like some maritime centipede. Guy would just be dropping off again; well, too bad.

The Armorican emerged on all fours, groaning, but he snapped awake at the sight. '*Merde de mégère*! We cannot outrun that! Not while it can go against the wind with those banks of oars. But I do not think it will be a pirate. If they had such galleys there would be no Empire any longer.'

They waited, breath baited, while the great shape loomed higher and higher, its course set between them and the shore. Suddenly Volker caught Guy's arm, and pointed. High on the curving stern rose a tall pole, capped with a golden arc that held a wide shape with outflung wings. 'The standard!' breathed Guy. 'The standard of the old Empire – laurels and eagle! Only the Southern Empire uses those now. *Mon gars* – we have arrived!'

They were close enough to hear the roll of the time-drums as the trireme surged by them, three tiers of oars rippling high like beating wings, dripping a trail of foam behind them. The beaked ram crested a wave for a moment, showing the great baulk of steel-sheathed timber with eyes at its base. 'Just like Diderik's!' muttered Volker. 'So this one's from Syracusa too!'

On the top deck of the warship a lookout saw them staring and waved lazily, never dreaming that the beamy, battered little boat wallowing in the wash below could possibly be an interloper all the way from the distant North. Volker looked back at the long, foamy trail still visible across the sea. It curved away in a very wide curve southward. 'Well,' said Guy quietly, 'we timed our crossing passably well. For that is southward by the sun, and we must be at the eastward end of the Italian coast, near the Cape Hydrunto by Ulrich's charts. We have only to steer after that wake as it curves around to the west again, and we will be on course for Sicilia.'

It was not quite that simple. The winds that had driven them with easy speed now made them tack wildly across the Gulf of Tarentum as they struggled to avoid being blown out into the open Ionian Sea. To Volker's northern eyes the sun-parched coastline seemed like a desert, a mass of scrub and stunted olive groves and barren, sandy soils that reflected the sun with a blinding glare. He wondered how anyone could live here in this heat; yet there were villages dotted at every convenient harbour, and sometimes the rooftops of a more substantial town. These were often gathered around the ramparts of coastal towers, ancient relics of the Old Empire of Rome, crumbling yet immensely strong. They began to encounter more heavy shipping, trading vessels of all kinds passing peacefully to and fro. Evidently Ulrich's notes were right, and this area was free of pirates. The reason became apparent when they met more and more patrol galleys; the Ionian, at least, was still Imperial property, and strongly defended. But nobody bothered the *Walross*, even when they had to put into a little village for fresh water; its mayor, easily bribed with a length of rich woollen cloth from the cargo, gave them a mighty dinner full of garlic, oil, peppers and rough red wine which left Guy beaming and Volker stretched out groaning on the deck. But he soon sat up when, sailing out of harbour, they saw the setting sun blaze red across the open sea ahead, and saw that once again the coastline was turning away westward.

'So what is before us must be the Stretto di Messina!' whooped Guy. 'And beyond that, *mon gars*, is Sicilia!'

'And what else?' demanded Volker soberly, and belched. G flat; if they all ate like this down here he wasn't going to need a horn.

'What else indeed? But we will not know until we try.'

'We'd better be right about Diderik. He could be in Egypt or Libya by now, or headed for Mauretania or Hispania . . .'

'Not in that ship. And his crew, they were not Africans, for the most part. No, he called them up from Sicilia; he must have fellow Tartarists there as he did in Nürnberg. So he is likely to make landfall there, most likely at Syracusa. My guess is that he is as anxious to

372

find this temple as you are . . . though doubtless for very different purposes. For now, we will set our course that way, and hope.'

Even at dusk the straits were busy with the traffic of the southern empire, and Volker had to keep a careful watch for the great grain ships and coastal barges that plied back and forth from the mainland; but most sought anchorage for the night, and out in the main channel the way cleared. Volker returned to his work on the horn. Repeated coats of pitch seemed to be achieving something; at any rate when he blew down it the harmonics didn't always set his teeth on edge. Stopping up more of the innumerable holes was helping, too; every time he lit on some especially horrible sounding fingering he converted it into a more melodious one. The trouble was, parts of it seemed to be tuned in ordinary tones, others interspersed with quarter-tones and worse, and still more in weird intervals he couldn't put a name to, yet clearly had some kind of underlying relationship. It seemed to be designed for a committee to play; no one musician could possibly exploit all the fingering patterns at once, no one human anyhow. He was trying to correct that, but in doing so he sensed he was somehow cramping the horn's qualities. It had been crafted to be what it was, and he could only reduce and limit it. He blew a soft note, and it came out clean and clear; nothing happened, except that the taut sail sagged for a moment, threshing. Hastily he grabbed the tiller and turned it away from the wind a point; the sail boomed taut, and he eased it gradually back on course. If he kept this up he might have quite a serviceable musical instrument; the question was, would it still have any power?

As the bow swung sluggishly back on its heading, he saw, more or less ahead, a needlepoint of ruby light just where sea and sky met, like the first harbinger of the sunrise. But it was far too early for that, and this light was too small, too bright, too red. And he soon saw that it waxed and waned, with a suggestion of disturbing activity in the sky beneath. It sparkled like an angry star, like the eye of a demon glaring over the world's edge. It was like nothing he had seen before, a sharp spark gleaming against the ragged shreds of cloud. It lasted for hours while he watched, a tiny distant spark pulsing away steadily until the true dawn gradually began to overtake and drown it in a broader glow. But as it did so he saw something else; he saw the cloud that had reflected it, oddly dark and solid against the rest, and beneath it . . .

He turned to the companionway, opened his mouth to shout, then grinned, scooped up the horn and, sticking to a safer fingering, blew a rousing military *appel*. The result was quite impressive, harsh but not destructive. Guy was on deck almost before he'd finished, struggling to do up the laces on his battered doublet and getting them all in the wrong holes. 'That is a louse-ridden trick to play on an old soldier, *fiston du diable*!' he protested, blinking himself awake. 'It makes my legs to work before my mind is awake! It sends alarms running through my very blood! See, I shake with the pestilential chill of them! Now, where did I put that bottle. . . .'

'Time enough,' interrupted Volker. 'There's something you should see.'

'If I can!' he grumbled. 'This eyesight of yours is costing me sleep!'

'Well, it's nothing for *you* to fret—' began Volker, confused.

'*Fret*?' howled De Guillac. 'Not even over serious matters do I do that! Not even though I have hardly moistened my mouth with wine in a month or more! I mean, *espèce d'oreille pointu*, you are forever tearing me from my bed minutes too soon! To see what no normal human being can see, only you and this insanitary and ill-bred thing of feathers!'

'I'm sorry,' said Volker, very straight-faced. 'But I can't help it! All my life I've seen no further than any normal man, and then suddenly . . . It may be in my blood, but I don't know why it got out so suddenly!'

'*Tiens*! Well, it may be a skill you must learn, like riding. It seems you will never learn to gallop; yet once you learn it can be hard to keep to a simple canter once again. No matter! What now?'

Guy heard Volker out, whistled softly, then took the spyglass and scanned the horizon. After a moment he turned away, rubbing his eyes. '*Sacré Dieux*! I am seeing everywhere red dots, now . . . I have read a holy book of the Hebrews in which there is something like this – a pillar of smoke by day, a pillar of fire by night. Their god would be uncomfortable company.'

'I think I've read about something, too. This is right on our course for Syracusa. Couldn't they have built something like the *Pharos* at Alexandria – a beacon for travellers?'

Guy shook his head. 'To grow such a monstrous mass of smoke you must needs burn the *Pharos* itself and all the city with it. See how it spreads out against the sky. No . . . We should have another look at your master's maps.'

He nodded as Volker spread the tattered paper out before him. 'This spot of light, I should have known what it was without seeing it! For better or for worse, our long journey nears its end.'

'It's a landmark, then? Must be a big one – a volcano?'

'The very greatest, in a region where they are so common that legend makes it where Zeus imprisoned the Titans, or the workshop of Vulcan's Kyklops. That is Aetna Mons, Mount Etna! Just along the coast from Syracusa! And in fractious mood, it appears. Fire by night, smoke by day, a beacon for all seafarers turning

375

eastward through these narrow straits. And a signal for us . . . though not of safety, I fear! Well, the smoke shows us the dawn breeze is turning our way. So let us ride in on its wings!'

Guy unlashed the tiller, while Volker, lighter and more agile, bounded around the decks letting out the sheets and hauling the great boom about. Guy leant his weight on the rebellious tiller, and slowly and clumsily the patched bows of the *Walross* swung around. The shallow hull wallowed alarmingly a moment in the swell, with strange slapping and sucking sounds echoing up from below. Then the sail boomed taut again and they were gathering speed, riding the wavecrests, running before the wind towards the tower of smoke.

Aetna loomed higher and higher off their starboard bow as they approached, a great grey ruin of a mountain fully two miles high that seemed to thrust up through the yellowish landscape of lesser peaks around it. Its jagged crown was seamed with black and dull red scorchings like some horrible ulcerated brand. Now and then a brighter red glowed in its crevices, and thin threads of fire oozed slowly out, extruded like infected pus. Here and there it coughed out swift puffs of dusty smoke, sometimes sending a spatter of hot pellets splashing and sizzling down into the shallows of the bay like bombard shot. To Volker's eyes the whole summit was quivering like the flank of a panting beast, and even with a following wind the air stank of sulphur smoke and hot pumice. A soft grumbling roar shivered through the sea, making the hull reverberate, and he had the uncomfortable suspicion the horn was picking it up somehow and responding.

'I don't like the look of that one bit,' he said.

'Nor I!' said Guy emphatically. 'Nor I! *Ma foi*, it smoulders like a bully spoiling for a fight! Why build a capital so close?'

'They live a lot closer than that!' Volker exclaimed. 'Ye gods, there are villages all over its slopes. Vineyards, olive groves—'

'A volcano makes good soil. For me, they are welcome; I would warm my feet at less ambitious hearths —'

'And there's a city – a big harbour! Right at the foot!' He scrabbled with the map. 'No; that's Catana – Catania they call it these days. So we ought to be looking just . . . ahead . . . there . . .'

'Speak for yourself!' complained Guy.

But before long the Armorican could see it, too, sparkling in the harsh noon glare, a long shimmering line of white. To Volker's eyes it had already resolved itself into what looked like a model in white marble, a jumble of walls and towers and columns picked out in minute detail, miniature ships behind the walls of vast harbours, almost impossible to realise at their true scale. Only as they drew slowly closer did it really strike home to them.

It was like nowhere Volker had ever seen before. His own city of Bremen presented a wide front to the sea, but nothing like as splendid. A chain of huge breakwaters in smoothly iridescent volcanic stone had long ɛ go stretched out and embraced the original Little and Great Harbours in one huge sheltered pool, divided only by the peninsula of Ortygia, where the city had been founded. But even before the Old Empire it had spread out far along the coast, taking in the region of Achradina and Epipolai; Tychia, with a host of temples, and the Neapolis or New City had been built inland, and walls had been built around all this by the *tyrannos* Dionysios, Sicily's most powerful ruler till the coming of the Emperors. They had built on his work, redoubling its area and building new walls from beyond the fortress of Euryalos to the north and southward along the drained Lysimeleian Marshes towards Heliopolis, rebuilding the rich temples, halls and theatres he had raised and making them richer still, quarrying the white limestone of the region and importing the finest white marble in vast quantities from the mainland, and even from barbarian Caria.

Now a phalanx of immense and beautiful buildings lined the seafront, palaces and fortresses and temples fronted with obelisks, statues, rows of columns, or clumps of waving palms, domed in dusty green copper or sullen glaring gold; and every building blazed white against the deep blue sky behind, while the palms and the masts of the moored shipping stood out stark against them. Beyond the seafront the city walls stretched out over the land on either side, their limestone only slightly less white than the marble buildings, and crested here and there with tall turreted gates. From behind them rose a jumble of rooftops, mostly white and flat but occasionally splashed with red or yellow tiles, and here and there a slender reaching tower, scaled like a dark snake with glazed tiles.

Volker and Guy exchanged occasional glances as they laboriously turned their craft into the channel named on their skimpy chart as the Arethusan, after the freshwater spring at Ortygia. The shadow of the walls fell suddenly chill and dark across them, and the vast warships moored in grim rows across in the Little Harbour, impossible numbers of them. The Southern Empire might be narrower and more decayed than the young and thrusting Burgundian realm in the north; but here at its heart it was still immensely strong and daunting.

'A formidable place to approach, even for one who knows it,' observed the Armorican soberly.

'It's amazing!' breathed Volker. 'Makes Worms look like nothing, for all the temples and palaces. And the Nibelungenhalle – Hel-fire, you could drop it wholesale into any one of these palaces, gilt roof tiles and all.

There must be twice as many people here . . . no, more. Easily.'

'And if repute is anything to go by, half of them bandits and the rest merely light of finger. What are we going to do about our boat, *mon gars*? And our cargo? We are here to fulfil your pledge, and to rescue our friends; but we should keep something to get home in, and perhaps also with. Here we have neither guide nor friend; here we can rely on nothing.'

'Except our enemies, maybe,' was Volker's only reply.

At the harbour-mouth a guardboat stopped them. Its grubby white sail was marked with the imperial standard, but it was unmistakably a *dhow*, and many of the guardsmen who came clattering aboard in light armour were brown-faced North Africans, amiable and chattering. Only the officer was recognisably Sicilian, hard-faced, hawk-nosed and unsmiling, speaking a peculiarly old-fashioned but comprehensible Latin dialect. He demanded where the ship had come from, clearly didn't believe the answer, and equally clearly didn't much care. What he was really concerned with was piracy and smuggling; whatever else had slipped, the southern Empire still kept a tight rein on its trade. He called for a detailed account of their cargo, and raised his eyebrows at the exotic goods that trailed down the manifest, furs and spices, tough walrus-hide cordage that seamen prized above gold, and all the richest produce of the North.

'Impressive. I have not seen such quantities of these goods these last twenty years. There will be duty to pay on all of this, of course.' Guy and Volker looked at each other in alarm; this was something they hadn't thought of. What was left of Ulrich's gold wouldn't cover a hundredth of what this cargo was worth, and they would need money here in the city. The officer unbent slightly. 'By the concession of our deified Emperor

379

foreign merchants need not pay it all at once, provided the goods are deposited in an Imperial warehouse, or the ship sealed and guarded at an Imperial quay, at a nominal extra charge.'

'Guarded, eh?' mused Volker.

'Night and day. Customers may be granted access under escort, but . . .' He smiled thinly. 'I would advise nobody to remove one ear of corn upon which duty has not been paid. The penalties may also involve the removal of ears.' It was obviously one of his standard little jokes, but Volker and Guy had no trouble summoning up a smile.

'Ah, but of course the noble and high-born officer understands we would never *dream* of attempting such a thing!' oiled Guy, with a leer of such appalling craftiness that his eyes almost crossed. Volker went for the subtler approach and took on a look of such schoolboy innocence that the officer looked ready to arrest him there and then. Pretty obviously the *Walross* was going to get guarded like the Imperial regalia – which couldn't have suited them better.

The sheer size of the waterfront crowds was daunting, not to say deafening, a swirling, jostling mass of jabbering humanity and jumbled races. Italians, hard-faced Sicilians, light-skinned Berbers and Egyptians, coffee-coloured Moors and Libyans, darker Arab nomads, black-faced Fulanis from Africa Inferior, and brown peoples Volker guessed must be from the fabled land of Hind – all paraded past him, dressed in everything from stiff pipeclayed white *togas* to loincloths so ragged they hardly seemed worth the trouble. And the moment Volker and Guy took their first step past the tall sentries at the end of the commercial pier it seemed that every single one of them, from whiskered ancients to tiny children, turned and converged on the newcomers, offering to sell, rent or barter almost every thing or service Volker could imagine, and one or two he wouldn't have dared.

'How fresh-plucked are my grapes, excellenzia! How juicy my pineapples!'

'Bwana! How luxurious is our caravanserai, how bugless its divans!'

'Pashas! How sweet is my rahat-loukoum!'

'Miei signori! How lonely is my beautiful sister—'

'Al-shaykh! How mind-blowing is my kif—'

'Sahib! How succulent is my pa'an—'

'Baksheesh, effendi! How starving are my children, effendi! How mangy my aged relations!'

'How do we get out of this?' groaned Volker, beating aside offers of vintage wines, embroidered silk caftans, gaudy floral wreaths, fresh spring water that nobody had piddled in, sheep's eyes, manuscripts from Elephantis apparently illustrating the lovelife of double-jointed dwarvish perverts, portions of strange-looking skewered meats, and any number of sisters, cousins, mothers, brothers and goats.

'One must admire their enterprise!' panted Guy, who had lingered a moment to scroll through the latest from Elephantis, and was now hanging on to his sword, his purse and his hat, of which ghostly fingers had instantly begun relieving him. Together they plunged towards the gables of a tiny cafe, and as they reached it the proprietor drove off their tormentors with a blast of Sicilian invective, before offering a choice of food and drink or his sister. Guy took one good look at the man and ordered a meal.

It was excellent, after days of shipboard provisions, and washed down with flagons of Sicilian wine even Guy was quite polite about. Over coffee, served killingly strong and sweet in the Egyptian manner, Volker struck up a conversation with the proprietor. He thought of asking after Diderik's ship, but if it was Sicilian the proprietor would hardly have paid attention to it – and

381

might not say anything if he had. Temples? Too many to number, as they had expected; and a cautious mention of the name left him entirely blank. 'Just one more thing, *padrone*,' added Volker, as he cleared his palate with the boiled water. 'Could you possibly give us directions to the Imperial Library?'

'And the baths,' added Guy. 'Salted food within and days of salt-soaked clothes without – much longer, *mousaillon*, and you may serve me up as a herring!'

The proprietor swelled with pride and his blue chins wobbled. 'Ah, *signori*, in our beautiful city you will find the best of delights for the mind and the body, close together! There above the Agora, under the western aspect of the Imperial Palace, there you will find the Philippium, which houses on its three sides the Imperial Library, the Imperial Baths, and the Imperial Theatre, and all free to citizens . . . and at a nominal charge, of course, to distinguished foreigners such as yourselves.'

'It sounds very pleasant,' grinned Guy. 'All you need is a *maison de joie* on the fourth side.'

'Ah, *signor*, that is open to the city, and the city provides! Speaking of which . . .'

'We have, alas! no time. You paid, Volker? Very well, *m'sieu le patron*! And our compliments to your sister.'

There was no danger of losing their way. The streets were wide and straight and the Imperial Palace was a towering landmark for the whole city, a place of colonnades and galleries, its high white walls speckled with jewel-bright mosaics of the gods – including, Volker was surprised to note, Christ, Mithras, Osiris and what appeared to be a large Hebrew character. Evidently the Emperors didn't intend to miss a trick. But they soon encountered other less impressive aspects of the streets; straight and wide, yes, but cleanliness was another matter. Volker blessed his northern boots and wondered how these Sicilians could stand just sandals. And among the crowds many of the poorest dressed – perhaps even most – had ears notched or half removed, men, women and children all. He was about to remark on it to Guy when he saw a miserable-looking black youth being led by a metal chain and collar, his ear still streaming blood.

'Yes,' said Guy sombrely, seeing Volker's indignation, 'there must be a slave market nearby. See, there goes a whole string of the wretches! Black, white, anyone who has fallen foul of the authorities, or merely had the misfortune to be born to slave parents. It is the old Roman system still.'

Volker bridled. The Burgundian Empire despised slavery; prisoners of war, serious debtors and criminals could be indentured for a few years, but under strict legal limits. 'A wonder they put Christ on their palace, then. I've never had much time for Christians, but they forbid slavery, don't they?'

Guy smiled cynically. 'Most people do, unless their prosperity demands it. Our lands grew up without it, so much the better. But this is the way here, and though I feel as you do, I will keep my mouth shut on the subject. These are touchy folk, I think.'

'In that case, the sooner we get to this Imperial Library the better. You haven't had a decent fight since our run-in with Diderik.'

'I?' said Guy, with a brave attempt at mildness, 'I, who am without question the quietest and gentlest of my family—'

'—on the odd occasion when you happen to be sober? Yes. And since you happen to be more or less sober now . . .'

'I am offended, *monsire* Volker. I am deeply affronted. I am—'

'—going to soak your head in the Imperial Baths. I *know* you, Guy: I saw what happened with that chambermaid at the *Goldener Hirsch*.'

383

Guy shrugged expressively. 'A little harmless fun . . .'

'Yes, but did you have to pull her in *twice*? I could swear you're at least two parts merman.' He laughed. 'All right, go on. After all, what could happen to me in a library?'

An hour later – by the library water-clock, whose echoing drip was beginning to drive him mad – Volker had the answer. What could happen to him was confusion, doubly and trebly confounded. Strauben's library had consisted of twelve manuscripts and a small shelf of badly block-printed books. The Civic Library in Nürnberg had three large rooms. The Imperial Library in Worms had ten.

The Imperial Library of Syracusa was the size of a small palace. Its entrance hall alone had more books than any library Volker had ever seen, and beyond it was a four-sided *basilica* on two levels. The racks nearest the door were lined with scrolls, carefully stored in neat wooden compartments. He picked one at random, and found it covered in businesslike symbols that he recognized as Hebrew. Those in the next rack were covered in artistic-looking squiggles that he supposed to be some kind of African writing, but most of the rest were in Greek. They covered a bewildering range of subjects – it looked as though the whole rack had been knocked over, and the scrolls replaced in random sequence. To his surprise, few of them showed much sign of use.

The southern aisle, nearest the square, was entirely taken up with fanfolded documents: he looked at one, and found a seemingly endless list of names, numbers and symbols that meant nothing at all to him. This was one of the busiest parts of the building, full of suspicious looking characters rattling pocket abaci and scribbling furiously on bits of paper. Runners were coming and going constantly through a small side door.

He took a cautious look at one man's work, but all he saw was a jumble of letters and symbols that looked remarkably like Eisenbardt's *el gibber*. Confusingly, this seemed to be the Sports section; it looked more like a department of higher mathematics. Clearly chariot-racing had a lot more to do with the philosophy of numbers and probability than with the breeding, control and driving of horses.

The opposite aisle – the Religious section – was almost equally busy, and teeming with a strange and ill-matched assortment of characters. A clean-shaven man in a dirty toga was working his way through a Greek scroll letter by letter – every so often he would stop and write something down, tongue firmly between his teeth, in a childish schoolboy hand. Glancing over his shoulder. Volker saw at least seven mutually contradictory statements on the subject of adultery. Those suggesting exotic punishments for it were carefully underlined. At the next table two men were arguing, apparently about the date. One was banging heavily on a *Menologia* insisting that this was the feast day of Digenis Akritas and therefore suitable for a dragon-hunt. The other, unrolling a long scroll of African glyphs, was arguing that it was more proper to commemorate Simeon Stylites by fasting on the column at the bottom of his garden. Volker found books on Mithraism, Judaism, Baal-worship, fertility cults, the gods of Egypt, the gods of Rome, the gods of Greece, and the patron gods of the Empire, but nowhere could he find mention of a Templa Volcana.

He decided to look under *Geographia*.

Maps of Syracusa were unhelpful. Many showed the rash of temples and shrines scattered across the city, but the Templa Volcana was not among them, and none of the indices mentioned it. At the next table a tall man with an aquiline nose was making careful notes from the *Codex Geographia Probabile Tartaris*, including sketches of its seven likely levels and the various titans and demons who were said to inhabit them. He seemed to be checking out suitable punishments for an endless list of political opponents, and discouraged Volker's curiosity with a piercing stare that reminded him of the owl. He had left it in the square outside, perched, rather pretentiously, on a bust of Homer.

Reluctantly, he walked across to the desk at the end of the aisle to ask for help.

The librarian was a small, round, man with a round moon face, round eyes fixed in an expression of perpetual surprise, and a halo of fluffy white hair around the crown of his head. His face had once been small and round as well, but now it was crinkled like a well-stored apple.

'So you're looking for t-t-temples?' he asked, helpfully. 'L-lots of books about t-temples . . . architecture, s-statuary, p-painting, ob-obscene rites . . .'

'Actually, it's one *particular* temple . . .'

'S-say no more, young sir. T-temple of Artemis Ephesion. *Very* popular, es-es-p-pecially this time of year. L-lovely g-girls . . .'

Volker cursed silently. If the librarian was any more helpful, everyone in the gallery would soon know his business. 'My interest is purely academic—'

'Excellent – re-reduced r-rates for just *watching* . . .'

'—and I had a different temple in mind. *Outside* the city, perhaps.'

'Outside?' The librarian was baffled. He scratched his head with an extraordinary backward movement of his hand. 'N-nothing I can think of *there* . . .'

'The Templa Volcana,' said Volker, as quietly as he could. 'It will be very old, I think. Perhaps forgotten by now . . .'

'The Templa . . . ?' A strange sequence of expressions flickered across the wrinkled face and eventually settled on delighted amazement. 'My d-dear young sir, you

d-don't mean you're a schol-schol-*scholar*?' He drew
Volker gently aside as if he were an honoured foreign
dignitary; the hairy, long-fingered hand on Volker's
forearm was trembling. 'Do f-forgive me sir . . . so *few*
these days . . . all these t-tourists . . . this way . . .
have the very m-manuscript . . .'

He drew Volker towards a tall stack, tugging urgently
at his sleeve as though the book he wanted might get
up and walk away – which was entirely possible, given
the number of magicians, sorcerers, necromancers,
rhabdomancers and illusionists in the building. The
little librarian dived straight for a cobwebby shelf full
of massive, skin-bound books, and groaned.

'Oh dear, I'm afraid it's *out*. I'm really qu-qu-*quite*
mortified . . . *Ah*!' Wrinkles radiated from his huge
smile like a rosy sunrise. 'Of course! The next b-bay, I
think. On the t-table . . .'

He trotted happily round the corner of the stack,
dragging Volker's sleeve. 'There, young sir: a f-f-fellow
scholar with the s-same interest! Wha-wha-what could
be . . . ?'

Volker was no longer listening; the manuscript lying
open on the table demanded all his attention. It was
hardly what he had imagined. The greater part was
covered in southron hieroglyphics, and the crude map
scrawled across its left-hand side bore little relation to
the city outside. The title, *Templa Volcana*, was in a
scratchy uncial hand, and worryingly ambiguous. Was
there one temple or two? Even the map gave no real
clue. Puzzled, Volker looked up – straight into the
narrow, glinting eyes of Diderik.

Guy de Guillac had gone to heaven, without the tedious
necessity of dying.

He had begun with a luxuriant wallow in a bubbling
hot tub, happily ogling the thinly clad girls selling wine,
sweetmeats and exotic delicacies. Guy was feeling

spendthrift; more importantly, he was hungry; *most* importantly, he was thirsty. The wine was excellent, and the girl who brought it was slim, dark and smelled faintly of jasmine. The Armorican savoured a dozen vintages, admired the fine-blown crystal they arrived in, and looked forward with relish to a closer acquaintance with the girl.

But the Imperial Baths offered many other pleasures. Amid gilded mosaics of dubious encounters between gods, nymphs, satyrs and huldra (in every possible combination) he submitted to the rigours of high civilization – steam rooms, skilled barbers, and sensual oils. Through a warm haze of contentment he admired highborn Syracusan ladies, winked at their daughters, and leered happily at their maids. For the moment, at least, all his cares were forgotten. It was a mere whim of Fortune that brought him back to the steam-room just as two rather unusual characters were leaving it.

The first of them Guy disliked on sight – a tall, gangling man with a long, curling beard that failed to hide his receding chin. The other, a self-consciously graceful youth with sallow skin and outrageous eye makeup, burst into a giggling, high-pitched laugh just as the Armorican turned the corner. Instinct, and the ancestral pride of his entire family, sent Guy's right hand clawing for the hilt of his sabre – just as he remembered he'd left it at the door.

'But the fellow is so *crude*!' said giggling youth. 'And *Diddleick* . . . what kind of name is *that*'

'Diderik,' said the gangler, reprovingly. 'And he gave specific instructions not to . . .'

'Oh, in*struc*tions!' The youth waved a languid hand. 'Who cares about the in*struc*tions of a northern bar*bar*ian?'

Guy smiled for pure joy. He was about to savour a unique combination of pleasures. 'Good day, *gentlemen*.

388

You have not, perhaps, met many travellers from the north?'

Both men ignored him, but Guy had never regarded himself as part of anyone's furniture. With an economical gesture he grabbed both newly laundered togas and lifted their occupants a foot or so off the ground. 'Messieurs, it seems to this northern barbarian that the folk of your city lack courtesy.'

The gilded youth gave a falsetto squeal and drummed his feet against Guy's left kneecap. 'Let me *go*, you horrible man! *Now*, or I call my bodyguards!'

'Not so,' said Guy amiably. '*I* shall call them. *Ohé! Messieurs les andouilles*! You with the brains in your nether parts! Why do you not rush to the aid of this drooling little *limace* who may loosely be termed your master?'

'Erm – excuse me,' said a trembling, nasal voice at his right shoulder. 'I'd rather like it if you could – er – put me down. I mean, if it's not too much trouble.'

Guy smiled as three massive, muscle-bound hulks emerged from the steamroom. 'My great pleasure, *m'sieu.*'

Dropping the youth unceremoniously on the marble tiling, Guy lifted the gangler above his head, and passed him from hand to hand until the man was spinning like a windmill. The hulks hesitated, and were lost. The beard described an interesting geometrical curve before its screaming owner bowled all three of them arse over apex. Nonchalantly, Guy gathered up the gilded youth and kicked him into the tangle of arms, legs and bodies that blocked the entrance to the steam-room.

'That', said a silky voice at his back, 'was a mistake, my friend.'

Guy's only response was a raised eyebrow, which the owner of the voice failed to notice; he was already doubled up over the Armorican's fist. The two thugs behind him were hard to surprise: one had already drawn a knife the length of Guy's forearm. The Armorican feinted, dived to one side, and sprinted back towards the main pool with the thugs in hot pursuit. At the water's edge a young Apollo was self-consciously scraping oil from his skin with a curved strigil. He yelled as the razor-sharp blade was snatched from his grasp by a manicured hand attached to a huge and hairy arm.

Guy bared his teeth and turned to face his pursuers. 'Now, *messieurs – en garde!*'

The first thug chuckled, shielded his left arm with his toga, and hunkered down in the unmistakable stance of a professional knife-fighter. His grin froze when he realized that his knife, and several of the fingers that had held it, were now rolling gently across the marble-tiled floor. His crony yelped and turned to run, upsetting Apollo's oil-jar in the process. Guy, hard on his heels, found himself slithering helplessly down a high corridor lit by chandeliers towards a heavy velvet curtain, most of which wrapped itself round his head. Moments later the tiled floor disappeared, to be replaced by large amounts of water. As he thrashed and spluttered his way out of the entangling fabric, Guy found he had exchanged heaven for paradise.

He was treading water in a pool the size of his ancestral dining hall – and it was full of naked women.

Volker lurched back in horror, his eyes locked with Diderik's. He barely noticed the slave girl, the barbarian and the two overdressed acolytes who stood around the old Tartarist, and before he could do or say anything a fireball filled his vision.

A squeak of outrage from the librarian cut clear through Volker's yell of terror. The fireball fizzled and scattered in a shower of multicoloured sparks, and as Volker dived for cover behind the nearest stack he heard the little man's voice, trembling with rage and miraculously cured of its stutter. '*My . . . dear . . . sir*! Positively *no* tinder-boxes, spark inducers, links or fire-spells on library premises!' At the same moment Thorgrim's battle cry '*Odin og Frigg!*' echoed through the vaults overhead, and the stack next to Volker shuddered, listed, and keeled gently sideways like a felled pine. He barely escaped a spectacular chain reaction as the next stack, and the next, teetered and fell in their turn. No wonder the scrolls nearest the door had been so jumbled – obviously the scholars of Syracusa used other tools of argument besides rhetoric and writing ink. Generations of knowledge spilled from their crowded shelves in a choking cloud of dust as a panic-stricken bat skittered up into the rafters and a dozen anaemic-looking rats sailed past Volker's left ear. One seemed to be wearing spectacles.

The librarian had gone; Volker preferred not to imagine where. The little man had saved his life – and also, apparently, given Thorgrim the chance to escape. Diderik's two acolytes crawled out from a tumbled heap of leather, vellum, paper, papyrus and splintered wood, groaning theatrically. The slave girl was staggering under a rain of blows from Diderik's cane, without once making the slightest sound . . .

The girl was Dani. He simply hadn't recognized her. The ornate gilded harness that masked her eyes also secured a brutal gag that lengthened her face by an inch and a half, and her wrists were linked to each other, to her waist and to Diderik by fine steel chains.

Rage drove out reason. He stumbled to his feet, gathering all the power of his *huldra* ancestors into a single, devastating invocation as he stepped forward to confront Diderik for the last time—

—and collapsed with a whoosh as the roof fell on his head and knocked all the breath out of his lungs.

'I thank you,' said the roof, in a quiet voice remark-

391

ably like Thorgrim's. 'But perhaps more than my fall is broken?'

'I'm . . . all . . . right,' wheezed Volker, between desperate gasps for air. 'How . . . many?'

'What you see.' The Icelander waved his hands, still manacled in front of him. 'The two winesacks have magic, but none to match their master's. But there are servants and bullies all around.'

'Why?'

Thorgrim shrugged. 'He had, perhaps, warning of your coming.'

'Anyone else?' asked Volker dispiritedly.

'None here.' The big man was clearly disappointed. 'The other Tartarist *affald* and their bullies are gone to the baths.'

Diderik had recovered his composure, and Volker could almost feel the small, steely eyes cutting through the wreckage around him in search of the horn. Volker reached for the case, reassuring himself it was still securely strapped to his back, just as another fireball exploded above their heads. The tinder-dry shelving burst into flames, and a flock of burning folios fluttered skywards into the vault, but Thorgrim was already dragging him clear, grabbing a copy of Virgil's *Aeneid* to flatten an officious librarian who barred their way. 'Too heavy,' he growled, thrusting the massive tome on to an empty shelf, 'too many words! This way, Volker!'

'No! Got to . . . fight them!' gasped Volker. 'Get . . . manuscript!'

The big Norseman shook his head. 'We cannot stand against them all; best to win freedom while we can.'

Before Volker could answer, the stacks either side of him vanished in twin curtains of flame, and moments later a deafening alarm bell rang out from one of the galleries. Blinded, deafened, and smarting from a dozen superficial burns, Volker ran unthinkingly where Thorgrim led him, trusting the Icelander's talent to steer them clear of spellcasters, magic fire, and anything more potent that Diderik might have in store. By now the library was a scene of panic-stricken pandemonium. As terrified readers struggled to get out, and devoted staff struggled to get in, every doorway became a solid, milling mass of shouting and infuriated humanity. For the moment, at least, there was no escape from Diderik and his minions.

'Raining,' muttered Thorgrim.

'In *here*?' Volker glanced up towards the roof, and was immediately blinded by a small hail of water droplets. Behind them the flames were already dying down – clearly the library had magical protection of its own. But the incident had given him an idea.

He grabbed Thorgrim's sleeve. 'This way – up the stairs!'

'In a *fire*—?'

'Come *on*!'

The spiral staircase to the gallery had apparently been designed for kobolds; climbing it was a little like running up the inside of a fretwork drainpipe, and the horn case was for ever banging against the metalwork with a ringing C sharp. Luckily there was so much noise from the stacks that no one else could hear it. Glancing back, Volker could see a small army of librarians converging on the fire with sand, water, and spell-power. Little rivulets of water emerged at high pressure from mid-air, apparently diverted from an aqueduct. But the same, gentle shower was still falling from directly above the burning stacks . . .

The metalwork above him fizzled and glowed red, and a choking brown smoke drifted up from the soles of Volker's boots. Thorgrim, just below, bellowed in pain and snatched his hand away from the rail. The enemy were just below and very much in range. Before Volker dived for cover he even caught a glimpse of

Diderik, still holding Dani's chain in one hand and the horn in the other.

Why in Hel doesn't he use it? He knows what it can do . . .

He was about to make a break for the roof when Thorgrim pulled him back. 'We have company, my friend . . . a magician.'

Volker mouthed a silent curse. Diderik had obviously anticipated them, and posted lookouts in the gallery. Just then something splattered against the stack behind his back. He jerked away as the whole structure collapsed in a festering heap of mould, rot and fungus, but tripped and fell over something on the floor. As he staggered to his feet he heard a singing whine by his right ear, and felt a trickle of blood down the side of his face. Just above his head was a razor-edged metal wheel, buried to its hub in a copy of Caesar's *Gallic Wars*.

'Good,' muttered Thorgrim. 'There is a work that has always needed cutting.'

Volker, still pinned down by the crossfire, was examining the floor. He had tripped on a metal bar that ran at right angles to the stacks. For a moment he was baffled; then he grinned, and whispered to Thorgrim.

Seconds later the metal disk whined back towards its thrower, while something remarkably like a sizzling ball of flame soared towards the magician at the other end of the gallery. As both men dived for cover, there was a rattling concatenation of sound like a dozen metal-rimmed cartwheels rolling over a cobbled street. It was loud enough to drown two anguished screams – and the noise of running footsteps as Volker and Thorgrim raced up the next staircase and out on to the roof.

'Shelves on wheels,' said Thorgrim. 'Why?'

'Get . . . more . . . books in,' gasped Volker. 'or flatten . . . more Tartarists.'

The Icelander grinned savagely. 'Later they may bind

them in their own skins and catalogue them – under N for *nithing*.'

'Right now . . . settle for . . . way down.' Volker had expected the library roof to link up with other roofs around the square. It did not. There was a twenty-foot gap between the Library and the Baths, and the roof of the Baths was at least fifteen feet higher. Peering over the edge, between statues of distinguished citizens poised as if for suicide, he found himself looking forty feet straight down into the library gardens. There was nothing behind him but the roof, and a curious series of wooden structures mounted on trestlework frames.

Thorgrim scowled. 'They come now. You will use the horn?'

Volker shook his head. 'I can't. It still isn't properly tuned. I can't control it, and we can't risk Dani.'

The Icelander nodded philosophically. 'So. A glorious last stand?'

'I suppose so.'

'Good,' said the Icelander. 'It touches my honour always to run from these *svineskidt* Tartarists.' He selected a large red tile from the roof, weighed it in both hands, and dropped it casually down the ladder they had used to reach the roof. He was rewarded by a scream, a crash, and the sound of assorted bodies striking the floor in no particular order. Volker followed his example – this time a vituperative curse proved at least one of their pursuers was still in the line of fire. With a smug grin Thorgrim sent two more tiles after the first, ducking back as a fireball sailed up through the hatch, arced high over the roof, and vanished into one of the wooden structures.

There was an echoing hiss followed by a billowing cloud of steam.

Volker chuckled. 'Of course! Water tanks! *That's* what made it rain down there!'

'*Naa*?' Now Thorgrim, too, noticed the pipes running

out of each tank into the roof space; the nearest was gurgling like a toper swallowing a yard of ale as it fed the sprinklers below. Casually, the Icelander wrenched up a length of lead piping, snapping it off at the joints, and whacked it happily against his hand. 'Clear of the hatch,' he said quietly. 'Let them think we fear them.'

Long moments passed before a curly-haired head appeared above the edge of the hatch – and yelped as strong hands grabbed the shoulders that supported it and a resounding blow struck it from behind. Thorgrim helped himself to the thug's sword, and hammered at his chain with the hilts until one link gave up the struggle. He grunted in satisfaction, then swore savagely as a sound from the far side of the building betrayed a second line of Tartarist attack. Bounding up the roof, sword in hand, he leapt down among the enemy with a berserk howl – just as a second head emerged from the hatch. Volker hit it hard with the discarded lead pipe and followed the Icelander, ignoring the muffled curses as yet another pile of bodies gathered at the base of the ladder.

Thorgrim was beset by two well-armed thugs, but his desperate attack had frustrated the surviving acolyte. Fireballs were indiscriminate, and the Tartarist could not afford to blast his own men off the roof. Instead he danced from side to side just behind them, waiting for a clear shot, and making himself an excellent target. Volker yearned to use the horn, but with a large, resonant water-tank by his left shoulder the effects were incalculable. Instead he scraped a little corroded lead from the water-pipe into his crucible, called up a simple fire spell, and hurled the result at the Tartarist.

The burning flakes made a passable-looking fireball that scattered Thorgrim's opponents and sent the sorcerer tumbling backwards in an undignified tangle of arms, legs and billowing robes. Thorgrim roared with laughter, and kicked both panic-stricken thugs down the roof after their master. Volker saw the cold anger in the Tartarist's face as he struggled to his feet in the gutter, and opened his mouth to shout a warning, but a massive fireball was already roaring up the roof towards the Icelander.

After that, things became rather confused.

Thorgrim leapt improbably high – a skill he frequently boasted about – and the fireball passed under his feet, exploding noisily at the base of the water-tank and shattering several supporting struts. The tank creaked, groaned despairingly, and finally gave up the struggle, tipping several hundred gallons of water down the roof. The fireball-thrower and his henchmen were swept off the edge of the building. Thorgrim, still laughing, regained his footing to one side of the wreckage – then stepped on a loose tile, slipped, and tumbled after the Tartarists with a despairing cry. Volker, horrified, made the mistake of stepping on to the wet roof, and found that he, too, was slithering towards the gutter. He bounced off it with a bruising thud, and sailed out into space.

Guy de Guillac was surrounded by noise.

Several dozen naked women of various ages from pre-pubescent to semi-senile were screaming simultaneously in a large, vaulted and very echoey space. Some were swimming or wading away from him in panicky flight while others were swimming or wading towards him, apparently with murder in mind.

'*Mesdames, mesdemoiselles*, I mean you no harm! *Hélas*, I am an innocent victim of circumstance!'

His protests had little obvious effect, and in any case the screaming largely drowned them out. Two of the approaching women carried strigils, with the clear intention of removing some treasured body parts from the innocent victim of circumstance. Guy began a dignified but fairly rapid retreat – and found he had backed into something large, soft and suggestively yielding.

'So,' said a remarkably masculine voice. 'You would, eh? You barbarian beast!'

A heavy object slammed into the back of his skull, not once but several times. He staggered forward, almost measuring his length in the water, and threw himself sideways just in time to dodge another head-splitting blow. The club was an iron ladle from the steam-room; and the club-wielder was indisputably the largest woman he had ever seen in his life. To his chagrin she was standing between him and the door, waist-deep in the pool, wearing nothing but a voluminous, and by now rather diaphanous, pair of shorts.

'*Madame*, I protest . . .'

His protest fell on deaf ears. The ladle lashed out again, and again he was forced to dive to one side, narrowly avoiding a close encounter with a strigil.

'Beast!' roared the Amazon happily. 'Rapist! *Heretic!*'

At this critical moment the chinless gangler sprinted in through the door – straight on to the oily track that Guy had left at the edge of the pool. His legs shot out from under him, but his velocity carried him forward, and he sailed feet first through the air to strike the Amazon squarely in the back. He was still floundering in the water when the ladle caught him a sickening blow on the skull, and he sank beneath the surface in a trail of bubbles as two of his henchmen splashed into the water on either side.

By now half the women in the pool had grabbed impromptu weapons, and the two big thugs were set upon from all sides. The Amazon belaboured them mercilessly, but the punches and kicks they delivered in return had no useful effect. They simply made large areas of female flesh wobble in a strangely suggestive way.

Guy made an undramatic exit from the side of the

pool, trying to look like an innocent bystander. His performance lacked conviction, but most of the women were too involved with the thugs to notice. He got to the doorway with nothing worse than a swelling bump on the head, sighed and sidled quietly out.

'*Ooh*! That's *him*! *That's* the bar*barian*!'

With a muttered invocation to the gods of his family, Guy turned wearily to face this new threat – and ducked as a knife whistled past his ear and embedded itself in the doorframe. He tugged it free and returned it to its owner slightly below waist height. The knife-man emitted a falsetto squeal as he clutched his groin, doubled up and staggered away, but Guy had other, more serious problems. The two men either side of the gilded youth carried no weapons, and needed none. Both had the indefinable confidence of practised magic users, but neither could see the preoccupied girl attendant bringing a heaped tray of exotic fruits up to the ladies' baths.

She curtsied confusedly to Guy as he selected a large and slightly over-ripe melon, weighed it in one hand for less than a heartbeat, and hurled it at the left-hand magician. It struck the man's face with a satisfying squelch. His companion's savage sending went slightly awry; it shattered the wall-mosaic above Guy's head, scattering jagged fragments of tile and stone across the spot where the Armorican had stood a moment before.

The girl screamed, just as the battle beyond the doorway spilled noisily into the corridor, carrying the hapless Guy forward on a living tide of battling womenfolk. The gilded youth squeaked with horror and floundered to one side, sending the magic-user's second spell rocketing into the roofspace. With a grinding roar the chandelier above their heads parted company with its anchorage and crashed to the ground. Beneath the bent and twisted metal assorted limbs twitched randomly.

'Out like a candle,' murmured the Armorican, side-stepping the carnage. '*Adieux, messieurs, et bonne chance en Tartare.*' Whistling happily to himself, he went to find his clothes, his sword, and Volker.

The market square of the Philippium, a strangely pungent sea of awnings, street-vendors, bargain-hunters, cutpurses and adventurers, came up to meet Volker at sickening speed.

Off to one side he saw the flailing figure of the Norseman hit and demolish the awning of a large fish-stall. He barely had time to yell before he himself was enveloped in a steaming sea of ripping canvas that decanted him into a pile of soft fruit. He staggered unbelievingly to his feet like a grape-treader who had sampled too much of the merchandise. Ignoring the stream of colourful invective from the stallholder, he tried to cope with the idea that somehow, thanks to some capricious and over-generous god, he was still alive.

Even more surprisingly, so was Thorgrim. The big Icelander seemed quite at home in a chaotic jumble of fish, lobsters, crabs and molluscs, and quite oblivious to the dozen or so cats converging on him hungrily from every corner of the square.

Most surprisingly of all, no one, apart from the stallholders, was paying them much attention; in fact there was quite a movement towards the back of the square, where a small fire had started . . .

If we got out of this alive, so could Diderik's people. And I haven't seen Diderik lately, either.

'Thorgrim!'

'*Hvad?*'

'Time we were leaving.'

He scattered a few compensatory coins in the general direction of the stallholders, and was very nearly killed in the rush as eager, clawing hands materialized from every side. He was still dusting himself down when he saw the unmistakable figure of Guy de Guillac sauntering down the steps of the Imperial Baths. The Armorican was resplendent: his clothes cleaned, darned and restored to their former glory, his hat reshaped and glittering with a new feather, his boots and belts polished to a mirror sheen, and his sabre gleaming in the bright sunlight. His beard was trimmed and oiled, his moustaches had been waxed and curled within an inch of their lives, and the lace at his cuffs was crisp, white and freshly starched.

Just then a gangling, bearded man tore out of the main doors. He was in a deplorable state – his robes were in tatters, he had two swelling black eyes, and had apparently been arguing with a basketful of kittens. Close behind him came a wicked-looking crew of thugs and cutthroats waving an assortment of weapons, and a tall, thin-faced man who did not appear to need any.

The gangler stared around the square, panting and wide-eyed, saw Guy at the foot of the steps, and pointed a trembling finger. '*There! There he is!*'

The thin-faced man smiled unpleasantly and raised his hand.

With a bellowing roar Thorgrim threw himself at the Armorican and hurled him to the round as a bolt of fire hammered over their heads and converted the nearby spice stall to a pungent ball of flame. In the bout of coughing and sneezing that followed, Guy and the Icelander made good their escape. They had just joined Volker by the fountain at the centre of the square when another familiar figure appeared by the ruins of a basket stall.

'*There,*' shouted Diderik's fat acolyte, '*there they are!*'

A fireball arced towards them, and they scattered wildly as it whizzed over their heads and fell with a screaming sizzle into the waters of the fountain. There was a thudding explosion, and the gaping onlookers ran howling as boiling droplets came showering down. Steam swirled across the square.

'In here!' yelled Thorgrim, bounding through one of the pairs of wide doors on the third side of the square. 'While they cannot see us!' Guy and Volker clattered after him. A flunkey in gorgeous livery squealed and leaped violently aside as the Norseman waved his sword at him and plunged past, but Guy, purple in the face, caught hold of a huge standing board and hung gasping. Volker went to help him, then stared at the long placard posted on it. So did Guy.

The length of paper – much more crudely printed than anything northern – bore the Imperial Arms, and beneath it, after some minuscule lines of names, in huge capitals:

IL RAPPRESENTAZIONE;
LE TRIONFI DEL'OSIRIDE
osia
ISIDE ABBANDONATA
Melodramma per Musica
di
Giovanni Quasistasio
Musica e corí di
Claudio Monteazzuri

'My gods, no!' yelled Volker. 'Thorgrim, come back! It's a theatre! An opera!'

'Where better?' wheezed Guy. 'We'll slip in and out the back, unobtrusively, like mere phantoms!'

A flaring bolt of light struck the board and the placard burst into flames. Guy shied and ran, yanking Volker after him. '*En avant*, my little friend! They play the overture!'

Thorgrim, confronted by doors, kicked them open and plunged through, his borrowed sword levelled. He stopped dead, astonished; or tried to. But the floor wasn't level, and his onrush carried him, arms flailing, down a narrow stepped aisle into the middle of an

402

enormous crowd. They were sitting in rows of marble tiers that stretched out in a wide arc around three sides of a hall as big as the whole baths, staring with apparent intensity at something going on along the fourth wall, something that seemed to involve twangling music and high quavering voices. At least they were till Thorgrim's dramatic entrance, when everyone within reach turned on him, and with various friendly Sicilian gestures hissed, '*Sssssshhhhh*!'

'*Thorgrim*!' came Volker's yell from outside. 'Not that way! Along here!' It was punctuated by the sizzle and crash of another fireball.

'*Sssshhhht*!'

'*Taci*!'

'*Basta*!'

'*Silenzio*!'

'*Animale*!'

Thorgrim turned and ran under a barrage of cushions, sausage-ends, wine-jugs and sandals. A dignified old gentleman in a purple-edged senatorial robe whacked at him with his walking-stick, a little old lady belaboured him with a bag stuffed, apparently, with jagged rocks and mace-heads. Somebody bit him on the shin.

'*Odin og Frigg*!' protested the bewildered Norseman as he was hauled away down a corridor outside. 'What was that about? The arena, with the wild beasts in the audience?'

'Don't worry, Thorgrim,' panted Volker as they ran, 'that was culture. We'll explain it to you later!'

'Do! Or I shall revert to barbarism. It may be less bloodthirsty!'

A shout and a clatter of sandals warned them to look around. Some of the Tartarist thugs had spotted them and were heading down the corridor after them. Thorgrim glanced at the distance to the double door at the end, then swung around and raised his sword. 'A god place to discourage them,' he grunted.

'Where better?' agreed Guy. Thorgrim aimed a vicious slash at the leading Tartarist, and Volker saw what he meant; the swordfight filled the corridor, and the others couldn't get past. As Thorgrim held the leader off, Guy casually reached under the Norseman's arm and ran him through.

'You see, *mes amis*, we are not gentlemen,' said Guy with a flash of teeth under his moustache. The thug dropped with a bubbling groan. 'Not when you out-number us ten to one, with your filthy sorcerers tagging along behind. So who will be next to even up the odds?'

But the thugs had evidently learnt their tactics in back alleys narrower than this. With a sudden yell the three largest charged, shoulder to shoulder in a human wedge. Thorgrim's halberd might have skewered them, but no sword could withstand that weight. He was forced back against the wall. Guy was thrust staggering aside and the leader came face to face with Volker. With a smirk of triumph he brought his sword down hard. Volker met it with the horn-case. Ulrich's spells held firm; the blade snapped, and Volker kicked out with all the force of his long leg. With a high-pitched shriek remarkably like the stage noises filtering through, the thug folded; Volker brought the case down on the back of his head with a satisfying crunch, and the man sprawled out unconscious. Guy stepped back over him, hotly engaged with another ruffian even larger than himself, while Thorgrim was performing the near-impossible feat of holding off two by periodically kicking them in the shins or stamping on their open sandals. Gradually the little knot of fighters was being driven back down the corridor.

'I'll get the door!' yelled Volker. Neither man spared him a word; Guy's opponent was evidently no mean swordsman, and a lot fresher, while Thorgrim was fending off a third assailant whose shins he couldn't reach. But if they could bar or block that door, they'd cut off some of their opponents, at least. As they reached it Volker flung the doors wide, and brushed aside the heavy curtain behind to look for a bolt or bar. There wasn't one. He turned to find something to block it – and froze.

He wasn't in a corridor any more. A vast echoing space opened around him, shadowy and dim, scattered with heaps of indistinct clutter, hung with tangles like hellish creepers and vines, filled with the stink of hot dry dust. Through the gloom, silhouetted against brightness beyond, moved shapes, graceful half-naked human shapes, except that above their shoulders reared the monstrous heads of animals, long-snouted, with glassy, hostile eyes and towering jewelled crowns.

He gaped, but only for an instant. Then he turned back to the others. Guy and his opponent were whirling around one another in a furious glitter of blades, too dangerous to reach, but Thorgrim's opponents were leaping aside to outflank him. Volker put a stop to that by tripping one and braining another with the case; Thorgrim, liberated, lashed out and his last adversary's head leaped from its shoulders in a horrible fountain. The animal shapes squealed and scattered. But there were more thugs charging through, and the sorcerers would not be far behind them. Volker looked around frantically, and saw an iron ladder set into the wall. It led to some kind of gallery in the gloom above, with what looked like a door at its far end. He tugged at Thorgrim's sleeve and yelled, *'Guy! Over here! Come on!'*

But the Armorican and his opponent had vanished into the gloom, dodging this way and that around the clutter, lost in a frenzy of battle. 'Come!' growled Thorgrim. 'At least we can draw off the others!' He sprang for the ladder, and Volker after him. Somebody was climbing down it now, hissing what was evidently a furious question, but when he got a look at Thorgrim with his dripping sword he climbed back up a lot faster and disappeared yelping into the gallery. A sword whanged into the iron beside Volker's leg and he too climbed a lot more quickly, running into Thorgrim. A hand yanked at his ankle and he swung the horn-case down; the thug ducked the first swing and ran straight into the next. He reeled a minute, cross-eyed, then slid back on to the man behind. There was a crash from below and a great puff of dust. Volker saw the thugs scatter; not scared, surely? That didn't look good. Maybe they were going after Guy.

Thorgrim had reached the gallery and swung him up. They looked around, amazed. A couple of crudely painted replica mummy cases stood at the head of the stairs. On one side the high stone walls, no longer marble-sheathed, went up into darkness. On the other, beyond a thin iron railing, there was emptiness. It was like being in the upper branches of some vast forest, with all the tangles of cordage around them; mysterious arrangements of pulleys and cogs poked out here and there, and dirty sandbags dangled in clusters like unpleasant fruit. 'The rigging is good,' grinned Thorgrim, 'but the ships – where are they? This, too, this is culture?'

'It's how they move the scenery,' panted Volker. 'And lower the *deus ex machina* – the gods who come down from the machinery to sort out the plot. It's traditional . . . oh, top smirking and help me get this bloody door open!'

But the fleeing man must have locked it behind him. Two heavy kicks hadn't shifted it when they heard the door at the far end crash open, and there were the thugs, racing along the narrow gallery. 'Nothing for it!' roared the Norseman. '*Odin!*' He charged headlong to meet them, and Volker with him. But before they met, a sudden uproar from below caused both sides to halt and look down, open-mouthed.

They were above the stage, behind the arch called the *proscenium* and out of sight of the audience. But into sight, among a group of curious looking people dressed in overdone formal robes piled high with gaudy Pharaonic accessories, charged Guy and his opponent, still trading furious blows. A scatter of animal-headed types ran shrieking across the stage. A large rotund figure in a hawk mask tried to intervene, and was knocked staggering by somebody's fist.

'The Triumphs of Osiris!' exclaimed Volker.

'What?' demanded Thorgrim.

'That's what the title meant. *The Triumphs of Osiris, or Isis Abandoned*. I think we just rewrote Egyptian legend; that was Osiris who got flattened!'

Thorgrim clapped a hand on his shoulder. The thugs, confident they had cornered their quarry, were also leaning over, laughing and pointing. They only realized their mistake when Thorgrim reached the nearest and largest, seized his belt and heaved. The man went over the edge with a strangled shriek, and Volker winced; but he landed heavily in some cordage beneath and hung there, gibbering with fright. The others piled in on Thorgrim and Volker, and a frantic mêlée developed, everyone flailing at each other with fists and swords and knees, but afraid to swing too far or too hard in case an injudicious swipe took them over the rail. A punch in the stomach doubled Volker up, a kick took his legs from under him. He sat down hard, and his feet shot out into emptiness, a horrible queasy feeling; but as he landed he jerked the horn-case up hard, and his attacker went face down in the thick dust, writhing. He scrambled up, and found he was on the far side of the fight, while Thorgrim was still furiously engaged with the thugs. He moved to help him, but the Norseman yelled 'No! Get the horn away! Get that idiot Armorican!'

One of the thugs turned and leaped, and there was no time to argue. Volker lashed out, not with the case but with his own fist. It was powered with all his anger and frustration, and it caught the man full on an already broken nose. He spun around, dropping his sword, and toppled backward over the rail. This time there were no ropes. He fell into the scenery with a rending crash, and more screams rose from below. A cardboard and canvas pyramid slid slowly down out of the flies, landed with a booming thud, and toppled slowly on to Osiris, who was just staggering shakily to his feet. Thorgrim seized his moment, kicked his nearest opponent smartly in the stomach, and leapt for the ropes. The thugs jabbed their swords at him, but he was too far out; fingering his nose at them, he swung to another rope.

'*Avanti!*' bellowed one of the thugs and swung out after him; others followed, agile as monkeys. But so was Thorgrim – in fact he was acting as if he'd been born in a tree. He crossed blades with one, slashed at another's rope so he had to swing out of the way with a squeal, and then, glancing up at the sandbag counterweights, cut the end of his own rope free. He swung right past his pursuers, striking at them and their ropes, to the narrow anchorage point on the far wall. A sandbag fell on to the gallery and burst in a cloud of choking volcanic pumice, right in the face of the man Thorgrim had toppled, as he clambered back up. With a coughing scream he slid back, barely catching the rail with one hand.

Volker tensed, and yelled a warning. Thorgrim had swung back out again on another loop of rope, but with little momentum, and the nearest thug was twisting along towards him, sword levelled. They kicked out their legs to make the ropes swing, back and forth, twisting around and back, each time a little nearer, a little faster, until with a sudden lithe twist the thug wrapped the rope around his body and leant out. That increased his reach and his speed, and with sword outstretched he swung in towards the Norseman like a flung javelin, unstoppable. Thorgrim didn't try. Instead, at what seemed like the last instant, he swung himself upward, out of the way, and the thug passed by beneath. Thorgrim stabbed downwards, as if fishing, and the thug yelled; but he did not let go, and swung around again, streaming blood and screaming curses. The others were closing in now; Thorgrim, catching sight of Volker, made a furious gesture at the door, and then, bending down, he slashed hard at the nearest thug. The man ducked back with a yelp, and Thorgrim's blade slashed through his own rope. Another sandbag whistled down on to the gallery and burst like a bombard shot. A huge backdrop of what appeared to be the Rape of the Sabine Women, with acres of flesh tones, went whistling down out of the flies. Thorgrim, gathering speed, shot up past it and disappeared with a howl into the blackness of the flytower. Out of the cloud of pumice a horrible figure came lurching, staggering, grey and groaning horribly, as if one of the property mummy-cases had spewed out its occupant. It was Thorgrim's first victim, now doubly sandbagged, and he advanced on Volker with eyes narrowed and huge hands opening and closing like a strangler's. Volker knew being torn limb from limb when he saw it. He slammed the door right in the man's face and fled down the rickety termite-gnawed stair outside. For once he guessed right, and plunging through the lefthand door he came out into the counterpart of the dim area he'd first entered, on the far side of the stage.

Out in the light there swords still clanged, and weirdly costumed people were still running on and off, yelling. Terrified chorus members were trapped behind bits of scenery, all of which was covered with great ragged slashes. Nobody paid any attention to Osiris, back on his knees and struggling with muffled oaths to remove the mask. The falling pyramid had driven it tight over his shoulders, imprisoning his upper arms. Volker pushed past a man with a great fat belly and a hippopotamus head. He held the horn-case in both hands, wishing he'd had the chance to snatch up a sword or something, not that he'd be much use with it, but he could manage a stab in the back as well as anyone. As Guy himself had said, this was no time for playing the gentleman.

He thrust forward, ignoring the startled shouts of the audience, to find that he was almost too late. Guy and his opponent were streaming with blood from their cuts, gripping their weapons with both hands to keep them steady, but still hewing at each other with startling speed. Guy seemed to be staggering slightly, backing away upstage towards the newly arrived backdrop, barely parrying the hammering strokes his enemy drove home. Volker lifted the horn-case; but at the speed they were moving he might hit the wrong man. Just then, though, Guy's feet appeared to skid, his stroke went wide and the huge man was at him with a great lunge. But Guy spun on one sure foot, the stroke slid past him by a hair's-breadth and impaled one of the fleshier areas of Sabine Women. Guy parried it hard, the big thug staggered back and Guy unleashed a harrowing rain of cuts and lunges, so fast the big man could only block them and give ground downstage, back, back until suddenly he was trampling among the footlight lanterns and there was emptiness at his heels. He lost his balance, flailed desperately, and Guy lunged like a striking snake. His sabre smashed down the other's guard and drove up to its hilt under the big man's breastbone with an audible thud, leaving him flailing there suspended. With a certain deliberation the Armorican poised himself on one foot, planted his boot in his adversary's stomach and slid him off the blade. He crashed down into the abandoned orchestra and on to a large floor-standing lyre with a fearful, shattering twang.

Guy gazed down thoughtfully at the wreck, and bowed slightly. It was not aimed at the open-mouthed audience, but it had its effect. They rose in a storm of applause. It was all he needed; he blossomed like a rose, forgetting where he was, bowing and blowing kisses, picking up the flowers they were throwing. If anything could have made the cast forget their fright, it was the sight of somebody else getting their applause. What appeared to be Isis, by the horned-moon head-dress, stormed out of the wings in a swish of flowing silks, gesticulating furiously, and shoved Guy aside. He turned, his eyes widened and he clapped his hand to his heart and bowed.

'*Ma demoiselle*, believe me, I could not regret more the necessity of interrupting your most angelic endeavours! To see such fury in those lovely eyes of yours, I am crushed, I am heartbroken! May I kiss the fair hand that—'

The fair hand bunched and hit him an unscientific left to the jaw. 'But, creature of divine elegance!' he protested, reeling slightly, 'Can I but quench the wrath that makes your ivory bosom heave with such inspiring—'

'*Cane! Vil assassino! Gonzo! Bifalco! Figlio di*—' The gestures were anything but elegant; the voice was baritonal. Volker stormed forward, pushed the protesting singer rudely aside, and grabbed Guy by his blood-stained ruffles.

'That is a man!' protested the Armorican, wide-eyed.

'More or less, yes! Listen, you moron—'

'But she – he was singing soprano!'

'He's a *castrato*, idiot!'

Comprehension began to sink in. 'You mean . . . one

of those they do that to, just to preserve their singing voices?'

'That's right!'

'*Sacrés dieux*! What do they have to sing about?'

'You'd be surprised!' said Volker grimly. From all he'd heard *castrati* were very popular with the ladies, because there was no chance of unwelcome results. He bridled. 'And I may just give you the chance to find out! You bloody . . . idiot! Why didn't you come after Thorgrim and me? Now he's off the gods know where and they're all still after us!'

Guy almost jumped physically as his eyes unglazed. '*Merde, tu parles*! But if we are rid of the *sorciers*—'

A cold laugh echoed from the edge of the stage. '*Nol sperate, signori*! You will first let fall your weapons and then turn around – or we will give the public a truly flaming finale! I counsel you, do nothing to alarm me!'

'*It's not Diderik*!' mouthed Volker, as he and Guy stooped to lay down their weapons.

Guy nodded imperceptibly. With one of the others there might just be a chance, if they timed their move right. But as they turned they saw not one but two of the acolytes step out of the wings, the fat fireball-thrower wringing his palms and beaming, as if just daring them to try something.

'Come along, gentlemen! After all, if we linger I am sure the Imperial Guard will be roused from its afternoon slumbers to deal with all this . . . entertainment.' He patted Osiris, still struggling, on the beak. 'and while *we* are of unimpeachable respectability, they may well decide to have a word with you, a long and shall we say torturous one? Who knows, you might be better off with us!'

The slightly thinner one stepped forward and raised his short cane in a scabby hand. '*Basta*! Come at once, or it will be as if the heavens have fallen upon you—'

Volker's ears caught the faint whistle an instant

before it happened. A brown blur shot down on the thinner acolyte's head and drove it down between his shoulders. His legs flew up and his cane danced away into the orchestra as he fell flat in a cloud of pumice dust. The fat acolyte stared up and raised his hand, his mouth opened in what might have been a spell or a scream or an oath, or all three. The second sandbag appeared to land right in it, and his knees knocked with the impact. It didn't burst, but flew open at the top and settled inside out over his head as he sagged down like a deflating sail, trickling little rivulets of pumice.

With a mighty fanfare of creaking and groaning machinery, a gaudy gilt chariot driven by a team of tatty gilt horses came grinding down out of the darkness above, its descent slightly spoilt by the fact that one of its occupants was furiously cranking a wheel, while the other held a sword at his throat. Osiris, still tearing at his mask with fingers like hairy sausages, almost staggered underneath it, till Volker grabbed him and hurled him back. With a final toothgrating screech the chariot landed, and out of it, like a somewhat used Norse deity, stepped Thorgrim. The divine dignity wasn't helped by an ear-to-ear grin, but the audience knew a good entrance when they saw it, and roared to their feet.

Guy exhaled and bounded to meet him. '*Mille millions de mille sabords*! Seldom have I been so glad to be upstaged!'

Volker pounded him on the back. 'I was afraid you wouldn't get down!'

The Norseman shrugged. 'All that culture, it is much like ship's rigging – easy to see how it works, with that little monkey to help. And I found a pile of sandbags marked "For Fighting Fires Only". So . . .'

Volker yelped as a bunch of roses struck him in the back of the neck. 'So indeed! But we've got to get out of here before Diderik pops up out of somewh . . .' He

413

stopped. The applause already had. And his friends were suddenly rigid, staring back over his shoulder. Slowly he turned around. Guy's sword lay where he'd let it fall, alongside the horn-case. And between them, impossibly, stood Diderik, his cane ready in his horny hand. Close behind him, chained and docile, stood Dani.

There was no sparkle in the little man's eyes now, only a crazy glitter. And his voice held none of his usual cackle; it was cold and hard as black ice. 'A theatre is a useful place. There are so many means of staying out of the way and observing while the less competent clear the way.' Behind his heels Volker saw the outline of the trapdoor he had stepped through, a close fit in the planking. Diderik had taken care to step completely off it. He prodded a contemptuous toe at the prostrate body of one acolyte. 'You have cost me too much already, masters; no more talking.' He gestured to the few remaining thugs, hanging nervously back in the shadows. 'One of you get the black case . . . *gently*, mind! The others, cut some rope, tie up these creatures! They will not resist.'

Oh no?

The same thought must have leaped into the others' heads. But Diderik was infinitely more formidable than his acolytes, and if he couldn't read minds he read the sudden tension in their muscles. Volker saw his cane shift slightly, twirl, and the air was suddenly hotter, full of invisible wires that snagged and tightened around their limbs like jellyfish tendrils. Volker tore at nothing and saw his flesh dent, his fingers whiten as the circulation was cut off. He could barely breathe, let alone move. Diderik swayed with the effort, his waxy face set beneath its sagging skin; but he showed no sign of weakening. The thugs were approaching . . . nervously, but they were obviously more afraid of Diderik. Volker looked in agony at Dani, but she had sunk

414

to her knees, head bent, as if she didn't want to see. Her chained hands rested on the trapdoor . . .

With a sudden hollow rumble she vanished. Her chain rattled over the edge of the trap like an anchor falling. Diderik, still clutching it wrapped around his wrists, was yanked bodily off his feet with a screech. He landed at the trap's edge, clawing at the chain to untangle himself. It went slack for a moment as the trap bottomed; then there was an even more furious jerk, and Diderik was hauled right over the edge, his scrawny little legs flailing the air like a mantis'. He dropped with a crash. Volker jumped for the trap, but the door shot up again. He fumbled with the catch as Dani had, then caught Guy's warning yell. One of the thugs was sneaking off with the horn-case. With a howl of frustration Volker jumped up and struck a pose, fingers outthrust as if to cast some appalling spell. The thug froze, and Volker jumped him.

It took about a second for the thug to find out first, that he hadn't been ensorcelled into something nasty, and second, that Volker had not been brought up brawling in Sicilian gutters. He was twisting off Volker's left ear and making progress towards gouging out his right eye when he suddenly gave up, sprang up and leaped curiously over the edge of the stage with a crash. Thorgrim swung a negligent boot as Volker scrambled up, clutching the horn-case protectively; Guy was throttling the thug who had been trying to tie him up. The others were out of sight.

Thorgrim shouted, and tossed Guy his sabre. He let his adversary drop to the stage and caught it.

'As well we are going while we can!' said Thorgrim heavily.

'But Dani – we've got to go after her—'

'You know yourself we could do her no good!' said Guy, equally heavily. 'The horn, we must deal with that first – and before the *sbirri* come to arrest us for our little performance!'

He reached out as he spoke. Osiris, still encased, blundered past him. Guy dug his fingers under the rim of the mask and hauled upward, so hard he actually lifted the man off the ground. For an instant short fat legs flailed the air, then with a horrendous noise head and mask parted company. Osiris was revealed as a plump bear of a man, wide startled eyes and snub nose staring out of a bush of hair and beard. He staggered as he landed, lost his balance and before Guy could drop the mask and catch him he followed several others backwards into the orchestra. A terrifying boom arose, as if he'd exploded on impact, followed by high-pitched Sicilian obscenities. Peering nervously over the edge they saw the legs again, protruding from the skin of an enormous kettledrum.

Guy raised an eyebrow to the silent, gaping audience. '*Signore e signorina . . . la commedia é finita*! And now, my infants . . . run like Tartarus!'

Chapter 9

The earth beneath them was as grey as the air overhead, where the sun did not turn it to a ghastly glaring bronze. Every dragging step lifted little choking clouds of the dusty soil, and by now it was easier to suffer that than try and lift their feet too often. From time to time a quick shudder in the earth raised the dust on its own, or a soft pattering rain of ashes fell for a few seconds. There was a continual grumble, as much in the ground as the air, and a smoky furnace stink in their nostrils.

'About fifty miles, the man said,' groaned Guy, another continual grumble. 'If we could not have taken the boat, at least we should have ridden the horses a little further. You did not mention the last ten miles were uphill. *Je dirai même plus*, up volcano.'

'I didn't know myself,' answered Volker curtly. He had some sympathy; Guy's involuntary exhibition bout had lost him a fair amount of blood from various minor wounds, and the long ride had re-opened most of them. But he couldn't help adding, for perhaps the tenth time, 'Anyway, it's not up, it's across. And the Imperial Customs wouldn't have let us take the boat. They'd have figured we meant to unload it further along the shore somewhere.'

That had become clear when, despite their haste, Thorgrim had insisted on going back to the *Walross* for his beloved Hlavisbana. Volker hadn't had the heart to argue; they'd need every fighting advantage they could get, now Diderik knew where they were headed. But the customs men on the pier had looked very askance, insisted on searching them, and finally made out import documents for '*halibardo antico, uno, poco carbonato*' – one old halberd, slightly charred – and insisted on charging Thorgrim duty. At least that had been reasonable, encouraged perhaps by Thorgrim's waving the blade under their noses and offering to sharpen their pens with it. When he actually did it they became quite co-operative.

'The horses . . . well, yes. Only I wanted to be careful. We didn't know what to expect, after all; better to leave them at the town and foot it. Three horses make three riders twice as easy to spot.'

Thorgrim snorted. 'In this barren *Nastrand* of a country three fleas would stand out. At least by the dust they kicked up. But as you say, we did not know.'

'It need not be so barren,' said Guy reflectively, though fatigue caught at the edges of his words. 'This is good soil. A south slope, volcanic ash, steady sun – good for *vignerons*. I could make fine grapes spring up along this whole hillside . . .'

'*Naa*,' grunted Thorgrim. 'And the hill, I think, could spring them higher. What use are your vintages if they go up with a bang and come down in Libya Major?'

'We have a wine a little like that, in the *campagne* southeast of my land, near Gascony. It bubbles so hard the cork must be held in by wire bonds, and frequently explodes out when these are removed, now and again striking the server on the nose or eye.'

'It sounds merry,' allowed Thorgrim. 'But somewhat aggressive. At least a good ale does not fight back. Though there was one that drank King Domaldi of the Swedes.'

'You mean that he drank?' demanded Volker. The silliness of the conversation was making him light-headed.

'*Nej*, it drank him. One night at a Thing he rose in

418

the darkness to make water. They had buried a great vat of ale to keep it cool, and the cover was not secure. They did not find him till they had downed most of it next day, and agreed it was the best in those lands for many a year.'

'Expensive, though.'

Thorgrim shrugged. 'It was truly said that kings always brew the best ale.'

'A bit rough on him, doing it that way.'

'Oh, I am not so sure. When they found him he was grinning.'

Volker shuddered. 'I can imagine, but I don't think he'd seen the joke.' He hefted his water bottle, and reluctantly allowed himself one flat alkaline sip. 'Gah! What're we doing, talking about vats of ale, anyhow? And bottles of Campagne?'

'Skirting the flank of a very uneasy volcano,' answered Guy. 'And still more uneasy in ourselves. A dry land, dry air, dry mouth – *vision funeste*. We take refuge in fantasy.'

Volker glanced up at that immense summit, more than a mile above. 'It does look uneasy, doesn't it? But we're in no immediate danger here.'

Guy glared. 'Are we not? I am not so sure. We might not be caught in the first blast of an eruption. Lava can run faster than a speeding horse at times, I am told; and I could hardly run a step.' He groaned. 'What becomes of me? When I entered that accursed inn at Nürnberg I still counted myself a young man. Well, below middle age. See what these last few months have done to me!'

'Months?' Volker shook his head in wonder. 'Has it only been months? It feels like years . . . And I thought the end would just be getting to the temple. But even if we do, there's still the other horn – and Dani.'

'And Diderik. We have ridden fast, but he may have moved faster.' They were silent a moment, and then

Guy sighed. 'And once at the temple, what then? With all due respects to your late master, he might have left us more details about this vital aspect of your mission.'

Volker echoed the sigh. 'Ulrich must have thought he'd have more time to finish his account. And he couldn't allow for the rain washing away so much of his blood-spell. He expected to be safe till the journey started, at least.' *And he would have been – if he hadn't protected me.*

Guy grunted. 'Well, let us hope that there is somebody in authority still at this temple. If it is still there, and not covered in dust or lava, or swallowed up by the fires below! What a place to build one!'

Volker gazed up at the smoky activity around the blackened tip of the cone. 'I wonder!' he remarked. 'If the location hasn't got something to do with it. If the only way to destroy these horns could be by dropping them into the volcano where they were forged. Or something like that!'

Thorgrim shrugged. 'It sounds somewhat implausible to me, but then I am no sorcerer. And speaking of such . . .'

'Is there someone near?' demanded Volker. 'Do you smell them out?' he glanced about wildly, wondering what scrubby bush or lava crevice might conceal.

Thorgrim sniffed. 'I smell nothing but sulphur dust. And yet . . . away somewhere ahead, yes, there is some source of magic. Something odd. I . . . do not think it is that little trollkarl. This feels . . . old, old and weak. Or not so weak, perhaps; but asleep, using nothing but a faint trickle of its power. As if something dreamt of magic and stirred a little in its sleep.'

'Something?' Weariness had dropped from Guy's voice.

'It is hard to put into words. I have never met anything like it before.'

'Not at Nebelstein?' Volker prompted.

'No. This – it hangs in the air like a thin fog, without form or colour. Even the direction . . . Beyond the next ridge, perhaps.'

'Not far, then,' sniffed Guy. 'Best we approach the crest on our bellies, then. Could it be the temple, Volker?'

'Maybe. The map wasn't precise . . . Damn it, some of these pebbles have got razor edges! Like broken glass!'

'Volcanic glass,' said Thorgrim, squirming along beside him. 'I have seen some like it in Iceland, thrown up by a great convulsion . . . aagh! But we are almost at the crest now. If we peer around these boulders, so we do not stand out clearly against the sky . . . *I Lokis navn*! What would that be – down there?'

Volker was silent, swallowing, his mouth drier even than it had a right to be. 'I think . . .' he began. 'It looks . . . very much as if . . . that could be it.'

Beyond them the flank of Aetna fell away in a smooth curve, to rise again opposite, forming a wide shallow valley like a sunken scar on the mountain. The slopes were smooth sandy soil, but strewn with half-buried boulders and patches of sagging scree; and they were barren and bare. A fierce yellow tinge in the soil hinted at the reason: sulphur deposits. Volker's alchemical training also recognized the filthy rotten-egg smell in the air as sulphurated hydrogen; too much of that might make this an unhealthy place to linger. But that was far from his mind, because at the head of the little fold in the mountainside he saw something that was no boulder. But nor was it any temple he had ever expected.

It looked old, very old, from another time altogether. Its walls, whatever they were built of, were the colour of old parchment in this sickly light, and stained here and there with darker sooty scorches that might be relics of past eruptions. Against the hillside it lay, half-enveloped, as if the hill were a long slow wave in the process of breaking over it. But its great smooth dome, evidently the work of some master builder, still rose clear above the slope, curving down towards the frontage. This was the most unusual part, for it held not one arching door, but two, side by side beneath a huge rounded lintel. From above the lintel two vast curving buttresses of some darker material soared out, blossoming into high angled pillars rooted in the ashen soil, forming majestic ceremonial arches to either side of the doors.

'It . . . has the air almost Oriental,' breathed Guy in astonishment, rubbing absent-mindedly at one of his swordcuts. 'From the land of Hind, perhaps, or fabled Cathay.'

'Serckland, you mean?' Thorgrim mused. 'It might be. It is like nothing I have seen in my travels. Your eyes, Volker – they, perhaps, see a little more?'

'Little enough. But so much here comes from Africa, since the fall of Roma Mater – maybe this did, too. I've read they have domed buildings there, faced with smooth white clay. This could have been like that. But those pillars – they're too big. And they look as if they might be carved, somehow, like Imperial monuments. They're impressive, but they don't do anything.'

'They could have held up a portico, against that lintel; that would have been even more impressive. But I see no sign of one, or its remains.'

'There are other signs a man might look for,' remarked Thorgrim mildly. 'This gritty soil would be good at showing tracks, footprints even.'

Volker swallowed; Guy twitched his moustache uncomfortably. The temple became less intriguing, more mysterious, a shadowy, brooding nest of problems. What did it hold? Were there priests, a congregation? In this stinking, unhealthy air nobody would live there – nobody human, anyhow. But there were a dozen small villages within walking distance, even for some elderly priest to hobble out each day, or rustic worshippers on rare festival days to lead oxen in procession to the altars of some half-forgotten god. So there might be a lot of people there, or nobody. And of course, there might be Diderik and his unmerry men.

'He could do it – just.' Guy matched Volker's unspoken thought. 'By fast boat up the coast, or by riding harder than we did. Unlikely, but I would put nothing past that little swine.'

'And by magic?' wondered Thorgrim. 'He is powerful, that one. He could command powers to carry him that you and I would not care to.'

'He might,' agreed Volker. 'But not his entourage. And though he could probably blast us all on the spot by himself, he seems to feel the need of help.' He paused, and chuckled.

'What is so droll?'

Volker snorted. 'I was just thinking . . . I know it sounds silly, but – he couldn't be just a bit *scared* of us, could he? I mean, a Tartarist master sorcerer, who can darken the sun and summon blasphemous horrors from the nether pits and all that sort of thing – scared of, well, *us*?'

They chuckled for a moment. Guy bared his teeth. 'If I were not who I am,' he said quietly, 'I might be very scared of us, indeed. Us as we are now. Us together.'

Thorgrim nodded. 'That is so. But a man will take stronger measures against what he fears.'

Volker grimaced, and raised his head to take another look at the temple. It lay quiet and still, as if undisturbed by the passing centuries. 'Then you'd expect him to turn up with a small army. But I'd swear there hasn't been any large number of people down that valley lately.'

'A trail can be brushed out,' agreed Thorgrim. 'But not entirely, if many had passed.'

'Then I'd say we could risk a closer look,' said Volker.

423

'The sooner the better, in fact. What do you say, Guy – *Guy*?'

For a moment he thought Aetna had redoubled its sullen roaring. A rumbling snore set the dust quivering in imitation of the crater above.

'Afraid of us as we are now?' grunted Volker as they hauled the exhausted Armorican to his feet. 'Oh, wonderful. In case we snore them to death, maybe.'

'You could try placing his nose in the horn,' suggested Thorgrim.

Volker shook his head. 'There are some things man was never meant to hear . . . *Wake up, Guy!*'

The big Gallian groaned. 'I feel as if I have been to dinner with our local vampires.'

'Your *local* . . .'

'Armorica is known for *loups-garous*, but they concern themselves chiefly with the peasants. In aristocratic circles vampires are the most socially acceptable family curse – save perhaps for those of Hibernian stock such as the Demoiselles O'Murphy, whose people boast a very melodious *bean sidhe*. Shapely, too, by all accounts. But that is considered ostentatious in the best circles.'

Thorgrim nodded. 'We content ourselves with the occasional nightwalker and roofrider. Even their upkeep is too expensive for all but larger landowners, chieftains, jarls and so on.'

Volker boggled. 'Too expensive?'

'Why yes. Only nobles can afford to have large enough families. Lesser ones are soon exterminated, and the – *hvad skal man sige* – bloodline is lost. It serves them right for undying beyond their means.'

They turned and trudged uphill now, keeping below the skyline of the sulphurous valley. From time to time Thorgrim paused to peer back along it, with an expression of increasing puzzlement.

'Why do you keep stopping?' demanded Volker irritably, heaving at an inert de Guillac. 'It only gives Guy a chance to go back to sleep.'

'It is that it reminds me of something, that valley. Something I do not like . . .'

'It reminds me of a lot of things I don't like, and Diderik's the current favourite. The longer we wait, the likelier he is to get here.' Volker sighed. 'And yet I want him to, don't I? With the other horn, with Dani. And how we're going to get them off him . . . *Wake up, you Gallic oaf! We're going on!*'

But there was not much further they could go, without revealing themselves. 'We could go round behind the temple,' suggested Volker. 'Come down the side, and inch around to the door.'

'That will take hours, we will be in plain sight, and it is much steeper!' Thorgrim objected. 'No, I have been weighing it up, and it comes to me that I have had enough of creeping around like a mouse. I will go ahead some way, and you two follow. If I feel there is trouble, or anything happens to me, you will have time to get the horn away.'

Volker was about to protest, but Guy's heavy hand restrained him. 'It makes too much sense. I would dispute the lead with you, Norseman, but you are in better trim, and you have your nose for this kind of thing. Use it, and do not go rushing in like a berserk!'

Thorgrim snorted, and made his way crouching over the crest of the ridge and down on to the rocky slope, dodging from boulder to boulder. 'This is the man who tells me not to turn berserk? This is the man who drinks his way into sorcery and out the other side . . . This is the man who . . .' His grumbles died away as he disappeared down the slope.

'How long should we wait?' demanded Volker.

'Not long, *fiston*, not long. Enough to make us two targets, not one, that is all. In fact . . .' He lumbered to his feet, drew his sabre, and went padding along in

Thorgrim's tracks. The Norseman wasn't as far ahead as Volker had expected, and he soon found why. The slope looked gentle enough, but the ashen soil was loose and crumbly, and the rocks that spattered it made it even worse. Instead of a clean swift descent they had to scuff and scramble their way back and forth across the slope, skidding and falling on the sharp gravel, trying not to send a minor avalanche down on the others. Finally the inevitable happened. Thorgrim lost his balance, tried to dig in Hlavisbana to catch himself, and only succeeded in dislodging more ash. A half-moon shape slid out of the slope with a powdery rush and broadened; a small boulder worked loose, the crumbling arc widened, and Volker felt his feet going from under him. With a yelp he caught at a larger rock and hung there a moment; Guy scrambled after him, caught the edge of the crumbling and fell flat on his back. Volker's rock came loose; Guy shot past, gathering speed, and Volker tumbled after him in a bouncing hail of pebbles. Somewhere along the way they gathered up Thorgrim, and came to rest in a flail of limbs and oaths and minor contusions from the stones rattling by.

A sulphurous silence fell, broken only by wheezing. 'If somebody will kindly put up a tombstone,' remarked Guy at last, 'I see no need to proceed any further.'

'You might, if you have life enough to turn your head,' answered Thorgrim, in a very strange voice.

Volker sat up with a groan, wiping yellow sand from his eyes; and he stared. Like insects tumbling into an antlion's trap, the slip had borne them headlong to the valley floor, and deposited them right in front of the gaping doors of the Templa Volcana.

Or rather, doorways; for there were no doors in them, only the ashy sand piled up in a great smooth sweep, like a model of the wind. Volker looked for hinges, but could see none, nor any marks where they might have been. All beyond was darkness. They scrambled up, cautiously, wincing at wounds and bruises but paying them little heed, retrieving their weapons from the slide. Volker opened the case and took out the horn. The wind seemed to swirl in it, like a faint eerie moan. Thorgrim took a short stub of candle from his pack; Guy shivered, fumbled in his pockets for a tinderbox. Hunched about the candle to shield it from the wind, they crunched over the wave of sand towards the side of one great arch. Volker glanced up at the nearest pillar as they passed. It was dull black, like slate, and apparently carved in broad, crude spirals. So was the buttress; in fact, it was a seamless part of it, curving over and down towards the uneven sand. He could see now that the pillar leant outward slightly, an unusual architectural trick creating a very dynamic sort of effect. Whatever mind built this temple had a touch of sophistication, crude as it might look.

At the edge of the darkness they paused, looking to left and right, holding their breath and listening. There was nothing but the faint susurrus of the wind in the ashy sand. Little particles trickled down into their footprints, but slowly. If anyone had passed this way in the last few hours, they would have been seen. Slowly, sword levelled, Guy shouldered past Thorgrim and down, treading lightly in the crunching soil. He hissed a soft word, and Thorgrim held a candle suddenly aloft. Dim yellow light flooded across the inner surface of the dome, and was mirrored back down at them. Guy swore horribly; Thorgrim hissed something in his own tongue; but Volker only stared. The horn fell from his hand, and swung by its hide cord, this way and that, unheeded.

The temple was empty. There was only a single, huge hall; no rooms, partitions, antechambers, nothing but the space contained beneath that awesome dome. Its inner surface was high, smooth and glossy; but that might have been the swirling of the sand that lay in windrows over whatever floor there might be, hiding it completely. There were no marks in it beyond Guy's first footprints. There were no furnishings, no hangings, no decorations – nothing, except a low rough-edged rise that protruded slightly through the sand at the centre, like the crudest of altars. The side facing the doors was encrusted with sand, stuck, apparently, to some dark stain across it.

Volker felt himself beginning to shake uncontrollably. *'Ulrich! Damn you, Ulrich! What've you done to me? There's nobody here!'*

Guy glanced around at him quickly. 'Do not jump to conclusions too swiftly, where magic is in play. There may be more to it than this!'

'What more could there be?' demanded Volker. He might have been crying or laughing, he wasn't sure which. 'Look at it! There's nobody! Maybe there never has been! Nobody comes here!'

Guy frowned suddenly, squinted, then leaned forward and prodded the piled-up sand at the front of the altar with his sword. With a little sigh it sagged and slid. He stepped back with an oath. Thorgrim's candle flame shook. Volker felt the hair on his neck bristle. White things gleamed up through the sand, the arches of a ribcage, the empty eyesocket of a skull. Shreds of wizened, yellowing skin and hair still clung to it.

'Nobody comes here!' repeated Guy in a stunned voice.

'I beg to correct you upon that point,' said a dry voice behind them.

The three of them caught each others' eyes and turned. 'I am here. Hold them fast!'

Diderik stood in the doorway, a gnarled silhouette against the baleful light. Ahead of them, already stepping inside, were two tall men. Volker registered little of their faces, of the long robes they wore; what he saw

428

was the sudden tension in their hands as they raised them. It was a gesture that shrieked *mage!* to him, and evidently to the others also. Thorgrim's halberd swung down, Guy's sabre lifted for a swift slashing charge. But even as they moved dark bundles seemed to leap from the hands of the tall men, leap and explode into a mass of flying strips. With a noise like a fusillade of cracking whips they showered down on Thorgrim and Guy, wrapping themselves around weapon and flesh alike with entangling force.

'*Him!*' shrieked Diderik. 'The boy! Get the boy! He's the most dangerous!'

Aren't I just, though! With a savage, desperate delight and a great gasping breath Volker swung the second horn up to his lips, and blew. His fingers sought a fingering he'd chosen—

They never reached it.

The sound that emerged was bad enough in itself – a snarling, sweeping scythe-blow of a note that by itself would have sent its enemy reeling, cloven in mind and battered in body. But that great dome caught it, echoed it, drove it singing back and forth in a terrible clangour of deafening, clashing harmonics and subsonics that edged the very air. Not even in the forest had it been like that. The power in the built-up sound was appalling, like a rain of hammerblows. The walls juddered, the floor sand crawled into strange and terrible vibratory patterns. The men in its direct path took the brunt of it. Volker saw them jerked back as if thunderstruck, flung bodily from the floor and spun around in mid-air, torn and twisted; an arm was flung loose in a splash of scarlet among shredding robes, a head leaped and lolled on its neck. But even as the sorcerers died, the awful vibrations rebounded on him, juddered and pounded him. Beside him Thorgrim was scooped off his feet in a great swathe of ash; Guy was rolled over and over the vibrating floor, jerking like a stringless puppet, both strong men as helpless as feathers in a gale. Volker was torn from his feet and twisted till his spine creaked. The horn was dashed from his lips, and with it the core of that horrendous reverberation; otherwise they would have died the next instant, as the sorcerers had. Even its final echo was enough to send Volker sprawling down against the horrid wrecks at the altar foot, stunned and helpless.

He did not lose consciousness, only comprehension. He gaped and lolled as the shadow-shapes clustered around him, caught his feebly flailing limbs and jerked cords tight around them with blood-stopping force. He heard a voice order them outside, felt himself bumped and scraped across the sand without understanding why. Only outside, in fresher air, did his senses begin to return. They were about to gag him, but he rolled over and vomited with awful force, till there was nothing more for his heaving stomach to spill. After that his head grew clearer, and he looked around. Guy lay there, pale-faced, open-eyed, his dark clothes crusted with blood he could ill afford to lose. Thorgrim, with a nosebleed matting his moustache, was struggling furiously against his bonds. Something thudded to the ground beside him, in a furious scrabble. Volker twisted about, despite complaining muscles, and saw Dani there, trying to kick the legs from the man who had forced her to sit. He snorted contemptuously and cuffed her across the face once or twice. She let out a muffled wail and rolled away.

The wail died away, and a pair of dark eyes lifted and looked anxiously into Volker's. 'You okay?' she hissed. The gag had been knocked aside. 'Made for somebody bigger-headed than me,' she grinned, licking a split lip. 'Almost worked loose when that bastard slapped me before. Figured another couple of slaps ought to do it! You okay?'

'Not . . . really . . . I'm not hurt badly, but . . . what difference will it make now?'

'We're not dead yet!' she hissed. 'Listen, the temple . . . that damn gag, I tried to warn you . . . it's not what Ulrich meant . . .'

She stopped suddenly. Footsteps were coming back, a shadow falling over them. It was Diderik. He had exchanged his cane for an ornate staff of some black wood inlaid with garnets; and dangling from his hands were both horns.

He gazed down on them with a cold light in his eyes, empires distant from the cackling little merchant he had played. 'You hardly needed me, did you?' he remarked contemptuously, prodding Volker with his toes. 'Really you did not. You're quite capable of catching yourself. So much so, my dear young idiot, that I confess I'm puzzled. I genuinely would like to know – was there something I didn't know? Some effect I hadn't thought of, that you were banking on to protect you? Some shieldspell? Or just plain—' He shook his head wonderingly. 'Of all the imbecilic tricks – sounding *that* horn within *there*! Even the other one would have been perilous, but *that* . . .'

He looked at the second horn with extreme wonder. 'I truly cannot imagine why you're still alive. A poor player, perhaps? Oh, I knew you were foolish. I hoped you would be, and you proved me right – racing straight here after your friends like that, instead of getting at least one horn back to the Imperial Inquisition at Worms, as you should. That level of sentimentality one might expect. Even an accomplished man like Ulrich was not wholly free of it. But I, even I, could never have guessed that you'd do half my work for me by not only coming out here yourselves, but bringing the horn . . . the *horn*! *Here*! Of all places!'

He was not gloating, Volker realized. He really did seem astonished. 'And then *using* it! How anyone who knew anything at all about it could do such a thing I cannot imagine . . .'

He broke off. A very strange look settled on his face, and stooping forward he clamped a pallid hand over Volker's face and held it steady, staring into his beady dark eyes. 'You . . .' he muttered. 'You . . . really *don't* know anything about it . . . do you? You genuinely don't . . .'

His eyes wandered. It was as if he'd been hit by the horn. 'Wha . . . I . . . Then Ulrich never told you everything! He must just have told you the name of this temple, nothing more . . . and you thought . . . Tell me!' He kicked Volker painfully on the kneecap. 'Tell me!'

Volker heaved at his bonds, and said nothing. The little sorcerer shot out a hand, grabbed Dani by the hair and jerked it, hard. She yelped and snarled at him, still pretending to be gagged. *'Tell me!'*

Volker sighed. He had no illusions about what was coming; but there was no need to give Dani extra pain. What did one more answer matter? 'Just the name . . . no more . . .'

'Of course there was more!'

Volker swore to himself. 'The way the words went, in the rain . . . The blood . . .' Diderik peered, puzzled, then seemed to realize what Volker was talking about. His eyes widened. 'The way he said it,' mused Volker, more for himself. 'It sounded as if I was meant to bring it here to be destroyed . . . he must have meant destroy the temple, too . . .'

'Temples,' corrected Diderik absentmindedly. He seemed utterly flabbergasted. 'So . . . I needn't have revealed myself on the Poiana river! I could just have sat tight. And you would have brought both horns all the way here for me. And never suspected a thing. . . . And you gave me all that trouble . . .'

A violent shock seemed to pass through the little

432

man. He convulsed, his face sagged. For the first time he looked truly as old as he must really be; a thousand years seemed to drift down on him like dust, leaching the colour and the life out of him. 'You could have beaten me!' he said, breathless. He sank to his knees on the sand. 'You could have beaten me . . . no! You *would* have beaten me! You did so much, as it was. If you had known the truth of this, you would have beaten me – *me!* – at every turn.'

He looked this way and that, shaking his head. 'And only a chance you did not! I never thought it was so close! I, I . . .' He became aware that his men were watching him, and visibly pulled himself together.

'Well!' he said, rising. His voice and manner became sombre, unmenacing, matter of fact, cackling and gloating gone. He might have been discussing a serious business matter with respected equals. 'I could torment you in a myriad ways, but it would gain me nothing. It could be said I owed you an explanation. That would cost me nothing. The Great Deed must begin without delay, and I had planned to use you as sacrificial flesh to prime the reaction. But these carrion . . .' He jerked a toe at the shattered remains of his sorcerers as they were dragged by. 'They will do as well. So you will have a chance to see what you have had a hand in. But spare me your vulgar hopes, your last-minute attempts at escape! If you ran from here to Syracusa or beyond, the scale of what is to happen would still envelop you and many others besides, greater ones than yourselves. Yet even they will be the first of many.' Something of the old glitter crept back into his eyes as he surveyed them. 'Like all wise men I choose to work through others when I can. Because of that you may have underestimated me, also. Watch, then, and learn the true power that a man with learning, courage and no weak restraints may wrest from out the Pit!'

He lifted the first horn, and contemplated it for a

moment. Then, with a careless strength Volker would have not credited, he ripped the beautiful silver key-work from around it and cast it, bent and twisted, to the sand. Then he slung the horns over his narrow shoulders, and leaning on his gaudy staff he waved his men irritably back from the doors of the temple. They retreated hastily, dragging Volker and the rest with them, to the base of the slope some way back. Diderik seemed to hesitate for a moment; then he fell to his knees in the sand. He stayed there a moment, prostrate; and then, scrambling to his feet with his old demonic vitality, he stepped for the first time into the right-hand door of the Temple.

As he passed, dwarfed beneath that mighty arch, he lifted his arms wide, his long sleeves billowing in the breeze. Only a second ago, Volker realized, there had been no breeze. And this one was blowing from behind Diderik – *out* of the enclosed Temple, down the valley. His robes fluttered wildly as it grew, like some black butterfly. Something else was moving, too. Little by little at first, swelling to a continuous stream, the sulphurous sand was being blown out of the temple. Higher still rose the wind, to a jagged, screeching blast; clouds of sand boiled out and were borne away down the valley. Through stinging eyes Volker saw Diderik make a sudden, circling gesture with his staff; and the wind changed, swirling, eddying, spinning.

'He makes a whirlwind!' croaked Guy, then cut off short as a knife pressed against the side of his neck. Evidently he was right. Little sand devils sprang up, shimmered and wavered this way and that, then swam together. A thin whirling stalk sprang up, thickened, then grew, up and out. The billowing clouds were plucked from the air; sand and stones were plucked from the ground in a screaming mass and pitched sky-ward. The column rose to an awesome height, but stayed as if rooted where it had started. Below the gates the ground was being sucked away at an amazing rate, faster than a hundred men could dig, as if Diderik meant to strip away the very foundations. Certainly there was something there, something deep. Volker strained to make it out, through the churning column – then scoffed at what he saw.

An illusion of Diderik's, a stupid trick . . . it had to be. Or at the very least some strange, perverted work of an earlier age, that was being laid bare. Yet when, quite suddenly, the screaming wind was stilled, and the last load of stones and sand fell back with a rattle into the vast pit that had been dug, he could not choke back a cry of horror and disbelief. Nor could the others; but it was lost, entirely drowned, amid the triumphant baying of the Tartarists.

Now he saw why Diderik had said 'Temples'. That was exactly what they were.

Where the sand had been blasted away the dome curved down and inwards, not to foundations but to a massive structure of shapes. Deformed and strange as they were, he had no trouble recognizing them, eerie mirrors of those pitiful remains within. Across the pit stretched a stained arch. Behind it, far behind, a massive column of brown discs stood out from the pit's rear wall, vanishing down into the half-seen reaches of a great cage-like structure – oh, they were all clear enough, all recognizable. Volker found himself giggling hysterically at the idea of people who could want to build things like that – collarbone, vertebrae, a ribcage filled only with the stinking sand. Above them, at a crazy angle, loomed a huge cantilever only slightly dislocated from its massive socket on the side of the dome. No mistaking that, either; a jawbone. But the *size* . . .

And the curve of the dome, the doors through which they'd dared to enter, stood revealed, as the forehead and eyesockets of an enormous skull.

The sheer monstrosity of it taxed Volker's sanity. And

435

monstrous not only in size; for even without flesh that skull was a distorted, loathsome thing, a leering parody of human mortality. Human in general pattern, but lumpy, bulbous, distorted, with a jawbone whose heavy hinges supported a bestial jaw that narrowed like a leopard's, with teeth only at its tip, an asymmetric tusklike jumble. The nasal aperture above it had a hundred chambers, strangely shaped. On either side of it great overhanging cheekbones shelved out beneath the eyesockets. Minutes before they had stepped through those misshapen openings into the empty braincase beyond. The awful altar within had been the socket of the spine, the entry for the spinal cord. And the buttresses and pillars that flanked the sockets were two great excrescences like malformed antlers, curling out of the forehead like a ram's, flanking that horrible face before they curled inwards, narrowing to blunt points at the level of its jutting teeth.

'It has to be a building!' choked Dani past her gag. 'Nothing that size could've lived! It'd be crushed under its own weight!'

'*Merde alors!* But if they sculpted that, what was the model? Could even a Tartarist dream up such a . . . thing?'

'And would they mould the braincase so perfectly?' Volker demanded. 'Even as a challenge? And worse – would they build so accurate a jaw?'

'Sure!' objected Dani. 'Just like the rest!'

'So it could come *unhinged?*'

Dani gave a little gasp.

'It is in my mind to vomit,' said Thorgrim suddenly, in a strained voice. Volker looked at him, startled. The Norseman had a proverbially strong stomach. Then he remembered Thorgrim sometimes interpreted his special sense as smell. There must be magic brewing here; magic that came to him as an appalling stench . . . Volker swallowed. As a building the Temple Volcana

436

was bad enough. But as the dry hulk of something that had lived . . . Surely no living thing could *be* that size? No *normal* thing. But what about something magical?

Diderik appeared in one vast eyesocket and sprang down, exultant. He shouted to the Tartarists, and they scuttled like ants about the monstrous shape to do his bidding. *'Chairete!* It is revealed! It returns, to appal the day! To defy the unjust gods!' He hopped and chattered like a demented ape, pointing this way and that, chivvying his followers as they furiously painted symbols about the exposed bones, characters from all alphabets, hieroglyphs and wedge-shaped cuneiform patterns, runes and strange designs that branched off from a central line like leaves from a tree, cage-like characters of slashing brushwork. Innocent in themselves, in that jumble of furious scrawling they took on a sinister colour, interspersed as they were with crazy tangles whose very lack of meaning seemed to express a sinister nihilism. Some of them, though, Volker recognized. He wished he didn't; he'd found their faint images chalked upon the floor of old Strauben's laboratory, trodden too deep to be completely erased, or faintly scorched in outline against the ancient floorboards.

Diderik flung up his arms, and turning to the prisoners he kicked a flurry of sand in their faces. 'Behold, you who would have challenged it, the might of Tartarus!' He whirled around on the loose surface, robes outspread, like a barbarian dervish. 'For three lifetimes and more have I endured to look upon His mighty form! Breed of Uranos, warlord of Kronos, prince of primal Kaos! Whose only order is endless turmoil, whose only government is continual revolution, whose only constant is change! Rightful Anarch of the unending cycle, to whom creation and destruction are one!'

Still raving, he lurched forward into the pit, and blue fire sputtered out, once, twice. As its glare faded he scrambled up the shifting sand, and Volker saw with a shock that the horns no longer dangled from his shoulders.

He staggered on the rim of the pit, still exulting, dwarfed by the angle of that monstrous jaw. 'In the morning of the world he dared to challenge the usurping gods! Their cramping order . . . their cramping laws and whining restraints! He was betrayed, he was broken, cast down beneath a mountain of fire! Cast down and left to lie, blighting the land with his corruption, the fount of his being riven from him!' He paused, panting, and swept his staff skyward. 'Yet devotion and sacrifice maintained him, blood kept his shadow strong even in Tartarus. Until now . . . Now! *Now!* Now comes the evening, when the gods are weak, when Kaos shall return and its faithful be exalted! Now comes unending Night!'

The onlookers were forgotten, ignored. Dropping all they held, the Tartarists sank down to the sand, grovelled, beat their foreheads and ground their faces into it in blind obeisance. They wailed and chanted what sounded like gibberish, they tore at their clothes, scraped their skin till blood ran into the sand. One man lashed at himself with the cords he held; one woman slowly sank her nails into her cheeks and dug great bloody furrows below her eyes, as if to signify tears. They caught their blood in cupped hands, and hurled it to sprinkle and splash upon those arid, brittle bones. Only Diderik stood, staff outstretched, quivering with tension. The falling sun stained his face with the reflected light of the sulphurous sand, filled his beady eyes with flame. Across each of those gaping sockets lay the broken bodies of his lesser sorcerors. Slowly he turned, looking up to them, gestured slightly, and spoke a single word.

Typhon.

Scarlet light sprang from his staff-tip. As if struck by some vast hammer, the bodies exploded, spraying into

438

fragments that spattered the darkness. Volker gulped; that would have happened to them, alive. And Diderik was anything but merciful. He must think what was coming would be worse.

'Who was this Typhon?' demanded Thorgrim. Like the others, he was straining furiously at his bonds. 'Hard to die like a dog before a thing of which you know nothing!'

Guy snarled with frustration. 'Typhon, child of the Northlands, was akin to your primal Giants! One of the embodied spirits of the chaos that reigned before the Gods were, the forces of evil and discord whose reign they ended, whom they destroyed and cast down! Into Tartarus! Into the realm of fire! *Typhaeus Tartarus! Typhoios Titanos* – a Titan!'

From each empty eye, where the bodies had been, a single fat drop of dark blood oozed, like a monstrous tear. It grew, spread, ran along the runnels and channels of the bare bones, leaving a pinkness in its path, a pale, fatty trail that seemed to cling and spread. Down on to the jaw it dropped, to the lower bones, spreading, racing, filling up each crevice, each channel with the same deposit, that dripped and spread in its turn. A great waft of the odour reached the prisoners and rolled over them; they gagged and retched. It seemed as if the earth itself revolted and heaved beneath them, toppling them this way and that among little showers of stones; but it was not that.

Beyond them the steep end of the valley collapsed with a roar, sliding down into sudden vacancy. The ground itself was splitting, and out of it, like some unclean burrowing thing, rose the shape of a vast skeletal hand. It was as horrible as the head, human and yet unhuman, a great thicket of thin bony fingers that swelled with tarry blackness and filled out even as they watched, clenching and convulsing with the horrible

439

animation of some crawling sea creature. Oozing ichor dripped down onto the sand. It bubbled.

A yawning creak, like the grinding of stone, and more of the slope fell. From the congealed sulphur flow that had entombed it the vast head tore slowly free, lolling horribly. The lower jaw swung and sagged, but ragged tendons already tethered it to the flaring cheekbones; they tautened, and the great teeth clashed with a flinty ring.

The head sagged. Steaming drops oozed and bubbled between the teeth. The cultists wailed, and it seemed to stir again. The hand scrabbled at the ground, leaving slimy furrows. Beyond the head the ground leaped up, its crust cracking to reveal another hand, dripping with congealing flesh. Black veins stood out over what had been the bare lintel of the doors, pulsing slowly at the roots of the monstrous horns. Within the chamber beyond something was forming, stirring, still leaking those long slow tears of yellowish mucus, threaded thin with blood.

The cultists cowered, rapt, hardly daring to raise their eyes, without a thought for the prisoners 'We could run!' raged Thorgrim. He had struggled around so Guy could reach the knots on his ropes, but the Armorican's own wrists were too well bound to let him get a proper grip. He jerked his head at the horses, left tied to boulders, rearing and plunging in their terror. 'We could be far away before they so much as suspected!'

'It is hopeless!' growled Guy. 'If you could use your teeth . . .'

'On this rope? If we had a day to spare, maybe. We have need of something with an edge! Volker?'

'Can hardly move my fingers . . . blood stopped! Anyway . . . what good's running going to do when *that* thing's . . .'

'Then why do you still struggle?' Behind them somewhere came another rumble, another wild ecstatic wail from the worshippers. The stench billowed about them.

'Ask the gods! Maybe . . . warn people, at least. Maybe Dani could . . . Dani . . . *Dani?*'

He thought her mind had snapped, almost hoped it had if it would spare her what was coming. She was sitting up, struggling no longer but weaving her head about slowly, this way, that way, her lips half parted in a sort of inner ecstasy. Then she shivered and hunched up, pulling her shoulders in and leaning forward. For an instant her face slackened, then went taut with effort, neck muscles standing out as if she meant to break the cords by sheer force. Her head snapped back, and suddenly her eyes seemed to clear, as if now she really *was* looking for something.

'What is it, Dani?' he hissed. 'What do you see?'

Out of the boiling dust a shadow swooped, stooping so low that they ducked instinctively in fright. Something fell, rattling among the pebbles between them, gleaming blackly as it came to rest. They stared an instant, then with a muffled roar Guy rolled over and pounced on the heavy sliver of volcanic glass. With a soft sigh of wings the owl came to rest on Dani's shoulder, and in unison, with the identical look of serene and haughty composure, the two heads turned to face the others.

Guy, with his back to Thorgrim, was sawing frantically at the Norseman's bonds. 'Beware of your wrists!' he hissed.

'Much longer and we will have no need of hands!' retorted the Icelander. 'Cut, man! *Cut!*' Volker heard him suck in his breath, strain . . . and there was a sudden sharp snap. The Norseman rolled over in a mess of unravelling cords, and they huddled together to conceal him.

'Now me!' growled Guy. 'Take the glass, man . . . so! So!'

Thorgrim breathed hard as he sawed away, matched by Guy as he wrenched at the parting ropes. Then Guy too was rolling over, and Volker saw him seize Dani's wrists and slash away at the complex knot, while the owl swivelled its head to peer at him. All in seconds, yet it felt like centuries as the earth heaved beneath them.

'This . . . grows blunt!' hissed the Norseman. 'If I made for their baggage there . . . fetched Hlavisbana . . .'

'No! You might be seen!' Volker panted. 'And we, left here bound! We must go together, there will be no second chances . . .'

The earth shivered under him, the sand swirled and ran as if snaky things coursed beneath it. Suddenly the owl spread its wings with a crack, and Dani's shoulders tensed, then sagged. She groaned and fell over, and hard hands seized her wrists. He winced as the slashing stone passed, slicing the skin on his arms, again and again. Wishing he had the muscles the others had, and wishing Thorgrim would hurry up, he heaved despairingly at the ropes . . . and was amazed to feel them burst apart. He opened his mouth to say something, but just then the agony of returning circulation struck him speechless. He wavered, arms open; and to his utter astonishment – and by the look of it, hers – Dani swung into them.

With an upsurge of strength he clawed at that hateful harness; it defeated him, but with his numbed fingers he still managed to twist off the bolt of the gag and cast it aside. She drew a great gasping breath, and caught him in a grip that was almost tighter than the ropes; he tasted the blood from her bruised mouth. His head reeled as she thrust him away, panting, equally unable to speak.

'Time enough for that later!' growled Thorgrim. 'The horses . . .'

'Where would we ride to? Who could we warn?'

'The Imperials . . . they have strong sorcerers, too . . . someone might do *something*!'

'Last time it took the gods! They must know! Why don't *they* do something?'

'We might not like it! Last time they destroyed the face of all the earth . . .'

A sudden convulsion threw them all off their feet, amid a deafening, rending roar. The slope juddered and split; boulders crashed down, sand and soil sprayed around their heads. The horses neighed wildly, burst their tethers and fled, scattering the baggage. The cultists flew back in a disorderly rabble, shrieking and gesticulating, clutching at each other in an orgiastic rapture of terror and worship, ignoring their prisoners. In front of them a vast hand came crashing down, a hand of half-raw flesh, its sinews flexing as its forest of fingers rippled; but they dug hard into the ground, and beneath their weight it split, heaved and erupted as if Aetna were seeking a new outlet for her deepest fires. The Northerners, clinging to each other for support as the valley slopes came crashing down around them, found themselves gaping through the sulphurous clouds at the vast shadow that arose there – a shadow that heaved, changed shape, swung and lifted, high, higher . . .

The ground shuddered as if in horror at what it was releasing. They fought for balance, but they could not tear their stinging eyes from the monstrous, inchoate form. Their heads tilted back, straining their necks as that impossible rise went on, until at last it loomed even above the choking mists it had raised, high against the searing sunset. Then, for the first time, they saw it clearly.

Among the cultists a woman screamed, a shrill tiny sound that was abruptly cut off. Dani jammed a knuckle in her mouth to muffle a startled yelp; Volker gave a low moan. Thorgrim was silent, running a hand down over his face as if to wipe away the sight. It was Guy, breathing like an exhausted rhinoceros, who summed up their general reaction most succinctly.

'*Merde alors!*'

The monstrous form wavered there as if weary, bulbous head hanging, long arms dangling, thin fingers flexing like the waving tendrils of some predatory sea-creature. Its shape was manlike, but ill-made, distorted, some gross imitation or fearsome parody. The grey-green flesh that now coated it was incomplete, cracked, open in places like vast running sores, dull grey and yellow with suppuration and rot. Some were closing, slowly; others filling and caking with hardening putrescence that dripped on to the shattered sand beneath. Where the skin was intact it was scaly, dark, of no single colour but shining with a faint oily iridescence like the trail of a slug; there was no sign of hair, or any other covering, or any mark of sex. At every joint a bony spike protruded, sometimes cracked, sometimes blunt, sometimes broken away to leave a crater of horn. The face was shadowed, save where the eyesockets poured runnels of stringy slime over the ghastly cliff-edged cheekbones, trickling down the grooves of ridged, reptilian cheeks. The skin sagged on breast and belly, over muscles that had nothing human in their shaping, and gave no sign of breath. It did not look alive. Swaying, lolling loosely in its half-decay, it looked like a gigantic caricature of a gallows-bird, left wind-swung in his chains to rot beside the high roads he had preyed on, and the stench of it could have been no worse. It might be a hundred feet tall.

Together, without a word spoken, the Northerners scrambled up. Without the horses they had little chance; but if they could just get to firmer ground and run . . . Carefully, silently, they began to back away.

Then they froze. From the settling dust a shrill voice

cried out . . . a voice they knew. Dimly they saw Diderik, robes coated in yellow sand and clinging filth, shouting up at the vast abomination he had brought about, shouting and gesturing with his staff, harsh, insistent words.

'Behold!' screamed the ancient sorcerer. 'They that were hurled to the ends of the earth are recovered! That which we cherished, and that which was hidden from us! That which was stolen from us, that which was used against us, yet which we made ours again! That which was found in our despite, yet was brought to us by by the very unbelievers who would have destroyed it! The pure tone finds its counter, the harmony its discord! The Two are reunited – and the One is made whole! From the toils of Tartarus his shadow is drawn back! From its unjust prison his undying body is lifted! *Typhon is risen!*'

And lifting their heads in one ecstatic gaze of worship the cultists bayed in response. '*Risen! Risen indeed!*'

As if they were heard—

With an audible grinding of bone on half-formed cartilage, with a ghastly sucking sound of flesh still half liquescent, the monstrous head lifted. The face framed by those immense spiralling horns was repulsive, slate-like, sweating droplets of fat across its slow-forming scales, shedding flakes of caked sand and filth. The vast nose was blunt and broad, nostrils strangely flattened and slot-like; the mouth beneath it absurdly pinched and narrow, the lips thin and scaly as some giant lizard's. Even closed as they were the lower tusks protruded, stained and rotten and slablike as ancient gravestones. Black veins stood out along the cheeks, seamed by cracks and ulcerations. One burst for a moment, spraying out a tarry liquid, then seethed, closed, and settled.

Diderik positively capered in his delirium. 'From the prisoning stuff of the still-molten rock into which he

445

was treacherously hurled down – from the substance and soil to which it had decayed, from the blood and bone of his votaries, his undying flesh is formed anew! *Behold his power!'*

'Behold . . . ' they moaned, heaping the stifling sand upon their heads, grinding their faces in it. *'Behold! Behold! Behold!'*

Only then did Volker see just what he had done, and understand at last what it was he had borne for Ulrich, what it was he had so dutifully and so disastrously sought out. Seen from this far off the contorted black surface of those 'pillars' looked strangely familiar; and the dull blackness of the two horns leaped into his mind. He saw, with a weird helpless inevitability, that one was just a coarser version of the other. They had not been instruments in themselves, those horns, nor any thing on their own; they were no more than the final twists and narrowings of those tortuous columns rooted in that monstrous brow. And, welding them somehow with those two blasts of fire, Diderik had put them back. Put them back, so that their open ends now passed on either side of those gaping tusks, extending the columns so that they could reach that stiff reptilian mouth, as they never could have otherwise. Now their tips lay hard against those scaly, inflexible lips, as they had against his own. Those two horns, for all their awesome powers, had never been more than the mouthpieces of instruments immensely greater.

The cultists were bobbing and wailing faster than ever. Together, still wordlessly, the four Northerners backed off, clutching at each other for balance on the ruined ground, and also for a touch of humanity in the face of that awesome monstrosity. They could hardly take their eyes off it, even to find their way; always it drew them back, with the sickening attraction of some deadly void. The cultists' baggage lay all over the place, strewn by the bolting horses and heaving earth. When something clinked underfoot Volker didn't even look down till Thorgrim gave an outraged gasp, ducked and clutched his halberd to him like a long-lost lover. Guy looked around, found a sword, tossed it aside and an instant later grabbed his own from under a heavy pack. Dani, too, scooped up some things; there were no bows, but she had a long knife. It wasn't her own; it had a matt black blade traced with unpleasant looking characters in silver, but clutching it seemed to strengthen her, too. Volker didn't have that consolation; the only weapons he'd come to rely on he didn't even want to think about now. And before that living mountain even the gesture of a weapon looked ridiculous. What good would any be now? What good was anything?

And then, with a positive shriek of laughter, Diderik swung around and faced them. As if, all the time, he had been aware of their efforts, and indulged them only to have more to mock at.

'*Behold!*' he gibbered. 'Hear me, you who would have opposed us, the mighty counterpoints of Kaos! Let the unisons of doom ring out, and shatter the music of the spheres! *Behold the Horns of Typhon!*'

Under the bony ridge of the skull, between those immense curling horns, the sockets they had stepped through wept no longer. Lids had closed over their pus-ridden hollowness, lids that seemed to swell even as they watched. Lids that cracked the crust of rheumy substances that sealed them in a shower of yellow flakes, that lifted with the awesome grinding weight of vault doors sealed by the passing centuries. And behind them, high overhead, light glittered through the dust and smoke. Where they had trodden vast eyes now glittered, green and inhuman as some monstrous sea-creature's. The sockets ran and suppurated, but the pupils, like cavernous black slots, held them steadily, and blazed with a malice and contempt so vast it oppressed Volker like a burden. Yet he knew the thing hardly saw him for what he was, knew nothing of him, contemplated him as a man might contemplate some low crawling thing in the instant before he raised his foot and stamped it into shapelessness. That malevolence was no more and no less than its world-view, the first instinctive basis of every thought that might pass through that remoulded brain and the dark spirit it housed. Diderik's shrilling and shrieking taunts seemed as irrelevant as a cricket's squeaking in the grass. The four Northerners waited, hopeless and helpless, clutching their ridiculous weapons.

The hands lifted, whole now save for patches of weeping ulceration, fingers rippling like grass fronds. They spread wide, framing the face, and came together at the crest of the skull to touch the vast hornroots. The cultists brayed and chanted, Diderik gibbered; the sagging chest heaved with a single howling breath that drew the dust spiralling into the leaden skies, and the threshing multitude of fingers rippled down the horns in a strangely familiar gesture. Volker's heart shook and pounded. They were moving upon the rows of holes. It was the gesture of a musician about to play. The scaly lips tautened, pressed against the protruding tusks in a kind of pursing, and blew.

Typhon was a living instrument. His skull must resonate with the sounds he blew. Till those horns had been broken off . . . by whom? By someone very powerful, someone immensely powerful, torn or smashed off so they no longer reached Typhon's mouth, and hurled far, very far, this way and that. The tips of those horns had commanded immense powers; what inconceivable, cataclysmic things would be possible when the great instruments were complete?

Sound answered him.

Sound he heard, sound he felt, sound that stabbed and shook him. The ground shuddered with an earthquake as a gigantic foot struck it. Boulders leaped and shattered, sand spurted up in walls or spilled down hissing into the jagged cracks that crazed the ground at every thudding step. Volker clapped his hands to his ears.

'It's *dancing*!' he screamed, half blinded by the pain. He could see it in his mind, that vast shape shifting, stamping, a dance of death that split walls, smashed down towers, sank great ships, crushed all before it. With Diderik to call the tune . . . Diderik to direct it . . . Diderik's dance, a dance of destruction and terror to which all mankind must bow. Diderik dancing with a giant's steps, to a killing music . . .

Except it was not killing. The steps crashed down, but the sound itself, though it shook the very centre of him like a leaf in a gale, was not beyond bearing. The rhythm faltered, and the fearful steps slowed . . .

The music changed. Now it blared with furious intent, blared and roared and thudded like a caged beast pounding at the bars. The steps took it up; but even as they caught the rhythm it changed again, took on a frantic, searching pace, sliding wildly through intervals Volker could hardly imagine, leaping crazily from key to key. As if – some part of his numbed brain told him – as if the thing was racing through some weird and alien sequence of scales or modes, beginning many but never completing them. As if, somehow, each one failed it and was cast aside as it raced on to the next, like a wild beast racing round and round its cage, frenziedly tearing at every door or bar in search of an exit. It was a terrible cacophony, one minute jagged runs and piercing squeals that seemed to tear at the very air or threatened to spill his brains from his skull, the next a moment of awesome, healing beauty, harmonies the gods might play, then an instant, insane leap back into meaningless, churning sensation. One moment he was screaming as it splashed molten lead through his veins, the next he was racked by fantastic sensual visions, impossible orgies enveloping him like an endless ocean, Dani arching over him in a shower of meteors like the star-filled sky. Then the vision tore down the middle like a ripping canvas as a tide of boiling colour burst through, and everything disintegrated into sheer chaotic turbulence. Those visions of madness passed in their turn. Suddenly the music was noise once again, and he could see.

He was on his knees on the shaking earth, with the others sprawled around him looking wildly about them. Dani twisted around. *'Look out!'* she screamed, and tried to scramble up. Down through the haze a vast toeless foot, half scaly hoof, came crashing, almost on top of them; the impact shot them bodily into the air, twenty feet or more. Fallen sand broke their fall, and they rolled free, staring aghast as the monster staggered back, ignoring them completely. The vast head rolled on its shoulders, blowing music that sounded more like some horrendous screech. The cultists screamed and scattered in all directions; one or two didn't quite make it, stumbling over a crack that had snaked open directly in their path. The vast foot smashed down, and Volker shut his eyes. Through the cacophony he heard a faint tinny screech, full of malicious mirth. Diderik was laughing. The cultists ran back in terror from the next blundering step, and the laughter changed to an angry cry. Scarlet fire blossomed in the murk, and voices screamed. The cry was suddenly cut off.

'It runs mad!' wheezed Thorgrim. 'It treads down its own!'

Through the boiling clouds the cultists surged, scattering in panic then clinging back together in terror, swaying this way and that as they saw the monstrous feet rise and fall, racing towards the Northerners in a murderous panic. Thorgrim and Guy felled the first two; the rest broke like stampeding animals and went by on either side, only to flow back together at the next

450

shattering footfall. Cracks were racing up the mountain-side now, little avalanches tore loose, and steam spurted from sagging hollows in the thin soil.

'If that thing gets loose it'll level the island!' gasped Dani.

'It could be in the capital within an hour!' yelled Guy. 'What is the matter with it? Has Diderik bungled?'

A swaying foot stamped down in the midst of a pack of cultists; Dani winced as it lifted. There was nothing but a dark smear on the flattened soil.

'Can't you hear?' demanded Volker, trying to stifle a lunatic urge to laugh. 'The music—'

'What is it?' shrugged the Norseman. But Guy's jaw sagged in dawning comprehension. He was about to speak when the whole valley shook even more violently. Above them the mountain soughed and exhaled like a wrathful beast, and from its peak a great fountain of fire burst out. Grey-black smoke so dense it looked almost solid climbed in a billowing column, and a rain of blazing fragments sizzled and spattered down across the hillside.

They looked up, and one horrified thought crossed all their minds. Aetna . . . the forge of Hephaestus . . . Were the gods already smelting the first great thunderbolts to blast all life from the earth?

'It'll crush us long before that!' Volker yelled. 'Or they will! It's out of control! We've got to get out of here!'

'How?' bellowed Guy. 'Run to this side? Or that? Stampede like those Tartarist sheep? We cannot outrun those great strides!'

'What about *up*?' Volker shouted.

'Up? By *magic*? Your brain has curdled, boy! If I could levitate even myself alone, do you think I would have had half the trouble I have had on this putrid journey?'

'Back on the barges! You levitated a whole heap of weapons!'

451

'My spell only held them where they were already up, that is less hard than lifting them! To lift four people – *pah!* We would need to command the forces of the wind itself! And I have not even any wine!'

'Oh yes you do!' grinned Dani, ducking as boulder fragments flew by. She thrust a flask at him. 'All that baggage scattered about . . . I figured it might came in handy . . .'

Guy gazed at her with instant adoration, while his fingers were already twisting off the stopper. He sniffed. 'Libyan, *fiu!* But better than dying with a dry throat. But still it is hopeless, *mes chers!* Wine or no wine, I have not so much power! No more than Volker, or this fair one!'

'Or I, least of all!' said Thorgrim stolidly, ignoring the screech of sand around his head. 'Yet in this place there is magic to be had. Can you not draw upon what that *troldhjørning* flings around, so that the very air stinks of it? All of you . . . *together?*'

Volker gaped at Dani, she at him. Then she caught his hand, and he felt as if his brain had caught fire. He seized Guy's hand. The Armorican lowered the flask from his lips, and smashed it to the ground. The dregs ran scarlet on the sand. '*Foi du Draconnier!*' he barked.

> *Faut faire l'essaic, quoi'qu'il nous apporte,*
> *La gloire vivante ou la sombre mort!*

'Does that by any chance mean *yes*?' inquired the Norseman politely. Guy swelled with fury.

'All of you . . . yes, even you, you sink of magic, you smeller of spells . . . speak as I do! Now . . .'

He stopped, and the sword jerked in his hand. Thorgrim cursed, and swung down the halberd. Out of the dust, halting and lurching, staggered the shrunken form of Diderik.

His robes were clotted with sand and filth, his hair

452

was wild, and bloody foam oozed from his purpled lips. There were footprints on his robe; the maddened cultists had trampled him, either in their panic, or when he had turned his fire upon them. Behind him the cacophony was growing louder, higher. His gnomelike face sagged with the weight of pain and failure, and his face twitched with terror of the thing he had unleashed. But his eyes were a cold blaze of wrath, and it fell upon Volker like a scatter of stabbing darts.

'*You!*' he bubbled. '*You* . . . this is your work, your doing! Only you could have caused this! Only you, boy, could so have ruined my plans . . .'

Volker shook his head furiously, too outraged to be afraid. '*I*? You called up a whirlwind, and when it blows you away, you blame me? I've done nothing.'

'No,' gasped Diderik, clutching at his side. 'Oh no, boy! You do not fool me so easily! Ulrich chose you more wisely than I could ever have dreamed! And a thousand years of waiting and hoping, of search and scholarship and fearful sacrifices, all that I worked for, is brought to an end by one wretched mongrel child! Well, now we all perish, toads beneath the harrow; yet I'll not leave you to easy oblivion!' He thrust out his staff. 'You at least will end in *agony*!'

Dani screamed, a scream of anger, and the owl dropped like a thunderbolt on to Diderik's face, slashing and tearing with claw and beak at those malevolent eyes. The Tartarist screeched and twisted about, hurled the owl away – then gave a horrified shriek. He swung up his staff again, hurling a streak of blue flames that seared the eyes. Not at Volker, but up, up into the choking mirk; and it was terror, not wrath, that cracked his voice. '*No! I gave you life! I command you . . .*'

The dreadful music soared up unbearably, setting teeth on edge, towards the brink of hearing. The voice vanished. The massive foot, untouched by word or sorcery, slammed down with a ghastly crunching thud, the sound some tough-shelled vermin might make beneath an ironshod heel, and ground deep.

The Northerners ducked as the sand hissed down over them. *'Guy!'* shouted Volker, and flung his long arms wide. 'The winds! *Potestate Numi!'*

Guy seized his arm and echoed him. *'Potestate Numi! Venti implorabile, experge! Subventa nos! Venti amicabile! In salutem removendum est!'*

Dani, arm around Volker's neck, added her voice to his; but Thorgrim hesitated, stumbling over the Latin. Nothing seemed to happen; and then the Norseman burst out *'To Hela with this hog-language – kom du nu her og hjaelp, du Nordvind!'*

Against that eerie wail his voice sounded infinitesimal; but on the last word it seemed to change and grow, swelling to a great hissing roar. Above them a swelling shadow like a falling cloud blotted out the light. But abruptly a blasting breath of cold punched Volker's breath out of him and crusted his face with rime, a sudden blaze of blue dazzled his eyes. Somewhere, almost at his heels, a massive impact juddered the air, but still greater forces gripped him now. In an instant's giddying confusion he felt himself whirled up like a driven snowflake, spun and twisted in all directions with the very blood congealing in his veins. Then a massive wall of pure whiteness reared up in front of him, and before he could draw another breath he crashed down into its icy, enveloping folds.

He floundered in the freezing softness, clawing at his eyes, struggling to see. In his ears the shrieking rose higher, higher, stabbing into his brain like twin needles. Ice cracked and fell from his hair and clothes, from the stubble on his upper lip where his breath had congealed. His eyes cleared, streaming and stinging with water. He was lying embedded in what was very likely the first deep snowdrift ever to form on the steaming flanks of Aetna, and his limbs, chilled as they were, felt more or less intact. Familiar grunts and complaints rose from the snow around him. He looked down . . . and stiffened.

The Titan's eyes, drawn wide and agonized, seemed to be staring into his own. Against the leaden clouds that monstrous head reared; only now it was barely below him. Then the eyes clamped tight in the terrible rictus that distorted the face. The fearful thing arched back in a spasm of agony, muscles knotting beneath the oil-dark skin, limbs convulsing with a terrible quivering tension. Another rictus shivered through the body, it folded forward, seemed almost to inflate . . .

'*Down!*' yelled Volker, and (not without malice afore-thought) flung himself on top of Dani. So did everyone else. But even as the swearing heap crashed back into the melting drift, that tormented wail suddenly changed.

There was no word for what sang around them. If the world was a harp, and one string plucked, that might approach it. He seemed to see the whole universe stretched out like a tray of gems for him to reach out and take. And at the centre of every facet, seen clearly for the first time, a different image of his own aston-ished face.

But the sound it ended in was a lot easier to describe. The blast blew right across the valley, up and down the mountainside. It wasn't exactly an explosion, though it was deafening enough. There was a soggy, hollow popping quality to it which Volker never quite defined, until some time later he heard Guy hurl a rotten cantel-oupe at a tavern wall. The rain of fragments, too, was not dissimilar, though magnified by the same enormous factor. But the canteloupe simply wasn't in the same league, when it came to the stink.

'If there is anyone left alive in that valley,' said Thorgrim some time later, 'I do not envy them.'

'I think they would be very lonely for the rest of their lives,' agreed Guy disgustedly, picking fragments off his clothing. 'Also deaf, no doubt. But I believe Typhon had taken care of those little details before his . . . departure.'

'Thanks to Thorgrim he didn't take care of us, too,' added Volker, exhausted. 'We were almost strong enough, together – but Thorgrim gave us that last extra push. You should study, my Norse friend. Maybe that talent of yours isn't as passive as you think.'

'That's right!' agreed Dani. She contemplated the remaining snow, now blasted out in a great star-shaped streak across the hillside, and sneezed violently. 'Only – and understand, I'm not complaining, okay? – did you have to choose the *North* Wind?'

Thorgrim shrugged: 'What other one? Anyhow, it gave you a good soft landing.'

'Yeah, and probably the first summer cold to hit Sicilia since the Great Ice packed up and went home.' She sneezed again. 'Yuch! I can't wait to lose my sense of smell. Oh well, at least the snow's some use.' She scooped up a double handful and began scrubbing down her tattered doeskins. 'And listen, while we're on the subject . . . just what in the name of all the gods and their little pink pet poodles *happened*? If someone doesn't come up with an answer pretty soon, *I* might just explode! And when it comes to hitting the wind-mill, let me tell you, you haven't seen *anything* yet!'

'My dear,' sighed Guy, 'it would be a privilege to be covered in any of you—'

She boxed his ear.

'—but since you manifest such patience I could hardly refuse you. It is our estimable young friend here who destroyed him.'

'*What*? You? *Volker*?' Dani gaped at him. 'I don't believe it!'

'I could,' nodded Thorgrim. 'Most definitely I could.

But it seemed to me, *kaere ven*, that you were just as terrified as the rest of us. I saw no spellcasting.'

'That', said Guy smugly, 'is because you did not have the privilege of travelling south with us. Now where is it? Ah . . .' He picked up a black fragment he had thrown away. 'This obscene object which sought to disappear at speed down the seat of my trousers, it holds the clue. It is a piece – a very small piece – of that second horn. And on the inside it is covered in pitch. Do you not remember what Diderik was raving about, the two horns . . . one the pure tone, one the discord? When we lost the first horn, Volker naturally sought to turn the other to serve him. It would not; it was hideous, destructive, ungovernable. So he retuned it. He altered its music.'

'I *knew* I was hearing something different!' shouted Volker. 'The way his music was changing . . .'

'Precisely,' nodded Guy. 'It was in that music that Typhon's power lay. With it he must have been a foe for the gods, indeed. We caught some snatches of his deadly dance – and look at what that did to us. But music itself is neutral. Even with great power like Typhon's behind it, it is neither good nor bad. It was the discords, the clashes, with which Typhon could disrupt the harmony of the spheres – as your old master might have told you, Volker.'

'I should have guessed,' said Volker, wonderingly. He sat down in the snow-melt mud. He felt about ready to start making pies of it. 'So when Typhon tried to blast out his discords, he found himself playing my revised tuning – and everything came out wrong. Even the harmonics were wrong – wrong to the tenth power, maybe, along those vast tubes. It probably hurt like Hela, right there in his head. He got an occasional flash of his real destructive sound . . . but only by accident, when he was playing the opposite. No wonder he got confused!' He shook his head in wonder. 'Typhon was a musician – of a sort. But he couldn't think in opposites. It's hard enough just to transpose a piece as you go along; he'd have had to compose a sort of supercounterpoint. He must have been trying; that was when it just degenerated into sheer noise. But he was hurting, and the harder he tried the worse it got. Right at the end there he was panicking, I think. Playing it faster, higher, harder, until . . .'

Guy chuckled. 'Until, quite literally, he hit one big right chord . . . or wrong one, from his point of view. One big bang of harmony . . . and the resonances tore him apart. And Sicilia, and perhaps many wider places with better vintages do not get them prematurely trodden. *Pas mal joué, mon p'tit!'*

Volker clutched his head in awe. 'Gods, you make it sound as if . . . I mean, I don't deserve any credit! I was just doing what . . . needed to be done. I mean, not even old Ulrich could've foreseen . . .' He registered Guy's sardonically raised eyebrow. 'Hey, hold on a minute!'

Guy smiled enigmatically. 'Could he not? I am not sure I could plumb the depths of our late *patron*'s powers. But ask yourself this . . . why did he not at once destroy the first horn when he had it? It was the only way of finding the second, true; but it would still have been safer. My guess is that he had tried, and found that neither he nor any other mage could damage those horns sufficiently. Or perhaps with one horn restored Typhon could have grown back the other. But this is certain, that in choosing you to aid him he sought to add to a knowledge of magic one of music, which was to both him and Diderik a closed book. And it was that which destroyed Typhon.'

Thorgrim grinned. 'So the credit is indeed yours, my friend. As was the harmony that made the monster pull himself apart.'

Guy nodded. 'Harmony, goodness, happiness . . .

whatever words you choose. A positive power that was utterly alien to him, yet one he could not help generating. He was broadcasting it far and wide.'

'So that was why we got all those . . . visions,' said Dani. 'Of . . . harmony.' She blushed. So did Volker. She saw him blushing, and blushed all the more.

'They quite brought back my student days in Lutecia,' agreed Guy wistfully.

'My first bearslaying . . .' mused Thorgrim. The others looked askance at him. 'I made love to my foster-father's house-girl on the rug,' he explained. They all looked relieved.

'That . . . extraordinary sound . . .' said Guy, awed. 'Was that . . . did he somehow tap into the celestial harmony itself?'

'I don't think so,' Volker said thoughtfully. 'As I understand old Strauben's treatise, that would have rearranged the world rather drastically – maybe even affected causality, probability, things like that. I don't think we'd still be here to have heard it. But maybe he hit a remote harmonic, a distant echo . . .' He shivered, and glanced at Dani. 'It was amazing. But no better than some other things.'

To his surprise she grinned. 'How would you know? That was all your nasty little imagination.'

'And yours. I'd never've dreamt a priestess could think up things like that.'

'Hmph. How would you know? You haven't tried them for real.'

He steepled his fingers. Those harmonies were still ringing in his blood, exultant, liberating. 'We could make an appointment . . . *ouch!*'

'I told you he liked you!' she cooed, reaching out to tickle the rather battered-looking owl that was digging its claw into his shoulder. 'He's been telling me how nice you were to him all the way down here. Spoiling him rotten.'

'He's welcome.' Volker leaned up and scratched the bird's fluffy neck-feathers. 'He was good company. Helpful, too. The two of you made a lovely mess of Diderik. I could get used to having him around.'

She surveyed him wryly. 'Now don't tell me you're trying to seduce my owl away from me. That's an elvish kind of trick.'

'Why not? We *huldrafolk* are supposed to have a way with animals. Even human ones. We can be very seductive when we put our minds to it.'

'*Huldra* . . . that's a change in you! Why are you so happy with it all of a sudden?'

Volker shrugged. 'Oh, it's not so sudden. It's been happening since the forest, I suppose. When I let that half of me go for the first time, began to use my senses, my qualities . . . After all, they're mine. Not my father's. Whoever he is – or was – I'm my own man. Or *huldra*. A lot of my problems have come from denying that, from living out of . . . harmony.' He paused. 'You know . . . it's funny, but it's almost as if . . . that single note showed me that . . .'

'Funny,' she echoed him flatly. 'And me . . . what about me? Maybe it showed me something too. Torn between priestess and . . . I don't know what. Not yet. Scholar. Adventuress . . .'

'Not ratcatcher, anyhow.'

She chuckled. 'No. You've taken care of that much.'

'I wouldn't mind taking care of the rest.'

She reached out, caressed his cheek . . . and rounded it off with a gentle slap. The owl nibbled his ear. 'And what would you be doing meanwhile?'

'Oh, I don't know. I might go back and study. Magic, music – old Ulrich was right, they're in my nature. I might as well make the best of them. But I'd hate to do it alone.'

'Me too . . . But I don't know – I don't know . . . That music . . . I'm afraid of forgetting it, one day.'

460

Volker grinned again. 'We should stick together, then. We can jog each other's memory.'

'Which is all very well for you young featherheads who think you can live on air,' interrupted a choleric voice, 'but may I recall you to a livelier grasp of the situation?'

Guy's theatrical gesture took in the entire universe.

'We are presently standing, or sitting for those who prefer the mud, upon the slopes of a Sicilian volcano. We are clad in dust, dry blood, the remains of a once-proud wardrobe, and the assorted contents of a briefly revived Titan, no longer fresh. We are without defence except for one sabre and one halberd, both somewhat used, without witnesses to testify to our various heroisms and without, in fact, any particular purpose to our existence.'

Dani opened her mouth to add something, and sneezed violently.

'To lower the tone still further,' put in Thorgrim, 'we are also without food, drink, or any means of transport except what remains of our bodies. This is a matter of more immediate concern.'

'In short,' demanded Guy, 'although this matter of horns has been fun, after a fashion . . . where has it got us?'

Volker stood up, and stretched. A quantity of mud fell off his hose, but he hardly cared. He rounded on his crestfallen friends with the benefit of a powerful grin.

'Where, eh? I'll tell you where! First of all, Thorgrim, it's got us within reach of five or six of those horses that bolted, and which . . . being half-elf . . . I just happen to see grazing by that patch of trees over there.'

Thorgrim peered into the evening light. 'I will take your word for it,' he said dubiously.

'With a bit of luck we should be able to catch them. They might even have something to eat in their saddle-

461

bags. And if not, we should be able to stagger back to our own horses. Downhill all the way, after all. As to the rest, Guy . . . they can carry us back to Syracusa, richest city in the world. And there, waiting for us, is one cargo of desirable goods abandoned by its original owners – who won't be back to claim it – and salvaged by us. That's where this whole business has got us. And you've got to admit, it's a whole lot better than where we all started.'

Guy cheered up considerably. 'A whole lot, as you say. But the Draconnier is no merchant, to know how best to dispose of these goods . . .'

'You may not be; but I damn well am! That's my human half – all my mother's family were merchants, remember? Among the best in Bremen. And you know, Ulrich's idea wasn't that bad. With our combined magical talents we should attract a pretty fair price for them, after all.'

Volker grinned again. After all they'd been through it felt very good to be able to do just a little thing like that. And it was even better to know that somewhere out there hot baths and big meals and soft beds were waiting. Besides, there was another, private satisfaction in knowing that without the four of them, none of those things would still be there. He glanced at Dani, and wondered exactly what her feelings were about soft beds.

'Who knows . . . we may be natural businessmen!' He gestured down into the devastated valley. 'After all, we've just averted the market crash of all time . . . haven't we?'

THE WINTER OF THE WORLD
VOL 1: ANVIL OF ICE

Michael Scott Rohan

The chronicles of *The Winter of the World* echo down the ages in half-remembered myth and song – tales of mysterious powers of the Mastersmiths, of the forging of great weapons, of the subterranean kingdoms of the duergar, of Gods who walked abroad, and of the Powers that struggled endlessly for dominion.

'An exciting adventure . . . Rohan creates a haunting sense of mythology rather than fantasy. This remarkable novel reveals a gifted writer of stories and pages turn as if by magic'
Jean M. Auel

'A wonderful story'
Raymond E. Feist

'An outstanding piece of fantasy fiction'
Andre Norton

'A very good and a very powerful writer . . . The concept of the Ice itself as the ultimate enemy is a remarkable feat, compelling reading'
Anne McCaffrey

0 7088 8210 2
FANTASY

CHASE THE MORNING

Michael Scott Rohan

SAIL AWAY TO A WORLD OF MAGIC

Steve is a hollow man, both in his job and his personal life, until one night, near the docks of his home city. A night that changes his life.

As a dockyard fight turns into something much more fantastic and deadly, Steve finds himself drawn into a world he neither understands nor believes – at first. His meeting with the mercurial Jyp leads to a raid on his office by beings not-quite-human, and the kidnapping of Clare, his secretary. Aware of strong feelings for the first time in years, Steve enlists the aid of Jyp and his roistering friends to sail after Clare and her captors . . . to *Chase the Morning*.

With the *Winter of the World* Trilogy, Michael Scott Rohan proved himself one of the modern masters of fantasy. Now he has gone beyond even that, in this marvellous blend of the worlds we know and a world of magic, pirates . . . and death!

0 7088 8338 9
FANTASY

RUN TO THE STARS
Michael Scott Rohan

Earth in the thirtieth century is a bleak place – a creeping self-righteous puritanism is abroad, and one official is only too willing to betray his neighbour for advancement in the State hierarchy.

Digging too deep into a bureaucratic cover-up, Mark Bellamy, Chief of Security, finds himself accused of murder and treason. This leaves him no choice but to *Run to the Stars*.

Along with thirty thousand others, he will leave on Earth's Second Colony ship. It will mean twenty-two years of space travel with no definite goal at the end – but Mark is willing to take the risk. For there is no alternative. He must soar into the stars, forging a new world and an unknown destiny – or else perish at the hands of bureaucratic assassins . . .

0 7088 8312 5
SCIENCE FICTION

THE DRAGON IN THE STONE
Allan Scott

In the twilight world there is an endless struggle for power between the Light Elves and the Dark Elves. Over the millennia the battle has swayed first to one side then the other – but now the Light Elves are near to final defeat. A defeat that will open a way into this world for the forces of evil.

Peter Brockman, a young American archaeologist of Danish descent, becomes involved in the final stages of this supernatural struggle when he visits the Danish village of Egerød, trying to trace his ancestors. The old man he finds in the churchyard will prove to be a pivotal character in the destiny of both worlds. And both of them are somehow bound to the mysterious Watcher . . . *The Dragon in the Stone.*

0 7088 8354 0
FANTASY

Orbit Books now offers an exciting range of quality titles by both established and new authors which can be ordered from the following address:
Little, Brown and Company (UK) Limited,
Cash Sales Department,
P.O. Box 11,
Falmouth,
Cornwall TR10 9EN.

Alternatively you may fax your order to the above address. Fax No. 0326 376423.

Payments can be made as follows: cheque, postal order (payable to Little, Brown and Company) or by credit cards, Visa/Access. Do not send cash or currency. UK customers and B.F.P.O. please allow £1.00 for postage and packing for the first book, plus 50p for the second book, plus 30p for each additional book up to a maximum charge of £3.00 (7 books plus).

Overseas customers including Ireland, please allow £2.00 for the first book plus £1.00 for the second book, plus 50p for each additional book.

NAME (Block Letters) ....

ADDRESS ....

....

☐ I enclose my remittance for _____

☐ I wish to pay by Access/Visa Card

Number ☐☐☐☐☐☐☐☐☐☐☐☐☐☐☐☐

Card Expiry Date ☐☐☐☐